Diary of a
Drug Fiend

Diary of a Drug Fiend

Aleister Crowley

MINT EDITIONS

Diary of a Drug Fiend was first published in 1922.

This edition published by Mint Editions 2021.

ISBN 9781513214894 | E-ISBN 9781513212890

Published by Mint Editions®

MINT
EDITIONS
minteditionbooks.com

Publishing Director: Jennifer Newens
Design & Production: Rachel Lopez Metzger
Project Manager: Micaela Clark
Typesetting: Westchester Publishing Services

Contents

BOOK I
PARADISO

I

A Knight Out

Yes, I certainly was feeling depressed.

I don't think that this was altogether the reaction of the day. Of course, there always is a reaction after the excitement of a flight; but the effect is more physical than moral. One doesn't talk. One lies about and smokes and drinks champagne.

No, I was feeling quite a different kind of rotten. I looked at my mind, as the better class of flying man soon learns to do, and I really felt ashamed of myself. Take me for all in all, I was one of the luckiest men alive.

War is like a wave; some it rolls over, some it drowns, some it beats to pieces on the shingle; but some it shoots far up the shore on to glistening golden sand out of the reach of any further freaks of fortune.

Let me explain.

My name is Peter Pendragon. My father was a second son; and he had quarrelled with my Uncle Mortimer when they were boys. He was a struggling general practitioner in Norfolk, and had not made things any better for himself by marrying.

However, he scraped together enough to get me some sort of education, and at the outbreak of the war I was twenty-two years old and had just passed my Intermediate for M.D. in the University of London.

Then, as I said, the wave came. My mother went out for the Red Cross, and died in the first year of the war. Such was the confusion that I did not even know about it till over six months later.

My father died of influenza just before the Armistice.

I had gone into the air service; did pretty well, though somehow I was never sure either of myself or of my machine. My squadron commander used to tell me that I should never make a great airman.

"Old thing," he said, "you lack the instinct," qualifying the noun with an entirely meaningless adjective which somehow succeeded in making his sentence highly illuminating.

"Where you get away with it," he said, "is that you have an analytic brain."

Well, I suppose I have. That's how I come to be writing this up. Anyhow, at the end of the war I found myself with a knighthood which I still firmly believe to have been due to a clerical error on the part of some official.

As for Uncle Mortimer, he lived on in his crustacean way; a sulky, rich, morose, old bachelor. We never heard a word of him.

And then, about a year ago, he died; and I found to my amazement that I was sole heir to his five or six thousand a year, and the owner of Barley Grange; which is really an awfully nice place in Kent, quite near enough to be convenient for the prosperous young man about town which I had become; and for the best of it, a piece of artificial water quite large enough for me to use for a waterdrome for my seaplane.

I may not have the instinct for flying, as Cartwright said; but it's the only sport I care about.

Golf? When one has flown over a golf course, those people do look such appalling rotters! Such pigmy solemnities!

Now about my feeling depressed. When the end of the war came, when I found myself penniless, out of a job, utterly spoilt by the war (even if I had had the money) for going on with my hospital, I had developed an entirely new psychology. You know how it feels when you are fighting duels in the air, you seem to be detached from everything. There is nothing in the Universe but you and the Boche you are trying to pot. There is something detached and god-like about it.

And when I found myself put out on the streets by a grateful country, I became an entirely different animal. In fact, I've often thought that there isn't any "I" at all; that we are simply the means of expression of something else; that when we think we are ourselves, we are simply the victims of a delusion.

Well, bother that! The plain fact is that I had become a desperate wild animal. I was too hungry, so to speak, even to waste anytime on thinking bitterly about things.

And then came the letter from the lawyers.

That was another new experience. I had no idea before of the depths to which servility could descend.

"By the way, Sir Peter," said Mr. Wolfe, "it will, of course, take a little while to settle up these matters. It's a very large estate, very large. But I thought that with times as they are, you wouldn't be offended, Sir

Peter, if we handed you an open cheque for a thousand pounds just to go on with."

It wasn't till I had got outside his door that I realised how badly he wanted my business. He need not have worried. He had managed poor old Uncle Mortimer's affairs well enough all those years; not likely I should bother to put them in the hands of a new man.

The thing that really pleased me about the whole business was the clause in the will. That old crab had sat in his club all through the war, snapping at everybody he saw; and yet he had been keeping track of what I was doing. He said in the will that he had made me his heir "for the splendid services I had rendered to our beloved country in her hour of need."

That's the true Celtic psychology. When we've all finished talking, there's something that never utters a word, but goes right down through the earth, plumb to the centre.

And now comes the funny part of the business. I discovered to my amazement that the desperate wild animal hunting his job had been after all a rather happy animal in his way, just as the desperate god battling in the air, playing pitch and toss with life and death, had been happy.

Neither of those men could be depressed by misfortune; but the prosperous young man about town was a much inferior creature. Everything more or less bored him, and he was quite definitely irritated by an overdone cutlet. The night I met Lou, I turned into the Café Wisteria in a sort of dull, angry stupor. Yet the only irritating incident of the day had been a letter from the lawyers which I had found at my club after flying from Norfolk to Barley Grange and motoring up to town.

Mr. Wolfe had very sensibly advised me to make a settlement of a part of the estate, as against the event of my getting married; and there was some stupid hitch about getting trustees.

I loathe law. It seems to me as if it were merely an elaborate series of obstacles to doing things sensibly. And yet, of course, after all, one must have formalities, just as in flying you have to make arrangements for starting and stopping. But it is a beastly nuisance to have to attend to them.

I THOUGHT I WOULD STAND myself a little dinner. I hadn't quite enough sense to know that what I really wanted was human companions.

There aren't such things. Every man is eternally alone. But when you get mixed up with a fairly decent crowd, you forget that appalling fact for long enough to give your brain time to recover from the acute symptoms of its disease—that of thinking.

My old commander was right. I think a lot too much; so did Shakespeare. That's what worked him up to write those wonderful things about sleep. I've forgotten what they were; but they impressed me at the time. I said to myself, "This old bird knew how dreadful it is to be conscious."

So, when I turned into the café, I think the real reason was that I hoped to find somebody there, and talk the night out. People think that talking is a sign of thinking. It isn't, for the most part; on the contrary, it's a mechanical dodge of the body to relieve oneself of the strain of thinking, just as exercising the muscles helps the body to become temporarily unconscious of its weight, its pain, its weariness, and the foreknowledge of its doom.

You see what gloomy thoughts a fellow can have, even when he's Fortune's pet. It's a disease of civilisation. We're in an intermediate stage between the stupor of the peasant and—something that is not yet properly developed.

I went into the café and sat down at one of the marble tables. I had a momentary thrill of joy—it reminded me of France so much—of all those days of ferocious gambling with Death.

I couldn't see a soul I knew. But at least I knew by sight the two men at the next table. Everyone knew that gray ferocious wolf—a man built in every line for battle, and yet with a forehead which lifted him clean out of the turmoil. The conflicting elements in his nature had played the devil with him. Jack Fordham was his name. At sixty years of age he was still the most savage and implacable of publicists. "Red in tooth and claw," as Tennyson said. Yet the man had found time to write great literature; and his rough and tumble with the world had not degraded his thought or spoilt his style.

Sitting next him was a weak, good-natured, working journalist named Vernon Gibbs. He wrote practically the whole of a weekly paper—had done, year after year with the versatility of a practised pen and the mechanical perseverance of an instrument which has been worn by practice into perfect easiness.

Yet the man had a mind for all that. Some instinct told him that he had been meant for better things. The result had been that he had steadily become a heavier and heavier drinker.

I learnt at the hospital that seventy-five percent of the human body is composed of water; but in this case, as in the old song, it must have been that he was a relation of the McPherson who had a son,

> *"That married Noah's daughter*
> *And nearly spoilt the flood*
> *By drinking all the water.*
> *And this he would have done,*
> *I really do believe it,*
> *But had that mixture been*
> *Three parts or more Glen Livet."*

The slight figure of a young-old man with a bulbous nose to detract from his otherwise remarkable beauty, spoilt though it was by years of insane passions, came into the café. His cold blue eyes were shifty and malicious. One got the impression of some filthy creature of the darkness—a raider from another world looking about him for something to despoil. At his heels lumbered his jackal, a huge, bloated, verminous creature like a cockroach, in shabby black clothes, ill-fitting, unbrushed and stained, his linen dirty, his face bloated and pimpled, a horrible evil leer on his dripping mouth, with its furniture like a bombed graveyard.

The café sizzled as the men entered. They were notorious, if nothing else, and the leader was the Earl of Bumble. Everyone seemed to scent some mischief in the air. The earl came up to the table next to mine, and stopped deliberately short. A sneer passed across his lips. He pointed to the two men.

"Drunken Bardolph and Ancient Pistol," he said, with his nose twitching with anger.

Jack Fordham was not behindhand with the repartee.

"Well roared, Bottom," he replied calmly, as pat as if the whole scene had been rehearsed beforehand.

A dangerous look came into the eyes of the insane earl. He took a pace backwards and raised his stick. But Fordham, old campaigner that he was, had anticipated the gesture. He had been to the Western States in his youth; and what he did not know about scrapping was not worth being known. In particular, he was very much alive to the fact that an unarmed man sitting behind a fixed table has no chance against a man with a stick in the open.

He slipped out like a cat. Before Bumble could bring down his cane, the old man had dived under his guard and taken the lunatic by the throat.

There was no sort of a fight. The veteran shook his opponent like a bull-dog; and, shifting his grip, flung him to the ground with one tremendous throw. In less than two seconds the affair was over. Fordham was kneeling on the chest of the defeated bully, who whined and gasped and cried for mercy, and told the man twenty years his senior, whom he had deliberately provoked into the fight, that he mustn't hurt him because they were such old friends!

The behaviour of a crowd in affairs of this kind always seems to me very singular. Everyone, or nearly everyone, seems to start to interfere; and nobody actually does so.

But this matter threatened to prove more serious. The old man had really lost his temper. It was odds that he would choke the life out of the cur under his knee.

I had just enough presence of mind to make way for the head waiter, a jolly, burly Frenchman, who came pushing into the circle. I even lent him a hand to pull Fordham off the prostrate form of his antagonist.

A touch was enough. The old man recovered his temper in a second, and calmly went back to his table with no more sign of excitement than shouting "sixty to forty, sixty to forty."

"I'm on," cried the voice of a man who had just come in at the end of the café and missed the scene by a minute. "But what's the horse?"

I heard the words as a man in a dream; for my attention had suddenly been distracted.

Bumble had made no attempt to get up. He lay there whimpering. I raised my eyes from so disgusting a sight, and found them fixed by two enormous orbs. I did not know at the first moment even that they were eyes. It's a funny thing to say; but the first impression was that they were one of those thoughts that come to one from nowhere when one is flying at ten thousand feet or so. Awfully queer thing, I tell you— reminds one of the atmospherics that one gets in wireless; and they give one a horrible feeling. It is a sort of sinister warning that there is some person or something in the Universe outside oneself: and the realisation of that is as frankly frightening as the other realisation, that one is eternally alone, is horrible.

I slipped out of time altogether into eternity. I felt myself in the presence of some tremendous influence for good or evil. I felt as though

I had been born—I don't know whether you know what I mean. I can't help it, but I can't put it any different.

It's like this: nothing had ever happened to me in my life before. You know how it is when you come out of ether or nitrous-oxide at the dentist's—you come back to somewhere, a familiar somewhere; but the place from which you have come is nowhere, and yet you have been there.

That is what happened to me.

I woke up from eternity, from infinity, from a state of mind enormously more vital and conscious than anything we know of otherwise, although one can't give it a name, to discover that this nameless thought of nothingness was in reality two black vast spheres in which I saw myself. I had a thought of some vision in a story of the middle ages about a wizard, and slowly, slowly, I slid up out of the deep to recognise that these two spheres were just two eyes. And then it occurred to me—the thought was in the nature of a particularly absurd and ridiculous joke—that these two eyes belonged to a girl's face.

Across the moaning body of the blackmailer, I was looking at the face of a girl that I had never seen before. And I said to myself, "Well, that's all right, I've known you all my life." And when I said to myself "my life," I didn't in the least mean my life as Peter Pendragon, I didn't even mean a life extending through the centuries, I meant a different kind of life— something with which centuries have nothing whatever to do.

And then Peter Pendragon came wholly back to himself with a start, and wondered whether he had not perhaps looked a little rudely at what his common sense assured him was quite an ordinary and not a particularly attractive girl.

My mind was immediately troubled. I went hastily back to my table. And then it seemed to me as if it were hours while the waiters were persuading the earl to his feet.

I sipped my drink automatically. When I looked up the girl had disappeared.

IT IS A TRIVIAL OBSERVATION enough which I am going to make. I hope at least it will help to clear any one's mind of any idea that I may be an abnormal man.

As a matter of fact, every man is ultimately abnormal, because he is unique. But we can class man in a few series without bothering ourselves much about what each one of them is in himself.

I hope, then, that it will be clearly understood that I am very much like a hundred thousand other young men of my age. I also make the remark, because the essential bearing of it is practically the whole story of this book. And the remark is this, after that great flourish of trumpets: although I was personally entirely uninterested in what I had witnessed, the depression had vanished from my mind. As the French say, "*Un clou chasse l'autre.*"

I have learnt since then that certain races, particularly the Japanese, have made a definite science starting from this fact. For example, they clap their hands four times "in order to drive away evil spirits." That is, of course, only a figure of speech. What they really do is this: the physical gesture startles the mind out of its lethargy, so that the idea which has been troubling it is replaced by a new one. They have various dodges for securing a new one and making sure that the new one shall be pleasant. More of this later.

What happened is that at this moment my mind was seized with sharp, black anger, entirely objectless. I had at the time not the faintest inkling as to its nature, but there it was. The café was intolerable—like a pest-house. I threw a coin on the table, and was astonished to notice that it rolled off. I went out as if the devil were at my heels.

I remember practically nothing of the next half-hour. I felt a kind of forlorn sense of being lost in a world of incredibly stupid and malicious dwarfs.

I found myself in Piccadilly quite suddenly. A voice purred in my ear, "Good old Peter, good old sport, awfully glad I met you—we'll make a night of it."

The speaker was a handsome Welshman still in his prime. Some people thought him one of the best sculptors living. He had, in fact, a following of disciples which I can only qualify as "almost unpleasantly so."

He had no use for humanity at the bottom of his heart, except as convenient shapes which he might model. He was bored and disgusted to find them pretending to be alive. The annoyance had grown until he had got into the habit of drinking a good deal more and a good deal more often than a lesser man might have needed. He was a much bigger man than I was physically, and he took me by the arm almost as if he had been taking me into custody. He poured into my ear an interminable series of rambling reminiscences, each of which appeared to him incredibly mirthful.

For about half a minute I resented him; then I let myself go and found myself soothed almost to slumber by the flow of his talk. A wonderful man, like an imbecile child nine-tenths of the time, and yet, at the back of it all, one somehow saw the deep night of his mind suffused with faint sparks of his genius.

I had not the slightest idea where he was taking me; I did not care. I had gone to sleep inside. I woke to find myself sitting in the Café Wisteria once more.

The head waiter was excitedly explaining to my companion what a wonderful scene he had missed.

"Mr. Fordham, he nearly kill' ze Lord," he bubbled, wringing his fat hands. "He nearly kill' ze Lord."

Something in the speech tickled my sense of irreverence. I broke into a high-pitched shout of laughter.

"Rotten," said my companion. "Rotten! That fellow Fordham never seems to make a clean job of it anyhow. Say, look here, this is my night out. You go 'way like a good boy, tell all those boys and girls come and have dinner."

The waiter knew well enough who was meant; and presently I found myself shaking hands with several perfect strangers in terms which implied the warmest and most unquenchable affection. It was really rather a distinguished crowd. One of the men was a fat German Jew, who looked at first sight like a piece of canned pork that has got mislaid too long in the summer. But the less he said the more he did; and what he did is one of the greatest treasures of mankind.

Then there was a voluble, genial man with a shock of gray hair and a queer twisted smile on his face. He looked like a character of Dickens. But he had done more to revitalise the theatre than any other man of his time.

I took a dislike to the women. They seemed so unworthy of the men. Great men seem to enjoy going about with freaks. I suppose it is on the same principle as the old kings used to keep fools and dwarfs to amuse them. "Some men are born great, some achieve greatness, some have greatness thrust upon them." But whichever way it is, the burden is usually too heavy for their shoulders.

You remember Frank Harris's story of the Ugly Duckling? If you don't, you'd better get busy and do it.

That's really what's so frightful in flying—the fear of oneself, the feeling that one has got out of one's class, that all the old kindly familiar things below have turned into hard monstrous enemies ready to smash you if you touch them.

The first of these women was a fat, bold, red-headed slut. She reminded me of a white maggot. She exuded corruption. She was pompous, pretentious, and stupid. She gave herself out as a great authority on literature; but all her knowledge was parrot, and her own attempts in that direction the most deplorably dreary drivel that ever had been printed even by the chattering clique which she financed. On her bare shoulder was the hand of a short, thin woman with a common, pretty face and a would-be babyish manner. She was a German woman of the lowest class. Her husband was an influential Member of Parliament. People said that he lived on her earnings. There were even darker whispers. Two or three pretty wise birds had told me they thought it was she, and not poor little Mati Hara, who tipped off the Tanks to the Boche.

Did I mention that my sculptor's name was Owen? Well, it was, is, and will be while the name of Art endures. He was supporting himself unsteadily with one hand on the table, while with the other he put his guests in their seats. I thought of a child playing with dolls.

As the first four sat down, I saw two other girls behind them. One I had met before, Violet Beach. She was a queer little thing—Jewish, I fancy. She wore a sheaf of yellow hair fuzzed out like a Struwwelpeter, and a violent vermilion dress—in case anyone should fail to observe her. It was her affectation to be an Apache, so she wore an old cricket cap down on one eye, and a stale cigarette hung from her lip. But she had a certain talent for writing, and I was very glad indeed to meet her again. I admit I am always a little shy with strangers. As we shook hands, I heard her saying in her curious voice, high-pitched and yet muted, as if she had something wrong with her throat:—

"Want you to meet Miss——"

I didn't get the name; I can never hear strange words. As it turned out, before forty-eight hours had passed, I discovered that it was Laleham—and then again that it wasn't. But I anticipate—don't try to throw me out of my stride. All in good time.

In the meanwhile I found I was expected to address her as Lou. "Unlimited Lou" was her nickname among the initiate.

Now what I am anxious for everybody to understand is simply this. There's hardly anybody who understands the way his mind works; no two minds are alike, as Horace or some old ass said; and, anyhow, the process of thinking is hardly ever what we imagine.

So, instead of recognising the girl as the owner of the eyes which had gripped me so strangely an hour earlier, the fact of the recognition simply put me off the recognition—I don't know if I'm making myself clear. I mean that the plain fact refused to come to the surface. My mind seethed with questions. Where had I seen her before?

And here's another funny thing. I don't believe that I should have ever recognised her by sight. What put me on the track was the grip of her hand, though I had never touched it in my life before.

Now don't think that I'm going off the deep end about this. Don't dismiss me as a mystic-monger. Look back each one into your own lives, and if you can't find half a dozen incidents equally inexplicable, equally unreasonable, equally repugnant to the better regulated type of mid-Victorian mind, the best thing you can do is to sleep with your forefathers. So that's that. Goodnight.

I told you that Lou was "quite an ordinary and not a particularly attractive girl." Remember that this was the first thought of my "carnal mind" which, as St. Paul says, is "enmity against God."

My real first impression had been the tremendous psychological experience for which all words are inadequate.

Seated by her side, at leisure to look while she babbled, I found my carnal mind reversed on appeal. She was certainly not a pretty girl from the standpoint of a music-hall audience. There was something indefinably Mongolian about her face. The planes were flat; the cheek-bones high; the eyes oblique; the nose wide, short, and vital; the mouth a long, thin, rippling curve like a mad sunset. The eyes were tiny and green, with a piquant elfin expression. Her hair was curiously colourless; it was very abundant; she had wound great ropes about her head. It reminded me of the armature of a dynamo. It produced a weird effect—this mingling of the savage Mongol with the savage Norseman type. Her strange hair fascinated me. It was that delicate flaxen hue, so fine—no, I don't know how to tell you about it, I can't think of it without getting all muddled up.

One wondered how she was there. One saw at a glance that she didn't belong to that set. Refinement, aristocracy almost, were like a radiance about her tiniest gesture. She had no affectation about being an artist. She happened to like these people in exactly the same way as a Methodist old maid in Balham might take an interest in natives of Tonga, and so she went about with them. Her mother didn't mind. Probably, too, the way things are nowadays, her mother didn't matter.

You mustn't think that we were any of us drunk, except old Owen. As a matter of fact, all I had had was a glass of white wine. Lou had touched nothing at all. She prattled on like the innocent child she was, out of the sheer mirth of her heart. In an ordinary way, I suppose, I should have drunk a lot more than I did. And I didn't eat much either. Of course, I know now what it was—that much-derided phenomenon, love at first sight.

Suddenly we were interrupted. A tall man was shaking hands across the table with Owen. Instead of using any of the ordinary greetings, he said in a very low, clear voice, very clear and vibrant, as though tense with some inscrutable passion:—

"Do what thou wilt shall be the whole of the Law."

There was an uneasy movement in the group. In particular, the German woman seemed distressed by the man's mere presence.

I looked up. Yes, I could understand well enough the change in the weather. Owen was saying—

"That's all right, that's all right, that's exactly what I do. You come and see my new group. I'll do another sketch of you—same day, same time. That's all right."

Somebody introduced the new-comer—Mr. King Lamus—and murmured our names.

"Sit down right here," said Owen, "what you need is a drink. I know you perfectly well; I've known you for years and years and years, and I know you've done a good day's work, and you've earned a drink. Sit right down and I'll get the waiter."

I looked at Lamus, who had not uttered a word since his original greeting. There was something appalling in his eyes; they didn't focus on the foreground. I was only an incident of utter insignificance in an illimitable landscape. His eyes were parallel; they were looking at infinity. Nothing mattered to him. I hated the beast!

By this time the waiter had approached.

"Sorry, sir," he said to Owen, who had ordered a '65 brandy.

It appeared that it was now eight hours forty-three minutes thirteen and three-fifth seconds past noon. I don't know what the law is; nobody in England knows what the law is—not even the fools that make the laws. We are not under the laws and do not enjoy the liberties which our fathers bequeathed us; we are under a complex and fantastic system of police administration nearly as pernicious as anything even in America.

"Don't apologise," said Lamus to the waiter in a tone of icy detachment. "This is the freedom we fought for."

I was entirely on the side of the speaker. I hadn't wanted a drink all evening, but now I was told I couldn't have one, I wanted to raid their damn cellars and fight the Metropolitan Police and go up in my 'plane and drop a few bombs on the silly old House of Commons. And yet I was in no sort of sympathy with the man. The contempt of his tone irritated me. He was inhuman, somehow; that was what antagonised me.

He turned to Owen.

"Better come round to my studio," he drawled; "I have a machine gun trained on Scotland Yard."

Owen rose with alacrity.

"I shall be delighted to see any of you others," continued Lamus. "I should deplore it to the day of my death if I were the innocent means of breaking up so perfect a party."

The invitation sounded like an insult. I went red behind the ears; I could only just command myself enough to make a formal apology of some sort.

As a matter of fact, there was a very curious reaction in the whole party. The German Jew got up at once—nobody else stirred. Rage boiled in my heart. I understood instantly what had taken place. The intervention of Lamus had automatically divided the party into giants and dwarfs; and I was one of the dwarfs.

During the dinner, Mrs. Webster, the German woman, had spoken hardly at all. But as soon as the three men had turned their backs, she remarked acidly:—

"I don't think we're dependent for our drinks on Mr. King Lamus. Let's go round to the Smoking Dog."

Everybody agreed with alacrity. The suggestion seemed to have relieved the unspoken tension.

We found ourselves in taxis, which for some inscrutable reason are still allowed to ply practically unchecked in the streets of London. While eating and breathing and going about are permitted, we shall never be a really righteous race!

II

Over the Top!

I t was only about a quarter of an hour before we reached "The Dog"; but the time passed heavily. I had been annexed by the white maggot. Her presence made me feel as if I were already a corpse. It was the limit.

But I think the ordeal served to bring up in my mind some inkling of the true nature of my feeling for Lou.

The Smoking Dog, now ingloriously extinct, was a night club decorated by a horrible little cad who spent his life pushing himself into art and literature. The dancing room was a ridiculous, meaningless, gaudy, bad imitation of Klimmt.

Damn it all, I may not be a great flyer, but I am a fresh air man. I detest these near-artists with their poses and their humbug and their swank. I hate shams.

I found myself in a state of furious impatience before five minutes had passed. Mrs. Webster and Lou had not arrived. Ten minutes—twenty—I fell into a blind rage, drank heavily of the vile liquor with which the place was stinking, and flung myself with I don't know what woman into the dance.

A shrill-voiced Danish siren, the proprietress, was screaming abuse at one of her professional entertainers—some long, sordid, silly story of sexual jealousy, I suppose. The band was deafening. The fine edge of my sense was dulled. It was in a sort of hot nightmare that I saw, through the smoke and the stink of the club, the evil smile of Mrs. Webster.

Small as the woman was, she seemed to fill the doorway. She preoccupied the attention in the same way as a snake would have done. She saw me at once, and ran almost into my arms excitedly. She whispered something in my ear. I didn't hear it.

The club had suddenly been, so to speak, struck dumb. Lou was coming through the door. Over her shoulders was an opera cloak of deep rich purple edged with gold, the garment of an empress, or (shall I say?) of a priestess.

The whole place stopped still to look at her. And I had thought she was not beautiful!

She did not walk upon the ground. "*Vera incessu patuit dea*," as we used to say at school. And as she paced she chanted from that magnificent litany of Captain J. F. C. Fuller, "Oh Thou golden sheaf of desires, that art bound by a fair wisp of poppies! I adore thee, Evoe! I adore thee, I A O!"

She sang full-throated, with a male quality in her voice. Her beauty was so radiant that my mind ran to the breaking of dawn after a long night flight.

"In front the sun climbs slow, how slowly, but westward, look! the land is bright!"

As if in answer to my thought, her voice rolled forth again:—

"O Thou golden wine of the sun, that art poured over the dark breasts of night! I adore Thee, Evoe! I adore Thee, I A O!"

The first part of the adoration was in a sort of Gregorian chant varying with the cadence of the words. But the chorus always came back to the same thing.

I a-dore Thee, Evoe ! I adore Thee, I   A   O !

EE-AH-OH gives the enunciation of the last word. Every vowel is drawn out as long as possible. It seemed as if she were trying to get the last cubic millimetre of air out of her lungs everytime she sang it.

"O Thou crimson vintage of life, that art poured into the jar of the grave! I adore Thee, Evoe! I adore Thee, I A O!"

Lou reached the table, with its dirty, crazy cloth, at which we were sitting. She looked straight into my eyes, though I am sure she did not see me.

"O Thou red cobra of desire, that art unhooded by the hands of girls! I adore Thee, Evoe! I adore Thee, I A O!"

She went back from us like a purple storm-cloud, sun-crested torn from the breasts of the morning by some invisible lightning.

"O Thou burning sword of passion, that art torn on the anvil of flesh! I adore Thee, Evoe! I adore Thee, Evoe! I adore Thee, I A O!"

A wave of almost insane excitement swept through the club. It was like the breaking out of anti-aircraft guns. The band struck up a madder jazz.

The dancers raved with more tumultuous and breathless fury.

Lou had advanced again to our table. We three were detached from the world. Around us rang the shrieking laughter of the crazy crowd. Lou seemed to listen. She broke out once more.

"O Thou mad whirlwind of laughter, that art meshed in the wild locks of folly! I adore Thee, Evoe! I adore Thee, I A O!"

I realised with nauseating clarity that Mrs. Webster was pouring into my ears an account of the character and career of King Lamus.

"I don't know how he dares to come to England at all," she said. "He lives in a place called Telepylus, wherever that is. He's over a hundred years old, in spite of his looks. He's been everywhere, and done everything, and every step he treads is smeared with blood. He's the most evil and dangerous man in London. He's a vampire, he lives on ruined lives."

I admit I had the heartiest abhorrence for the man. But this fiercely bitter denunciation of one who was evidently a close friend of two of the world's greatest artists, did not make his case look blacker. I was not impressed, frankly, with Mrs. Webster as an authority on other people's conduct.

"O Thou Dragon-prince of the air, that art drunk on the blood of the sunsets! I adore Thee, Evoe! I adore Thee, I A O!"

A wild pang of jealousy stabbed me. It was a livid, demoniac spasm. For some reason or other I had connected this verse of Lou's mysterious chant with the personality of King Lamus.

Gretel Webster understood. She insinuated another dose of venom.

"Oh yes, Mr. Basil King Lamus is quite the ladies' man. He fascinates them with a thousand different tricks. Lou is dreadfully in love with him."

Once again the woman had made a mistake. I resented her reference to Lou. I don't remember what I answered. Part of it was to the effect that Lou didn't seem to have been very much injured.

Mrs. Webster smiled her subtlest smile.

"I quite agree," she said silkily, "Lou is the most beautiful woman in London tonight."

"O Thou fragrance of sweet flowers, that art wafted over blue fields of air! I adore Thee, Evoe! I adore Thee, I A O!"

The state of the girl was extraordinary. It was as if she possessed two personalities in their fullest possibilities—the divine and the human. She was intensely conscious of all that was going on around her, absolute mistress of herself and of her environment; yet at the same time she was lost in some unearthly form of rapture of a kind which, while essentially unintelligible to me, reminded me of certain strange and fragmentary experiences that I had had while flying.

I suppose everyone has read *The Psychology of Flying* by L. de Giberne Sieveking. All I need do is to remind you of what he says:—

"All types of men who fly are conscious of this very obscure, subtle difference that it has wrought in them. Very few know exactly what it is. Hardly any of them can express what they feel. And none of them would admit it if they could. . . One realises without any formation into words how that one is oneself, and that each one is entirely separate and can never enter into the recesses of another, which are his foundation of individual life."

One feels oneself out of all relation with things, even the most essential. And yet one is aware at the same time that everything of which one has ever been aware is a picture invented by one's own mind. The Universe is the looking-glass of the soul.

In that state one understands all sorts of nonsense.

"O Thou foursquare Crown of Nothing, that circlest the destruction of Worlds! I adore Thee, Evoe! I adore Thee, I A O!"

I flushed with rage, understanding enough to know what Lou must be feeling as she rolled forth those passionate, senseless words from her volcanic mouth. Gretel's suggestion trickled into my brain.

"This beastly alcohol brutalises men. Why is Lou so superb? She has breathed the pure snow of Heaven into her nostrils."

"O Thou snow-white chalice of Love, that art filled up with the red lusts of man! I adore Thee, Evoe! I adore Thee, I A O!"

I tingled and shivered as she sang; and then something, I hardly know what, made me turn and look into the face of Gretel Webster. She was sitting at my right; her left hand was beneath the table, and she was looking at it. I followed her glance.

In the little quadrilateral of the veins whose lower apex is between the first and middle fingers, was a tiny heap of sparkling dust. Nothing I had ever seen before had so attracted me. The sheer bright infinite beauty of the stuff! I had seen it before of course, often enough, at the hospital; but this was quite a different thing. It was set off by its environment as a diamond is by its setting. It seemed alive. It sparkled intensely. It was like nothing else in Nature, unless it be those feathery crystals, wind-blown, that glisten on the lips of crevasses.

What followed sticks in my memory as if it were a conjurer's trick. I don't know by what gesture she constrained me. But her hand slowly rose not quite to the level of the table; and my face, hot, flushed, angry and eager, had bent down towards it. It seemed pure instinct, though I have little doubt now that it was the result of an unspoken suggestion. I drew the little heap of powder through my nostrils with one long breath. I felt even then like a choking man in a coal mine released at the last moment, filling his lungs for the first time with oxygen.

I don't know whether this is a common experience. I suspect that my medical training and reading, and hearing people talk, and the effect of all those ghoulish articles in the newspapers had something to do with it.

On the other hand, we must make a good deal of allowance, I think, for such an expert as Gretel Webster. No doubt she was worth her wage to the Boche. No doubt she had picked me out for part of "Die Rache." I had downed some pretty famous flyers.

But none of these thoughts occurred to me at the time. I do not think I have explained with sufficient emphasis the mental state to which I had been reduced by the appearance of Lou. She had become so far beyond my dreams—the unattainable.

Leaving out of account the effect of the alcohol, this had left me with an intolerable depression. There was something brutish, something of the baffled rat, in my consciousness.

"O Thou vampire Queen of the Flesh, wound as a snake
around the throats of men! I adore Thee, Evoe! I adore Thee, I
A O!"

Was she thinking of Gretel or of herself? Her beauty had choked
me, strangled me, torn my throat out. I had become insane with dull,
harsh lust. I hated her. But as I raised my head; as the sudden, the
instantaneous madness of cocaine swept from my nostrils to my brain—
that's a line of poetry, but I can't help it—get on!—the depression lifted
from my mind like the sun coming out of the clouds.

I heard as in a dream the rich, ripe voice of Lou:—

"O Thou fierce whirlpool of passion, that art sucked up by the
mouth of the sun! I adore Thee, Evoe! I adore Thee, I A O!"

The whole thing was different—I understood what she was saying,
I was part of it. I recognised, for one swift second, the meaning of my
previous depression. It was my sense of inferiority to her! Now I was
her man, her mate, her master!

I rose to catch her by the waist; but she whirled away down the floor
of the club like an autumn leaf before the storm. I caught the glance of
Gretel Webster's eyes. I saw them glitter with triumphant malice; and
for a moment she and Lou and cocaine and myself were all inextricably
interlocked in a tangled confusion of ruinous thought.

But my physical body was lifting me. It was the same old, wild
exhilaration that one gets from rising from the ground on one's good
days. I found myself in the middle of the floor without knowing how
I had got there. I, too, was walking on air. Lou turned, her mouth a
scarlet orb, as I have seen the sunset over Belgium, over the crinkled
line of shore, over the dim blue mystic curve of sea and sky; with the
thought in my mind beating in tune with my excited heart. We didn't
miss the arsenal this time. I was the arsenal too. I had exploded. I was
the slayer and the slain! And there sailed Lou across the sky to meet me.

"O Thou outrider of the Sun, that spurrest the bloody flanks of
the wind! I adore Thee, Evoe! I adore Thee, I A O!"

We came into each other's arms with the inevitableness of gravitation.
We were the only two people in the Universe—she and I. The only force

that existed in the Universe was the attraction between us. The force with which we came together set us spinning.

We went up and down the floor of the club; but, of course, it wasn't the floor of the club, there wasn't the club, there wasn't anything at all except a delirious feeling that one was everything, and had to get on with everything. One was the Universe eternally whirling. There was no possibility of fatigue; one's energy was equal to one's task.

"O Thou dancer with gilded nails, that unbraidest the star hair of the night! I adore Thee, Evoe! I adore Thee, I A O!"

Lou's slim, lithe body lay in my arm. It sounds absurd, but she reminded me of a light overcoat. Her head hung back, the heavy coils of hair came loose.

All of a sudden the band stopped. For a second the agony was indescribable. It seemed like annihilation. I was seized with an absolute revulsion against the whole of my surroundings. I whispered like a man in furious haste who must get something vital done before he dies, some words to the effect that I couldn't "stick this beastly place any longer—"

"Let's get some air."

She answered neither yes nor no. I had been wasting words to speak to her at all.

"O Thou bird-sweet river of Love, that warblest through the pebbly gorge of Life! I adore Thee, Evoe! I adore Thee, I A O!"

Her voice had sunk to a clear murmur. We found ourselves in the street. The chucker-out hailed us a taxi. I stopped her song at last. My mouth was on her mouth. We were driving in the chariot of the Sun through the circus of the Universe. We didn't know where we were going, and we didn't care. We had no sense of time at all. There was a sequence of sensations; but there was no means of regulating them. It was as if one's mental clock had suddenly gone mad.

I have no gauge of time, subjectively speaking, but it must have been a long while before our mouths separated, for as this happened I recognised the fact that we were very far from the club.

She spoke to me for the first time. Her voice thrilled dark unfathomable deeps of being. I tingled in every fibre. And what she said was this:—

"Your kiss is bitter with cocaine."

It is quite impossible to give those who have no experience of these matters any significance of what she said.

It was a boiling caldron of wickedness that had suddenly bubbled over. Her voice rang rich with hellish glee. It stimulated me to male intensity. I caught her in my arms more fiercely. The world went black before my eyes. I perceived nothing anymore. I can hardly even say that I felt. I was Feeling itself! I was all the possibilities of Feeling fulfilled to the uttermost. Yet, coincident with this, my body went on automatically with its own private affairs.

She was escaping me. Her face eluded mine.

"O Thou storm-drunk breath of the winds, that pant in the bosom of the mountains! I adore Thee, Evoe! I adore Thee, I A O!"

Her breast sobbed out its song with weird intensity.

I understood in a flash that this was her way of resistance. She was trying to insist to herself that she was a cosmic force; that she was not a woman at all; that a man meant nothing to her. She fought desperately against me, sliding so serpent-like about the bounds of space. Of course, it was really the taxi—but I didn't know it then, and I'm not quite sure of it now.

"I wish to God," I said to myself in a fury, "I had one more sniff of that Snow. I'd show her!"

At that moment she threw me off as if I had been a feather. I felt myself all of a sudden no more good. Quite unaccountably I had collapsed, and I found myself, to my amazement, knocking out a little pile of cocaine from a ten-gramme bottle which had been in my trousers' pocket, on to my hand, and sniffing it up into my nostrils with greedy relish.

Don't ask me how it got there. I suppose Gretel Webster must have done it somehow. My memory is an absolute blank. That's one of the funny things about cocaine. You never know quite what trick it is going to play you.

I was reminded of the American professor who boasted that he had a first-class memory whose only defect was that it wasn't reliable.

I am equally unable to tell you whether the fresh supply of the drug increased my powers, or whether Lou had simply tired of teasing me, but of her own accord she writhed into my arms; her hands and mouth were heavy on my heart. There's some more poetry—that's the way it takes one—rhythm seems to come natural—everything is one grand harmony. It is impossible that anything should be out of tune. The voice of Lou seemed to come from an enormous distance, a deep, low, sombre chant:—

"O Thou low moan of fainting maids, that art caught up in the strong sobs of Love! I adore Thee, Evoe! I adore Thee, I A O!"

That was it—her engine and my engine for the first time working together! All the accidents had disappeared. There was nothing but the unison of two rich racing rhythms.

You know how it is when you are flying—you see a speck in the air. You can't tell by your eyes if it is your Brother Boche coming to pot you, or one of our own or one of the allied 'planes. But you can tell them apart, foe from friend, by the different beat of their engines. So one comes to apprehend a particular rhythm as sympathetic—another as hostile.

So here were Lou and I flying together beyond the bounds of eternity, side by side; her low, persistent throb in perfect second to my great galloping boom.

Things of this sort take place outside time and space. It is quite wrong to say that what happened in the taxi ever began or ended. What happened was that our attention was distracted from the eternal truth of this essential marriage of our souls by the chauffeur, who had stopped the taxi and opened the door.

"Here we are, sir," he said, with a grin.

Sir Peter Pendragon and Lou Laleham automatically reappeared. Before all things, decorum!

The shock bit the incident deeply into my mind. I remember with the utmost distinctness paying the man off, and then being lost in absolute blank wonder as to how it happened that we were where we were. Who had given the address to the man, and where were we?

I can only suppose that, consciously or subconsciously, Lou had done it, for she showed no embarrassment in pressing the electric bell. The door opened immediately. I was snowed under by an avalanche of crimson light that poured from a vast studio.

Lou's voice soared high and clear:—

"O Thou scarlet dragon of flame, enmeshed in the web of a spider! I adore Thee, Evoe! I adore Thee, I A O!"

　　　　　　　　　　　　　　　　　　　　　　　ALEISTER CROWLEY

A revulsion of feeling rushed over me like a storm; for in the doorway, with Lou's arms round his neck, was the tall, black, sinister figure of King Lamus.

"I knew you wouldn't mind our dropping in, although it is so late," she was saying.

It would have been perfectly simple for him to acquiesce with a few conventional words. Instead, he was pontifical.

"There are four gates to one palace; the floor of that palace is of silver and gold; lapis-lazuli and jasper are there; and all rare scents; jasmine and rose, and the emblems of death. Let him enter in turn or at once the four gates; let him stand on the floor of the palace."

I was unfathomably angry. Why must the man always act like a cad or a clown? But there was nothing to do but to accept the situation and walk in politely.

He shook hands with me formally, yet with greater intensity than is customary between well-bred strangers in England. And as he did so, he looked me straight in the face. His deadly inscrutable eyes burned their way clean through to the back of my brain and beyond. Yet his words were entirely out of keeping with his actions.

"What does the poet say?" he said loftily—"*Rather a joke to fill up on coke*—or words to that effect, Sir Peter."

How in the devil's name did he know what I had been taking?

"Men who know things have no right to go about the world," something said irritably inside myself. But something else obscurely answered it.

"That accounts for what the world has always done—made martyrs of its pioneers."

I felt a little ashamed, to tell the truth; but Lamus put me at my ease. He waved his hand towards a huge arm-chair covered with Persian tapestries. He gave me a cigarette and lighted it for me. He poured out a drink of Benedictine into a huge curved glass, and put it on a little table by my side. I disliked his easy hospitality as much as anything else. I had an uncomfortable feeling that I was a puppet in his hands.

There was only one other person in the room. On a settee covered with leopard skins lay one of the strangest women I had ever seen. She wore a white evening dress with pale yellow roses, and the same flowers were in her hair. She was a half-blood negress from North Africa.

"Miss Fatma Hallaj," said Lamus.

I rose and bowed. But the girl took no notice. She seemed in utter oblivion of sublunary matters. Her skin was of that deep, rich night-sky blue which only very vulgar eyes imagine to be black. The face was gross and sensual, but the brows wide and commanding.

There is no type of intellect so essentially aristocratic as the Egyptian when it happens to be of the rare right strain.

"Don't be offended," said Lamus, in a soft voice, "she includes us all in her sublime disdain."

Lou was sitting on the arm of the couch; her ivory-white, long crooked fingers groping the dark girl's hair. Somehow or other I felt nauseated; I was uneasy, embarrassed. For the first time in my life I didn't know how to behave.

A thought popped into my mind: it was simply fatigue—I needn't bother about that.

As if in answer to my thought, Lou took a small cut-glass bottle with a gold-chased top from her pocket, unscrewed it and shook out some cocaine on the back of her hand. She flashed a provocative glance in my direction.

The studio suddenly filled with the reverberation of her chant:—

"O Thou naked virgin of love, that art caught in a net of wild roses! I adore Thee, Evoe! I adore Thee, I A O!"

"Quite so," agreed King Lamus cheerfully. "You'll excuse me, I know, if I ask whether you have any great experience of the effects of cocaine."

Lou glowered at him. I preferred to meet him frankly. I deliberately put a large dose on the back of my hand and sniffed it up. Before I had finished, the effect had occurred. I felt myself any man's master.

"Well, as a matter of fact," I said superciliously, "tonight's the first time I ever took it, and it strikes me as pretty good stuff."

Lamus smiled enigmatically.

"Ah, yes, what does the old poet say? Milton, is it?

> *'Stab your demoniac smile to my brain,*
> *Soak me in cognac, love, and cocaine.'*"

"How silly you are," cried Lou. "Cocaine wasn't invented in the time of Milton."

"Was that Milton's fault?" retorted King Lamus. The inaptitude, the disconnectedness, of his thought was somehow disconcerting.

He turned his back on her and looked me straight in the face.

"It strikes you as pretty good stuff, Sir Peter," he said, "and so it is. I'll have a dose myself to show there's no ill-feeling."

He suited the action to the words.

I had to admit that the man began to intrigue me. What was his game?

"I hear you're one of our best flying men, Sir Peter," he went on.

"I have flown a bit now and then," I admitted.

"Well, an aeroplane's a pretty good means of travel, but unless you're an expert, you're likely to make a pretty sticky finish."

"Thank you very much," I said, nettled at his tone. "As it happens, I'm a medical student."

"Oh, that's all right, then, of course."

He agreed with a courtesy which somehow cut deeper into my self-esteem than if he had openly challenged my competence.

"In that case," he continued, "I hope to arouse your professional interest in a case of what I think you will agree is something approaching indiscretion. My little friend here arrived tonight, or rather last night, full up to the neck with morphia. Dissatisfied with results, she swallowed a large dose of Anhalonium Lewinii, reckless of the pharmaceutical incompatability. Presumably to pass away the time, she has drunk an entire bottle of Grand Marnier Cordon Rouge; and now, feeling herself slightly indisposed, for some reason at which it would be presumptuous to guess, she is setting things right by an occasional indulgence in this pretty good stuff of yours."

He had turned away from me and was watching the girl intently. My glance followed his. I saw her deep blue skin fade to a dreadful pallor. She had lost her healthy colour; she suggested a piece of raw meat which is just beginning to go bad.

I jumped to my feet. I knew instinctively that the girl was about to collapse. The owner of the studio was bending over her. He looked at me over his shoulder out of the corners of his eyes.

"A case of indiscretion," he observed, with bitter irony.

For the next quarter of an hour he fought for the girl's life. King Lamus was a very skilled physician, though he had never studied medicine officially.

But I was not aware of what was going on. Cocaine was singing in my veins. I cared for nothing. Lou came over impulsively and flung herself across my knees. She held the goblet of Benedictine to my mouth, chanting ecstatically:—

"O Thou sparkling wine-cup of light, whose foaming is the heart's blood of the stars! I adore Thee, Evoe! I adore Thee, I A O!"

We swooned into a deep, deep trance. Lamus interrupted us.

"You mustn't think me inhospitable," he said. "She's come round all right; but I ought to drive her home. Make yourselves at home while I'm away, or let me take you where you want to go."

Another interruption occurred. The bell rang. Lamus sprang to the door. A tall old man was standing on the steps.

"Do what thou wilt shall be the whole of the Law," said Lamus.

"Love is the law, love under will," replied the other.

It was like a challenge and countersign.

"I've got to talk to you for an hour."

"Of course, I'm at your service," replied our host. "The only thing is——" He broke off.

My brain was extraordinarily clear. My self-confidence was boundless. I felt inspired. I saw the way out.

A little devil laughed in my heart: "What an excellent scheme to be alone with Lou!"

"Look here, Mr. Lamus," I said, speaking very quickly, "I can drive any kind of car. Let me take Miss Hallaj home."

The Arab girl was on her feet behind me.

"Yes, yes," she said, in a faint, yet excited voice. "That will be much the best thing. Thanks awfully."

They were the first words she had spoken.

"Yes, yes," chimed in Lou. "I want to drive in the moonlight."

The little group was huddled in the open doorway. On one side the dark crimson tides of electricity; on the other, the stainless splendour of our satellite.

"O Thou frail bluebell of moonlight, that art lost in the gardens of the stars! I adore Thee, Evoe! I adore Thee, I A O!"

The scene progressed with the vivid rapidity of a dream. We were in the garage—out of it—into the streets—at the Egyptian girl's hotel—and then—

III

PHAETON

Lou clung to me as I gripped the wheel. There was no need for us to speak. The trembling torrent of our passion swept us away. I had forgotten all about Lamus and his car. We were driving like the devil to Nowhere. A mad thought crossed my mind. It was thrown up by my "Unconscious," by the essential self of my being. Then some familiar object in the streets reminded me that I was not driving back to the studio. Some force in myself, of which I was not aware, had turned my face towards Kent. I was interpreting myself to myself. I knew what I was going to do. We were bound for Barley Grange; and then, oh, the wild moonlight ride to Paris!

The idea had been determined in me without any intervention of my own. It had been, in a way, the solution of an equation of which the terms were: firstly, a sort of mad identification of Lou with all one's romantic ideas of moonlight; then my physical habit as a flying man; and thirdly, the traditional connection of Paris with extravagant gaiety and luxuriant love.

I was quite aware at the time that my moral sense and my mental sense had been thrown overboard for the moment; but my attitude was simply: "Goodbye, Jonah!"

For the first time in my life I was being absolutely myself, freed from all the inhibitions of body, intellect, and training which keep us, normally, in what we call sane courses of action.

I seem to remember asking myself if I was insane, and answering, "Of course I am—sanity is a compromise. Sanity is the thing that keeps one back."

It would be quite useless to attempt to describe the drive to Barley Grange. It lasted barely half a second. It lasted age-less æons.

Any doubts that I might have had about myself were stamped under foot by the undeniable facts. I had never driven better in my life. I got out the seaplane as another man might get out a cigarette from his case. She started like an eagle. With the whirr of the engine came Lou's soft smooth voice in exquisite antiphony:—

"O Thou trembling breast of the night, that gleamest with a rosary of moons! I adore Thee, Evoe! I adore Thee, I A O!"

We soared towards the dawn. I went straight to over three thousand. I could hear the beat of my heart. It was one with the beat of the engine.

I took the pure unsullied air into my lungs. It was an octave to cocaine; the same invigorating spiritual force expressed in other terms.

The magnificently melodious words of Sieveking sprang into my mind. I repeated them rapturously. It is the beat of the British engine.

"Deep lungfuls! Deep mouthfuls! Deep, deep mental mouthfuls!"

The wind of our speed abolished all my familiar bodily sensations. The cocaine combined with it to anæsthetise them. I was disembodied; an eternal spirit; a Thing supreme, apart.

"Lou, sweetheart! Lou, sweetheart! Lou, Lou, perfect sweetheart!"

I must have shouted the refrain. Even amid the roar, I heard her singing back.

"O Thou summer softness of lips, that glow hot with the scarlet of passion! I adore Thee, Evoe! I adore Thee, I A O!"

I could not bear the weight of the air. Let us soar higher, ever higher! I increased the speed.

"Fierce frenzy! Fierce folly! Fierce, fierce, frenzied folly!"

"O Thou tortured shriek of the storm, that art whirled up through the leaves of the woods! I adore Thee, Evoe! I adore Thee, I A O!"

And I felt that we were borne on some tremendous tempest. The earth dropped from beneath us like a stone into blind nothingness. We were free, free forever, from the fetters of our birth!

"Soar swifter! Soar swifter! Soar, soar swifter, swifter!"

Before us, high in the pale gray, stood Jupiter, a four-square sapphire spark.

"O Thou bright star of the morning, that art set betwixt the breasts of the Night! I adore Thee, Evoe! I adore Thee, I A O!"

I shouted back.

"Star seekers! Star finders! Twin stars, silver shining!"

Up, still up, I drove. There hung a mass of thundercloud between me and the dawn. Damn it, how dared it! It had no business to be there. I must rise over it, trample it under my feet.

"O Thou purple breast of the storm, that art scarred by the teeth
of the lightning! I adore Thee, Evoe! I adore Thee, I A O!"

Frail waifs of mist beset us. I had understood Lou's joy in the cloud. It was I that was wrong. I had not had enough cocaine to be able to accept everything as infinite ecstasy. Her love carried me out of myself up to her triumphal passion. I understood the mist.

"O Thou unvintageable dew, that art moist on the lips of the
Morn! I adore Thee, Evoe! I adore Thee, I A O!"

At that moment, the practical part of me asserted itself with startling suddenness. I saw the dim line of the coast. I knew the line as I know the palm of my hand. I was a little out of the shortest line for Paris. I swerved slightly to the south.

Below, gray seas were tumbling. It seemed to me (insanely enough) that their moving wrinkles were the laughter of a very old man. I had a sudden intuition that something was wrong; and an instant later came an unmistakable indication of the trouble. I was out of gas.

My mind shot back with a vivid flash of hatred toward King Lamus. "A case of indiscretion!" He'd as good as called me a fool to my face. I thought of him as the sea, shaking with derisive laughter.

All the time I had been chuckling over my dear old squad commander. Not a great flyer, am I? This will show him! And that was true enough. I was incomparably better than I had ever been before. And yet I had omitted just one obvious precaution.

I suddenly realised that things might be exceedingly nasty. The only thing to be done was to shut off, and volplane down to the straits. And there were points in the problem which appalled me.

Oh, for another sniff! As we swooped down towards the sea in huge wide spirals, I managed to extract my bottle. Of course, I realised instantly the impossibility of taking it by the nose in such a wind. I pulled out the cork, and thrust my tongue into the neck of the bottle.

We were still three thousand feet or more above the sea. I had plenty of time, infinite time, I thought, as the drug took hold, to make my decision. I acted with superb aplomb. I touched the sea within a hundred yards of a fishing smack that had just put out from Deal.

We were picked up as a matter of course within a couple of minutes. They put back and towed the 'plane ashore.

My first thought was to get more gas and go on, despite the absurdity of our position. But the sympathy of the men on the beach was mixed with a good deal of hearty chaff. Dripping, in evening dress, at four o'clock in the morning! Like Hedda Gabler, "one doesn't do these things."

But the cocaine helped me again. Why the devil should I care what anybody thought?

"Where can I get gas?" I said to the captain of the smack.

He smiled grimly.

"She'll want a bit more than gas."

I glanced at the 'plane. The man was perfectly right. A week's repairs, at the least.

"You'd better go to the hotel, sir, and get some warm clothes. Look how the lady's shivering."

It was perfectly true. There was nothing else to be done. We went together slowly up the beach.

There was no question of sleeping, of course. Both of us were as fresh as paint. What we needed was hot food and lots of it.

We got it.

It seemed as if we had entered upon an entirely new phase. The disaster had purged us of that orchestral oratorio business; but, on the other hand, we were still full of intense practical activity.

We ate three breakfasts each. And as we ate we talked; talked racy, violent nonsense, most of it. Yet we were both well aware that the whole thing was camouflage. What we had to do was to get married as quickly as we could, and lay in a stock of cocaine, and go away and have a perfectly glorious time forever and ever.

We sent for emergency clothes in the town, and went stalking a parson. He was an old man who had lived for years out of the world. He saw nothing particularly wrong with us except youth and enthusiasm, and he was very sorry that it would take three weeks to turn us off.

The good old boy explained the law.

"Oh, that's easy," we said in a breath. "Let's get the first train to London."

There are no incidents to record. We were both completely anæsthetised. Nothing bothered us. We didn't mind the waiting on the platform, or the way the old train lumbered up to London.

Everything was part of the plan. Everything was perfect pleasure. We were living above ourselves, living at a tremendous pace. The speed of the 'plane became merely a symbol, a physical projection of our spiritual sublimity.

The next two days passed like pantomime. We were married in a dirty little office by a dirty little man. We took back his car to Lamus. I was amused to discover that I had left it standing in the open half over the edge of the lake.

I made a million arrangements in a kind of whirling wisdom. Before forty-eight hours had passed we were packed and off for Paris.

I did not remember anything in detail. All events were so many base metals fused into an alloy whose name was Excitement. During the whole time we only slept once, and then we slept well and woke fresh, without one trace of fatigue.

We had called on Gretel and obtained a supply of cocaine. She wouldn't accept any money from her dear Sir Peter, and she was so happy to see Lou Lady Pendragon, and wouldn't we come and see her after the honeymoon?

That call is the one thing that sticks in my mind. I suppose I realised obscurely somehow that the woman was in reality the mainspring of the whole manœuvre.

She introduced us to her husband, a heavy, pursy old man with a paunch and a beard, a reputation for righteousness, and an unctuous way of saying the right kind of nothing. But I divined a certain shrewdness in his eyes; it belied his mask of ostentatious innocence.

There was another man there too, a kind of half-baked Nonconformist parson, one Jabez Platt, who had realised early in life that his mission was to go about doing good. Some people said that he had done a great deal of good—to himself. His principle in politics was a very simple one: If you see anything, stop it; everything that is, is wrong; the world is a very wicked place.

He was very enthusiastic about putting through a law for suppressing the evil of drugs.

We smiled our sympathetic assent, with sly glances at our hostess. If the old fool had only known that we were full of cocaine, as we sat and applauded his pompous platitudes!

WE LAUGHED OUR HEARTS OUT over the silly incident as we sat in the train. It doesn't appear particularly comic in perspective; but it's very hard to tell, at anytime, what is going to tickle one's sense of humour. Probably anything else would have done just as well. We were on the rising curve. The exaltation of love was combined with that of cocaine; and the romance and adventure of our lives formed an exhilarating setting for those superb jewels.

"Everyday, in every way, I get better and better."

M. Coué's now famous formula is the precise intellectual expression of the curve of the cocaine honeymoon. Normal life is like an aeroplane before she rises. There is a series of little bumps; all one can say is that one is getting along more or less. Then she begins to rise clear of earth. There are no more obstacles to the flight.

But there are still mental obstacles; a fence, a row of houses, a grove of elms or what not. One is a little anxious to realise that they have to be cleared. But as she soars into the boundless blue, there comes that sense of mental exhilaration that goes with boundless freedom.

Our grandfathers must have known something about this feeling by living in England before the liberty of the country was destroyed by legislation, or rather the delegation of legislation to petty officialdom.

About six months ago I imported some tobacco, rolls of black perique, the best and purest in the world. By-and-by I got tired of cutting it up, and sent it to a tobacconist for the purpose.

Oh, dear no, quite impossible without a permit from the Custom House!

I suppose I really ought to give myself up to the police.

Yes, as one gets into the full swing of cocaine, one loses all consciousness of the bumpy character of this funny old oblate spheroid. One is really very much more competent to deal with the affairs of life, that is, in a certain sense of the word.

M. Coué is perfectly right, just as the Christian Scientists and all those people are perfectly right, in saying that half our troubles come from our consciousness of their existence, so that if we forget their existence, they actually cease to exist!

Haven't we got an old proverb to the effect that "what the eye doesn't see, the heart doesn't grieve over?"

When one is on one's cocaine honeymoon, one is really, to a certain extent, superior to one's fellows. One attacks every problem with perfect confidence. It is a combination of what the French call *élan* and what they call *insouciance*.

The British Empire is due to this spirit. Our young men went out to India and all sorts of places, and walked all over everybody because they were too ignorant to realise the difficulties in their way. They were taught that if one had good blood in one's veins, and a public school and university training to habituate one to being a lord of creation, and to the feeling that it was impossible to fail, and to not knowing enough to know when one was beaten, nothing could ever go wrong.

We are losing the Empire because we have become "sicklied o'er with the pale cast of thought." The intellectuals have made us like "the poor cat i' the adage." The spirit of Hamlet has replaced that of Macbeth. Macbeth only went wrong because the heart was taken out of him by Macduff's interpretation of what the witches had said.

Coriolanus only failed when he stopped to think. As the poet says, "The love of knowledge is the hate of life."

Cocaine removes all hesitation. But our forefathers owed their freedom of spirit to the real liberty which they had won; and cocaine is merely Dutch courage. However, while it lasts, it's all right.

IV

AU PAYS DE COCAINE

I can't remember any details of our first week in Paris. Details had ceased to exist. We whirled from pleasure to pleasure in one inexhaustible rush. We took everything in our stride. I cannot begin to describe the blind, boundless beatitude of love. Every incident was equally exquisite.

Of course, Paris lays herself out especially to deal with people in just that state of mind. We were living at ten times the normal voltage. This was true in more senses than one. I had taken a thousand pounds in cash from London, thinking as I did so how jolly it was to be reckless. We were going to have a good time, and damn the expense!

I thought of a thousand pounds as enough to paint Paris every colour of the spectrum for a quite indefinitely long period; but at the end of the week the thousand pounds was gone, and so was another thousand pounds for which I had cabled to London; and we had absolutely nothing to show for it except a couple of dresses for Lou, and a few not very expensive pieces of jewellery.

We felt that we were very economical. We were too happy to need to spend money. For one thing, love never needs more than a pittance, and I had never before known what love could mean.

What I may call the honeymoon part of the honeymoon seemed to occupy the whole of our waking hours. It left us no time to haunt Montmartre. We hardly troubled to eat, we hardly knew we were eating. We didn't seem to need sleep. We never got tired.

The first hint of fatigue sent one's hand to one's pocket. One sniff which gave us a sensation of the most exquisitely delicious wickedness, and we were on fourth speed again!

The only incident worth recording is the receipt of a letter and a box from Gretel Webster. The box contained a padded kimono for Lou, one of those gorgeous Japanese geisha silks, blue like a summer sky with dragons worked all over it in gold, with scarlet eyes and tongues.

Lou looked more distractingly, deliriously glorious than ever.

I had never been particularly keen on women. The few love affairs which had come my way had been rather silly and sordid. They had not revealed the possibilities of love; in fact, I had thought it a somewhat overrated pleasure, a brief and brutal blindness with boredom and disgust hard on its heels.

But with cocaine, things are absolutely different.

I want to emphasise the fact that cocaine is in reality a local anæsthetic. That is the actual explanation of its action. One cannot feel one's body. (As everyone knows, this is the purpose for which it is used in surgery and dentistry.)

Now don't imagine that this means that the physical pleasures of marriage are diminished, but they are utterly etherealised. The animal part of one is intensely stimulated so far as its own action is concerned; but the feeling that this passion is animal is completely transmuted.

I come of a very refined race, keenly observant and easily nauseated. The little intimate incidents inseparable from love affairs, which in normal circumstances tend to jar the delicacy of one's sensibilities, do so no longer when one's furnace is full of coke. Everything soever is transmuted as by "heavenly alchemy" into a spiritual beatitude. One is intensely conscious of the body. But as the Buddhists tell us, the body is in reality an instrument of pain or discomfort. We have all of us a subconscious intuition that this is the case; and this is annihilated by cocaine.

Let me emphasise once more the absence of any reaction. There is where the infernal subtlety of the drug comes in. If one goes on the bust in the ordinary way on alcohol, one gets what the Americans call "the morning after the night before." Nature warns us that we have been breaking the rules; and Nature has given us common sense enough to know that although we can borrow a bit, we have to pay back.

We have drunk alcohol since the beginning of time; and it is in our racial consciousness that although "a hair of the dog" will put one right after a spree, it won't do to choke oneself with hair.

But with cocaine, all this caution is utterly abrogated. Nobody would be really much the worse for a night with the drug, provided that he had the sense to spend the next day in a Turkish bath, and build up with food and a double allowance of sleep. But cocaine insists upon one's living upon one's capital, and assures one that the fund is inexhaustible.

As I said, it is a local anæsthetic. It deadens any feeling which might arouse what physiologists call inhibition. One becomes absolutely reckless. One is bounding with health and bubbling with high spirits. It is a blind excitement of so sublime a character that it is impossible to worry about anything. And yet, this excitement is singularly calm and profound. There is nothing of the suggestion of coarseness which we associate with ordinary drunkenness. The very idea of coarseness or commonness is abolished. It is like the vision of Peter in the Acts of the Apostles in which he was told, "There is nothing common or unclean."

As Blake said, "Everything that lives is holy." Every act is a sacrament. Incidents which in the ordinary way would check one or annoy one, become merely material for joyous laughter. It is just as when you drop a tiny lump of sugar into champagne, it bubbles afresh.

Well, this is a digression. But that is just what cocaine does. The sober continuity of thought is broken up. One goes off at a tangent, a fresh, fierce, fantastic tangent, on the slightest excuse. One's sense of proportion is gone; and despite all the millions of miles that one cheerily goes out of one's way, one never loses sight of one's goal.

While I have been writing all this, I have never lost sight for a moment of the fact that I am telling you about the box and the letter from Gretel.

We met a girl in Paris, half a Red Indian, a lovely baby with the fascination of a fiend and a fund of the foulest stories that ever were told. She lived on cocaine. She was a more or less uneducated girl; and the way she put it was this: "I'm in a long, lovely garden, with my arms full of parcels, and I keep on dropping one; and when I stoop to pick it up, I always drop another, and all the time I am sailing along up the garden."

So this was Gretel's letter.

My Darling Lou,

I could not *begin* to tell you the other day how delighted I was to see you My Lady and with such a *splendid* man for your husband. I don't blame you for getting married in such a hurry; but, on the other hand, you mustn't blame your old friends for not being prophets! So I could not be on hand with the goods. However, I have lost no time. You know how poor I am, but I hope you will value the little present I am sending you, not for its own sake, but as a token of my *deep affection* for the loveliest and most charming girl I know. A word in your ear, my dear Lou: *the inside is sometimes better than the outside*. With my *very kindest* regards and best wishes

to dear Sir Peter and yourself, though I can't expect you to
know that I even exist at the present,

Yours ever devotedly,
GRETEL

Lou threw the letter across the table to me. For some reason or no
reason, I was irritated. I didn't want to hear from people like that at all.
I didn't like or trust her.

"Queer fish," I said rather snappily.

It wasn't my own voice; it was, I fancy, some deep instinct of self-
preservation speaking within me.

Lou, however, was radiant about it. I wish I could give you an idea of
the sparkling quality of everything she said and did. Her eyes glittered,
her lips twittered, her cheeks glowed like fresh blown buds in spring.
She was the spirit of cocaine incarnate; cocaine made flesh. Her mere
existence made the Universe infinitely exciting. Say, if you like, she was
possessed of the devil!

Any good person, so-called, would have been shocked and scared at
her appearance. She represented the siren, the vampire, Melusine, the
dangerous, delicious devil that cowards have invented to explain their
lack of manliness. Nothing would suit her mood but that we should
dine up there in the room, so that she could wear the new kimono and
dance for me at dinner.

We ate gray caviare, spoonful by spoonful. Who cared that it was
worth three times its weight in gold? It's no use calling me extravagant;
if you want to blame anyone, blame the Kaiser. He started the whole
fuss; and when I feel like eating gray caviare, I'm going to eat gray
caviare.

We wolfed it down. It's silly to think that things matter.

Lou danced like a delirious demon between the courses. It pleased
her to assume the psychology of the Oriental pleasure-making woman.
I was her Pasha-with-three-tails, her Samurai warrior, her gorgeous
Maharaja, with a scimitar across my knee, ready to cut her head off at
the first excuse.

She was the Ouled Näil with tatooed cheeks and chin, with painted
antimony eyebrows, and red smeared lips.

I was the masked Toureg, the brigand from the desert, who had
captured her.

She played a thousand exquisite crazy parts.

I have very little imagination, my brain runs entirely to analysis; but I revel in playing a part that is devised for me. I don't know how many times during that one dinner I turned from a civilised husband in Bond Street pyjamas into a raging madman.

It was only after the waiters had left us with the coffee and liqueurs—which we drank like water without being affected—that Lou suddenly threw off her glittering garment.

She stood in the middle of the room, and drank a champagne glass half full of liqueur brandy. The entrancing boldness of her gesture started me screaming inwardly. I jumped up like a crouching tiger that suddenly sees a stag.

Lou was giggling all over with irrepressible excitement. I know "giggling all over" isn't English; but I can't express it any other way.

She checked my rush as if she had been playing full back in an International Rugger match.

"Get the scissors," she whispered.

I understood in a second what she meant. It was perfectly true—we had been playing it a bit on the heavy side with that snow. I think it must have been about five sniffs. If you're curious, all you have to do is to go back and count it up—to get me to ten thousand feet above the poor old Straits of Dover, God bless them! But it was adding up like the price of the nails in the horse's shoes that my father used to think funny when I was a kid. You know what I mean—Martingale principle and all that sort of thing. We certainly had been punishing the snow.

Five sniffs! it wasn't much in our young lives after a fortnight.

Gwendolen Otter says:—

> "Heart of my heart, in the pale moonlight,
> Why should we wait till tomorrow night?"

And that's really very much the same spirit.

> "Heart of my heart, come out of the rain,
> Let's have another go of cocaine."

I know I don't count when it comes to poetry, and the distinguished authoress can well afford to smile, if it's only the society smile, and step quietly over my remains. But I really have got the spirit of the thing.

"Always go on till you have to stop,
Let's have another sniff, old top!"

No, that's undignified.

"Carry on! over the top!"

would be better. It's more dignified and patriotic, and expresses the idea much better. And if you don't like it, you can inquire elsewhere.

No, I won't admit that we were reckless. We had substantial resources at our command. There was nothing whatever of the "long firm" about us.

You all know perfectly well how difficult it is to keep matches. Perfectly trivial things, matches—always using them, always easy to replace them, no matter at all for surprise if one should find one's box empty; and I don't admit for one moment that I showed any lack of proportion in the matter.

Now don't bring that moonlight flight to Paris up against me. I admit I was out of gas; but everyone knows how one's occupation with one's first love affair is liable to cause a temporary derangement of one's ordinary habits.

What I liked about it was that evidently Gretel was a jolly good sport, whatever people said about her. And she wasn't an ordinary kind of good old sport either. I don't see any reason why I shouldn't admit that she is what you may call a true friend in the most early Victorian sense of the word you can imagine.

She was not only a true friend, but a wise friend. She had evidently foreseen that we were going to run short of good old snow.

Now I want all you fellows to take it as read that a man, if he calls himself a man, isn't the kind of man that wants to stop a honeymoon with a girl in a Japanese kimono of the variety described, to have to put on a lot of beastly clothes and hunt all around Paris for a dope peddler.

Of course, you'll say at once that I could have rung for the waiter and have him bring me a few cubic kilometres. But that's simply because you don't understand the kind of hotel at which we were unfortunate enough to be staying. We had gone there thinking no harm whatever. It was right up near the Étoile, and appeared to the naked eye an absolutely respectable first-class family hotel for the sons of the nobility and gentry.

Now don't run away with the idea that I want to knock the hotel. It was simply because France had been bled white; but the waiter on our floor was a middle-aged family man and probably read Lamartine and Pascal and Taine and all those appalling old bores when he wasn't doing shot drill with the caviare. But it isn't the slightest use my trying to conceal from you the fact that he always wore a slightly shocked expression, especially in the way he cut his beard. It was emphatically not the thing whenever he came into the suite.

I am a bit of a psychologist myself, and I know perfectly well that that man wouldn't have got us cocaine, not if we'd offered him a Bureau de Tabac for doing it.

Now, of course, I'm not going to ask you to believe that Gretel Webster knew anything about that waiter—beastly old prig! All she had done was to exhibit wise forethought and intelligent friendship. She had experience, no doubt, bushels of it, barrels of it, hogsheads of it, all those measures that I couldn't learn at school.

She had said to herself, in perfectly general terms, without necessarily contemplating any particular train of events as follows:—

"From one cause or another, those nice kids may find themselves shy on snow at a critical moment in their careers, so it's up to me to see that they get it."

While these thoughts were passing through my mind, I had got the manicure scissors, and Lou was snipping the threads of her kimono lining round those places where those fiercely fascinating fingers of hers had felt what we used to call in the hospital a foreign body.

Yes, there was no mistake. Gretel had got our psychology, we had got her psychology, everything was going as well as green peas go with a duck.

Don't imagine we had to spoil the kimono. It was just a tuck in the quilting. Out comes a dear little white silk bag; and we open that, and there's a heap of snow that I'd much rather see than Mont Blanc.

Well, you know, when you see it, you've got to sniff it. What's it for? Nobody can answer that. Don't tell me about "use in operations on the throat." Lou didn't need anything done to her throat. She sang like Melba, and she looked like a peach; and she was a Pêche-Melba, just like two and two makes four.

You bet we sniffed! And then we danced all round the suite for several years—probably as much as eight or nine minutes by the clock—but what's the use of talking about clocks when Einstein has proved that time is only another dimension of space? What's the good of astronomers proving that the earth wiggles round 1000 miles an hour, and wiggles on 1000 miles a minute, if you can't keep going?

It would be absolutely silly to hang about and get left behind, and very likely find ourselves on the moon, and nobody to talk to but Jules Verne, H. G. Wells, and that crowd.

Now I don't want you to think that that white silk packet was very big.

Lou stooped over the table, her long thin tongue shot out of her mouth like an ant-eater in the Dictionary of National Biography or whatever it is, and twiddled it round in that snow till I nearly went out of my mind.

I laughed like a hyena, to think of what she'd said to me. "Your kiss is bitter with cocaine." That chap Swinburne was always talking about bitter kisses. What did he know, poor old boy?

Until you've got your mouth full of cocaine, you don't know what kissing is. One kiss goes on from phase to phase like one of those novels by Balzac and Zola and Romain Rolland and D. H. Lawrence and those chaps. And you never get tired! You're on fourth speed all the time, and the engine purrs like a kitten, a big white kitten with the stars in its whiskers. And it's always different and always the same, and it never stops, and you go insane, and you stay insane, and you probably don't know what I'm talking about, and I don't care a bit, and I'm awfully sorry for you, and you can find out any minute you like by the simple process of getting a girl like Lou and a lot of cocaine.

What did that fellow Lamus say?

> *"Stab your demoniac smile to my brain,*
> *Soak me in cognac, kisses, cocaine."*

Queer fish, that chap Lamus! But seems to me that's pretty good evidence he knew something about it. Why, of course he did. I saw him take cocaine myself. Deep chap! Bet you a shilling. Knows a lot. That's no reason for suspicion. Don't see why people run him down the way they do. Don't see why I got so leary myself. Probably a perfectly decent chap at bottom. He's got his funny little ways—man's no worse for that.

Gad, if one started to get worried about funny little ways, what price Lou! Queerest card in the pack, and I love her.

"Give me another sniff off your hand."

Lou laughed like a chime of bells in Moscow on Easter morning. Remember, the Russian Easter is not the same time as our Easter. They slipped up a fortnight one way or the other—I never can remember which—as long as you know what I mean.

She threw the empty silk bag in the air, and caught it in her teeth with a passionate snap, which sent me nearly out of my mind again. I would have loved to be a bird, and have my head snapped off by those white, small, sharp incisors.

Practical girl, my Lady Pendragon! Instead of going off the deep end, she was cutting out another packet, and when it was opened, instead of the birds beginning to sing, she said in shrill excitement, "Look here, Cockie, this isn't snow."

I ought to explain that she calls me Cockie in allusion to the fact that my name is Peter.

I came out of my trance. I looked at the stuff with what I imagine to have been a dull, glazed eye. Then my old training came to my rescue.

It was a white powder with a tendency to form little lumps rather like chalk. I rubbed it between my finger and thumb. I smelt it. That told me nothing. I tasted it. That told me nothing, either, because the nerves of my tongue were entirely anæsthetised by the cocaine.

But the investigation was a mere formality. I know now why I made it. It was the mere gesture of the male. I wanted to show off to Lou. I wished to impress upon her my importance as a man of science; and all the time I knew, without being told, what it was.

So did she. The longer I have known Lou, the more impressed I am with the extent and variety of her knowledge.

"Oh, Gretel is too sweet," she chirped. "She guessed we might get tired of coco, 'grateful and comforting' as it is. So the dear old thing sent us some heroin. And there are still some people who tell us that life is not worth living!"

"Ever try it?" I asked, and delayed the answer with a kiss.

When the worst was over, she told me that she had only taken it once, and then, in a very minute dose, which had had no effect on her as far as she knew.

"That's all right," I said, from the height of my superior knowledge. "It's all a question of estimating the physiological dose. It's very fine indeed. The stimulation is very much better than that of morphine. One gets the same intense beatific calm, but without the languor. Why, Lou, darling, you've read De Quincey and all those people about opium, haven't you? Opium's a mixture, you know—something like twenty different alkaloids in it. Laudanum: Coleridge took it, and Clive—all sorts of important people. It's a solution of opium in alcohol. But morphia is the most active and important of the principles in opium. You could take it in all sorts of ways. Injection gives the best results; but it's rather a nuisance, and there's always danger of getting dirt in. You have to look out for blood-poisoning all the time. It stimulates the imagination marvellously. It kills all pain and worry like a charm. But at the very moment when you have the most gorgeous ideas, when you build golden palaces of what you are going to do, you have a feeling at the same time that nothing is really worth doing, and that itself gives you a feeling of terrific superiority to everything else in the world. And so, from the objective point of view, it comes to nothing. But heroin does all that morphia does. It's a derivative of morphia, you know—Diacetyl-Morphine is the technical name. Only instead of bathing you in philosophical inertia, you are as keen as mustard on carrying out your ideas. I've never taken any myself. I suppose we might as well start now."

I had a vision of myself as a peacock strutting and preening. Lou, her mouth half open, was gazing at me fascinated with enormous eyes; the pupils dilated by cocaine. It was just the male bird showing off to his mate. I wanted her to adore me for my little scraps of knowledge; the fragments I had picked up in my abandoned education.

Lou is always practical; and she puts something of the priestess into everything she does. There was a certain solemnity in the way in which she took up the heroin on the blade of a knife and put it on to the back of her hand.

"My Knight," she said, with flashing eyes, "your Lady arms you for the fight."

And she held out her fist to my nostrils. I snuffed up the heroin with a sort of ritualistic reverence. I can't imagine where the instinct came from. Is it the sparkle of cocaine that excites one to take it greedily, and the dullness of the heroin which makes it seem a much more serious business?

I felt as if I were going through some very important ceremony. When I had finished, Lou measured a dose for herself. She took it with a deep, grave interest.

I was reminded of the manner of my old professor at U.C.H. when he came to inspect a new case; a case mysterious but evidently critical.

The excitement of the cocaine had somehow solidified. Our minds had stopped still, and yet their arrest was as intense as their previous motion.

We found ourselves looking into each other's eyes with no less ardour than before; but somehow it was a different kind of ardour. It was as if we had been released from the necessity of existence in the ordinary sense of the word. We were both wondering who we were and what we were and what was going to happen; and, at the same time, we had a positive certainty that nothing could possibly happen.

It was a most extraordinary feeling. It was of a kind quite unimaginable by any ordinary mind. I will go a bit further than that. I don't believe the greatest artist in the world could invent what we felt, and if he could he couldn't describe it.

I'm trying to describe it myself, and I feel that I'm not making out very well. Come to think of it, the English language has its limitations. When mathematicians and men of science want to exchange thoughts, English isn't much good. They've had to invent new words, new symbols. Look at Einstein's equations.

I knew a man once that knew James Hinton, who invented the fourth dimension. Pretty bright chap, he was, but Hinton thought, on the most ordinary subjects, at least six times as fast as he did, and when it came to Hinton's explaining himself, he simply couldn't do it.

That's the great trouble when a new thinker comes along. They all moan that they can't understand him; the fact annoys them very much; and ten to one they persecute him and call him an Atheist or a Degenerate or a Pro-German or a Bolshevik, or whatever the favourite term of abuse happens to be at the time.

Wells told us a bit about this in that book of his about giants, and so does Bernard Shaw in his *Back to Methuselah*. It's nobody's fault in particular, but there it is, and you can't get over it.

And here was I, a perfectly ordinary man, with just about the average allowance of brains, suddenly finding myself cut off from the world, in a class by myself—I felt that I had something perfectly tremendous to tell, but I couldn't tell even myself what it was.

And there was Lou standing right opposite, and I recognised instinctively, by sympathy, that she was just in the same place.

We had no need of communicating with each other by means of articulate speech. We understood perfectly; we expressed the fact in every subtle harmony of glance and gesture.

The world had stopped suddenly still. We were alone in the night and the silence of things. We belonged to eternity in some indefinable way; and that infinite silence blossoms inscrutably into embrace.

The heroin had begun to take hold. We felt ourselves crowned with colossal calm. We were masters; we had budded from nothingness into existence! And now, existence slowly compelled us to action. There was a necessity in our own natures which demanded expression and after the first intense inter-penetration of our individualities, we had reached the resultant of all the forces that composed us.

In one sense, it was that our happiness was so huge that we could not bear it; and we slid imperceptibly into conceding that the ineffable mysteries must be expressed by means of sacramental action.

But all this took place at an immense distance from reality. A concealed chain of interpretation linked the truth with the obvious commonplace fact that this was a good time to go across to Montmartre and make a night of it.

We dressed to go out with, I imagine, the very sort of feeling as a newly made bishop would have the first time he puts on his vestments.

But none of this would have been intelligible to, or suspected by, anybody who had seen us. We laughed and sang and interchanged gay nothings while we dressed.

When we went downstairs, we felt like gods descending upon earth, immeasurably beyond mortality.

With the cocaine, we had noticed that people smiled rather strangely. Our enthusiasm was observed. We even felt a little touch of annoyance at everybody not going at the same pace; but this was perfectly different. The sense of our superiority to mankind was constantly present. We were dignified beyond all words to express. Our own voices sounded far, far off. We were perfectly convinced that the hotel porter realised that he was receiving the orders of Jupiter and Juno to get a taxi.

We never doubted that the chauffeur knew himself to be the charioteer of the sun.

"This is perfectly wonderful stuff," I said to Lou as we passed the Arc de Triomphe. "I don't know what you meant by saying the stuff didn't have any special effect upon you. Why, you're perfectly gorgeous!"

"You bet I am," laughed Lou. "The king's daughter is all-glorious within; her raiment is of wrought gold, and she thrusts her face out to be kissed, like a comet pushing its way to the sun. Didn't you know I was the king's daughter?" she smiled, with such seductive sublimity that something in me nearly fainted with delight.

"Hold up, Cockie," she chirped. "It's all right. You're it, and I'm it, and I'm your little wife."

I could have torn the upholstery out of the taxi. I felt myself a giant. Gargantua was a pigmy. I felt the need of smashing something into matchwood, and I was all messed up about it because it was Lou that I wanted to smash, and at the same time she was the most precious and delicate piece of porcelain that ever came out of the Ming dynasty or whatever the beastly period is.

The most fragile, exquisite beauty! To touch her was to profane her. I had a sudden nauseating sense of the bestiality of marriage.

I had no idea at the time that this sudden revulsion of feeling was due to a mysterious premonition of the physiological effects of heroin in destroying love. Definitely stimulating things like alcohol, hashish and cocaine give free range to Cupid. Their destructive effect on him is simply due to the reaction. One is in debt, so to speak, because one has outrun the constable.

But what I may call the philosophical types of dope, of which morphine and heroin are the principal examples, are directly inimical to active emotion and emotional action. The normal human feelings are transmuted into what seem on the surface their spiritual equivalents. Ordinary good feeling becomes universal benevolence; a philanthropy which is infinitely tolerant because the moral code has become meaningless for it. A more than Satanic pride swells in one's soul. As Baudelaire says: "Hast thou not sovereign contempt, which makes the soul so kind?"

As we drove up the Butte Montmartre towards the Sacré Cœur, we remained completely silent, lost in our calm beatitude. You must understand that we were already excited to the highest point. The effect of the heroin had been to steady us in that state.

Instead of beating passionately up the sky with flaming wings, we were poised aloft in the illimitable ether. We took fresh doses of the dull soft powder now and again. We did so without greed, hurry or even desire. The sensation was of infinite power which could afford infinite deliberation. Will itself seemed to have been abolished. We were going nowhere in particular, simply because it was our nature so to do. Our beatitude became more absolute every moment.

With cocaine, one is indeed master of everything; but everything matters intensely.

With heroin, the feeling of mastery increases to such a point that nothing matters at all. There is not even the disinclination to do what one happens to be doing which keeps the opium smoker inactive. The body is left to itself so perfectly that one is not worried by its natural activities.

Again, despite our consciousness of infinity, we maintained, concurrently, a perfect sense of proportion in respect of ordinary matters.

V

A HEROIN HEROINE

I stopped the taxi in the Place du Tertre. We wanted to walk along the edge of the Butte and let our gaze wander over Paris.

The night was delicious. Nowhere but in Paris does one experience that soft suave hush; the heat is dry, the air is light, it is quite unlike anything one ever gets in England.

A very gentle breeze, to which our fancy attributed the redolence of the South, streamed up from the Seine. Paris itself was a blur of misty blue; the Pantheon and the Eiffel Tower leapt from its folds. They seemed like symbols of the history of mankind; the noble, solid past and the mechanical efficient future.

I leant upon the parapet entranced. Lou's arm was around my neck. We were so still that I could feel her pulses softly beating.

"Great Scott, Pendragon!"

For all its suggestion of surprise, the voice was low and winsome. I looked around.

Had I been asked, I should have said, no doubt, that I should have resented any disturbance; and here was a sudden, violent, unpleasant disturbance; and it did not disturb me. There was a somewhat tentative smile on the face of the man who had spoken. I recognised him instantly, though I had not seen him since we were at school together. The man's name was Elgin Feccles. He had been in the mathematical sixth when I was in the lower school.

In my third term he had become head prefect; he had won a scholarship at Oxford—one of the best things going. Then, without a moment's warning, he had disappeared from the school. Very few people knew why, and those who did pretended not to. But he never went to Oxford.

I had only heard of the man once since. It was in the club. His name came up in connection with some vague gossip about some crooked financial affair. I had it in my mind, vaguely enough, that that must have had something to do with the trouble at school. He was not the sort of boy to be expelled for any of the ordinary reasons. It was certainly something to do with the subtlety of his intellect. To tell you the truth, he had been a sort of hero of mine at school. He possessed all the qualities I most admired—and lacked—in their fullest expansion.

I had known him very slightly; but his disappearance had been a great shock. It had stuck in my mind when many more important things had left no trace.

He had hardly changed from when I had last seen him. Of middle height, he had a long and rather narrow face. There was a touch of the ecclesiastic in his expression. His eyes were small and gray; he had a trick of blinking. The nose was long and beaked like Wellington's; the mouth was thin and tense; the skin was fresh and rosy. He had not developed even the tiniest wrinkle.

He kept the old uneasy nervous movement which had been so singular in him as a boy. One would have said that he was constantly on the alert, expecting something to happen, and yet the last thing that anyone could have said about him was that he was ill at ease. He possessed superb confidence.

Before I had finished recognising him, he had shaken hands with me and was prattling about the old days.

"I hear you're Sir Peter now, by the way," he said. "Good for you. I always picked you for a winner."

"I think I've met you," interrupted Lou. "Surely, it's Mr. Feccles."

"Oh, yes, I remember you quite well. Miss Laleham, isn't it?"

"Please let's forget the past," smiled Lou, taking my arm.

I don't know why I should have felt embarrassed at explaining that we were married.

Feccles rattled off a string of congratulations.

"May I introduce Mademoiselle Haidée Lamoureux?"

The girl beside him smiled and bowed.

Haidée Lamoureux was a brilliant brunette with a flashing smile and eyes with pupils like pin-points. She was a mass of charming contradictions. The nose and mouth suggested more than a trace of Semitic blood, but the wedge-shaped contour of the face betokened some very opposite strain. Her cheeks were hollow, and crows' feet marred the corners of her eyes. Dark purple rims suggested sensual indulgence pushed to the point of weariness. Though her hair was luxuriant, the eyebrows were almost non-existent. She had pencilled fine black arches above them. She was heavily and clumsily painted. She wore a loose and rather daring evening dress of blue with silver sequins, and a yellow sash spotted with black. Over this she had thrown a cloak of black lace garnished with vermilion tassels. Her hands were deathly thin. There was something obscene in the crookedness of her fingers, which were covered with enormous rings of sapphires and diamonds.

Her manner was one of vivid languor. It seemed as if she always had to be startled into action, and that the instant the first stimulus had passed she relapsed into her own deep thoughts.

Her cordiality was an obvious affectation; but both Lou and myself, as we shook hands, were aware of a subtle and mysterious sympathy which left behind it a stain of inexpressible evil.

I also felt sure that Feccles understood this unspoken communion, and that for some reason or other it pleased him immensely. His manner changed to one of peculiarly insinuating deference, and I felt that he was somehow taking command of the party when he said:—

"May I venture to suggest that you and Lady Pendragon take supper with us at the Petit Savoyard?"

Haidée slipped her arm into mine, and Lou led the way with Feccles.

"We were going there ourselves," she told him, "and it will be perfectly delightful to be with friends. I see you're quite an old friend of my husband's."

He began to tell her of the old school. As if by accident, he gave an account of the circumstances which had led to his leaving.

"My old man was in the city, you know," I heard him say, "and he dropped his pile 'somewhere in Lombard Street'" (he gave a false little laugh), "where he couldn't pick it up, so that was the end of my academic career. He persuaded old Rosenbaum, the banker, that I had a certain talent for finance, and got me a job as private secretary. I really did take to it like a duck to water, and things have gone very well for me ever since. But London isn't the place for men with real ambition. It doesn't afford the scope. It's either Paris or New York for yours sincerely, Elgin Feccles."

I don't know why I didn't believe a word of the tale; but I didn't. The heroin was working beautifully. I hadn't the slightest inclination to talk to Haidée. In the same way she took no notice of me. She never uttered a word.

Lou was in the same condition. She was apparently listening to what Feccles was saying; but she made no remark, and preserved a total detachment. The whole scene had not taken three minutes. We reached the Petit Savoyard and took our seats.

The patron appeared to know our friends very well. He welcomed them with even more than the usual French fussiness. We sat down by the window.

The restaurant overhangs the steep slopes of the Montmartre like an eyrie. We ordered supper, Feccles with bright intelligence, the rest of us with utter listlessness. I looked at Lou across the table. I had never seen the woman before in my life. She meant nothing whatever to me. I felt a sudden urgent desire to drink a great deal of water. I couldn't trouble to pour myself out a glass. I couldn't trouble to call the waiter, but I think I must have said the word "water," for Haidée filled my goblet. A smile wriggled across her face. It was the first sign of life she had given. Even the shaking hands had been in the nature of a mechanical reflex rather than of a voluntary action. There was something sinister and disquieting in her gesture. It was as if she had the after-taste in her mouth of some abominable bitterness.

I looked across at Lou. I saw she had changed colour. She looked dreadfully ill. It mattered nothing to me. I had a little amusing cycle of thoughts on the subject. I remembered that I loved her passionately; at the same time she happened not to exist. My indifference was a source of what I can only call diabolical beatitude.

It occurred to me as a sort of joke that she might have poisoned herself. I was certainly feeling very unwell. That didn't disturb me either.

The waiter brought a bowl of mussels. We ate them dreamily. It was part of the day's work. We enjoyed them because they were enjoyable; but nothing mattered, not even enjoyment. It struck me as strange that Haidée was simply pretending to eat, but I attributed this to preoccupation.

I felt very much better. Feccles talked easily and lightly about various matters of no importance. Nobody took any notice. He did not appear to observe, for his own part, any lack of politeness.

I certainly was feeling tired. I thought the Chambertin would pick me up, and swallowed a couple of glasses.

Lou kept on looking up at me with a sort of anxiety as if she wanted advice of some kind and didn't know how to ask for it. It was rather amusing.

We started the entreé. Lou got suddenly up from her seat. Feccles, with pretended alarm on his face, followed her hastily. I saw the waiter had hold of her other arm. It was really very amusing. That's always the way with girls—they never know what's enough.

And then I realised with startling suddenness that the case was not confined to the frailer sex. I got out just in time.

If I pass over in silence the events of the next hour, it is not because of the paucity of incident. At its conclusion we were seated once more at the table.

We took little sips of very old Armagnac; it pulled us together. But all the virtue had gone out of us; we might have been convalescents from some very long and wasting illness.

"There's nothing to be alarmed about," said Feccles, with his curious little laugh. "A trifling indiscretion."

I winced at the word. It took me back to King Lamus. I hated that fellow more than ever. He had begun to obsess me. Confound him!

Lou had confided the whole story to our host, who admitted that he was familiar with these matters.

"You see, my dear Sir Peter," he said, "you can't take H. like you can C., and when you mix your drinks there's the devil to pay. It's like everything else in life; you've got to find out your limit. It's very dangerous to move about when you're working H. or M., and it's almost certain disaster to eat."

I must admit I felt an awful fool. After all, I had studied medicine pretty seriously; and this was the second time that a layman had read me the Riot Act.

But Lou nodded cheerfully enough. The brandy had brought back the colour in her cheeks.

"Yes," she said, "I'd heard that all before, but you know it's one thing to hear a thing and another to go through it yourself."

"Experience is the only teacher," admitted Feccles. "All these things are perfectly all right, but the main thing is to go slow at first, and give yourself a chance to learn the ropes."

All this time Haidée had been sitting there like a statue. She exhaled a very curious atmosphere. There was a certain fascination in her complete lack of fascination.

Please excuse this paradoxical way of putting it. I mean that she had all the qualities which normally attract. She had the remains of an astonishing, if bizarre, beauty. She had obviously a vast wealth of experience. She possessed a quiet intensity which should have made her irresistible; and yet she was absolutely devoid of what we call magnetism. It isn't a scientific word—so much the worse for science. It describes a fact in nature, and one of the most important facts in practical affairs.

Everything of human interest, from music-hall turns to empires, is run on magnetism and very little else. And science ignores it because it can't be measured by mechanical instruments!

The whole of the woman's vitality was directed to some secret interior shrine of her own soul.

Now she began to speak for the first time. The only subject that interested her in this wide universe was heroin. Her voice was monotonous.

Lou told me later that it reminded her of a dirge droned by Tibetan monks far off across implacable snow.

"It's the only thing there is," she said, in a tone of extraordinary ecstatic detachment. One could divine an infinite unholy joy derived from its own sadness. It was as if she took a morbid pleasure in being something melancholy, something monstrous; there was, in fact, a kind of martyred majesty in her mood.

"You mustn't expect to get the result at once," she went on. "You have to be born into it, married with it, and dead from it before you understand it. Different people are different. But it always takes some months at least before you get rid of that stupid nuisance—life. As long as you have animal passions, you are an animal. How disgusting it is to think of eating and loving and all those appetites, like cattle! Breathing itself would be beastly if one knew one were doing it. How intolerable life would be to people of even mediocre refinement if they were always acutely conscious of the process of digestion."

She gave a little shiver.

"You've read the Mystics, Sir Peter?" interrupted Feccles.

"I'm afraid not, my dear man," I replied. "Fact is, I haven't read anything much unless I had to."

"I went into it rather for a couple of years," he returned, and then stopped short and flushed.

The thought had apparently called up some very unpleasant memories. He tried to cover his confusion by volubility, and began an elaborate exposition of the tenets of St. Teresa, Miguel de Molinos, and several others celebrated in that line.

"The main point, you see," he recapitulated finally, "is the theory that everything human in us is before all things an obstacle in the way of holiness. That is the secret of the saints, that they renounce everything for one thing which they call the divine purity. It is not simply those things which we ordinarily call sins or vices—those are merely the elementary forms of iniquity—exuberant grossness. The real difficulty hardly begins till things of that sort are dismissed forever. On the road to saintship, every bodily or mental manifestation is in itself a sin, even when it is something which ordinary piety would class as a virtue. Haidée here has got the same idea."

She nodded serenely.

"I had no idea," she said, "that those people had got so much sense. I've always thought of them as tangled up with religious ideas. I understand now. Yes, it's the life of holiness, if you have to go to the trouble of putting it in the terms of morality, as I suppose you English people have to. I feel that contact of any sort, even with myself, contaminates me. I was the chief of sinners in my time, in the English sense of the word. Now I've forgotten what love means, except for a faint sense of nausea when it comes under my notice. I hardly eat at all—it's only brutes that want to wallow in action that need three meals a day. I hardly ever talk—words seem such waste, and they are none of them true. No one has yet invented a language from my point of view. Human life or heroin life? I've tried them both; and I don't regret having chosen as I did."

I said something about heroin shortening life. A wan smile flickered on her hollow cheeks. There was something appalling in its wintry splendour. It silenced us.

She looked down at her hands. I noticed for the first time with extreme surprise that they were extraordinarily dirty. She explained her smile.

"Of course, if you count time by years, you're very likely right. But what have the calculations of astronomers to do with the life of the soul? Before I started heroin, year followed year, and nothing worth while happened. It was like a child scribbling in a ledger. Now that I've got into the heroin life, a minute or an hour—I don't know which and I don't care—contains more real life than any five years' period in my unregenerate days. You talk of death. Why shouldn't you? It's perfectly all right for you. You animals have got to die, and you know it. But I am very far from sure that I shall ever die; and I'm as indifferent to the idea as I am to any other of your monkey ideas."

She relapsed into silence, leaned back and closed her eyes once more.

I make no claim to be a philosopher of any kind; but it was quite evident to the most ordinary common sense that her position was unassailable if anyone chose to take it. As G. K. Chesterton says, "You cannot argue with the choice of the soul."

It has often been argued, in fact, that mankind lost the happiness characteristic of his fellow-animals when he acquired self-consciousness. This is in fact the meaning of the legend of "The Fall." We have become as gods, knowing good and evil, and the price is that we live by labour, and—"In his eyes foreknowledge of death."

Feccles caught my thought. He quoted with slow emphasis:—

> *"He weaves and is clothed with derision,*
> *Sows and he shall not reap.*
> *His life is a watch or a vision,*
> *Between a sleep and a sleep."*

The thought of the great Victorian seemed to chill him. He threw off his depression, lighting a cigarette and taking a strong pull at his brandy.

"Haidée," he said, with assumed lightness, "lives in open sin with a person named Baruch de Espinosa. I think it's Schopenhauer who calls him 'Der Gottbetrunkene Mann.'"

"The God-intoxicated man," murmured Lou faintly, shooting a sleepy glance at Haidée from beneath her heavy blue-veined eyelids.

"Yes," went on Feccles. "She always carries about one of his books. She goes to sleep on his words; and when her eyes open, they fall upon the page."

He tapped the table as he spoke. His quick intuition had understood that this strange incident was disquieting to us. He wriggled his thumb and forefinger in the air towards the waiter. The man interpreted the gesture as a request for the bill, and went off to get it.

"Let me drive you and Sir Peter back to your hotel," said our host to Lou. "You've had a rather rough time. I prescribe a good night's rest. You'll find a dose of H. a very useful pick-me-up in the morning, but, for Heaven's sake, don't flog a willing horse. Just the minutest sniff, and then coke up gradually when you begin to feel like getting up. By lunch time you'll be feeling like a couple of two-year-olds."

He paid the bill, and we went out. As luck would have it, a taxi had just discharged a party at the door. So we drove home without any trouble.

Lou and I both felt absolutely washed out. She lay upon my breast and held my hand. I felt my strength come back to me when it was called on to support her weakness. And our love grew up anew out of that waste of windy darkness. I felt myself completely purged of all passion; and in that lustration we were baptised anew and christened with the name of Love.

But although nature had done her best to get rid of the excess of the poison we had taken, there remained a residual effect. We had arrived at the hotel very weary, though as a matter of course we had insisted on Feccles and Haidée coming upstairs for a final drink. But we could hardly keep our eyes open; and as soon as they were gone we made all possible haste to get between the sheets of the twin beds.

I need hardly tell my married friends that on previous nights the process of going to bed had been a very elaborate ritual. But on this occasion it was a mere attempt to break the record for speed. Within five minutes from the departure of Feccles and Haidée the lights were out.

I had imagined that I should drop off to sleep instantly. In fact, it took me sometime to realise that I had not done so. I was in an anæsthetic condition which is hard to distinguish from dreaming. In fact, if one started to lay down definitions and explained the differences, the further one got the more obscure would the controversy become.

But my eyes were certainly wide open; and I was lying on my back, whereas I can never sleep except on my right side, or else, strangely enough, in a sitting position. And the thoughts began to make themselves more conscious as I lay.

You know how thoughts fade out imperceptibly as one goes to sleep. Well, here they were, fading in.

I found myself practically deprived of volition on the physical plane. It was as if it had become impossible for me to wish to move or to speak. I was bathed in an ocean of exceeding calm. My mind was very active, but only so within peculiar limits. I did not seem to be directing the current of my thoughts.

In an ordinary way that fact would have annoyed me intensely. But now it merely made me curious. I tried, as an experiment, to fix my mind on something definite. I was technically able to do so, but at the same time I was aware that I considered the effort not worth making. I noticed, too, that my thoughts were uniformly pleasant.

Curiosity impelled me to fix my mind on ideas which are normally the source of irritation and worry. There was no difficulty in doing so, but the bitterness had disappeared.

I went over incidents in the past which I had almost forgotten by virtue of that singular mental process which protects the mind from annoyance.

I discovered that this loss of memory was apparent, and not real. I recollected every detail with the most minute exactitude. But the most vexatious and humiliating items meant nothing to me anymore. I took the same pleasure in recalling them as one has in reading a melancholy tale. I might almost go so far as to say that the unpleasant incidents were preferable to the others.

The reason is, I think, that they leave a deeper mark on the mind. Our souls have invented our minds, so to speak, with the object of registering conscious experiences, and therefore the more deeply an experience is felt the better our minds are carrying out the intention of our souls.

"*Forsitan hæc olim meminisse juvabit,*" says Æneas in Virgil when recounting his hardships. (Quaint, by the way! I haven't thought of a Latin tag a dozen times since I left school. Drugs, like old age, strip off one's recent memories, and leave bare one's forgotten ideas.)

The most deeply seated instinct in us is our craving for experience. And that is why the efforts of the Utopians to make life a pleasant routine always arouse subconscious revolt in the spirit of man.

It was the progressive prosperity of the Victorian age that caused the Great War. It was the reaction of the schoolboy against the abolition of adventure.

This curious condition of mind possessed an eternal quality; the stream of thoughts flowed through my brain like a vast irresistible river. I felt that nothing could ever stop it, or even change the current in any important respect. My consciousness had something of the quality of a fixed star proceeding through space by right of its eternal destiny. And the stream carried me on from one set of thoughts to another, slowly and without stress; it was like a hushed symphony. It included all possible memories, changing imperceptibly from one to another without the faintest hint of jarring.

I was aware of the flight of time, because a church clock struck somewhere far off at immense incalculable intervals. I knew, therefore, that I was making a white night of it. I was aware of dawn through the open French windows on the balcony.

Ages, long ages, later, there was a chime of bells announcing early Mass; and gradually my thought became more slow, more dim; the active pleasure of thinking became passive. Little by little the shadows crept across my reverie, and then I knew no more.

VI

THE GLITTER ON THE SNOW

I woke to find Lou fully dressed. She was sitting on the edge of my bed. She had taken hold of my hand, and her face was bending over mine like a pallid flower. She saw that I was awake, and her mouth descended upon mine with exquisite tenderness. Her lips were soft and firm; their kiss revived me into life.

She was extraordinarily pale, and her gestures were limp and languid. I realised that I was utterly exhausted.

"I couldn't sleep at all," she said, "after what seemed a very long time in which I tried to pull myself together. My mind went running on like mad—I've had a perfectly ripping time—perfectly top-hole! I simply couldn't get up till I remembered what that man Feccles said about a hair of the dog. So I rolled out of bed and crawled across to the H. and took one little sniff, and sat on the floor till it worked. It's great stuff when you know the ropes. It picked me up in a minute. So I had a bath, and got these things on. I'm still a bit all in. You know we did overdo it, didn't we, Cockie?"

"You bet," I said feebly. "I'm glad I've got a nurse."

"Right-o," she said, with a queer grin. "It's time for your majesty's medicine."

She went over to the bureau, and brought me a dose of heroin. The effect was surprising! I had felt as if I couldn't move a muscle, as if all the springs of my nerves had given way. Yet, in two minutes, one small sniff restored me to complete activity.

There was in this, however, hardly any element of joy. I was back to my normal self, but not to what you might call good form. I was perfectly able to do anything required, but the idea of doing it didn't appeal. I thought a bath and a shower would put me right; and I certainly felt a very different man by the time I had got my clothes on.

When I came back into the sitting-room, I found Lou dancing daintily round the table. She went for me like a bull at a gate; swept me away to the couch and knelt at my side as I lay, while she overwhelmed me with passionate kisses.

She divined that I was not in any condition to respond.

"You still need your nurse," she laughed merrily, with sparkling eyes and flashing teeth and nostrils twitching with excitement. I saw on the tip of one delicious little curling hair a crystal glimmer that I knew.

She had been out in the snowstorm!

My cunning twisted smile told her that I was wise to the game.

"Yes," she said excitedly, "I see how it's done now. You pull yourself together with H. and then you start the buzz-wagon with C. Come along, put in the clutch."

Her hand was trembling with excitement. But on the back of it there shimmered a tiny heap of glistening snow.

I sniffed it with suppressed ecstasy. I knew that it was only a matter of seconds before I caught the contagion of her crazy and sublime intoxication.

Who was it that said you had only to put salt on the tail of a bird, and then you could catch it? Probably that fellow thought that he knew all about it, but he got the whole thing wrong. What you have to do is to get snow up your own nose, and then you can catch the bird all right.

What did Maeterlinck know about that silly old Blue Bird?

Happiness lies within one's self, and the way to dig it out is cocaine.

But don't you go and forget what I hope you won't mind my calling ordinary prudence. Use a little common sense, use precaution, exercise good judgment. However hungry you may happen to be, you don't want to eat a dozen oxen *en brochette. Natura non facit saltum.*

It's only a question of applying knowledge in a reasonable manner. We had found out how to work the machine, and there was no reason in the world why we shouldn't fly from here to Kalamazoo.

So I took three quite small sniffs at reasonable intervals, and I was on the job once more.

I chased Lou around the suite; and I dare say we did upset a good deal of the furniture, but that doesn't matter, for we haven't got to pick it up.

The important thing was that I caught Lou; and by-and-by we found ourselves completely out of breath; and then, confound it, just when I wanted a quiet pipe before lunch, the telephone rang, and the porter wanted to know if we were at home to Mr. Elgin Feccles.

Well, I told you before that I didn't care for the man so much as that. As Stevenson observes, if he were the only tie that bound one to home, I think most of us would vote for foreign travel. But he'd played the game pretty straight last night; and hang it, one couldn't do less than invite the fellow to lunch. He might have a few more tips about the technique of this business anyhow. I'm not one of those cocksure fellows that imagine when they have one little scrap of knowledge, that they have drained the fount of wisdom dry.

So I said, "Ask him to be good enough to come up by all means."

Lou flew to the other room to fix her hair and her face and all those things that women always seem to be having to fix, and up comes Mr. Feccles with the most perfect manner that I have ever observed in any human being, and a string of kind inquiries and apologies on the tip of his tongue.

He said he wouldn't have bothered us by calling at all so soon after the case of indiscretion, only he felt sure he had left his cigarette case with us, and he valued it very much because it had been given him by his Aunt Sophronia.

Well, you know, there it was, right on the table, or rather, under the table, because the table was on top of it.

When we got the table on its legs again, we saw quite plainly that the cigarette case had been under it, and therefore must have been on top of it before it was overturned.

Feccles laughed heartily at the humorous character of the incident. I suppose it was funny in a sort of way. On the other hand, I don't think it was quite the thing to call attention to. However, I suppose the fellow had to have his cigarette case, and after all, when you do find a table upside down, it's not much good pretending that you don't notice it. And very likely, on the whole, the best way to pass over the incident pleasantly is to turn it into a kind of joke.

And I must say that Feccles showed the tact of a perfect gentleman in avoiding any direct allusion to the circumstances that caused the circumstances that were responsible for the circumstances that gave rise to the circumstances which it was so difficult to over-look.

Well, you know, this man Feccles had been a perfect dear the night before. He had seen Lou through the worst of the business with the utmost good taste at the moment when her natural protector, myself, was physically unable to apply the necessary what-you-may-call-it.

Well, of course, the way things were at the moment, I wished Feccles in the place that modern Christianity has decided to forget. But the least I could do was to ask him to lunch. But before I had time to put this generous impulse into words, Lou sailed in like an angel descending from heaven.

She went straight up to Feccles, and she positively kissed him before my eyes, and begged him to stay and have lunch. She positively took the words out of my mouth.

But I must admit that I wanted to be alone with Lou—not only then, but forever; and I was most consumedly glad when I heard Feccles say:—

"Why, really, that's too kind of you, Lady Pendragon, and I hope you repeat the invitation someother day, but I've got to lunch with two birds from the Bourse. We have a tremendous deal coming off. Sir Peter's got more money already than he knows what to do with, otherwise I'd be only too glad to let him in on the *rez-de-chaussée*."

Well, you know, that's all right about my being a millionaire, and all that. It's one thing being a single man running round London perfectly happy with a shilling cigar and a stall at the Victoria Palace, and it's quite another being on a honeymoon with a girl whom her most intimate friends call "Unlimited Lou."

Feccles did not know that I had spent more than a third of my annual income in a fortnight. But, of course, I couldn't tell the man how I was situated. We Pendragons are a pretty proud lot, especially since Sir Thomas Malory gave us that write-up in the time of Henry VIII. We've always been a bit above ourselves. That's where my poor old dad went gaga.

However, the only thing to do was to beg the man to find a date in the near future to fight Paillard to a finish.

I think Paillard is the best restaurant in Paris, don't you?

So out comes a little red pocket-book, and there is Mr. Feccles biting his pencil between his lips, and then cocking his head, first on one side and then on the other.

"Confound Paris!" he said at last. "A man gets simply swept away by social engagements. I haven't a thing for a week."

And just then the telephone rang. Lou did a two-step across to the instrument.

"Oh, it's for you, Mr. Feccles," she said. "However did anyone know you were here?"

He gave his funny little laugh.

"It's just what I've been telling you, Lady Pendragon," he said, as he walked over to the receiver. "I'm a very much wanted man. Everyone seems to want me but the police," he giggled, "and they may get on to me any minute now, the Lord knows."

He became suddenly serious as he talked on the phone.

"Oh, yes," he said to the caller. "Very annoying indeed. What's that? Four o'clock? All right, I'll be round."

He hung up. He came back to us radiant, holding out his hands.

"My dear friends," he said. "This is a special providence—nothing less. The lunch is off. If your invitation holds, I shall be the happiest man in Europe."

Well, of course, there couldn't be two men like that in Europe. I was infernally bored. But there was nothing to do except to express the wildest joy.

It didn't add to my pleasure to see that Lou was really pleased. She broke out into a swift sonata.

"Let's lunch up here," she said. "It's more *intime*. I hate feeding in public. I want to dance between the courses."

She rang down for the head-waiter while I gave Feccles a cigarette, lamenting my lack of forethought in not having insinuated a charge of trinitro-toluol amid the tobacco.

Lou had a passionate controversy with the head waiter. She won on points at the end of the sixth round. Half an hour later we started the gray caviare.

I don't know why everyone has to rejoice on gray caviare; but it's no use trying to interfere with the course of civilisation. I ate it; and if I were in similar circumstances tomorrow, I would do it again.

In the immortal words of Browning, "You lied, D'Ormea, I do not repent." Beside which, this was no ordinary lunch. It was big with the future.

It was an unqualified success from the start. We were all in our best form. Feccles talked freely and irresponsibly with the lightness of champagne. He talked about himself and his amazing luck in financial matters; but he never stayed long enough on any subject to make a definite impression or, you might say, to allow of a reply. He interspersed his remarks with the liveliest anecdotes, and apologised towards the end of the meal for having been preoccupied with the deal which he had on at the moment.

"I'm afraid it's literally obsessing me," he said. "But you know it makes, or rather will make, a big difference to my prospects. Unfortunately, I'm not a millionaire like you, old thing. I've been doing very well, but somehow, it's gone as easy as it came. But I've scraped up twenty thousand of the best to buy an eighth share in this oil proposition that I told you about."

"No," put in Lou, "you didn't tell us what it was."

"I made sure I had," he laughed back; "I've got it fairly on the brain, especially since that lunch was put off. I need another five thou', you see, and I was going to dig it out of those birds. The only difficulty was that I can't exactly borrow it on my face, can I? and I don't want to let those birds into 'the know'—they'd simply snap the whole thing up for themselves. By the way, that reminds me of a very good thing I heard of the other day——" and he rattled off an amusing story which had no connection with what he had been saying before.

I didn't listen to what it was. My brain was working very fast with the champagne on top of the other things. His talk had brought to my mind that I should have to wire for another thousand today or tomorrow. I was aware of a violent subconscious irritation. The man's talk had dealt so airily with millions that I couldn't help recognising that I was a very poor man indeed, by modern standards. Five or six thousand a year, and perhaps another fifteen hundred from the rents of the Barley Grange estate, and that infernal income-tax and so on—I was really little better than a pauper, and there was Lou to be considered.

I had always thought jewellery vulgar; a signet ring and a tie pin for a man—for a woman, a few trinkets, very quiet, in good taste—that was the limit.

But Lou was absolutely different. She could wear any amount of the stuff and carry it off superbly. I had bought her a pair of ear-rings in Cartier's yesterday afternoon—three diamonds in a string, the pendant being a wonderful pear-shaped blue-white, and as she ate, and drank, and talked, they waggled behind the angle of her jaw in the most deliciously fascinating way, and it didn't vulgarise her at all.

I realised that, as a married man, it was my duty to buy her that string of pearls with the big black pearl as a pendant, and there was that cabochon emerald ring! How madly that would go with her hair. And then, of course, when we got back to England, she must be presented at Court, not but what we Pendragons don't feel it a little humiliating— that meant a tiara, of course.

And then you know what dressmakers are!

There's simply no end to the things that a civilised man has to have when he's married! And here was I, to all intents and purposes, a case for out-door relief.

I came out of my reverie with a start. My mind was made up.

Lou was laughing hysterically at some story of a blind man and a gimlet.

"Look here, Feccles," I said. "I wish you'd tell me a little more about this oil business. To tell you the truth, I'm not the rich man you seem to think——"

"My dear fellow——" said Feccles.

"In fact, I assure you," said I. "Of course, it was all very well when I was a bachelor. Simple tastes, you know. But this little lady makes all the dif'."

"Why, certainly," replied Feccles, very seriously. "Yes, I see that perfectly. In fact, if I may say so, it's really a duty to yourself and your heirs, to put yourself on Easy Street. But money's been frightfully tight since the war, as you know. What with the collapse in the foreign exchanges, the decrease in the purchasing power of money, and the world's gold all locked up in Washington, things are pretty awkward. But then, you know, it's just that sort of situation which provides opportunities to a man with real brains. Victorian prosperity made us all rich without our knowing anything about it or doing anything for it."

"Yes," I admitted, "the gilt edges seem to have come off the gingerbread securities."

"Well, look here, Pendragon," he said, pulling his chair half round so as to face me squarely, and making his points by tapping his Corona on a plate, "the future lies with just two things as far as big money's concerned. One's oil, and the other is cotton. Now, I don't know a thing about cotton, but I'll give any sperm whale that ever blew four thousand points in twelve thousand up about oil, and you can lay your shirt on the challenger."

"Yes, I see that," I replied brightly. "Of course, I don't know the first thing about finance; but what you say is absolutely common sense. And I've got a sort of flair for these things, I believe."

"Why, it's very curious you should say that," returned Feccles, as in great surprise. "I was thinking the same thing myself. We know you've got pluck, and that's the first essential in any game. And making money is the greatest game there is. But beside that, I've got a hunch that you've got the right kind of brain for this business. You're as shrewd as they make 'em, and you've got a good imagination. I don't mean the wild fancies that you find in a crank, but a good, wholesome, sound imagination."

In the ordinary way, I should have been embarrassed by so direct a compliment from a man who was so evidently in the know, a man who was holding his own with the brightest minds all over the world. But in my present mood I took it as perfectly natural.

Lou laughed in my ear. "That's right, Cockie, dear," she chirruped. "This is where you go right in and win. I've really got to have those pearls, you know."

"She's quite right," agreed Feccles. "When you're through with this honeymoon, come round with me, and we'll take our coats off and get into the game for all we're worth and a bit more, and when we come out, we'll have J. D. Rockefeller as flat as a pancake."

"Well," said I, "no time like the present. I don't want to butt in, but if I could be any use to you about this deal of yours——"

Feccles shook his head.

"No," he said, "this isn't the sort of thing at all. I'm putting my last bob into the deal; but it's a risky business at the best, and I wouldn't take a chance on your dropping five thou' on the very first bet. Of course, it is rather a good thing if it comes off——"

"Let's have the details, dear boy," I said, trying to feel like a business man bred in the bone.

"The thing itself's simple enough," said Feccles. "It's just a case of taking up an option on some wells at a place called Sitka. They used to be all right before the war—but in my opinion they were never properly developed. They haven't been worked ever since, and it might take all sorts of money to put them on the map again. But that's the smaller point. What I and my friends know and nobody else has got on to is that if we apply the Feldenberg process to the particular kind of oil that Sitka yields, we've got practically a world's monopoly of the highest class oil that exists. I needn't tell you that we can sell it at our own price."

I saw in a flash the magnificent possibilities of the plan.

"Of course, I needn't tell you to keep it as dark as a wolf's mouth," continued Feccles. "If this got out, every financier in Paris would buy the thing over our heads. I wouldn't have mentioned it to you at all except for two things. I know you're on the square—that goes without saying; but the real point is this, that I told you I rather believe in the Occult."

"Oh, yes," cried Lou, "then, of course, you know King Lamus."

Feccles started as if he had received a blow in the face. For a moment he was completely out of countenance. It seemed as if he were going to say several things, and decided not to. But his face was black as thunder. It was impossible to mistake the meaning of the situation.

I turned to Lou with what I suppose was rather a nasty little laugh.

"Our friend's reputation," I said, "appears to have reached Mr. Feccles."

"Well," said Feccles, recovering himself with a marked effort, "I rather make a point of not saying anything against people, but as a matter of fact, it is a bit on the thick side. You seem to know all about it, so there's no harm in my saying the man's an unspeakable scoundrel."

All my hatred and jealousy surged up from the subconscious. I felt that if Lamus had been there I would have shot him like a dog on sight.

My old school-fellow skated away from the obnoxious topic.

"You didn't let me finish," he complained. "I was going to say I have no particular talent for finance and that sort of thing in the ordinary way, but I have an intuition that never lets me down—like the demon of Socrates, you remember, eh?"

I nodded. I had some faint recollection of Plato.

"Well," said Feccles, tapping his cigar, with the air of a Worshipful Master calling the Lodge to order, "I said to myself when I met you last night, 'it's better to be born lucky than rich, and there's a man who was born lucky.'"

It was perfectly true. I had never been able to do anything of my own abilities, and after all I had tumbled into a reasonably good fortune.

"You've got the touch, Pen," he said, with animation. "Anytime you're out of a job, I'll give you ten thousand a year as a mascot."

Lou and I were both intensely excited. We could hardly find the patience to listen to the details of our friend's plan. The figures were convincing; but the effect was simply to dazzle us. We had never dreamed of wealth on this scale.

I got the vision for the first time in my life of the power that wealth confers, and I realised equally for the first time how vast were my real ambitions.

The man was right, too, clearly enough, about my being lucky. My luck in the war had been prodigious. Then there was this inheritance, and Lou on the top of that; and here I'd met old Feccles by a piece of absolute chance, and there was this brilliant investment. That was the word—he was careful to point out that it was not a speculation, strictly speaking—absolutely waiting for me.

We were so overjoyed that we could hardly grasp the practical details. The amount required was four thousand nine hundred and fifty pounds.

Of course, there was no difficulty in getting a trifle like that, but as I told Feccles, it would mean my selling out some beastly stock or something which might take two or three days. There was no time to lose; because the option would lapse if it weren't taken up within the week, and it was now Wednesday.

However, Feccles helped me to draft a wire to Wolfe to explain the urgency, and Feccles was to call on Saturday at nine o'clock with the papers.

Meanwhile, of course, he wouldn't let me down, but at the same time he couldn't risk pulling off the coup of his life in case there was a hitch, so he would get a move on and see if he couldn't raise five thousand on his own somewhere else, in which case he'd let me have some of his own stock anyway. He wanted me in the deal if it was only for a sovereign, simply because of my luck.

So off he ran in a great hurry. Lou and I got a car and spent the afternoon in the Bois du Boulogne. It seemed as if the cocaine had taken hold of us with new force, or else it was the addition of the heroin.

We were living at the same terrific speed as on that first wild night. The intensity was even more extraordinary; but we were not being carried away by it.

In one sense, each hour lasted a fraction of a second, and yet, in another sense, every second lasted a life-time. We were able to appreciate the minutest details of life to the full.

I want to explain this very thoroughly.

"William the Conqueror, 1066, William Rufus, 1087."

One can sum up the whole period of the reign of the Duke of Normandy in a phrase. At the same time, an historian who had made a special study of that part of English History might be able to write ten volumes of details, and he might, in a sense, have both aspects of his knowledge present to his mind at the same moment.

We were in a similar condition. The hours flashed by like so many streaks of lightning, yet each discharge illuminated every detail of the landscape; we could grasp everything at once. It was as if we had acquired a totally new mental faculty as superior to the normal course of thought as the all-comprehending brain of a great man of science is to that of a savage, though the two men are both looking with the same optical instruments at the same blackbeetle.

It is impossible to convey, to anyone who has not experienced it, the overwhelming rapture of this condition.

Another extraordinary feature of the situation was this; that we seemed to be endowed with what I must call the power of telepathy, for want of a better word. We didn't need to explain ourselves to each other. Our minds worked together like those of two first-class three-quarters who are accustomed to play together.

Part of the enjoyment, moreover, came from the knowledge that we were infinitely superior to anything we might happen to meet. The mere fact that we had so much more time to think than other people assured us of this.

We were like a leash of greyhounds, and the rest of the world so many hares, but the disproportion of speed was immensely increased. It was the airman against the wagoner.

We went to bed early that night. We had already got a little tired of Paris. The pace was too slow for us. It was rather like sitting at a Wagner opera. There were some thrilling moments, of course, but most of the time we were bored with long and monotonous passages like the dialogue between Wotan and Erde. We wanted to be by ourselves; no one else could keep up with the rush.

The difference between sleep and waking, again, was diminished, no, almost abolished. The period of sleep was simply like a brief distraction of attention, and even our dreams continued the exaltation of our love.

The importance of any incident was negligible. In the ordinary way one's actions are to a certain extent inhibited. As the phrase goes, one thinks twice before doing so and so. We weren't thinking twice anymore. Desire was transformed into action without the slightest check. Fatigue, too, had been completely banished.

We woke the next morning with the sun. We stood on the balcony in our dressing-gowns and watched him rise. We felt ourselves one with him, as fresh and as fervent as he. Inexhaustible energy!

We danced and sang through breakfast. We had a phase of babbling, both talking at once at the top of our voices, making plans for the day, each one as it bubbled in our brains the source of ecstatic excitement and inextinguishable laughter.

We had just decided to spend the morning shopping when a card was brought up to the room.

I had a momentary amazement as I read that our visitor was the confidential clerk of Mr. Wolfe.

"Oh, bother the fellow," said I, and then remembered my telegram of the day before.

I had a swift pang of alarm. Could something be wrong? But the cocaine assured me that everything was all right.

"I'll have to see the fellow, I suppose," I said, and told the hall-boy to send him upstairs.

"Don't let him keep you long," said Lou, with a petulant pout, and ran into the bedroom after a swift embrace, so violent that it disarranged my new Charvet necktie.

The man came up. I was a little bored by the gravity of his manner, and rather disgusted by its solemn deference. Of course, one likes being treated as a kind of toy emperor in a way, but that sort of thing doesn't go with Paris. Still less does it go with cocaine.

It annoyed me that the fellow was so obviously ill at ease, and also that he was so obviously proud of himself for having been sent to Paris on important business with a real live knight.

If there's one thing flying teaches one more than another, it is to hate snobbery. Even the Garter becomes imperceptible when one is flying above the clouds.

I couldn't possibly talk to the man till he was a little more human. I made him sit down and have a drink and cigarette before I would let him tell me his business.

Of course, everything was perfectly in order. The point was simply this, that the six thousand pounds wasn't immediately available, so, as I needed it urgently, it was necessary for me to sign certain papers which Mr. Wolfe had drawn up at once, on receipt of my wire, and it would be better to have it done at the consulate.

"Why, of course, get a taxi," I said; "I'll be down in a minute."

He went downstairs. I ran in to Lou and told her that I had to go to the consul on business: I'd be back in an hour and we could do our shopping.

We took a big sniff of snow and kissed goodbye as if I were starting on a three years' expedition to the South Pole. Then I caught up my hat, gloves, and cane, and found my young man at the door.

The drink and the air of Paris had given him a sense of his own dignity. Instead of waiting humbly for me to get into the car, he was sitting there already; and though his greeting was still solemnly deferential, there was a little more of the ambassador about it. He had repressed the original impulse to touch his hat.

I myself felt a curious sense of enjoyment of my own importance. At the same time, I was in a violent hurry to get back to Lou. My brain was racing with the thought of her. I signed my name where they told me, and the consul dabbed it all over with stamps, and we drove back to the hotel, where the clerk extracted a locked leather wallet from a mysterious inside hip pocket and counted me out my six thousand in hundred-pound notes.

Of course, I had to ask the fellow to lunch, it was only decent, but I was very glad when he excused himself. He had to catch the two o'clock train back to town.

"Good God, what a time you've been," said Lou, and I could see that she had been filling it in in a wonderful way. It was up to her neck. She danced about like a crazy woman with little jerky movements which I couldn't help seeing signified nervous irritability. However, she was radiant, beaming, glowing, bursting with excitement.

Well, you know, I don't like to be left in the lurch. I had to catch up. I literally shovelled the snow down. I ought to have been paid a shilling an hour by the County Council. The world is full of injustice.

However, we certainly didn't have anytime to have questions asked in Parliament. There was Lou almost in tears because she had nothing to wear; practically no jewellery—the whole idea of being a knight is that when you see a wrong it is your duty to right it.

Fortunately, there was no difficulty at the present moment. All we had to do was to drive down to the Rue de la Paix. I certainly almost fell down when I saw all those pearls on her neck. And that cabochon emerald! By George, it did go with her hair!

These shop men in Paris are certainly artists. The man saw in a moment what was wrong. There was nothing to match the blue of her dress, so he showed us a sapphire and diamond bracelet and a big marquise ring that went with it in a platinum setting. That certainly made all the difference! And yet he seemed to be very uneasy. He was puzzled; that's what it was.

Then his face lightened up. He had got the idea all right. You can always trust these chaps when you strike a really good man. What was missing was something red!

I told you about Lou's mouth; her long, jagged, snaky, scarlet streak always writhing and twisting as if it had a separate life of its own and were perpetually in some delicious kind of torture!

The man saw immediately what was necessary. The mouth had to be repeated symbolically. That's the whole secret of art. So he fished out a snake of pigeon's blood rubies.

ALEISTER CROWLEY

My God! it was the most beautiful thing I had ever seen in my life, except Lou herself. And you couldn't look at it without thinking of her mouth, and you couldn't think of her mouth without wanting to kiss it, and it was up to me to prove to Paris that I had the most beautiful woman in the world for my wife, and that could only be done in the regular way by showing her off in the best dresses and the most wonderful jewellery. It was my duty to her as my wife, and I could afford it perfectly well because I was a tolerably rich man to start with anyhow, and besides, the five thousand I was putting into Feccles' business would mean something like a quarter of a million at least, on the most conservative calculations, as I had seen with my own eyes.

And that was all clear profit, so there was no reason in the world why one shouldn't spend it in a sensible way. Mr. Wolfe himself had emphasised the difficulty of getting satisfactory investments in these times.

He told me how many people were putting their money into diamonds and furs which always keep their value, whereas government securities and that sort of thing are subject to unexpected taxation, for one thing, depreciation for another, with the possibility of European repudiation looming behind them all.

As a family man, it was my duty to buy as many jewels for Lou as I could afford. At the same time, one has to be cautious.

I bought the things I mentioned and paid for them. I refused to be tempted by a green pearl tie pin for myself, though I should have liked to have had it because it would have reminded me of Lou's eyes everytime I put it on. But it was really rather expensive, and Mr. Wolfe had warned me very seriously about getting into debt, so I paid for the rest of the stuff, and we went off, and we thought we'd drive out to the Bois for lunch, and then we took some more snow in the taxi and Lou began to cry because I had bought nothing for myself. So we took some more snow, we had plenty of time, nobody lunches before two o'clock. We went straight back to the shop and bought the green pearl, and that got Lou so excited that the taxi was like an aeroplane; if anything, more so.

It's stupid to hang back. If you start to do a thing, you'd much better do it. What's that fellow say? "I do not set my life at a pin's fee." That's the right spirit. "Unhand me, gentlemen, I'll make a ghost of him that lets me."

That's the Pendragon spirit, and that's the flying man's spirit. Get to the top and stay at the top and shoot the other man down!

VII

The Wings of the Oof-Bird

The lunch at the Restaurant de la Cascade was like a lunch in a dream. We seemed to be aware of what we were eating without actually tasting it. As I think I said before, it's the anæsthesia of cocaine that determines the phenomena.

When I make a remark like that, I understand that it's the dead and gone medical student popping up.

But never you mind that. The point is that when you have the right amount of snow in you, you can't feel anything in the ordinary sense of the word. You appreciate it in a sort of impersonal way. There's a pain, but the pain doesn't hurt. You enjoy the fact of the pain as you enjoy reading about all sorts of terrible things in history at school.

But the trouble about cocaine is this; that it's almost impossible to take it in moderation as almost anyone, except an American, can take whisky. Every dose makes you better and better. It destroys one's power of calculation.

We had already discovered the fact when we found that the supply we had got from Gretel, with the idea that it would last almost indefinitely, was running very short, when the dressing-gown came to solve the problem.

We had only been a few days on the stunt, and what we had got from three or four sniffs, to begin with, meant almost perpetual stoking to carry on. However, that didn't matter, because we had an ample supply. There must have been a couple of kilograms of either C. or H. in that kimono. And when you think that an eighth of a grain is rather a big dose of H., you can easily calculate what a wonderful time you can have on a pound.

You remember how it goes—twenty grains one penny-weight, three penny-weights one scruple—I forget how many scruples one drachm, eight drachms one ounce, twelve ounces one pound.

I've got it all wrong. I could never understand English weights and measures. I have never met anyone who could. But the point is you could go on a long time on one-eighth of a grain if you have a pound of the stuff.

Well, this will put it all right for you. Fifteen grains is one gramme, and a thousand grammes is a kilogramme, and a kilogramme is two point two pounds. The only thing I'm not sure about is whether it's a sixteen-ounce pound or a twelve-ounce pound. But I don't see what it matters anyway, if you've got a pound of snow or H. you can go on for a long while, but apparently it's rather awkward orchestrating them.

Quain says that people accustomed to opium and its derivatives can take an enormous amount of cocaine without any bother. In the ordinary way, half a grain of cocaine can cause death, but we were taking the stuff with absolute carelessness.

One doesn't think of measuring it as one would if one took it by hypodermic. One just takes a dose when one feels one needs it. After all, that's the rule of nature. Eat when you're hungry. Nothing is worse for the health than settling down to a fixed ration of so many meals a day.

The grand old British principle of three meat meals has caused the supply of uric acid to exceed the demand in a most reprehensible manner.

Physiology and economics, and, I should think, even geology, combine to protest.

Now we were living an absolutely wholesome life. We took a sniff of cocaine whenever the pace slackened up, and one of heroin when the cocaine showed any signs of taking the bit in its teeth.

What one needs is sound common sense to take reasonable measures according to the physiological indications. One needs elasticity. It's simply spiritual socialism to tie oneself down to fixed doses whether one needs them or not. Nature is the best guide. We had got on to the game.

Our misadventure at the Petit Savoyard had taught us wisdom. We were getting stronger on the wing every hour.

That chap Coué is a piker, as they say in America. "Everyday, in every way, I get better and better," indeed? The man must simply have been carried away by the rhyme. Why wait for a day? We had got to the stage where every minute counted.

As the Scotchman said to his son, half-way through the ten-mile walk to kirk, when the boy said, "It's a braw day the day." "Is this a day to be ta'king o' days?"

Thinking of days makes you think of years, and thinking of years makes you think of death, which is ridiculous.

Lou and I were living minute by minute, second by second. A tick of the clock marked for us an interval of eternity.

We were the heirs of eternal life. We had nothing to do with death. That was a pretty wise bird who said, "Tomorrow never comes."

We were out of time and space. We were living according to the instruction of our Saviour: "Take no thought for the morrow."

A great restlessness gripped us. Paris was perfectly impossible. We had to get to some place where time doesn't count.

The alternation of day and night doesn't matter so much; but it's absolutely intolerable to be mixed up with people who are working by the clock.

We were living in the world of the Arabian Nights; limitations were abhorrent. Paris was always reminding us of the Pigmies, who lived, if you call it living, in a system of order.

It is monstrous and ridiculous to open and close by convention. We had to go to some place where such things didn't annoy us. . .

An excessively irritating incident spoilt our lunch at the Cascade. We had made a marvellous impression when we came in. We had floated in like butterflies settling on lilies. A buzz went round the tables. Lou's beauty intoxicated everybody. Her jewellery dazzled the crowd.

I thought of an assembly of Greeks of the best period unexpectedly visited by Apollo and Venus.

We palpitated not only with our internal ecstasy but with the intoxicating sense that the whole world admired and envied us. We made them feel like the contents of a waste-paper basket.

The head waiter himself became a high priest. He rose to the situation like the genius he was. He was mentally on his knees as he ventured to advise us in the choice of our lunch.

It seemed to us the tribute of inferior emperors. And there was that fellow King Lamus five or six tables away!

The man with him was a Frenchman of obvious distinction, with a big red rosette and a trim aristocratic white moustache and beard. He was some minister or other. I couldn't quite place him but I'd seen him often enough in the papers: somebody intimate with the president. He had been the principal object of interest before we came in.

Our arrival pricked that bubble.

Lamus had his back to us, and I supposed he didn't see us, for he didn't turn round, though everyone else in the place did so and began to buzz.

I didn't hate the man anymore; he was so absurdly inferior. And this was the annoying thing. When he and his friend got up to leave, they passed our table all smiles and bows.

And then, the deuce! The head waiter brought me his card. He had scribbled on it in pencil: "Don't forget me when you need me."

Of all the damned silly impertinence! Absolutely gratuitous insufferable insolence! Who was going to need Mr. Gawd Almighty King Lamus?

I should have handed out some pretty hot repartee if the creature hadn't sneaked off. Well, it wasn't worth while. He didn't count anymore than the grounds in the coffee.

But the incident stuck in my mind. It kept on irritating me all the afternoon. People like that ought to be kicked out once and for all.

Why, hang it, the man was all kinds of a scoundrel. Everyone said so. Why did he want to butt in? Nobody asked him to meddle.

I said something of the sort to Lou, and she told him off very wittily.

"You've said it, Cockie," she cried. "He's a meddler, and his nature is to be rotten before he's ripe."

I remembered something of the sort in Shakespeare. That was the best of Lou; she was brilliantly clever, but she never forced it down one's throat.

At the same time, as I said, the man stuck in my gizzard. It annoyed me so much that we took a lot more cocaine to get the taste out of our mouths.

But the irritation remained, though it took another form. The bourgeois atmosphere of Paris got on my nerves.

Well, there was no need to stay in the beastly place. The thing to do was to hunt up old Feccles and pay him the cash, and get to some place like Capri where one isn't always being bothered by details.

I was flooded by a crazy desire to see Lou swim in the Blue Grotto, to watch the phosphorescent flames flash from her luminous body.

We told the chauffeur to stop at Feccles's hotel, and that was where we hit a gigantic snag.

Monsieur Feccles, the manager said, had left that morning suddenly. Yes, he had left his heavy baggage. He might be back at any moment. No, he had left no word as to where he was going.

Well, of course, he would be back on Saturday morning to get the five thousand. It was obvious what I was to do. I would leave the money for him, and take the manager's receipt, and tell him to send the papers on to the Caligula at Capri.

I started to count out the cash. We were sitting in the lounge. A sense of absolute bewilderment and helplessness came over me.

"I say, Lou," I stammered, "I wish you'd count this. I can't make it come right. I think I must have been going a bit too hard."

She went through the various pockets of my portefeuille.

"Haven't you some money in your pocket?" she said.

I went through myself with sudden anxiety. I had money in nearly every pocket; but it only amounted to so much small change. A thousand francs here and a hundred francs there, a fifty-pound note in my waistcoat, a lot of small bills——

In the meanwhile, Lou had added up the contents of my porte-feuille. The total was just over seventeen hundred.

"My God! I've been robbed," I gasped out, my face flushing furiously with anger.

Lou kept her head and her temper. After all, it wasn't her money! She began to figure on a scrap of the hotel note paper.

"I'm afraid it's all right," she announced, "you dear, bad boy."

I had become suddenly sober. Yes, there was nothing wrong with the figures. I had paid cash to the jeweller without thinking.

By Jove, we were in a hole! I felt instinctively that it was impossible to telegraph to Wolfe for more money. I suppose my face must have fallen; a regular nose dive. Lou put her arm around my waist and dug her nails into my ribs.

"Chuck it, Cockie," she said, "we're well out of a mess. I always had my doubts about Feccles, and his going off like this looks to me as if there were something very funny about it."

My dream of a quarter of a million disappeared without a moment's regret. I had been prudent after all. I had invested my cash in something tangible. Feccles was an obvious crook. If I had handed him that five thousand, I should never have heard of him or of it again.

I began to recover my spirits.

"Look here," said Lou, "let's forget it. Write Feccles a note to say you couldn't raise the money by the date it was wanted, and let's get out. We ought to economise, in any case, Let's get off to Italy as we said.

The exchange is awfully good, and living's delightfully cheap. It's silly spending money when you've got Love and Cocaine."

My spirit leapt to meet hers. I scribbled a note of apology to Feccles, and left it at the hotel. We dashed round to the Italian consulate to have our passport viséd, got our sleeping cars from the hotel porter, and had the maid pack our things while we had a last heavenly dinner.

VIII

Vedere Napoli E Poi—Pro Patria—Mori

We had just time to get down to the Gare de Lyon for the *train de luxe*. A sense of infinite relief enveloped us as we left Paris behind; and this was accompanied with an overwhelming fatigue which in itself was unspeakably delicious. The moment our heads touched the pillows we sank like young children into exquisite deep slumber, and we woke early in the morning, exhilarated beyond all expression by the Alpine air that enlarged our lungs; that thrilled us with its keen intensity; that lifted us above the pettiness of civilisation, exalting us to communion with the eternal; our souls soared to the primæval peaks that towered above the train. They flowed across the limpid lakes, they revelled with the raging Rhone.

Many people have the idea that the danger of drugs lies in the fact that one is tempted to fly to them for refuge whenever one is a little bored or depressed or annoyed. That is true, of course; but if it stopped there, only a small class of people would stand in real danger.

For example, this brilliant morning, with the sun sparkling on the snow and the water, the whole earth ablush with his glory, the pure keen air rejoicing our lungs; we certainly did say to ourselves, our young eyes ablaze with love and health and happiness, that we didn't need any other element to make our poetry perfect.

I said this without a hint of hesitation. For one thing, we felt like Christian when the burden of his sins fell off his back, at getting away from Paris and civilisation and convention and all that modern artificiality implies.

We had neither the need to get rid of any depression, nor that to increase our already infinite intoxication; ourselves and our love and the boundless beauty of the ever changing landscape, a permanent perfection travelling for its pleasure through inexhaustible possibilities!

Yet almost before the words were out of our mouths, a sly smile crept over Lou's loveliness and kindled the same subtly secret delight in my heart.

She offered me a pinch of heroin with the air of communicating some exquisitely esoteric sacrament; and I accepted it and measured her a similar dose on my own hand as if some dim delirious desire devoured us. We took it not because we needed it; but because the act of consummation was, so to speak, an act of religion.

It was the very fact that it was not an act of necessity which made it an act of piety.

In the same way, I cannot say that the dose did us any particular good. It was at once a routine and a ritual. It was a commemoration like the Protestant communion, and at the same time a consecration like the Catholic. It reminded us that we were heirs to the royal rapture in which we were afloat. But also it refreshed that rapture.

We noticed that in spite of the Alpine air, we did not seem to have any great appetite for breakfast, and we appreciated with the instantaneous sympathy which united us that the food of mortals was too gross for the gods.

That sympathy was so strong and so subtle, so fixed in our hearts, that we could not realise the rude, raw fact that we had ever existed as separate beings. The past was blotted out in the calm contemplation of our beatitude. We understood the changeless ecstasy that radiates from statues of the Buddha; the mysterious triumph on the mouth of Monna Lisa, and the unearthly and ineffable glee of the attitude of Haidée Lamoureux.

We smoked in shining silence as the express swept through the plains of Lombardy. Odd fragments of Shelley's lines on the Euganean hills flitted through my mind like azure or purple phantoms.

"The vaporous plain of Lombardy
Islanded with cities fair."

A century had commercialised the cities for the most part into cockpits and cesspools. But Shelley still shone serene as the sun itself.

"Many a green isle needs must be
In this wide sea of misery."

Everything he had touched with his pen had blossomed into immortality. And Lou and I were living in the land which his prophetic eyes had seen.

I thought of that incomparable idyll, I will not call it an island, to which he invites Æmilia, in Epipsychidion.

Lou and I, my love and I, my wife and I, we were not merely going there; we had always been there and should always be. For the name of the island, the name of the house, the name of Shelley, and the name of Lou and me, they were all one name—Love.

> *"The wingèd words with which my song would pierce*
> *Into the heights of love's rare universe*
> *Are chains of lead about its flight of fire,*
> *I pant, I sink, I tremble, I expire."*

I noticed, in fact, that our physical selves seemed to be acting as projections of our thought. We were both breathing rapidly and deeply. Our faces were flushed, suffused with the sunlight splendour of our bloods that beat time to the waltz of our love.

Waltz? No, it was something wilder than a waltz. The Mazurka, perhaps. No, there was something still more savage in our souls.

I thought of the furious fandango of the gipsies of Granada, of the fanatical frenzy of the religious Moorish rioters chopping at themselves with little sacred axes till the blood streams down their bodies, crazily crimson in the stabbing sunlight, and making little scabs of mire upon the torrid trampled sand.

I thought of the mœnads and Bacchus; I saw them through the vivid eyes of Euripides and Swinburne. And still unsatisfied, I craved for stranger symbols yet. I became a Witch-Doctor presiding over a cannibal feast, driving the yellow mob of murderers into a fiercer Comus-rout, as the maddening beat of the tom-tom and the sinister scream of the bull-roarer destroy every human quality in the worshippers and make them elemental energies; Valkyrie-vampires surging and shrieking on the summit of the storm.

I do not even know whether to call this a vision, or how to classify it psychologically. It was simply happening to me—and to Lou—though we were sitting decorously enough in our compartment. It became increasingly certain that Haidée, low-class, commonplace, ignorant girl that she was, had somehow been sucked into a stupendous maelstrom of truth.

The normal actions and reactions of the mind and the body are simply so many stupid veils upon the face of Isis.

What happened to them didn't matter. The stunt was to find some trick to make them shut up.

ALEISTER CROWLEY

I understood the value of words. It depended, not on their rational meaning, but upon their hieratic suggestion.

"In Xanadu did Kubla Khan
A stately pleasure-house decree."

The names mean nothing definite, but they determine the atmosphere of the poem. Sublimity depends upon unintelligibility.

I understood the rapture of the names in Lord Dunsany's stories. I understood how the "barbarous names of evocation" used by magicians, the bellowings and whistlings of the Gnostics, the Mantras of Hindoo devotees, set their souls spinning till they became giddy with glory.

Even the names of the places that we were passing in the train excited me just as far as they were unfamiliar and sonorous.

I became increasingly excited by the sight of the Italian words, "E pericoloso sporgersi." That wouldn't mean much, no doubt, to anyone who spoke Italian. To me, it was a master-key of magic. I connected it somehow with my love for Lou. Everything was a symbol of my love for Lou except when that idiotic nuisance, knowledge, declared the contrary.

We were whirling in this tremendous trance all the morning. There kept on coming into my mind the title of a picture I had once seen by some crazy modern painter: "Four red monks carrying a black goat across the snow to Nowhere."

It was obviously an excuse for a scheme of colour; but the fantastic imbecility of the phrase, and the subtle suggestion of sinister wickedness, made me pant with suppressed exaltation.

The "first call for lunch" came with startling suddenness. I woke up wildly to recognise the fact that Lou and I had not spoken to each other for hours, that we had been rushing through a Universe of our own creation with stupendous speed and diabolical delight. And at the same time I realised that we had been automatically "coking up" without knowing that we were doing so.

The material world had become of so little importance that I no longer knew where I was. I completely mixed up my present journey with memories of two or three previous Continental excursions.

It was the first time that Lou had ever been farther than Paris, and she looked to me for information as to time and place. With her, familiarity had not bred contempt, and I found myself unable to tell her the most ordinary things about the journey. I didn't even know in which direction we were travelling, whether the Alps came next, or which tunnel we were taking; whether we passed through Florence, or the difference between Geneva and Genoa.

Those who are familiar with the route will realise how hopelessly my mind was entangled. I hardly knew morning from evening. I have described things with absolute confidence which could not possibly have taken place.

We kept on getting up and looking at the map on the panels of the corridor, and I couldn't make out where we were. We compared times and distances only to make confusion worse confounded.

I went into the most obstruse astronomical calculations as to whether we ought to put our watches on an hour or back an hour at the frontier; and I don't know to this day whether I came to any correct conclusion. I had an even chance of being right; but there it stopped.

I remember getting out to stretch our legs at Rome, and that we had a mad impulse to try to see the sights during the twenty minutes or so we had to wait.

I might have done it; but on the platform at Rome I was brought up with a shock. An impossible thing had happened.

"Great Scot," cried a voice from the window of a coach three ahead of our own. "Of all the extraordinary coincidences! How are you?"

We looked up, hardly able to believe our ears. Who should it be but our friend Feccles!

Well, of course, I'd rather have seen the devil himself. After all, I'd behaved to the man rather shabbily; and, incidentally, made a great fool of myself. But what surprised me on second glance was that he was travelling very much incognito. He was hardly recognisable.

I don't think I mentioned he had fair hair with a bald patch, and was clean shaven. But now his hair was dark; and a toupée silently rebuked Nature's inclemency. A small black moustache and imperial completed the disguise. But in addition, his manner of dressing was a camouflage in itself. In Paris he had been dressed very correctly. He might have been a man about town of very good family.

But now he was dressed like a courier, or possibly a high-class commercial traveller. His smartness had an element of commonness very well marked. I instinctively knew that he would prefer me not to mention his name.

At this moment the train began to move, and we had to hop on. We went at once to his compartment. It was a coupé, and he was its sole occupant.

I have already described the shock which the reappearance of Feccles had administered to my nerves. Normally, I should have felt very awkward indeed, but the cocaine lifted me easily over the fence.

The incident became welcome; an additional adventure in the fairy tale which we were living. Lou herself was all gush and giggles to an extent which a month earlier I should have thought a shade off. But everything was equally exquisite on this grand combination honeymoon.

Feccles appeared extremely amused by the encounter. I asked him with the proper degree of concern if he had had my note. He said no, he'd been called suddenly away on business, I told him what I had written, with added apologies.

The long journey had tired me deep down. I took things more seriously, though the cocaine prevented my realising that this was the case.

"My dear fellow," he protested. "I'm extremely annoyed that you should have troubled yourself about the business at all. As a matter of fact, what happened is this. I went round to see those men at four o'clock, as arranged on the 'phone, and they were really so awfully decent about the whole thing that I had to let them in for five thousand, and they wrote me their cheque on the spot. Now, of course, you mustn't imagine that I'd let an old pal down. Anytime you find yourself with a little loose cash, just weigh in. You can have it out of my bit."

"Well, that's really too good of you," I said, "and I won't forget it. It'll be all right, I suppose, now you've got the thing through, to wait till I get back to England."

"Why, of course," he replied. "Don't think about business at all. It was really rotten of me to talk shop to a man on his honeymoon."

Lou took up the conversation. "But do tell us," she began, "why this thusness. It suits you splendidly, you know. But after all, I'm a woman."

Feccles suddenly became very solemn. He went to the door of the coupé and looked up and down the corridor; then he slid the door to and began to speak in a whisper.

"This is a very serious business," he said, and paused.

He took out his keys and played with them, as if uncertain how far to go. He thrust them back into his pocket with a decisive gesture.

"Look here, old chap," he said, "I'll take a chance on you. We all know what you did for England during the war—and take one thing with another, you're about my first pick."

He stopped short. We looked at him blankly, though we were seething with some blind suppressed excitement whose nature we could hardly describe.

He took out a pipe, and began to nibble the vulcanite rather nervously. He drew a deep breath, and looked Lou straight in the face.

"Does it suggest anything to you," he murmured, almost inaudibly, "a man's leaving Paris at a moment's notice in the middle of a vast financial scheme, and turning up in Italy, heavily camouflaged?"

"The police on your track!" giggled Lou.

He broke into hearty, good-natured laughter.

"Getting warm," he said. "But try again."

The explanation flashed into my mind at once. He saw what I was thinking, and smiled and nodded.

"Oh, I see," said Lou wisely and bent over to him and whispered in his ear. The words were:—

"Secret Service."

"That's it," said Feccles softly. "And this is where you come in. Look here."

He brought out a passport from his pocket and opened it. He was Monsieur Hector Laroche, of Geneva, so it appeared; by profession a courier.

We nodded comprehensively.

"I was rather at my wits' end when I saw you," he went on. "I'm on the trail of a very dangerous man who has got into the confidence of some English people living in Capri. That's where you're going, isn't it?"

"Yes," we said, feeling ourselves of international importance.

"Well, it's like this. If I turn up in Capri, which is a very small place, without a particularly good excuse, people will look at me and talk about me, and if they look too hard and talk too much, it's ten to one I'm spotted, not necessarily for what I am, but as a stranger of suspicious character. And if the man I'm after gets on his guard, there'll be absolutely nothing doing."

"Yes," I said, "I see all that, but—well, we'd do anything for good old England—goes without saying, but how can we help you out?"

"Well," said Feccles, "I don't see why it should put you out very much. You needn't even see me. But if I could pose as your courier, go ahead and book your rooms and look after your luggage and engage boats and that sort of thing for you, I shouldn't need to be explained. As things are, it might even save you trouble. They're the most frightful brigands round here; and anything that looks like a tourist, especially of the honeymoon species, is liable to all sorts of bother and robbery."

Well, the thing did seem almost providential; as a matter of fact, I had been thinking of getting a man to keep off the jackals, and this was killing two birds with one stone.

Lou was obviously delighted with the arrangement.

"Oh, but you must let us do more than that," she said. "If we could only help you spot this swine!"

"You bet I will," said Feccles heartily, and we all shook hands on it. "Anytime anything happens where you could be useful, I'll tell you what to do. But of course you'll have to remember the rules of the service— absolute silence and obedience. And you stand or fall on your own feet, and if the umpire says 'out,' you're out, and nobody's going to pick up the pieces."

This honeymoon was certainly coming out in the most wonderful way. We had left the cinema people at the post. Here we were, without any effort of our own, right in the middle of the most fascinating intrigues of the most mysterious kind. And all that on the top of the most wonderful love there was in the world, and heroin and cocaine to help us make the most of the tiniest details.

"Well," said I to Feccles, "this suits me down to the ground. I'm trying to forget what you said about my brain, because it isn't good for a young man to be puffed up with intellectual vanity. But I certainly am the luckiest man in the world."

M. Hector Laroche gave us a delightful hour, telling of some of his past exploits in the war. He was as modest as he was brave; but for all that, we could see well enough what amazing astuteness he had brought to the service of our country in her hour of peril. We could imagine him making rings round the lumbering minds of the Huns with their slow pedantic processes.

The only drawback to the evening was that we couldn't get him to take any snow. And you know what that means—you feel the man's somehow out of the party. He excused himself by saying that the regulations forbade it. He agreed with us that it was rotten red-tape, but "of course, they're right in a way, there are quite a lot of chaps that wouldn't know how to use it, might get a bit above themselves and give something away—you know how it is."

So we left him quietly smoking, and went back to our own little cubby and had the most glorious night, whispering imaginary intrigues which somehow lent stronger wing to the real rapture of our love. We neither of us slept. We simply sailed through the darkness to find the dawn caressing the crest of Posilippo and the first glint of sunrise signalling ecstatic greetings to the blue waters of the Bay of Naples.

When the train stopped, there was Hector Laroche at the door, ordering everybody about in fluent Italian. We had the best suite in the best hotel, and our luggage arrived not ten minutes later than we did, and breakfast was a perfect poem, and we had a box for the opera and our passages booked for the following day for Capri, where a suite was reserved for us at the Caligula. We saw the Museum in the morning and automobiled out to Pompeii in the afternoon, and yet M. Laroche had managed everything for us so miraculously well that even this very full day left us perfectly fresh, murmuring through half-closed lips the magic sentence:—

"Dolce far niente."

THE MAJORITY OF PEOPLE SEEM to stumble through this world without any conception of the possibilities of enjoyment. It is, of course, a matter of temperament.

But even the few who can appreciate the language of Shelley, Keats and Swinburne, look on those conceptions as Utopian.

Most people acquiesce in the idea that the giddy exaltation of *Prometheus Unbound*, for example, is an imaginary feeling. I suppose, in fact, that one wouldn't get much result by giving heroin and cocaine, however cunningly mixed, to the average man. You can't get out of a thing what isn't there.

In ninety-nine cases out of a hundred, any stimulant of whatever nature operates by destroying temporarily the inhibitions of education.

The ordinary drunken man loses the veneer of civilisation. But if you get the right man, the administration of a drug is quite likely to suppress his mental faculties, with the result that his genius is set free. Coleridge is a case in point. When he happened to get the right quantity of laudanum in him, he dreamed Kubla Khan, one of the supreme treasures of the language.

And why is it incomplete? Because a man called from Porlock on business and called him back to his normal self, so that he forgot all but a few lines of the poem.

Similarly, we have Herbert Spencer taking morphia everyday of his life, decade after decade. Without morphia, he would simply have been a querulous invalid, preoccupied with bodily pain. With it, he was the genius whose philosophy summarised the thought of the nineteenth century.

But Lou and I were born with a feeling for romance and adventure. The ecstasy of first love was already enough to take us out of ourselves to a certain extent. The action of the drugs intensified and spiritualised these possibilities.

The atmosphere of Capri, and the genius of Feccles for preventing any interference with our pleasure, made our first fortnight on the island an unending trance of unearthly beauty.

He never allowed us a chance to be bored, and yet, he never intruded. He took all the responsibilities off our hands, he arranged excursions to Anacapri, to the Villa of Tiberius and to the various grottos. Once or twice he suggested a wild night in Naples, and we revelled in the peculiar haunts of vice with which that city abounds.

Nothing shocked us, nothing surprised us. Every incident of life was the striking of a separate note in the course of an indescribable symphony.

He introduced us to the queerest people, drove us into the most mysterious quarters. But everything that happened wove itself intoxicatingly into the tapestry of love.

We went out on absurd adventures. Even when they were disappointing from the ordinary standpoint, the disappointment itself seemed to add piquancy to the joke.

One couldn't help being grateful to the man for his protecting care. We went into plenty of places where the innocent tourist is considered fair game; and his idiomatic Italian invariably deterred the would-be sportsman. Even at the hotel, he fought the manager over the weekly bill, and compelled him to accept a much lower figure than his dreams had indicated.

Of course, most of his time was occupied with keeping watch on the man he was trailing; and he kept us very amused with the account of his progress.

"I shall never be grateful enough to you, if I bring this off as I think I shall," he said. "It will be the turning point in my official career. I don't mind telling you they've treated me rather shabbily at home about one or two things I've done. But if I bag this bird, they can hardly say no to anything I may ask."

At the same time, it was clear that he took a genuine friendly interest in his love-birds, as he called us. He had had a disappointment himself, he said, and it had put him off the business personally, but he was glad to say it hadn't soured his nature, and he took a real pleasure in seeing people so ideally happy as we were.

The only thing, he said, that made him a little uneasy and discontented was that he hadn't got in touch with the people who ran the Gatto Fritto, which was an extremely exciting and dangerous kind of night club which indulged in pleasures of so esoteric a kind that no other place in Europe had anything to compare with it.

IX

THE GATTO FRITTO

It was about the end of the third week, I discover from Lou's Diary (I had lost all count of time myself), that he came in one day with a smile of subtle triumph in his eyes.

"I've got on to the ropes," he said, "but I think I ought in fairness to warn you that the Gatto Fritto is a pretty hot place. I wouldn't mind taking you as long as you go in disguise and have a gun in your pocket, but I really can't take it on my conscience to have Lady Pendragon along."

I was so full up with cocaine I hardly knew what he was saying. It was the easiest way out to nod assent and watch the clouds fighting each other to get hold of the sun.

I was betting on that big white elephant on the horizon. There were two black cobras and a purple hippopotamus against him; but I couldn't help that. With those magnificent tusks he ought to be able to settle their business, and only to look at his legs you could see the old sun hadn't got a dog's chance. I can't see why people haven't the sense to keep still when a fight of this kind is in progress. What's the referee for, anyway?

It was extremely annoying of Lou to protest in that passionate shrill voice of hers that she was going to the Gatto Fritto, and if she didn't she'd take to keeping cats herself, and fry them, and make me eat them!

I don't know how long she went on. It was perfectly gorgeous to hear her. I knew what it meant just as soon as we could get rid of that swine Feccles.

Hang it all, one doesn't want another man on one's honeymoon!

So there was Feccles turning to me in a sort of limp, helpless protest, imploring me to put my foot down about it.

So I said, "Feccles, old top, you're the right sort. I always liked you at school, and I shall never forget what you've done for me these last thirty or forty years or whatever it is we've been in Capri, and Lloyd George can trust you to nip that blighter you're after, why shouldn't I trust you to see us through this fun at the Gatto Fritto?"

Lou clapped her hands, screaming with merriment, but Feccles said:—

"Now, that's all right. But this is a very serious business. You're not going about it in the right spirit. We've got to go about it very quietly and soberly, and then open up when the word comes Over the top."

We pretended to pull ourselves together to please him, but I couldn't blind my eyes to the fact that I was likely to lose my money, because the white elephant had turned into a quite ordinary Zebu or Brahman cow, or at the best a two-humped or Bactrian dromedary, in any case, an animal entirely unfitted by nature to carry the money of a cautious backer.

Agitated by this circumstance, I was hardly in a condition to realise the nature of the proposals laid before the meeting by Worshipful Brother Feccles, Acting Deputy Grand Secretary General.

But roughly they were to this effect: That we were to lock up all our money and jewellery, except a little small change, as an act of precaution, and Feccles would arrive in due course, with disguises for me and Lou as Neapolitan fisherfolk, and we were to take nothing but a revolver apiece and a little small change, and we were to slip off the terrace of the hotel after dark without anyone seeing, and there would be a motor-boat across to Sorrento; and there would be an automobile, so we could get into Naples at about one o'clock in the morning, and then we were to go to a certain drinking place, the Fauno Ebbrio, and as soon as the coast was clear he would pick us up and take us along to the Gatto Fritto, and we would know for the first time what life was really like.

Well, I call that a perfectly straight, decent, sensible programme. It's the duty of every Englishman to learn as much of foreign affairs as he can without interfering with his business. That sort of knowledge will always come in useful in case of another European War. It was knowing that sort of thing that had put Feccles where he was in the Secret Service, the trusted confident of those mysterious intelligences that watch over the welfare of our beloved country.

Thank you, that will conclude the evening's entertainment.

I will say this for Feccles. He always understood instinctively when he wasn't wanted. So immediately the arrangements were made, he excused himself hastily, because he had to go down to the Villa where his victim was staying, and fix a dictaphone in the room where he was going to have dinner.

So I had Lou all to myself until he came with the disguises the next day in the afternoon. And I wasn't going to waste a minute.

I admit I was pretty sick about the way the white cloud let me down. I'd have gone after the silly old sun myself if I hadn't been a married man.

However, there we were alone, alone forever, Lou and I in Capri, it was all much too good to be true! Sunlight and moonlight and starlight! They were all in her eyes. And she handed out the cocaine with such a provocative gesture! I knew what it was to be insane. I could understand perfectly well why the silly fools that aren't insane are afraid of being insane. I'd been that way myself when I didn't know any better.

This rotten little race of men measures the world by its own standard. It is lost in the vastness of the Universe, and is consequently afraid of everything that doesn't happen to fit its own limits.

Lou and I had discarded the miserable measures of mankind. That sort of thing is all right for tailors and men of science; but we had sprung in one leap to be conterminous with the Universe. We were as incommensurable as the ratio of a circle to its diameter. We were as imaginary and unreal from their point of view as the square root of minus one.

We didn't ask humanity to judge us. It was simply a case of mistaken identity to regard us as featherless bipeds at all. We may have looked like human beings to their eyes; in fact, they sent in bills and things as if we had been human beings.

But I refuse to be responsible for the mistakes of the inferior animals. I humour them to some extent in their delusions, because they're lunatics and ought to be humoured. But it's a long way between that and admitting that their hallucinations have any basis in fact.

I had been in their silly world of sense a million years or so ago, when I was Peter Pendragon.

But why recall the painful past? Of course, one doesn't come to one's full strength in a minute. Take the case of an eagle. What is it as long as it's in the egg? Nothing but an egg with possibilities. And the first day it's hatched you don't expect it to fly to Neptune and back. Certainly not!

But everyday, in every way, it gets better and better. And if I ever tempted to flop and remember my base origin as a forked radish, why all I needed was a kiss from Lou, or a sniff of cocaine to put me back in Paradise.

I can't tell you about those next twenty-four hours. Suffice it to say that all world's records were broken and broken again. And we were simply panting like two hungry wolves when Feccles turned up with the disguises and the guns!

He repeated those instructions, and added one word of almost paternal counsel in a very confidential tone.

"You'll excuse me, I know; I'm not suggesting for a moment you're not perfectly capable of taking care of yourself, but you haven't been in these parts before, and you must never forget the quick, violent tempers of these Southern Italians. It's like one of these sudden gusts that the fishermen are so afraid of. It doesn't mean anything in particular; but it's often ugly enough at the moment, and what you have to do is to keep out of any kind of a row. There may be a lot of drunken ruffians in the Fauno Ebbrio. Sit near the door; and if anybody starts scrapping, slip out quietly and walk up and down till it's over. You don't want to get mixed up with a fuss."

I could see the wisdom of his remarks, although, on the other hand, I was personally spoiling for a fight. The one fly in the apothecary's ointment of the honeymoon, though I didn't notice it, was that something in me missed the excitement of the daily gambling with death to which the war had accustomed me.

The slightest reminder of the wilder passions—a couple of boatmen quarrelling, or even a tourist protesting about some trifle, sent the blood to my head. I only wanted a legitimate excuse for killing a few hundred people.

But nature is wise and kind, and I was always able to take it out of Lou. The passions of murder and love are inseparably connected in our ancestry. All civilisation has done is to teach us to pretend to idealise them.

The programme went off without the slightest hitch. Our room opened on to a terrace in deep shadow. At this time of year there was hardly anyone in the hotel, of course. A little flight of steps at the side of the terrace took us under an arch of twisted vines into the barely more than mule-path that does duty for a road in Capri.

No one took any notice of us. There were only strolling lovers, parties of peasants singing as they walked to the guitar, and two or three tired happy fishermen strolling home from the wine-shop.

We found the motor-boat at the quay, and lay lapsed in delight. It seemed hardly a minute later when we found ourselves in Sorrento couched in a huge roadster. Without a word spoken, we were off at top speed. The beauty of the drive is notorious; and yet:—

> *"We were the first that ever burst*
> *Into that silent sea."*

The world had been created afresh for our sakes. It was an ever-changing phantasmagoria of rapturous sounds and sights and scents; and it all seemed a mere ornamentation for our love, the setting for the jewel of our sparkling passion.

Even the last few miles into Naples, where the road runs through tedious commercialised suburbs, took on a new aspect. The houses were a mere irregular skyline. Somehow they suggested the jagged contour of a score of Debussy.

But all this, exquisite as it was, gripping as it was, was in a way superficial. At the bottom of our hearts there seethed and surged a white hot volcanic lake of molten, of infernal, metal.

We did not know what hideous, what monstrous abominations were in store for us at the Gatto Fritto.

I have set down how the action of the drugs had partially stripped off the recent layers of memory. It had achieved a parallel result much more efficiently on the moral plane. The toil of countless generations of evolution had been undone in a month. We still preserved, to a certain extent, the conventions of decency; but we knew that we did so only from apelike cunning.

We had reverted to the gorilla. No action of violence and lust but seemed a necessary outlet for our energies!

We said nothing to each other about this. It was, in fact, deeper and darker than could be conveyed by articulate speech.

Man differs from the lower animals indeed, first of all, in this matter of language. The use of language compels one to measure one's thoughts. That is why the great philosophers and mystics, who are dealing with ideas that cannot be expressed in such terms, are constantly compelled to use negative adjectives, or to rebuke the mind by formulating their thoughts in a series of contradictory statements. That is the explanation of the Athanasian Creed. Its clauses puzzle the plain man.

One must oneself be divine to comprehend divinity.

The converse proposition is equally true. The passions of the pit find outlet only in bestial noises.

The automobile stopped at the end of the dirty little street where the Fauno Ebbrio lurks. The motorman pointed to the zig-zag streak of light that issued from it, and cast a sinister gleam on the opposite wall.

A bold, black-haired, short-skirted girl with a gaudy shawl and huge gold ear-rings was standing in the door. What with the long journey and the drugs and other things, we were a little drunk—just enough to realise that it was part of our policy to pretend to be a little more drunk than we were.

We let our heads roll from side to side as we staggered to the door. We sat down at a little table and called for drink. They served us one of those foul Italian imitations of liqueurs that taste like hair-wash.

But instead of nauseating us, it exalted us; we enjoyed it as part of the game. Dressed as low-class Neapolitans, we threw ourselves heartily into the part.

We threw the fiery filth down our throats as if it had been Courvoisier '65. The drink took effect on us with surprising alacrity. It seemed to let loose those swarming caravans of driver ants that eat their way through the jungle of life like a splash of sulphuric acid flung in a woman's face.

There was no clock in the den, and of course we had left our watches at home. We got a little impatient. We couldn't remember whether Feccles had or had not told us how long he was likely to be. The air of the room was stifling. The lowest vagabonds of Naples crowded the place. Some were jabbering like apes; some singing drunkenly to themselves; some shamelessly caressing; some sunk in bestial stupor.

Among the last was a burly brute who somehow fascinated our attention.

We thought ourselves quite safe in speaking English; and for all I know we were talking at the top of our voices. Lou maintained that this particular man was English himself.

He was apparently asleep; but presently he lifted his head from the table, stretched his great arms, and called for a drink, in Italian.

He drained his glass at a gulp, and then came suddenly over to our table and addressed us in English.

We could tell at once from his accent that the man had originally been more or less of a gentleman, but his face and his tone told their own story. He must have been going downhill for many years—reached the bottom long ago, and found it the easiest place to live.

He was aggressively friendly in a brutal way, and warned us that our disguises might be a source of danger; anyone could see through them, and the fact of our having adopted them might arouse the quick suspicion of the Neapolitan mind.

He called for drinks, and toasted King and Country with a sort of surly pride in his origin. He reminded me of Kipling's broken-down Englishman.

"Don't you be afraid," he said to Lou. "I won't let you come to any harm. A little peach like you? No blooming fear!"

I resented the remark with almost insane intensity. To hell with the fellow!

He noticed it at once, and leered with a horrible chuckle.

"All right, mister," he said. "No offence meant," and he threw an arm round Lou's neck, and made a movement to kiss her.

I was on my feet in a second, and swung my right to his jaw. It knocked him off the bench, and he lay flat.

In a moment the uproar began. All my old fighting instincts flashed to the surface. I realised instantly that we were in for the very row that Feccles had so wisely warned us to avoid.

The whole crowd—men and women—were on their feet. They were rushing at us like stampeding cattle. I whipped out my revolver. The wave surged back as a breaker does when it hits a rock.

"Guard my back!" I cried to Lou.

She hardly needed telling. The spirit of the true Englishwoman in a crisis was aflame in her.

Fixing the crowd with my eyes and my barrel, we edged our way to the door. One man took up a glass to throw; but the *padrone* had slipped out from behind the bar, and knocked his arm down.

The glass smashed to the floor. The attack on us degenerated into a volley of oaths and shrieks. We found ourselves in the fresh air—and also in the arms of half a dozen police who had run up from both ends of the street.

Two of them strode into the wine-shop. The uproar ceased as if by magic.

And then we found that we were under arrest. We were being questioned in voluble, excited Italian. Neither Lou nor I understood a word that was said to us.

The sergeant came out of the dive. He seemed an intelligent man. He understood at once that we were English.

"Inglese?" he asked. "Inglese?" and I forcibly echoed "Inglese, Signore Inglese," as if that settled the whole matter.

English people on the Continent have an illusion that the mere fact of their nationality permits them to do anything soever. And there is a great deal of truth in this, after all, because the inhabitants of Europe have a settled conviction that we are all harmless lunatics. So we are allowed to act in all sorts of ways which they would not tolerate for a moment in any supposedly rational person.

In the present instance, I have little doubt that, if we had been dressed as ourselves, we should have been politely conducted to our hotel or put into an automobile, without anymore fuss, perhaps, than a few perfunctory questions intended to impress the sergeant's men with his importance.

But as it was, he shook his head doubtfully.

"Arme vietate," he said solemnly, pointing to the revolvers which were still in our hands.

I tried to explain the affair in broken Italian. Lou did what was really a much more sensible thing by taking the affair as a stupendous joke, and going off into shrieks of hysterical laughter.

But as for me, my blood was up. I wasn't going to stand any nonsense from these damned Italians. Despite the Roman blood that is legitimately the supreme pride of our oldest families, we always somehow instinctively think of the Italian as a nigger.

We don't call them "dagos" and "wops," as they do in the United States, with the invariable epithet of "dirty"; but we have the same feeling.

I began to take the high hand with the sergeant; and that, of course, was quite sufficient to turn the balance against us.

We found ourselves pinioned. He said in a very short tone that we should have to go to the Commissario.

I had two conflicting impulses. One to shoot the dogs down and get away; the other to wish, like a lost child, that Feccles would turn up and get us out of the mess.

Unfortunately for either, I had been very capably disarmed, and there was no sign of Feccles.

We were marched to the police station and thrown into separate rooms.

I cannot hope to depict the boiling rage which kept me awake all night. I resented ill-temperedly the attempts of the other men to be sympathetic. I think they recognised instinctively that I had got into trouble through no fault of my own, and were anxious to show kindness in their own rough way to the stranger.

The worst of the whole business was that they had searched us and removed our stand-by, the dear little gold-topped bottle! I might have got myself into a mood to laugh the whole thing off, as had so often happened before; and I realised for the first time the dreadful sinking of heart that comes from privation.

It was only a hint of the horror so far. I had enough of the stuff in me to carry me through for a bit. But, even as things were, it was bad enough.

I had a feeling of utter helplessness. I began to repent having repulsed the advances of my fellow prisoners. I approached them and explained that I was a "*Signor Inglese*" with "*molto danaro*"; and if anyone could oblige me with a sniff of cocaine, as I explained by gesture, I should be practically grateful.

I was understood immediately. They laughed sympathetically with perfect comprehension of the case. But as it happened, nobody had managed to smuggle anything in. There was nothing for it but to wait for the morning. I lay down on a bench, and found myself the prey of increasingly acute irritation.

The hours passed like the procession of Banquo's heirs before the eyes of Macbeth; and a voice in me kept saying, "Macbeth hath murdered sleep, Macbeth shall sleep no more!"

I had an appallingly disquieting sensation of being tracked down by some invisible foe. I was seized with a perfectly unreasonable irritation against Feccles, as if it were his fault, and not my own, that I was in this mess.

Strangely enough, you may think, I never gave a thought to Lou. It mattered nothing to me whether she were suffering or not. My own personal physiological sensations occupied the whole of my mind.

I was taken before the Commissario as soon as he arrived. They seemed to recognise that the case was important.

Lou was already in the office. The Commissario spoke no English, and no interpreter was immediately available. She looked absolutely wretched.

There had been no conveniences for toilet, and in the daylight the disguise was a ridiculous travesty.

Her hair was tousled and dirty; her complexion was sallow, mottled with touches of unwholesome red. Her eyes were bleared and bloodshot. Dark purple rims were round them.

I was extremely angry with her for her unprepossessing appearance. It then occurred to me for the first time that perhaps I myself was not looking like the Prince of Wales on Derby Day.

The commissary was a short, bull-necked individual, evidently sprung from the ranks of the people. He possessed a correspondingly exaggerated sense of his official importance.

He spoke almost without courtesy, and appeared to resent our incapacity to understand his language.

As for myself, the fighting spirit had gone out of me completely. All I could do was to give our names in the tone of voice of a schoolboy who has been summoned by the head master, and to appeal for the "Consule Inglese."

The commissary's clerk seemed excited when he heard who we were, and spoke to his superior in a rapid undertone. We were asked to write our names.

I thought this was getting out of it rather nicely. I felt sure that the "Sir" would do the trick, and the "V.C., K.B.E." could hardly fail to impress.

I'm not a bit of a snob; but I really was glad for once to be of some sort of importance.

The clerk ran out of the room with the paper. He came back in a moment, beaming all over, and called the attention of the commissary to one of the morning newspapers, running his finger along the lines with suppressed excitement.

My spirits rose. Evidently some social paragraph had identified us.

The commissary changed his manner at once. His new tone was not exactly sympathetic and friendly, but I put that down to the man's plebeian origin.

He said something about "Consule," and had us conducted to an outer room. The clerk indicated that we were to wait there—no doubt, for the arrival of the consul.

It was not more than half an hour; but it seemed an eternity. Lou and I had nothing to say to each other. What we felt was a blind ache to get away from these wretched people, to get back to the Caligula; to have a bath and a meal; and above all, to ease our nerves with a good stiff dose of heroin and a few hearty sniffs of cocaine.

X

The Bubble Bursts

We felt that our troubles were over when a tall bronzed Englishman in flannels and a Panama sauntered into the room.

We sprang instinctively to our feet, but he took no notice beyond looking at us out of the tail of his eye, and twisting his mouth into a curious little compromise between a smile and a query.

The clerk bowed him at once into an inner room. We waited and waited. I couldn't understand at all what they could have been talking about in there for so long.

But at last the soldier at the door beckoned us in. The vice-consul was sitting on a sofa in the background. With his head on one side, he shot a keen fixed glance out of his languid eyes, and bit his thumbnail persistently, as if in a state of extreme nervous perplexity.

I was swept by a feeling of complete humiliation. It was a transitory feverish flush; and it left me more exhausted than ever.

The commissario swung his chair around to our saviour, and said something which evidently meant, "Please open fire."

"I'm the vice-consul here," he said. "I understand that you claim to be Sir Peter and Lady Pendragon."

"That's who we are," I replied, with a pitiful attempt at jauntiness.

"You'll excuse me, I'm sure," he said, "if I say that—to the eyes of the average Italian official—you don't precisely look the part. Have you your passports?"

The mere presence of an English gentleman had a good effect in pulling me together.

I said, with more confidence than before, that our courier had arranged to take us to see some of the shows in Naples that the ordinary tourist knows nothing about, and in order to avoid any possible annoyance, he had advised us to adopt this disguise—and so on for the rest of the story.

The vice-consul smiled—indulgently, as I thought.

"I admit we have some experience," he said slowly, "of young people like yourselves getting into various kinds of trouble. One can't expect everyone to know all the tricks; and besides, if I understand correctly, you're on your honeymoon."

I admitted the fact with a somewhat embarrassed smile. It occurred to me that honeymoon couples were traditionally objects of not unkindly ridicule from people in a less blessèd condition.

"Quite so," replied the vice-consul. "I'm not a married man myself; but no doubt it is very delightful. How do you like it in Norway?"

"Norway?" I said, completely flabbergasted.

"Yes," he said. "How do you like Norway; the climate, the *lax*, the people, the fiords, the glaciers?"

There was some huge mistake somewhere.

"Norway?" I said, with a rising inflection.

I was on the brink of hysteria.

"I've never been to the place in my life. And if it's anything like Naples, I don't want to go!"

"This is a rather more serious matter than you seem to suppose," returned the consul. "If you're not in Norway, where are you?"

"Why, I'm here, confound it," I retorted with another weak flush of anger.

"Since when, may I ask?" he replied.

Well, he rather had me there. I didn't know how long I'd been away from England. I couldn't have told him the day or the month on a bet.

Lou helped me out.

"We left Paris three weeks ago tomorrow," she said positively enough, though the tone of her voice was weak and weary, with a sub-current of irritation and distress. I hardly recognised the rich, full tones that had flooded my heart when she chanted that superb litany in the "Smoking Dog."

"We spent a couple of days here," she said, "at the Museo-Palace Hotel. Since then, we've been staying at the Caligula at Capri; and our clothes, our passports, our money, and everything are there."

I couldn't help being pleased by the way in which she rose to the crisis; her practical good sense, her memory of those details that are so important in business, though the male temperament regards them as a necessary nuisance.

These are the things that one needs in an official muddle.

"You don't know any Italian at all?" asked the consul.

"Only a few words," she admitted, "though, of course, Sir Peter's knowledge of French and Latin help him to make sense out of the newspapers."

"Well," said the consul, rising languidly, "as it happens, that's just the point at issue."

"I know the big words," I said. "It's the particles that bother one."

"Perhaps then it will save trouble," said the consul, "if I offer you a free translation of this paragraph in this morning's paper."

He reached across, took it from the commissario, and began a fluent even phrasing.

"England is always in the van when it comes to romance and adventure. The famous ace, Sir Peter Pendragon, V.C., K.B.E., who recently startled London by his sudden marriage with the leading society beauty, Miss Louise Laleham, is not spending his honeymoon in any of the conventional ways, as might be expected from the gentleman's bold and adventurous character. He has taken his bride for a season's guideless climbing on the Jostedal Brae, the largest glacier in Norway."

I could see that the commissario was drilling holes in my soul with his eyes. As for myself, I was absolutely stupefied by the pointless falsehood of the paragraph.

"But, good God!" I exclaimed. "This is all absolute tosh."

"Excuse me," said the consul, a little grimly, "I have not finished the paragraph."

"I beg your pardon, sir," I answered curtly.

"Taking advantage of these facts," he continued to read, "and of a slight facial resemblance to Sir Peter and Lady Pendragon, two well-known international crooks have assumed their personalities, and are wandering around Naples and its vicinity, where several tradesmen have already been victimised."

He dropped the paper, put his hands behind his back, and stared me square in the eyes.

I could not meet his glance. The accusation was so absurd, so horrible, so unexpected! I felt that guilt was written on every line of my face.

I stammered out some weakly, violent objurgation. Lou kept her head better than I.

"But please, this is absurd," she protested. "Send for our courier. He has known Sir Peter since he was a boy at school. The whole thing is shameful and abominable. I don't see why such things are allowed."

The consul seemed in doubt as to what to do. He played with his watch-chain nervously.

I had sunk into a chair—I noticed they hadn't offered us chairs when we came in—and the whole scene vanished from my mind. I was aware of nothing but a passionate craving for drugs. I wanted them physically as I had never wanted anything in my life before. I wanted them mentally, too. They, and they only, would clear my mind of its confusion, and show me a way out of this rotten mess. I wanted them most of all morally. I lacked the spirit to stand up under this sudden burst of drum fire.

But Lou stuck to it gamely. She was on her mettle, though I could see that she was almost fainting from the stress of the various circumstances.

"Send for our courier, Hector Laroche," she insisted.

The consul shrugged his shoulders. "But where is he?"

"Why," she said, "he must be looking for us all over the town. When he got to the Fauno Ebbrio and found we weren't there, and heard what had happened, he must have been very anxious about us."

"In fact, I don't see why he isn't here now," said the consul. "He must have known that you were arrested."

"Perhaps something's happened to him," suggested Lou. "But that would really be too curious a coincidence."

"Well, these things do happen," admitted the consul.

He seemed somehow more at his ease with her, and better disposed, than when he was talking to me. Her magnetic beauty and her evident aristocracy could not help but have their effect.

I found myself admiring her immensely, in quite a new way. It had never occurred to me that she could rise to a situation with such superb *aplomb*.

"Won't you sit down?" said the consul, "I'm sure you must be very tired."

He put a chair for her, and went back to his seat on the sofa.

"It's a little awkward, you see," he went on. "I don't, as a matter of fact, believe all I read in the papers. And there are several very curious points about the situation which you don't seem to see yourself. And I don't mind admitting that your failure to see them makes a very favourable impression."

He paused and bit his lip, and pulled at his neck.

"It's very difficult," he continued at last. "The facts of the case, on the surface, are undeniably ugly. You are found in disguise in one of the worst places in Naples, and you have actually arms in your hands, which is *strengst verboten,* as they say in Germany. On the other hand, you give an account of yourself which makes you out to be such utter fools, if you will forgive the frankness of the expression, that it speaks volumes for your innocence, and there's no doubt about your being British——" he smiled amiably, "and I think I must do what I can for you. Excuse me while I talk to my friend here."

Lou turned on me with a triumphant smile; one of her old proud smiles, except that it was wrung, so to speak, out of the heart of unspeakable agony.

Meanwhile, the commissario was gesticulating and shouting at the consul, who replied with equal volubility but an apparently unsurmountable languor.

Then the conversation stopped suddenly short. The two men rose to their feet.

"I've arranged it with my friend here on the basis of his experience of the bold, bad, British tourist. You will come with me to the consulate under the protection of two of his men," he smiled sarcastically, "for fear you should get into any further trouble. You can have your things back except the guns, which are forbidden."

How little he knew what a surge of joy went through us at that last remark!

"I will send one of my clerks with you to Capri," he said, "and you will get your passports and money and whatever you need, and come back to me at once and put the position on a more regular footing."

We got our things from the sergeant, and made excuses for a momentary disappearance.

By George, how we did want it!

Five minutes later we were almost ourselves again. We saw the whole thing as an enormous lark, and communicated our high spirits to our companion. He attributed them, no doubt, to our prospects of getting out of the scrape.

Lou rattled on all the way about life in London, and I told the story—bar the snow part—of our elopement. He thawed out completely. Our confidence had reassured him.

We shook hands amid all-round genial laughter when we left under the guidance of a very business-like Italian, who spoke English well.

We caught the boat to Capri with plenty of time to spare, and regaled the consul's clerk with all sorts of amusing anecdotes. He was very pleased to be treated on such a friendly footing.

We went up to the Piazza in the Funicular with almost the sensation of soaring. It had been a devil of a mess; but five minutes more would see it at an end. And, despite my exaltation, I registered a vow that I would never do anything so foolish again.

Of course, it was evident what had happened to Feccles. He had somehow failed to learn of our arrest, and was waiting at the hotel with impatient anxiety for our return.

At the same time, it was rather ridiculous in that costume in broad daylight to have to ask the porter for one's key.

I could not at all understand his look of genuine surprise. That wasn't simply a question of clothes—I felt it in my bones. And there was the manager, bowing and scraping like a monkey. He seemed to have lost his self-possession. The torrent of his words of welcome ran over a very rough bed.

I couldn't really grasp what he was saying for a moment, but there was no mistaking the import of his final phrase.

"I'm so delighted that you've changed your mind, Sir Peter, but I felt sure you could never bear to leave Capri so soon. Our beautiful Capri!"

What the deuce was the fellow talking about? Change my mind? What I wanted to do was to change my clothes!

The consul's clerk made a few rapid explanations in Italian, and it almost hit me in the eye to watch the manager's face as he lifted his eyes and saw the two obvious detectives in the doorway.

"I don't understand," he said with sudden anxiety. "I don't understand this at all," and he bustled round to his desk.

"Where's our courier?" called out Lou. "It's for him to explain everything."

The manager became violently solemn.

"Your Ladyship is undoubtedly right," he broke out.

But the conventional words did not conceal the fact that his mental attitude was that of a man who has suddenly fallen through a trap-door into a cellar full of something spiky.

"There's some mistake here," he went on. "Let me see."

He called to the girl at the desk in Italian. She fished about in a drawer and produced a telegram.

He handed it over to me. It was addressed to Laroche.

"Urgent bisnes oblige live for Roma night. Pay bill packup join me Museo Palace Hotel Napls in time to cach miday train. Pendragon."

The words were mostly mis-spelt; but the meaning was clear enough. Someone must be playing a practical joke. Probably that paragraph in the paper was part of the same idea. So I supposed Laroche was in the hotel in Naples wondering why we didn't turn up.

"But where's our luggage?" cried Lou.

"Why," said the manager, "your Ladyship's courier paid the bill as usual. The servants helped him to pack your luggage, and he just managed to catch the morning boat."

"But what time was this?" cried Lou, and scanned the telegram closely.

It must have been received within a few minutes of our leaving the hotel.

The girl handed over another telegram addressed to the manager.

"Sir Petre add Lady Pendragom espress ther regrets at having so leve so sudenl and mill always have the warmest remebrances of the hapy times they had at the Caligula and hop so riture at the earliest possibile opportunity. Courier till attend to busines details."

It suddenly dawned on my mind that there was one scrap of fact imbedded in this fantastic farrago. The courier had attended to business details with an efficiency worthy of the best traditions of the profession.

The thing seemed to sink into Lou's mind like a person seeing his way through a chess problem. Her face was absolutely white with cold and concentrated rage.

"He must have watched us in Paris," she said. "He must have known that we had spent the money we were going to put into his swindle, and made up his mind that his best course was to get the jewellery and the rest of the cash."

She sat down suddenly, collapsed; and began to cry. It developed into violent hysterics, which became so alarming that the manager sent for the nearest doctor.

A knot of servants and one or two guests had gathered in the atrium of the hotel. The outside porter had become the man of the moment.

"Why, certainly," he announced triumphantly in broken English. "Mr. Laroche, he went off this morning on the seven o'clock boat. I tink you never catch him."

The events of the last few hours had got me down to my second wind, so to speak. I turned to the consul's clerk; and I spoke. But my voice seemed to come not so much from me as from the animal inside me; the original Pendragon, if you know what I mean; the creature with blind instincts and an automatic apparatus of thought.

"You see how it is," I heard myself saying, "no passports, no cash, no clothes—nothing!"

I was speaking of myself in the third person. The whole process of human life and action had stopped automatically as far as the hotel was concerned. The knot of babbling gossipers was like a swarm of mosquitoes.

The consul's clerk had taken in the situation clearly enough; but I could see that the detectives had become highly suspicious. They were itching to arrest me on the spot.

The clerk argued with them garrulously for an interminable time. The manager seemed the most uncomfortable man in Capri. He protested silently to heaven—there being nobody on earth to listen to him.

The situation was set going again by the reappearance of Lou on the arm of a chambermaid, followed by the doctor, who wore the air of a man who has once more met the King of Terrors in open combat, and knocked the stuffing out of him.

Lou was exceedingly shaky, paling and flushing by turns. I hated her. It was she who had got me into all this mess.

"Well," said the clerk, "we must simply go back to the consulate and explain what has happened. Don't be distressed, Lady Pendragon," he said. "There can be no doubt at all that this man will be caught in a very few hours, and you'll have all your things back."

Of course I had sense enough to know that he didn't believe a word of what he was saying. The proverb, "Set a thief to catch a thief," doesn't apply to Italy. If a thief were worth stealing, that would be another story.

There was no boat back to Naples that night. There was nothing to do but to wait till the morning. The manager was extremely sympathetic. He got us some clothes, if not exactly what we were accustomed to, at least better than the horrible things we were wearing. He ordered a special dinner with lots of champagne, and served it in the best suite but one in the house.

His instinctive Italian tact told him not to put us in the rooms we had had before.

He looked in from time to time with a cheery word to see how we were, and to assure us that telegraphic arrangements had been made to catch Mr. Laroche Feccles.

We managed to get pretty drunk in the course of the evening; but there was no exhilaration. The shock had been too great, the disillusion

ALEISTER CROWLEY

too disgusting. Above all, there was the complete absence of what had, after all, been the mainspring of our lives; our love for each other.

That was gone, as if it had been packed in our luggage. The only approach to sympathetic communion between us was when Lou, practical to the last, brought out our pitifully small supply of heroin and cocaine.

"That's all we've got," she whispered in anguish of soul, "till God knows when."

We were frightfully afraid, into the bargain, of its being taken from us. We were gnawed by fierce anxiety as to the issue of our affair with the police. We were even doubtful whether the consul wouldn't turn against us and scout our story as a string of obvious falsehoods.

The morning was chill. We were shaking with the reaction. Our sleep had been heavy, yet broken, and haunted by abominable dreams.

We could not even stay on deck. It was too cold, and the sea was choppy. We went down in the cabin, and shivered, and were sea-sick.

When we reached the consulate we were physical wrecks. One bit of luck, however, was waiting for us. Our luggage had been found in a hotel at Sorrento. Everything saleable had, of course, been removed by the ingenious Mr. Feccles, including our supply of dope.

But at least we had our passports, and some clothes to wear; and the finding of the luggage in itself, of course, confirmed our story.

The consul was extremely kind, and returned with us himself to the commissario, who dismissed us genially enough, obviously confirmed in his conviction that all English people were mad, and that we in particular ought to travel, if travel we must, in a bassinette.

It took three days to telegraph money from England. It was utterly humiliating to walk about Naples. We felt that we were being pointed at as the comic relief in a very low-class type of film.

We borrowed enough money to get on with, and, of course, we had only one use for it. We stayed in our room in a little hotel unfrequented by English, and crawled out by night to try to buy drugs.

That in itself is a sordid epic of adventure and misadventure. The lowest class of so-called guide was our constant companion. Weary in spirit, we dragged ourselves from one dirty doubtful street to another; held long whispered conferences with the scavenger type of humanity, and as often as not bought various harmless powders at an exorbitant price, and that at the risk of blackmail and other things possibly worse.

But the need of the stuff drove us relentlessly on. We ultimately found an honest dealer, and got a small supply of the genuine stuff. But even then we didn't seem to pick up. Even large doses did hardly more than restore us to our normal, by which I mean, our pre-drug selves. We were like Europe after the war.

The worst and the best we could do was to become utterly disgusted with ourselves, each other, Naples, and life in general.

The spirit of adventure was dead—as dead as the spirit of love. We had just enough moral courage after a very good lunch at Gambrinus, to make up our minds to get out of the entire beastly atmosphere.

Our love had become a mutual clinging, like that of two drowning people. We shook hands on the definite oath to get back to England, and get back as quick as we could.

I believe I might have fallen down even on that. But once again Lou pulled me through. We got into a veittura and took our tickets then and there.

We were going back to London with our tails between our legs, but we were going back to London!

BOOK II
INFERNO

I

Short Commons

August 17

We are at the Savoy. Cockie has gone to see his lawyer. He is looking awfully bad, poor boy. He feels the disgrace of having been taken in by that Feccles. But how was he to know?

It was all really my fault. I ought to have had an instinct about it.

I feel rotten myself. London is frightfully hot; much hotter than it was in Italy. I want to go and live at Barley Grange. No, I don't; what I want is to get back to where we were. There's frightfully little H. left. There's plenty of C.; only one wants so much.

I wonder if this is the right stuff. The effect isn't what it used to be. At first everything went so fast. It doesn't anymore.

It makes one's mind very full; drags out the details; but it doesn't make one think and talk and act with that glorious sense of speed. I think the truth is that we've got tired out.

Suppose I suggest to Cockie that we knock off for a week and get our physical strength back and start fresh.

I may as well telephone Gretel and arrange for a really big supply. If we're going to live at Barley Grange, we'll have to be cocaine hogs and lay in a big stock. There wouldn't be any chance of getting it down there; and besides one must take precautions. . .

Bother August! Of course Gretel's out of town—in Switzerland, the butler said. They don't know when she'll be back. I wonder when Parliament meets. . .

Cockie came back for lunch with a very long face. Mr. Wolfe gave him a good talking-to about money. Well, that's perfectly right. We had been going the pace.

Cockie wanted to take me out and buy me some jewellery to replace what was stolen; but I wouldn't let him, except a new watch and a wedding ring.

I've got a horrid feeling about that. It's frightfully unlucky to lose your wedding ring. I feel as if the new one didn't belong to me at all.

We had a long talk about Gretel being away. We tried one or two places, but they wouldn't give us any. I wish Cockie had taken out his diploma.

The papers are disgusting. It's the silly season, right enough. Everytime one picks one up, there's something about cocaine. That old fool Platt is on the war-path. He wants to "arouse public opinion to a sense of the appalling danger which threatens the manhood and womanhood of England."

One paper had a long speech of his reported in full. He says it's the plot of the Germans to get even with us.

Of course, I'm only a woman and all that; but it sounds to me rather funny.

We went to tea with Mabel Black. Everyone was talking about drugs. Everyone seemed to want them; yet Lord Landsend had just come back from Germany and he said you could buy it quite easily there, but nobody seemed to want to.

Then is the whole German people in a silent conspiracy to destroy us? I never took much stock in all those stories about the infernal cunning of the Hun.

We heard a lot about the underground traffic, though, and I think we ought to be able to get it pretty easily. . .

I don't know what's the matter with us both. It made us a bit better to meet the old crowd, and we thought we'd celebrate.

It didn't come off.

We had a wonderful dinner; and then a horrible thing happened, the most horrible thing in my life. Cockie wanted to go to a show! You might have hit me on the head with a poker. I don't attract him anymore; and I love him so much!

He went to the box office to see about tickets, and while he was gone—this was the really horrible thing—I found I was simply telling myself "I love him so much."

Love is dead. And yet that's not true. I do love him with all my heart and soul; and yet, somehow, I can't. I want to be able to love until I get back. Oh, what's the good of talking about it!

I know I love him, and yet I know I can't love anyone.

I took a whole lot of cocaine. It dulled what I felt. I was able to fancy I loved him.

We went to the show. It was awfully stupid. I was thinking all the time how I wanted to love, and how I wanted dope, and how I wanted to stop dope so that the dope might do me some good.

I couldn't really feel. It was a dull, blind sense of discomfort. I was awfully nervous, too. I felt as if I were somehow caught in a trap; as if

I had got into the wrong house by mistake and couldn't get out again. I didn't know what might be behind all those doors; and I was quite alone. Cockie was there; but he couldn't do a thing to help me. I couldn't call to him. The link between us was broken.

And yet apart from all the fear I had for myself, there was an even deeper fear on his account. There is something in me that loves him, something deeper than life; but it won't talk to me.

I sat through the show like being in a nightmare. I was clinging desperately to him; and he didn't seem to understand me and my need. We were strangers.

I think he was feeling rather good. He talked in a charming, light, familiar way; but every smile was an insult, every caress was a stab.

We got back to the Savoy, utterly worn out and wretched. We kept on taking H. and C. all night; we couldn't sleep, we talked about the drugs. It was just a long argument about how to take them. We felt we were somehow doing it wrong.

I had been so proud of his medical knowledge, and yet it didn't seem to throw any light.

It seems that in the medical books, they speak of what they call "Drug virginity." The thing was to get it back; and according to the books the only way to do it is to take nothing for a long time.

He said it was really just the same as any other appetite. If you have a big lunch you can't expect to be hungry at tea-time.

But then, what is one to do in the meanwhile?

August 18

We lay in bed very late. I didn't seem to miss my sleep; but I was too weak to get out of bed.

We had to buck ourselves up in the usual way, and manage to get downstairs for lunch.

London is quite empty and terribly dull. We met Mabel Black by accident walking in Bond Street. She is looking frightfully ill. I can see she dopes too hard. Of course, the trouble with her is she hasn't got a man. She has a lot of men round her. She could marry any day she liked.

We talked about it a bit. She hasn't got the energy, she said, and the idea of men disgusts her.

She wears the most wonderful boots. She has a new pair almost everyday, and hardly ever puts the same pair on twice. I think she's a little bit crazy. . .

London seems different somehow. I used to be interested in every funny little detail. I want to get back to myself. Drugs help me to get almost there; but there is always one little corner to turn and they never take one round. . .

We got back from Bond Street bored and stupefied. We went off unexpectedly to sleep; and when we woke it was this morning. I can't understand why a long sleep like that doesn't refresh one. We're both absolutely fagged.

Cockie said a meal would put us right, and he rang down for breakfast in bed. But when it came, we couldn't either of us eat it.

I remember what Haidée said about the spiritual life. We were being prepared to take our places in the new order of Humanity. It's perfectly right that one should have to undergo a certain amount of discomfort. You couldn't expect anything else. It's nature's way. . .

We picked ourselves up with five or six goes of heroin. It's no use taking cocaine unless you're feeling pretty good already. . .

The supply is really awfully small. Confound this silly holiday habit. It really isn't fair of Gretel to let us down like this.

We went to the Café Wisteria. Somebody introduced us to somebody that said he could get all he wanted.

But now there was a new nuisance. The police find it troublesome and dangerous to attend to the crime wave. Besides they're too busy enforcing regulations. England's altogether different since the war. You never know where you are. Nobody takes any interest in politics in the way they used to, and nobody bothers anymore about the big ideas.

I was taught about Magna Charta and the liberty of the individual, and freedom slowly broadening down from precedent to precedent, and so on and so forth.

All sorts of stupid interference with the rights of the citizen gets passed under our noses without our knowing what it is. For all I know, it may be a crime to wear a green hat with a pink dress.

Well, it would be a crime; but I don't think it's the business of the police.

I read in a paper the other day that a committee of people in Philadelphia had decided that a skirt must be not less than seven and a half inches from the ground—or not more. I don't know which and

I don't know why. Anyhow, the net result is that the price of cocaine has gone up from a pound an ounce to anything you like to pay. So of course everybody wants it whether they want it or not, and anybody but a member of parliament would know that if you offer a man twenty or thirty times what a thing is worth in itself, he'll go to a lot of trouble to make you want to buy it. . .

Well, we found this man was a fraud. He tried to sell us packets of snow in the dark. He tried to prevent Cockie examining the stuff by pretending to be afraid of the police.

But as it happened, Cockie's long suit was chemistry. He was the wrong man to try to sell powdered borax to at a guinea a sniff. He told the man he'd rather have Beecham's Pills.

What I love about Cockie is the witty way he talks. But somehow or other, the flashes don't come like they did—not so often, I mean. Besides which, he seems to be making his jokes to himself.

Most of the time, I don't get what he means. He talks to himself a great deal, for another thing. I get a feeling of absolute repulsion.

I don't know why it is. The least thing irritates me absurdly. I think it's because every incident, even the things that are pleasant, distracts my mind from the one thing that matters—how to get a supply and go down to Kent and lay off for a bit and have a really good time like we used to last month. I am sure love would come back if we did, and love's the only thing that counts in this world or the next.

I feel that it's only round the corner; but a miss is as good as a mile. It makes it somehow worse to be so near and yet so far. . .

A very funny thing has just struck me. There's something in one's mind that prevents one from thinking of the thing one wants to.

It was perfectly silly of us to be hunting round London for dope and getting mixed up with a rotten crowd like we did in Naples. It never struck us till tonight that all we had to do was to go round to King Lamus. He would give us all we needed at the proper price.

Funny, too, it was Cockie that thought of that. I know he hates the man, though he never said so except in an outburst which I knew didn't mean anything. . .

We went to the studio in a taxi. Curse the luck, he was out! There was a girl there, a tall, thin woman with a white face like a wedge. We gave several hints; but she didn't rise, and wretched as we were, we didn't want to spoil the market by telling her outright.

Lamus would be there in the morning, she said.

We said we'd be there at eleven o'clock.

We drove back. We had a rotten night economising. We didn't dare tell each other what we really feared: that somehow he might let us down. . .

I can't sleep. Cockie is lying awake with his eyes wide open, staring at the ceiling. He doesn't stir a muscle. It maddens me that he takes no interest in me. But after all, I take no interest in him. I am as restless as the wandering Jew. At the same time, I can't settle down to anything. I keep on scribbling this stuff in my diary. It relieves me somehow to write what I feel.

What is so utterly damnable is that I understand what I am doing. This complaining rambling rubbish is the substitute which has taken the place of love.

What have I done to forfeit love? I feel as if I had died and got forgotten in some beastly place where there was nothing but hunger and thirst. Nothing means anything anymore except dope, and dope itself doesn't really mean anything vital.

August 20

I am so tired, so tired, so tired! . . .

My premonition was right about Lamus. There was a very unpleasant scene. We were both frightfully wretched when we got there. (I can't get my hands and feet warm, and there's something wrong with my writing).

Peter Pan thought it best to remind him in a jocular way about his remark that we were to come when we needed him, and then introduced the subject of what we needed.

But he took the words brutally out of our mouths.

"You needn't tell me what you need," he said. "The lack is only too obvious."

He said it in a non-committal way so that we couldn't take offence; but we knew instinctively he meant brains.

However, Peter stuck to his guns, like the game little devil he is. That's why I love him.

"Oh, yes, heroin," said Lamus; "cocaine. We regret exceedingly to be out of it for the moment."

The brute seemed unconscious of our distress. He gave an imitation of an apologetic shop-walker.

"But let me show you our latest lines on morphine."

Cockie and I looked at each other wanly. Morphine would no doubt be better than nothing. And then, if you please, the beast pulled a review with a blue cover out of a revolving bookcase and read aloud a long poem. His intonation was so dramatic, he gave so vivid a picture that we sat spell-bound. It seemed as if he had long pincers twisted in our entrails, and were wrenching at them. He gave me the verses when he had finished.

"You ought to paste these," he said, "in your Magical Diary."

So I have. I hardly know why. There's a sort of pleasure in torturing oneself. Is that it?

Thirst!
Not the thirst of the throat
Though that be the wildest and worst
Of physical pangs—that smote
Alone to the heart of Christ,
Wringing the one wild cry
"I thirst!" from His agony,
While the soldiers drank and diced:
Not the thirst benign
That calls the worker to wine;
Not the bodily thirst
(Though that be frenzy accurst)
When the mouth is full of sand,
And the eyes are gummed up, and the ears
Trick the soul till it hears
Water, water at hand,
When a man will dig his nails
In his breast, and drink the blood
Already that clots and stales
Ere his tongue can tip its flood,
When the sun is a living devil
Vomiting vats of evil,
And the moon and the night but mock
The wretch on his barren rock,
And the dome of heaven high-arched
Like his mouth is arid and parched,
And the caves of his heart high-spanned
Are choked with alkali sand!

Not this! but a thirst uncharted;
Body and soul alike
Traitors turned black-hearted,
Seeking a space to strike
In a victim already attuned
To one vast chord of wound;
Every separate bone
Cold, an incarnate groan
Distilled from the icy sperm
Of Hell's implacable worm;
Every drop of the river
Of blood aflame and a-quiver
With poison secret and sour—
With a sudden twitch at the last
Like certain jagged daggers.
(With bloodshot eyes dull-glassed
The screaming Malay staggers
Through his village aghast).
So blood wrenches its pain
Sardonic through heart and brain.
Every separate nerve
Awake and alert, on a curve
Whose asymptote's name is "never"
In a hyperbolic "forever!"
A bitten and burning snake
Striking its venom within it,
As if it might serve to slake
The pain for the tithe of a minute.

Awake, forever awake!
Awake as one never is
While sleep is a possible end,
Awake in the void, the abyss
Whose thirst is an echo of this
That martyrs, world without end,
(World without end, Amen!)
The man that falters and yields
For the proverb's "month and an hour"
To the lure of the snow-starred fields

Where the opium poppy's aflower.

Only the prick of a needle
Charged from a wizard well!
Is this sufficient to wheedle
A soul from heaven to hell?
Was man's spirit weaned
From fear of its ghosts and gods
To fawn at the feet of a fiend?
Is it such terrible odds—
The heir of ages of wonder,
The crown of earth for an hour,
The master of tide and thunder
Against the juice of a flower?
Ay! in the roar and the rattle
Of all the armies of sin,
This is the only battle
He never was known to win.

Slave to the thirst—not thirst
As here it is weakly written,
Not thirst in the brain black-bitten,
In the soul more sorely smitten!
One dare not think of the worst!
Beyond the raging and raving
Hell of the physical craving
Lies, in the brain benumbed,
At the end of time and space,
An abyss, unmeasured, unplumbed—
The haunt of a face!

She it is, she, that found me
In the morphia honeymoon;
With silk and steel she bound me,
In her poisonous milk she drowned me,
Even now her arms surround me,
Stifling me into the swoon
That still—but oh, how rarely!—
Comes at the thrust of the needle,

Steadily stares and squarely,
Nor needs to fondle and wheedle
Her slave agasp for a kiss,
Hers whose horror is his
That knows that viper womb,
Speckled and barred with black
On its rusty amber scales,
Is his tomb—
The straining, groaning, rack
On which he wails—he wails!
Her cranial dome is vaulted,
Her mad Mongolian eyes
Aslant with the ecstasies
Of things immune, exalted
Far beyond stars and skies,
Slits of amber and jet—
Her snout for the quarry set
Fleshy and heavy and gross,
Bestial, broken across,
And below it her mouth that drips
Blood from the lips
That hide the fangs of a snake,
Drips on venomous udders
Mountainous flanks that fret,
And the spirit sickens and shudders
At the hint of a worse thing yet.

Olya! *the golden bait*
Barbed with infinite pain,
Fatal, fanatical mate
Of a poisoned body and brain!
Olya, *the name that leers*
Its lecherous longing and knavery,
Whispers in crazing ears
The secret spell of her slavery.

Horror indeed intense,
Seduction ever intenser,
Swinging the smoke of sense

From the bowl of a smouldering censer!
Behind me, behind and above,
She stands, that mirror of love.
Her fingers are supple-jointed;
Her nails are polished and pointed,
And tipped with spurs of gold:
With them she rowels the brain.
Her lust is critical, cold;
And her Chinese cheeks are pale,
As she daintily picks, profane
With her octopus lips, and the teeth
Jagged and black beneath,
Pulp and blood from a nail.

One swift prick was enough
In days gone by to invoke her:
She was incarnate love
In the hours when I first awoke her.
Little by little I found
The truth of her, stripped of clothing,
Bitter beyond all bound,
Leprous beyond all loathing.
Black, the plague of the pit,
Her pustules visibly fester,
Cancerous kisses that bit
As the asp caressed her.

Dragon of lure and dread,
Tiger of fury and lust,
The quick in chains to the dead,
The slime alive in the dust,
Brazen shame like a flame,
An orgy of pregnant pollution
With hate beyond aim or name—
Orgasm, death, dissolution!
Know you now why her eyes
So fearfully glaze, beholding
Terrors and infamies
Like filthy flowers unfolding?

Laughter widowed of ease,
Agony barred from sadness,
Death defeated of peace,
Is she not madness?

She waits for me, lazily leering,
As moon goes murdering moon;
The moon of her triumph is nearing;
She will have me wholly soon.
And you, you puritan others,
Who have missed the morphia craving,
Cry scorn if I call you brothers,
Curl lip at my maniac raving,
Fools, seven times beguiled,
You have not known her? Well!
There was never a need she smiled
To harry you into hell!

Morphia is but one
Spark of its secular fire.
She is the single sun—
Type of all desire!
All that you would, you are—
And that is the crown of a craving.
You are slaves of the wormwood star.
Analysed, reason is raving.
Feeling, examined, is pain.
What heaven were to hope for a doubt of it!
Life is anguish, insane;
And death is—not a way out of it!

"Olya," too, reminds me of myself. I have a morbid wish to be an impossible monster of cruelty and wickedness.

Lamus had told me that long ago. He said it was the phantasm which summed up my longing to "revert to type." *La nostalgie de la boue.*

Cockie lost all his dignity. He pleaded for just one sniff. We weren't really very bad, but the description of the thirst in that horrible poem had made us feel thirsty.

"My dear man," said Lamus very brutally. "I'm not a dope peddler. You've come to the wrong shop."

Cockie's head was drooping, and his eyes were glassy. But the need of dope drove him desperately to try every dodge.

"Hang it all," he said with a little flash of spirit. "You encouraged us to go on."

"Certainly," admitted Lamus, "and now, I'm encouraging you to stop."

"I thought you believed in do what you like; you're always saying it."

"I beg your pardon," came the sharp retort. "I never said anything of the kind. I said, 'Do what thou wilt,' and I say it again. But that's a horse of quite a different colour."

"But we need the stuff," pleaded Peter. "We've got to have it. Why did you induce us to take it?"

"Why," he laughed subtly, "it's my will to want you to do your will."

"Yes, and I want the stuff."

"Acute psychologist as you are, Sir Peter, you have failed to grasp my meaning. I fear I express myself badly."

Cockie was boiling inwardly, yet he was so weak and faint that he was like a lamb. I myself would have killed Lamus if I had had the means. I felt that he was deliberately torturing us for his own enjoyment.

"Oh, I see," said Cockie, "I forgot what you were. What's your figure?"

The point blank insult did not even make him smile. He turned to the tall girl who was at the desk, correcting proofs.

"Note the characteristic reaction," he said to her, as if we had been a couple of rabbits that he was vivisecting. "They don't understand my point of view. They misquote my words, after hearing them everytime we have met. They misinterpret four words of one syllable, 'Do what thou wilt.' Finally realising their lack of comprehension, they assume at once that I must be one of the filthiest scoundrels unhanged."

He turned back to Cockie with a little bow of apology.

"Do try to get some idea of what I'm saying," he said very earnestly.

I was bursting with hatred, brimming with suspicion, aghast with contempt. Yet he forced me to feel his sincerity. I crushed down the realisation with furious anger.

"I encourage you to take drugs," he went on, "exactly as I encourage you to fly. Drugs claim to be every man's master.

> *'Is it such terrible odds—*
> *The heir of ages of wonder,*
> *The crown of earth for an hour,*
> *The master of tide and thunder*
> *Against the juice of a flower?*
> *Ay! in the roar and the rattle*
> *Of all the armies of sin,*
> *This is the only battle*
> *He never was known to win.'*

You children are the flower of the new generation. You have got to fear nothing. You have got to conquer everything. You have got to learn to make use of drugs as your ancestors learnt to make use of lightning. You have got to stop at the word of command, and go on at the word of command according to circumstances."

He paused. The dire need of the drug kept Peter alert. He followed the argument with intense activity.

"Quite," he agreed, "and just at the moment, the word of command is 'go on.'"

The face of King Lamus flowered into a smile of intense amusement; and the girl at the desk shook her thin body as if she were being deliciously tickled.

Intuition told me why. They had heard the argument before.

"Very cleverly put, Sir Peter. It would look well in a broad frame, very plain, of dark mahogany, over the mantelpiece, perhaps."

For some reason or other, the conversation was pulling us together. Though we had had no dope, we both felt very much better. Cockie fired his big gun.

"It's the essence of your teaching, surely, Mr. Lamus, that every man should be absolute master of his own destiny."

"Well, well," admitted the Teacher with an exaggerated sigh, "I expected to be beaten in argument. I always am. But I, too, am the master of mine. 'If Power asks Why, then is Power weakness,' as we read in the Book of the Law; and it's not my destiny to give you any drugs this morning."

"But you're interfering with my Will," protested Cockie, almost vivaciously.

"It would take too long to explain," returned Lamus, "why I think that remark unfair. But to quote the Book of the Law once more,

'Enough of Because, be he damned for a dog.' Instead, let me tell you a story."

We tactfully expressed eagerness to hear it.

"The greatest mountaineer of his generation, as you know, was the late Oscar Eckenstein."

He went through a rather complicated gesture quite incomprehensible; but it vaguely suggested to me some ceremonial reverence connected with death.

"I had the great good fortune to be adopted by this man; he taught me how to climb; in particular, how to glissade. He made me start down the slope from all kinds of complicated positions; head first and so on; and I had to let myself slide without attempting to save myself until he gave the word, and then I had to recover myself and finish, either sitting or standing, as he chose, to swerve or to stop; while he counted five. And he gave me progressively dangerous exercises. Of course, this sounds all rather obvious, but as a matter of fact, he was the only man who had learnt and who taught to glissade in this thorough way.

"The acquired power, however, stood me in very good stead on many occasions. To save an hour may sometimes mean to save one's life, and we could plunge down dangerous slopes where (for example) one might find oneself on a patch of ice when going at high speed if one were not certain of being able to stop in an instant when the peril were perceived. We could descend perhaps three thousand feet in ten minutes where people without that training would have had to go down step by step on the rope, and perhaps found themselves benighted in a hurricane in consequence.

"But the best of it was this: I was in command of a Himalayan expedition some years ago; and the coolies were afraid to traverse a snow slope which overhung a terrific cliff. I called on them to watch me, flung myself on the snow head first, swept down like a sack of oats, and sprang to my feet on the very edge of the precipice.

"There was a great gasp of awed amazement while I walked up to the men. They followed me across the *mauvis pas* without a moment's hesitation. They probably thought it was magic or something. No matter what. But at least they felt sure that they could come to no harm by following a man so obviously under the protection of the mountain gods."

Cockie had gone deathly white. He understood with absolute clarity the point of the anecdote. He felt his manhood shamed that he was in the power of this blind black craving. He didn't really believe that Lamus was telling the truth. He thought the man had risked his life to get those coolies across. It seemed impossible that a man could possess such absolute power and confidence. In other words, he judged King Lamus by himself. He knew himself not to be a first-rate airman. He had flattered himself that he had dared so many dangers. It cut him like a whip that Lamus should despise what people call the heroic attitude; that he looked upon taking unnecessary risks as mere animal folly. To be ready to take them, yes. "I do not set my life at a pin's fee."

Lamus had no admiration for the cornered rat. His ideal was to make himself completely master of every possible circumstance.

Cockie tried to say something two or three times; but the words wouldn't come. King Lamus went to him and took his hand.

"Drugs are the slope in front of us," he said, "and I'm wily old Eckenstein, and you're ambitious young Lamus. And I say 'stop!' and when you show me that you can stop, when you have picked yourself together and are standing on the slope laughing, I'll show you how to go on."

We knew at the back of our minds that the man was inexorable. We hated him as the weak always hate the strong, and we had to respect and admire him, detesting him all the more for the fact.

II

Indian Summer

We went out gritting our teeth with mingled rage and dejection. We walked on aimlessly in silence. A taxi offered itself. We climbed into it listlessly and drove back here. We threw ourselves on our beds. The idea of lunch was disgusting. We were too weak and too annoyed to do anything. We could not trust ourselves to speak; we should have quarrelled. I fell into a state of sleepless agony. Our visit to the studio had burnt itself into my mind. I imagined the flesh of my soul sizzling beneath the white hot branding iron of Lamus's Will.

I reached out my hands for this diary. It has relieved me to write it down in all this detail.

I found myself on fire with passionate determination to fight H. and C. to a finish; and my hands were tied behind my back, my feet were fettered by a chain and ball. I wouldn't be made to stop by that beast. We'd get it despite him. We wouldn't be treated like children; we'd get as much as we wanted and we'd take it all the time, if it killed us.

The conflict in myself raged all the afternoon. Cockie had gone to sleep. He snored and groaned. He was like one's idea of a convict. He hadn't shaved for two days. My own nails were black. I felt sticky and clammy all over. I hadn't dressed myself. I had thrown my clothes on carelessly.

Cockie woke about dinner-time. We couldn't go down as we were. We were suddenly stung by the realisation that we were making ourselves conspicuous in the hotel. We had a horrible fear of being found out. They might do something. It was all the worse that we didn't quite know what. And we felt so helpless, almost too weak to move a finger.

Oh, couldn't we find some anywhere! . . .

My God! what a bit of luck. What a fool I am. There was one packet of H. in the pocket of my travelling dress. We crawled towards each other and shared it. After the long abstention, the effect was miraculous.

Cockie picked himself up almost fiercely. The desperate anguish of our necessity drove him to swift resolute action. He sent for the barber and the waiter. We had the maid pack our things. We paid the bill and left our heavy trunks in the hotel, explaining that we had been called away suddenly on business. We put our dressing cases into a taxi and said, "Euston, main line."

Cockie stopped the man at Cambridge Circus.

"Look here," he said in an eager whisper, "we want some rooms in Soho. Some French or Italian place."

The man was equal to the problem. He found us a dirty dark little room on the ground floor in Greek Street. The landlady was some kind of Southerner with a dash of black blood. Her face told us that she was exactly the kind of woman we wanted.

We paid the taxi. Cockie was very restless. He wanted to get the man to do what we wanted. He was itching all over, but he was afraid. We sat down on the bed, and began to make plans.

August 21

I don't remember anything. I must have gone off suddenly to sleep as I was. Cockie is out. . .

He has been going round town all night; the clubs and that. He got two sniffs from Mabel Black; but she was shy herself. He and Dick Wickham went down to Limehouse. No luck! They nearly got into a row with some sailors. . .

Madame Bellini has brought breakfast. Horrible, beastly food. We must eat some; I'm so weak. . .

She came in to clear it away and do the room. I got her talking about her life. She has been in England nearly thirty years. I worked round to the interesting subject. She doesn't know much about it. She thinks she can help. One of the women lodgers injects. She asked could we pay. It's really rather comic. Eight thousand a year and one of the most beautiful houses near London. And here we are in this filthy hole being asked "can we pay!" by a hag that never saw a sovereign in her life unless she stole it from some drunken client.

Cockie seems to have lost his sense. He flashed a fifty-pound note in her face. It was because he was angry at her attitude. She rather shut up. Either she thinks we're police spies or she's made up her mind to rob us.

The sight of the cash knocked her out of time! It destroyed her sense of proportion. It put all her ideas of straight dealing out of her mind. Her manner changed. She went off.

Pete told me to go and see the dope girl myself. It's the first time he ever spoke to me like that. All sexual feeling is dead between us. We've tried to work up the old passion. It was artificial, horrible, repulsive; a degradation and a blasphemy. Why is it? The snow intensified love beyond every possibility. Yet I love him more than ever. He's my boy. I think he must be ill. I wish I weren't so tired. I'm not looking after him properly, and I can't think about anything except getting H. I don't seem to mind so much about C. I never liked C. much. It made me dizzy and ill.

We have no amusements now. We get through the day in a dark, dreary dream. I can't fix my mind on anything. The more I want H. the less I am able to think and act as I should to get anything else I wanted.

Cockie went out slamming the door. It swung open again.

I couldn't go to the woman like this. I've written this to try to keep from crying.

But I am crying, only the tears won't come.

I'm snivelling like a woman I once saw when I visited the hospital.

I haven't got a handkerchief.

I can't bring myself to wash in that dirty cracked basin. We've brought no soap. The towel's soiled and torn. I must have some H. . .

I've just been to see Lillie Fitzroy. How can men give her money? Her hair is gray, crudely dyed. She has wrinkles and rotten teeth. She was in bed, of course. I shook her roughly to wake her. I've lost every feeling for others, and people see it, and it spoils my own game. I must pretend to have the kindness and gentleness which I used to have so much; which used to make people think me an amiable fool.

Someone told me once that adjectives spoilt nouns in literature, and you can certainly cut out that one.

She's a good sort, all the same, poor flabby old thing. She only takes M., and only gets that in solution ready to inject. She saw I was all in, and gave me a dose in the thigh. It doesn't touch the spot like H., but it stops the worst of the suffering. She never gets up till tea-time. I left her a fiver. She promised to see what she could do that night with the man who gets it for her.

She got very affectionate in a sentimental, motherly style, told me the story of her life, and so on, forever it seemed. Of course, I had to pretend to be interested to keep her in good humour. Everything might depend on that.

But it was awful to have to let her kiss me when I went away. I wonder if I should get like that if I went on with dope.

What absolute nonsense! For all I know, it may have prevented her going faster still. She must have had a beastly rotten life. The way she clawed at that five quid was the clue to her troubles; that and her ignorance of everything but the nastiest kind of vice and the meanest kind of crime.

The morphine has certainly done me a world of good. I am quite myself. I feel it by the way I am writing this entry. I have a quiet impersonal point of view. I have got back my sense of proportion. I can think of things consecutively and I feel physically much stronger, but I've got very sleepy again. . .

Joy! Cockie has just come in full of good news. He looks fine—as fine as he feels. He had a sample from a pedlar he met in the Wisteria. It's absolutely straight stuff. Pulled him round in a second. There are two of them in it; the man with the dope and the sentry. They talk business in the lavatory, and if another man comes in, the pedlar disappears. In case of real danger, he gets rid of his sample in a flash beyond any possibility of being traced. The loss is trifling; they can buy the stuff at a few shillings an ounce and sell it for I don't know how many times its weight in gold.

We shall have a great night tonight!

August 22

A hellish night!

Cockie kept his date with the pedlar, got ten pounds' worth of H. and fifteen of C., and the H. was nothing at all and the C., so adulterated that we took the whole lot and it was hardly worth talking about.

What filthy mean beasts people are! . . .

How can men take advantage of the bitter needs of others? It was the same in the war with the profiteers. It's always been the same.

I am writing this in a Turkish bath. I couldn't stand that loathsome house anymore. It has done me lots of good. The massage has calmed my nerves. I slept for a long while, and a cup of tea has revived me.

I tried to read a paper, but every line opens the wound. They seem to have gone mad about dope. . .

I suppose it's really quite natural. I remember my father telling me once that the inequality of wealth and all the trickery of commerce arose from artificial restriction.

Last night's swindle was made possible by the great philanthropist Jabez Platt. His Diabolical Dope Act has created the traffic which he was trying to suppress. It didn't exist before except in his rotten imagination. . .

I get such sudden spells of utter weariness. Dope would put me right. Nothing else has any effect. Everything that happens makes me want a sniff; and every sniff makes something happen. One can't get away from the cage, but the complexity makes me. . . there, I can't think what I started to say. My mind stops suddenly. It's like dropping a vanity bag. You stop to pick it up and the things are all over the place and it always seems as if something were missing. One can never remember what it is, but the feeling of annoyance is acute. It's mixed up with a vague fear. I've often forgotten things before—everyone does all the time, but it doesn't bother one.

But now, everytime that I remember that I've forgotten something, I wonder whether it's H. or C. or mixing the two that is messing up my mind. . .

My mind keeps on running back to that American nigger we met in Naples. He said snow made people "flighty and sceptical." It was such a queer expression. By sceptical he meant suspicious, I think. Anyhow, I've got that way. Flighty—I can't keep my mind on things like I could, except, of course, the one thing. And even that is confused. It's not a clear thought. It's an ache and a fear and a pain—and a sinister rapture. And I am suspicious of everybody I see.

I wonder if they think I'm taking it, and if they can do something horrid. I'm always on the look-out for people to play me some dirty trick, but that isn't a delusion at all. I've seen more meanness and treachery since the night I met Cockie than I knew in the rest of my life.

We seem to have got into a bad set somehow. And yet, my oldest friends—I can't trust them like I did. They're all alike. I wonder if that's a delusion? How can I tell? They do act funnily. I'm unsettled. How can one be sure of anything? One can't. The more one thinks of it, the more one sees it must be so.

Look how Feccles let us down. For all I know, there may be some motive at the back of even a really nice woman like Gretel—or Mabel Black. I'm really suspicious of myself. I think that's it.

I must go home. I hope to God Cockie's found some somewhere! . . .

I met Mabel Black coming out of the Burlington Arcade. She looked fine, all over smiles, a very short, white skirt and a new pair of patent leather boots almost up to her knees. She must find them frightfully hot. She rushed me into a tea place, awfully smart with rose-shaded lights reflected up to a blue ceiling; the combination made a most marvellous purple.

We got an alcove shut off by canary-coloured curtains and a set of the loveliest cushions I ever saw. Two big basket chairs and a low table. They have the most delightful tea in egg-shell china and Dolly cigarettes with rose leaves.

Mabel talked a hundred miles a minute. She has struck the biggest kind of oil—a romantic boy of sixty-five. He had bought her a riding crop with a carved ivory handle; the head of a race horse with ruby eyes and a gold collar.

I asked her laughingly if it was to keep him in order. But what she was really keen on was H. She had got a whole bottle and gave me quite a lot in an envelope.

The first go, oh, what joy! And then—how strange we all are! The minute I had it in my bag—in my blood—my mind began to work freely. The irritating stupefaction passed off like waking from a nightmare—a nightmare of suffocation—and it came to me with the force of a blow that the effect was not due to the H. at all, or hardly at all. When we got it again in Naples, it didn't do us much good.

Why was I translated into heaven this afternoon? Why had I found my wings?

The answer came as quick as the question. It's the atmosphere of Mabel and the relief of my worry. With that came a rational fear of the drug. I asked her if she hadn't had any troubles from taking it.

"You can't sleep without it," she said, but not as if it mattered much, "and it rather gets on one's nerves now and then."

She had to rush off to meet her beau for dinner. I went back to our dirty little den, brimming over with joy. I found Cockie sprawling on the bed in the depth of dejection. He did not move when I came in. I ran to him and covered him with kisses. His eyes were heavy and swollen and his nose was running.

I gave him my handkerchief and pulled him up. His clothes were all rumpled and of course he hadn't shaved. I couldn't resist the temptation of teasing my darling. My love had come back in flood. I tingled with the pain of feeling that he did not respond. I hugged the pain to my heart. My blood beat hard with the joy of power. I held him in my hand. One dainty act, and he was mine. I hadn't the strength to enjoy myself to the full. Pity and tenderness brought the tears to my eyes. I shook out a dose of the dull white wizardry.

He sniffed it up with stupid lethargy like a man who has lost hope of life, yet still takes his medicine as a routine. He came up gradually, but was hardly himself till after the third dose.

I took one, too, to keep him company, not because I needed it. I sent him out to get shaved and buy clean linen.

I take a curious delight in writing this diary. I know now why it is and it has rather startled me. It's just that chance phrase of King Lamus: "Your *magical* diary."

I have flirted a lot with Lamus, but it was mostly swank. I dislike the man in many ways.

By Jove, I know why that is, too. It's because I feel that he despises me intellectually, and because I respect him. Despite my dislike, I am eager to show him that I am not such a rotter after all.

One of his fads is to make his pupils keep these magical diaries. I feel that I've gone in for a competition; that I have to produce something more interesting than anything they do, whoever they are.

Here comes Peter Pan. He hasn't grown old after all. . .

We had a gorgeous feed at the dear old café. King Lamus came up to our table but he only said a few words.

"So you got it, I see."

Cockie gave him one back.

"I hate to injure your reputation as a prophet, Mr. Lamus, but it isn't stopping when you have to stop. I've got it, as you say, and now, with your kind permission, I'm going to show you that we can stop."

Lamus changed his manner like a flash. His contemptuous smile became like sunrise in spring.

"That's talking," he said. "I'm glad you've got the idea. Don't think I'm trying to put you off, but if you should find it more difficult than you imagine, don't be too proud to come to me! I really do know some fairly good tips."

I was glad that Peter took it in good part. Being in good form, he realised, I suppose, that it was a serious business. We might strike a snag.

August 23

The night has been a miracle!

We went on taking H. pretty steadily. I think the C. spoils it. Our love bloomed afresh as if it was a new creation. We were lapsed in boundless bliss!

> *"Awake, forever awake!*
> *Awake as one never is*
> *While sleep is a possible end,*
> *Awake in the void, the abyss."*

But not in the unutterable anguish of which the poet was writing. It is a formless calm. But love! We had never loved like this before. We had defiled love with the grossness of the body.

The body is an instrument of infinite pleasure; but excitement and desire sully its sublimity. We were conscious of every nerve to the tiniest filament; and for this one must be ineffably aloof from movement.

H. makes one want to scratch, and scratching is infinite pleasure. But that is only a relic of animal appetite.

After a little while, one is able to enjoy the feeling that makes one want to scratch in itself. It is an impersonal bliss perfectly indescribable and indescribably perfect.

I cannot measure the majesty of my consciousness; but I can indicate the change in the whole character of my consciousness.

I am writing this in the mood of the recording angel. I am living in eternity, and temporal things have become tedious and stupid symbols. My words are veils of my truth. But I experience quite definite delight in this diary.

King Lamus is always at the root of my brain. He is Jupiter and I have sprung from his thought; Minerva, Goddess of Wisdom!

The most tremendous events of life are unworthy trifles. The sublimity of my conceptions sweeps onward from nowhere to nowhere. Behind my articulate anthem is a stainless silence.

I am not writing for any reason, not even for myself to read; the action is automatic.

I am the first-born child of King Lamus without a mother. I am the emanation of his essence.

I lay all night without moving a muscle. The nearness of my husband completed the magnetic field of our intimacy. Act, word, and thought were equally abolished. The elements of my consciousness did not represent me at all. They were sparks struck off from our Selves. Those Selves were one Self which was whole. Any positive expression of it was of necessity partial, incomplete, inadequate. The Stars are imperfection of Night; but at least these thoughts are immeasurably faster and clearer than anything I have thought all my life.

If I were ever to wake up—it seems impossible that I ever should—this entry will probably be quite unintelligible to me. It is not written with the purpose of being intelligible or any other purpose. The idea of having a purpose at all is beneath contempt. It is the sort of thing a human being would have.

How can a supreme being inhabiting eternity have a purpose? The absolute, the all, cannot change; how then could it wish to change? It acts in accordance with its nature; but all such action is without effect. It is essentially illusion; and the deeper one enters into one's self the less one is influenced by such illusions.

As the night went on, I found myself less and less disturbed by my own exquisite emotions. I felt myself dissolving deliciously into absence of interruption to the serenity of my soul. . .

I think writing this has reminded me of what I used to think was reality. It was time to go out and have lunch. The luxurious lethargy seems insuperable. . .

It isn't hunger; it's habit. Some instinct, some obscure and obscene recollection of the lurking brute drives one to get up and go out. The dodge for doing this is to take three or four rather small sniffs in quick succession. C. would be much better, but we haven't got any.

September 1

What ages and ages have passed! These filthy lodgings have been Eden without the snake. Our lives have been Innocence; no toil, no thought. We did not even eat, except the little food the woman brought in.

We scared her, by the way. She can't or won't get us any H. or C. The morphine girl has disappeared.

I'm not sure and it doesn't matter, but I think the landlady—I can never remember the woman's name, she reminds me of those dreadful days in Naples—told us that she stole somethings from a shop and went to jail. It was a great nuisance, because I had to put my clothes on and call on Mabel. Luckily, she was in and had a whole lot of it.

We must have been increasing the dose very fast; but I can't be sure, because we don't keep track of it or of the days either. Counting things is so despicable. One feels so degraded. Surely that's the difference between spirit and matter. It's bestial to be bounded.

Cockie agrees with me about this. He thinks I'm writing rather wonderful things. But as soon as we come down to ordinary affairs, we quarrel all the time. We snap about nothing at all. The reason is evident.

Having to talk destroys the symphony of silence. It's hateful to be interrupted; and it interrupts one to be asked to pass a cigarette.

I wasn't going to be bothered to go out again, so I made Mabel give me all she could spare. She promised to get some more and send it round next Sunday. . .

We're not very well, either of us. It must be this dark, dirty room and the bad atmosphere; and the street noises get on my nerves.

We could go to Barley Grange, but it's too much trouble. Besides, it might break the spell of our happiness. We're both a little afraid about that.

It happened once before, and we don't want to take any chances. It wants a lot of clever steering to keep the course. For instance, we took too much one night and made ourselves sick. It took three or four hours to get back, and that was absolute hell. My heart is a little fretful at times. It's certainly great, Peter Pan having medical knowledge. He went out and got some strychnine and put me right.

Champagne helps H. quite a lot. You mustn't drink it off. The thing to do is to sip it very slowly. It helps one to move one's hands.

We sent out a boy and got in three dozen small bottles.

September 5

The world is a pig. It keeps on putting its nose where it isn't wanted. We are overdrawn at the bank. Cockie had to write to Mr. Wolfe.

"It ought to be stopped," he cried, "it amounts to brawling in church!"

A flash of the old Peter Pan!

September 8

The woman says it's Tuesday, and we're running awfully short. Why can't people keep their promises? I'm sure Mabel said Sunday.

III

The Grinding of the Brakes

September 9

Peter and I have had a long, nasty quarrel, and I had to pull his hair for him. It broke one of my nails. I've let them go very long. I don't know when I was manicured last.

For some reason, they're dry and brittle. I must have them done. I'd send the boy out, but I don't like the idea of a strange girl coming here. One never knows what may go wrong. It doesn't really matter, either. The body is merely a nuisance, and it hurts.

> *"So blood wrenches its pain*
> *Sardonic through heart and brain."*

I am beginning to hate that horrible poem. It haunts me. I don't know why I should remember it like I do.

Have I been reading it, I wonder? Or perhaps it is the incredible access of intellectual power which heroin gives that has improved my memory. Anyhow, the fact is that odd bits of it come swimming into my mind like goldfish darting in and out among streaming seaweed.

Oh, yes, my quarrel with Cockie. He said we mustn't risk being absolutely short of the suit; and I must go and get a new supply from Mabel before we ran clean out. I can't help seeing that Cockie is degenerating morally. He ought to be ashamed of himself. He ought to have made proper arrangements for a regular supply instead of relying on me.

He lies there all the time perfectly useless. He hasn't washed or shaved in a month, and he knows perfectly well that I detest dirt and untidiness. One of the things that attracted me most about him was his being so spruce and well-groomed and alert. He has changed altogether, since we came to London. I feel there is some bad influence at work on him. . .

This place is full of vermin. I found what had been annoying me. I think I shall bob my hair. I'm awfully proud of its length, but one must be practical. . .

I am lying down for a bit. It was a frightful nuisance getting ready to go out. Cockie nagged and bullied all the time.

I'm stiff all over, and it seems such waste of time to wash and dress, besides, the irritation of the interruption, and my clothes are impossible. I've been sleeping in them. I wish we'd brought some trunks from the Savoy. No, I don't, it would have been a lot of trouble, and interfered with our heroin honeymoon.

It's best the way it is. I wish I had Jacqueline here all the same. I need a maid, and she could have gone out and got things. But we both felt that anyone at all would be a pill. The old woman doesn't bother us, thank goodness. I'm sure she still thinks we're spies. Bother, what's this? . . .

Damn! It's a letter from Basil!

(Note. The original of this letter was destroyed. It is now printed from the carbon copy in the files of Mr. King Lamus. Ed.)

DEAR UNLIMITED LOU,

"Do what thou wilt shall be the whole of the Law. You will, I am sure, forgive me for boring you with a letter; but you know what a crank I am, and it is my mania just now to collect information about the psychology of people who are trying to advance spiritually in the way we spoke about when you so charmingly dawned on my studio the other morning.

"Do you find, in particular, that there is any difficulty in calling a halt? If so, is it not perhaps because you hear on all sides—especially from people quite ignorant of the subject, such as journalists, doctors and parrots—that it is in fact impossible to do so? Of course, I don't doubt that you immediately killed any such 'pernicious suggestion' by a counter-suggestion based on my positive statement, from experience, that people of strong character and high intelligence like yourself and Sir Peter—to whom please give my most cordial greetings!—were perfectly well able to use these things in moderation as one does soap.

"But, apart from this, do you find that the life of a 'Heroine' makes you abnormally 'suggestible?'

"As you know, I object to the methods of Coué and Baudouin. They ask us deliberately to abandon free will and clear mentality for the semi-hypnotic state of the mediæval peasant; to return like 'the sow that was washed to her wallowing in the mire' from which we have been extricated by evolution.

"Now, doesn't waltzing with the Hero's Bride or making Snow Men tend to put you into a state of mind which is too dreamy to resist the action of any strenuous idea which is presented to it strongly enough, is too dead to feeling to wish to resist, or so excitable that it is liable to be carried away by its admiration for any fascinatingly forceful personality?

"I should be so glad to have your views on these points; and, of course, your personal confirmation of my theory that people like you and Sir Peter can use these substances with benefit to yourselves and others, without danger of becoming slaves. I have trained myself and many others to stop at Will; but every additional affidavit to this effect is of great value to me in my present campaign to destroy the cowardly superstition that manhood and womanhood are incapable of the right and proper use of anything whatever in nature. We have tamed the wild lightning, after all; shall we run away from a packet of powder?

"Love is the law, love under will.

"With my kind regards to Sir Peter,

Yours ever,
BASIL KING LAMUS

Satirical, sneering stupidity—or is he a devil incarnate, as Gretel told us he was? Does he gloat? I loathe the beast—and I thought—once—well, never mind! Peter took the letter. Anything, anything to distract the mind from its boredom! Yet we haven't the energy to do anything: we take whatever comes to us, and clutch at it feebly. "It's true," said Cockie, to my amazement, "and we've got to be able to tell him we've won." There was a long quarrel—as there is over every incident of any sort. That is natural, with this eternal insomnia and sleeping at the wrong time. I hated Peter (and K.L.) the more because I knew all the time he was right. If K.L. is a Devil, it's up to us to get the last laugh. I tore the beastly letter into shreds. Peter has gone out—I hope he has gone to kill him. I want to be thrilled—just once more—if I had to be hanged for it myself.

Our watches have run down. It doesn't matter. I can call on Mabel anytime I like. I may as well go now. I'll drink a small bottle and go along. . .

It is night. Cockie has not returned. Just when I needed him most! I'm frightened of myself. I'm stark staring sober. I went to the glass to take my hat off. I didn't know who I was. There is no flesh on my face. My complexion's entirely gone. My hair is lustreless and dry, and it's coming out in handfuls. I think I must be ill. I've a good mind to send for a doctor. But I daren't. It has been a frightful shock! . . .

I must pull myself together and write it up.

It was about five o'clock when I got to Mount Street. If Mabel wasn't in, I could wait.

A strange man answered the door. It annoyed me. I felt frightened. Why had she changed Cartwright? I felt faint. Had something told me?

It embarrassed me to ask "Is Mrs. Black at home?" The man answered as if he had been asked the time.

"Mrs. Black is dead."

Something inside me screamed. "But I must see her," I cried insanely, feeling the ground cut suddenly from under my feet.

"I'm afraid it's impossible, madame," he said, misunderstanding me altogether. "She was buried yesterday morning."

So that was why she hadn't sent the stuff! I stood as if I was in a trance. I heard him explaining, mechanically. I did not take in what he was saying. It was like a record being made on a gramophone.

"She was only ill two days," the man said. "The doctors called it septic pneumonia."

I suppose I thanked him, and went away automatically. I found myself at home without knowing how I got here. Something told me that the real cause of her death was heroin, though, as a matter of fact, septic pneumonia can happen to anyone at any moment. I've known two or three people go off like that.

As my Uncle John used to say, conscience makes cowards of us all.

King Lamus was always saying that as long as one has any emotion about anything, love or fear or anything else, one can't observe things correctly. That's why a doctor won't attend his own family, and I can see coldly and clearly like a drowning man that whenever the idea of H. comes into my mind, I begin to think hysterically and come to the most idiotic conclusions; and heroin has twined itself about my life so closely that everything is connected with it one way or another.

ALEISTER CROWLEY

My mind is obsessed by the thought of the drug. Sometimes it's a weird ecstasy, sometimes a dreadful misgiving.

> *"Not thirst in the brain black-bitten*
> *In the soul more sorely smitten!*
> *One dare not think of the worst!*
> *Beyond the raging and raving*
> *Hell of the physical craving,*
> *Lies, in the brain benumbed,*
> *At the end of time and space,*
> *An abyss, unmeasured, unplumbed—*
> *The haunt of a face!"*

September 12

Peter came in just as I had finished writing this account. He seemed much more cheerful, and his arms were full of books.

"There," he said, throwing them on the bed, "that will refresh my memory, in case we have any trouble in stopping. I'll show Mr. King Lamus what it means to be a Pendragon."

I told him about Mabel. And now a strange thing happened. Instead of being depressed, we felt a current of mysterious excitement, rippling at first, then raging and roaring in every nerve. It was as if the idea of her death exhilarated us. He took me in his arms for the first time in— is it weeks or months? His hot breath coiled like a snake about my ear, and thrilled my hair like an electric machine. With a strange ghastly intensity his voice, trembling with passion, strummed the intoxicating words:—

> *"Olya! the golden bait*
> *Barbed with infinite pain,*
> *Fatal, fanatical mate*
> *Of a poisoned body and brain!*
> *Olya, the name that leers*
> *Its lecherous longing and knavery,*
> *Whispers in crazing ears*
> *The secret spell of her slavery."*

The room swam before my eyes. We were wreathed in spirals of dark blue smoke bursting with crimson flashes.

He gripped me with epileptic fury, and swung me round in a sort of savage dance. I had an intuition that he was seeing the same vision as I was. Our souls were dissolved into one; a giant ghost that enveloped us.

I hissed the next lines through my teeth, feeling myself a fire-breathing dragon.

> *"Horror indeed intense,*
> *Seduction ever intenser,*
> *Swinging the smoke of sense*
> *From the bowl of a smouldering censer!"*

We were out of breath. My boy sat on the edge of the bed. I crept up behind him. I shook out my hair all over his face, and dug my nails into his scalp.

We were living the heroin life, the life of the world of the soul. We had identified ourselves with the people of the poem. He was the poet, wreathed with poppies, with poisonous poppies that corrupted his blood, and I was the phantom of his delirium, the hideous vampire that obsessed him.

Little drops of blood oozed from his scalp and clotted to black under my greedy nails. He spoke the next lines as if under some cruel compulsion. The words were wrenched from him by some overwhelming necessity. His tone was colourless, as if the ultimate anguish had eaten up his soul. And all this agony and repulsion exercised a foul fascination. He suffered a paroxysm of pleasure such as pleasure itself had never been able to give him. And I was Olya, I was his love, his wife, world without end, the demon whose supreme delight was to destroy him.

> *"Behind me, behind and above,*
> *She stands, that mirror of love.*
> *Her fingers are subtle-jointed;*
> *Her nails are polished and pointed,*
> *And tipped with spurs of gold:*
> *With them she rowels the brain.*
> *Her lust is critical, cold;*
> *And her Chinese cheeks are pale,*
> *As she daintily picks, profane*
> *With her octopus lips, and the teeth*

Jagged and black beneath,
Pulp and blood from a nail."

I jerked his head back, and fastened my mouth on his. I sucked his breath into my lungs. I wanted to choke him; but there was time enough for that. I would torture him a few years longer first.

I leapt away from him. He panted heavily. When he got his breath back, he glared at me horribly with the pin-point pupils of his sightless eyes.

He began with romantic sadness, changing to demoniac glee.

"She was incarnate love
In the hours when I first awoke her.
Little by little I found
The truth of her, stripped of clothing,
Bitter beyond all bound,
Leprous beyond all loathing."

We shouted with delight, and fell into a fit of hysterical laughter. We came out of it completely exhausted. I must have slept for a while.

When I woke he was sitting at the table under the yellow gas jet, reading the books he had bought.

Somehow, the past had been washed out of us. We found ourselves intent on the idea of stopping H.; and the books didn't help very much. They were written in a very positive way. The writers quarrelled among themselves like a Peace Conference.

But they all agreed on two points: that it was beyond the bounds of human possibility to break off the habit by one's own efforts. At the best, the hope was pitifully poor. The only chance was a "cure" in a place of restraint. And they all gave very full details of the horrors and dangers of the process. The physician, they said, must steel his heart against every human feeling, and refuse inexorably the petitions of the patient. Yet he must always be ready with his syringe, in case of a sudden collapse threatening life itself.

There were three principal methods of cure: Cutting the drug off at once, and trust to the patient's surviving; then there was a long tedious method of diminishing the daily dose. It was a matter of months. During the whole of the time, the agony of the patient continues in a diluted form. It was the choice between plunging into boiling oil and being splashed with it everyday for an indefinite period. Then there was an intermediate method in which the daily amount was reduced by a series of jerks. As Peter said, one was to be sentenced to be flogged at irregular intervals without knowing exactly when. One would be living in a state of agonising apprehension which would probably be more morally painful than in either of the other ways.

In all cases alike there was no hint of any true comprehension of the actual situation. There was no attempt to remove the original causes of the habit; and they all admitted that the cure was only temporary, and that the rule was relapse.

There was also a horribly disquieting impression that the patient could not trust the honesty of the doctor. Some of them openly advocated attempts to deceive the patient by injecting plain water. Others had a system of giving other drugs in conjunction with the permitted dose, with the deliberate intention of making the patient so ill that he would rather bear the tortures of abstention than those devised by his doctor.

I felt too, that if I went to one of those places, I should never know what trick might be played on me next. They were cruel, clumsy traps set by ignorant and heartless charlatans. I began to understand the intensity of jealousy with which the regular physician regards the patent-medicine vender and the Christian scientist.

They were witch-doctors with a licence from government to torture and kill at extravagant prices. They guarded their prerogatives with such ferocity because they were aware of their own ignorance and incompetence; and if their victims found them out their swindle would be swept away. They were always trying to extend their tyranny. They were always wanting new laws to compel everybody, sick or well, to be bound to the vivisection table, and have some essential organ of the body cut out. And they were brazen enough to give the reason. They didn't understand what use it was! And everybody must be injected with all sorts of disgusting serums and vaccines ostensibly to protect them against some disease which there was no reason whatever to suppose they were likely to get. . .

The last three days have been too dreadful. This is the first time I have felt like writing, and yet I have been itching insanely to put down that hideously luxurious scene when our love broke out like an abscess. All the old fantastic features were there. They had assumed a diabolical disguise; but my mind has been in abeyance. We shut the medical books with a shudder, and slung them out of the window into the street. A little crowd gathered; they were picked up, and the passers-by began talking about what was to be done. We realised the rashness of our rage. The last thing was to attract attention! We pulled the frowsy old curtains across, and put out the light.

The reaction of our reading was terrific. We venomously contrasted the calm confidence of King Lamus with the croaking clamour of the "authorities."

Cockie summed up the situation with a quotation.

"Quoth the Raven, 'Nevermore!'"

Our thoughts splashed to and fro like an angry sea in a cave. These three days have been a flux of fugitive emotion. We are resolved to stop taking H.; and there the memory of Lamus's letter was like a rope held by a trustworthy leader for a novice on some crumbling crag.

If we could only have relied on that! But our minds were shaken by panic.

Those cursed medical cowards! Those pompous prophets of evil! Everytime we came back to the resolution to stop, they pulled us off the rock.

"It's beyond human power."

But they know which side their bread's buttered. It's their game to discourage their dupes.

But they had over-played their hand. They had painted their picture in too crude colours. They revolted us.

Again, the effect of Mabel's death, and the fact that our supplies were so short, combined to drive us into the determination to stop at whatever cost.

We struggled savagely hour by hour. There were moments when the abstinence itself purged us by sheer pain of the capacity to suffer. Our minds began to wander. We were whirled on the wings of woe across the flaming skies of anguish.

I remember Peter standing at the table, lost to all sense of actuality. He cried in a shrill, cracked voice:—

"Her cranial dome is vaulted,
Her mad Mongolian eyes
Aslant with the ecstasies

> *Of things immune, exalted*
> *Far beyond stars and skies,*
> *Slits of amber and jet——"*

I heard him across abysses of aching inanity. A thrill of Satanic triumph tingled in my soul, and composed a symphony from its screams. I leapt with lust to recognise myself in the repulsive phantasm pictured by the poet.

> *"Her snout for the quarry set*
> *Fleshy and heavy and gross,*
> *Bestial, broken across,*
> *And below it her mouth that drips*
> *Blood from the lips*
> *That hide the fangs of the snake,*
> *Drips on venomous udders*
> *Mountainous flanks that fret,*
> *And the spirit sickens and shudders*
> *At the hint of a worse thing yet."*

We had, on the other side, some spasms of weakness; a ghastly sensation of the sinking of the spirit. It's the same unescapable dread that seizes one when one is in a lift which starts down too quickly, or when one swoops too suddenly in a 'plane. Waves of weakness washed over us as if we were corpses cast up by the sea from a shipwreck. A shipwreck of our souls.

And in these hideous hours of helplessness, we drifted down the dark and sluggish river of inertia towards the stagnant and stinking morass of insanity.

We were obsessed by the certainty that we could never pull through. We said nothing at first. We were sunk in a solemn stupor. When it found voice at last, it was to whimper the surrender. The Unconditional Surrender of our integrity and our honour!

We eked out our small allowance of H. with doses of strychnine to ward off the complete collapse of all our physical faculties, and we picked ourselves up a bit on the moral plane by means of champagne.

In these moments of abdication we talked in fragile whispers, plans for getting supplies. We had both of of us a certain shame in admitting to each other that we were renegades. We felt that in future we should never be able to indulge frankly and joyously as we had hitherto done. We should become furtive and cunning; we should conceal from each other what we were doing, although it was obvious to us both.

I slipped out this afternoon on tiptoe, thinking Peter was asleep, but he turned like a startled snake just as I made for the door.

"Where are you going, Lou?"

His voice was both piteous and harsh. I had not thought of inventing a pretext; but a lie slipped readymade from my tongue.

"I am going to Basil, to see if he can't give me something to help us out."

I knew he didn't believe me, and I knew he didn't care where I went or what I did. He was not shocked at my lying to him—the first time I had ever done so.

I took a taxi round to the studio. My he was half truth. I was going to ask him to help in the cure; but my real object was to induce him, no matter how, to give me at least one dose. I didn't care how I got it. I would try pretending illness. I would appeal to our old relations, and I would look about slyly to see if I couldn't find some and steal it. And I didn't mean to let Peter know.

On the top of everything else was the torture of shame. I had always been proud of my pride. A subtle serenity made my brain swim when I got into the street. It delighted me to be alone—to have got rid of Peter. I felt him as a restraining influence, and I had shaken him off. I despised myself for having loved him. I wanted to go to the devil my own way.

I found Basil in, and alone. What luck! That hateful tall thin girl was out of the way.

Basil received me with his usual greeting. It stung me to the quick like an insult. What right had he to reproach me? And why should "Do what thou wilt" sound like a reproach?

As a rule he added something to the phrase. He slid into ordinary conversation with a kind of sinuous grace. There was always something feline about him. He reminded me of a beautiful, terrible tiger winding his way through thick jungle.

But today, he stopped short with dour decision. It was as if he had fired a shot, and was waiting to see the effect. But he motioned me silently into my usual arm-chair, lit a cigarette for me and put it into my mouth, switched in the electric kettle for tea, and sat on the corner of his big square table swinging his leg. His eyes were absolutely motionless; yet I felt that they were devouring my body and soul inch by inch.

I wriggled on my chair as I used to do at school when I didn't feel sure whether I had been found out in something or not.

I tried to cover my confusion by starting a light conversation; but I soon gave it up. He was taking no notice of my remarks. To him they were simply one of my symptoms.

I realised with frightful certitude that my plans were impossible. I couldn't fool this man, I couldn't play on his passions, I couldn't steal in his presence.

Despite myself, my lie had become the truth. I could only do what I said I was coming to do; to ask him to help me out. No, not even that. I had not got rid of Peter after all.

With King Lamus, I found I couldn't think of myself. I had to think of Peter. I was absolutely sincere when I said with a break in my voice, "Cockie's in an awful mess."

I had it in my mind to add, "Can't you do something to help him?" and then I changed it to "Won't you?" and then I couldn't say it at all. I knew it was wasting words. I knew that he could and he would.

He came over and sat on the arm of my chair, and took down my hair, and began playing with the plaits. The action was as absolutely natural and innocent as a kitten playing with a skein of wool.

It stabbed my vanity to the heart for a second to realise that he could do a thing like that without mixing it up with sexual ideas. Yet it was that very superiority to human instincts that made me trust him.

"Sir Peter's not here," he said lightly and kindly.

I knew that it had pleased him that I had not mentioned my own troubles.

"But it's you, my dear girl, that I see in my wizard's spy-glass, on a lee shore with your masts all gone by the board, and the Union Jack upside down flying from a stump, and your wireless hero tapping out S.O.S."

He dropped my hair and lighted his pipe. Then he began to play with it again.

"And some on boards, and some on broken pieces of the ship, they all came safe to land."

One's familiarity with the New Testament makes a quotation somehow significant, however little one may believe in the truth of the book.

I felt that his voice was the voice of a prophet. I felt myself already saved.

"You take some of this," he went on, bringing a white tablet from a little cedar cabinet, and a big glass of cold water. "Throw your head back, and get it well down, and drink all this right off. Here is another to take home to your husband, and don't forget the water. It will calm you down; your nerves have all gone west. I've got some people coming here in a few minutes. But this will help you through the night, and I'm coming round in the morning to see you. What's the address?"

I told him. My face blazed with the disgrace. A house where the top social note was a fifth-rate musician in a jazz-band, and the bottom where we don't give it a name.

He jotted it down as if it had been the Ritz. But I could feel in my over-sensitive state the disgust in his mind. It was as if he had soiled his pencil.

The tablet made me feel better; but I think that the atmosphere of the man did more than its share of the work. I felt nearly normal when I got up to go. I didn't want his friends to see me. I knew too well what I was looking like.

He stopped me at the door.

"You haven't any of that stuff, I take it?" he said.

And I felt an inexpressible sense of relief. His tone implied that he had taken charge of us.

"No," I said, "we used up the last grain sometime ago."

"I won't ask you to remember when," he replied. "I know too well how muddled one gets. And besides, when one starts this experiment, the clock doesn't tell one much, as you know."

My self-respect came back to me with a rush. He insisted on our regarding ourselves as pioneers of science and humanity. We were making an experiment; we were risking life and reason for the sake of mankind.

Of course, it wasn't true. And yet, who can tell the real root of one's motives? If he chose to insist that we were doing what the leaders of thought have always done, how could I contradict him?

A buoyant billow of bliss bounded in my brain. It might not be true; but, by God, we'd make it come true.

I suppose a light leapt in my eyes, and enabled him to read my thought.

"Respice finem! *Judge the end;*
The man, and not the child, my friend!"

he quoted gaily.

And then, to my absolute blank amazement, he took me back into the studio, got a bottle of heroin from the cedar cabinet and shook out a small quantity on to a scrap of paper. He twisted it up, and put it in my hand.

"Don't be surprised," he laughed, "your face tells me that it's all right. You hadn't got that look of a dying duck in a thunderstorm which shows that you're wholly enslaved. As Sir Peter very cleverly pointed out the other day, you can't stop unless you've got something to stop with. You're keeping your magical diary, of course."

"Oh, yes," I cried gladly, I knew how important he thought the record was.

He shook his head comically.

"Oh, no, Miss Unlimited Lou, not what I call a magical diary. You ought to be ashamed of yourself for not knowing the hours, minutes, and seconds since the last dose. *Nous allons changer tout cela.* You can take this if you like, and when you like. I merely put it up to you as a sort of sporting proposition that you should see how long you can manage to keep off it. But I trust you to make a note of the exact time when you decide on a sniff, and I trust you to tell me the truth. Get it out of your mind once for all that I disapprove of your taking it. It's entirely your business, not mine. But it's everyone's business to be true to himself; and you must regard me as a mere convenience, an old hand at the game whose experience may be of use to you in training for the fight."

I hurried home a different woman. I didn't want to save myself. I felt myself as a suit of armour made for the purpose of protecting Peter. My integrity was important not for my own sake but for his.

Peter is out, so I have written this up. How surprised he will be. . .

I wonder why he is so long, and where he has gone. It is very uncomfortable, waiting, with nothing to do. I should like a dose. The tablet has not made me sleepy; it seems to have calmed me. It has taken the edge off that hateful restlessness. I can bear it as far as that goes, if only I had something to do to take my mind off things. My mind keeps prowling around the little packet of paper in my bag. I turn a thousand corners; but it is always waiting behind all of them. There is something terrifying about the fatality of the stuff. It seems to want to convince you that it's useless to try to escape. One's thoughts always recur to lots of other subjects which we don't think of as obsessing. Why should we have this idea in connection with dope and be unable to do anything to throw it off? What's the difference?

IV

Below the Brutes

I wonder how I have lived through this. Peter came in last night just after I had closed my diary. I had never seen him like it before; his eyes were half out of his head, bloodshot and furious. He must have been drinking like a madman. He was trembling with rage. He came straight up to me, and hit me deliberately in the face.

"That'll teach you," he shouted, and called me a foul name.

I couldn't answer. I was too hurt, not by the blow, but by the surprise. I had pictured it so differently.

He staggered back into the middle of the room and pointed to the blood that was running down my face. The edge of his ring had cut the corner of my eye. The sight sent him into fits of hysterical laughter.

The only feeling in my mind was that he was ill; that it was my duty to nurse him. I tried to go to the door to get help. He thought I was escaping, and flung me back right across the room on to the bed, howling with rage.

"You can get away with it at once," he said, "but that's enough. You wait right here, and see whether Mr. Bloody King Lamus will come to fetch you. Don't fret; I expect he will. He likes dirt, the filthy beast!"

I burst out crying. The contrast between the two men was too shocking. And I belonged to this screaming swearing bully with his insane jealousy and his senseless brutality!

I would rather have swept out Basil's studio for the rest of my life than be Lady Pendragon.

What masters of irony the gods are! I had been swimming in a glowing flood of glory; I had been almost delirious to think I was the wife of a man in whose veins ran the blood of England's greatest king; of him whose glamour had gilded the centuries with romance; to think that I might hold such royal heirship under my heart. What radiant rapture!

And Peter himself had shown himself worthy of his ancestry. Had not he too beaten back the heathen and saved England?

So this was the end of my dream! This brawling ruffian was my man!

I sat stupefied while his incoherent insults battered my brain; but my indignation was not for myself. I had deserved all I was getting; but what right had this foul-mouthed coward to take in his mouth the name of a man like King Lamus?

My silence seemed to exasperate him more than if I had taken up the quarrel. He swayed and swore with blind ferocity. He didn't seem to know where I was. It was getting dark. He groped his way round the room looking for me; but he passed me twice before he found me. The third time he stumbled up against me, gripped me by the shoulder, and began to strike.

I sat as if I were paralysed. I could not even scream. Again and again he swore and struck me savagely, yet so weakly that I could not feel the blows. Besides, I was dulled to all possible pain. Presently he collapsed, and rolled over on the bed. I thought for a moment he was dead, and then he was seized by a series of spasms; his muscles twisted and twitched; his hands clawed at the air; he began to mutter rapidly and unintelligibly. I was horribly frightened.

I got up and lit the gas. The poor boy's face was white as death; but small, dark crimson flushes burnt on the cheek-bones.

I sat at the table for sometime and thought. I didn't dare send for a doctor. He might know what was the matter and take him away from me; take him to one of those torture-traps, and he'd never get out.

I knew what he wanted, of course; a little heroin would bring him round all right. I told him I had some. I had to tell him several times before he understood.

When he did, the mere thought helped to restore him; but there remained an ort of rage, and he told me to give it him, with a greedy snarl. If I had wanted to keep it from him, I shouldn't have let him know I had it.

I brought him the stuff, sitting down by his side and lifting his head with one hand while I gave it to him on the back of the other. My heart sank like a stone in deep water. The old familiar attitude, the old familiar act!—and yet how different in every point!

The convulsive movements stopped immediately. He sat up almost at once on one elbow. The only sign of distress was that he still breathed heavily. All his anger, too, had disappeared. He seemed tired, like a convalescent, but as tractable as a child. He smiled faintly. I don't know if he had any consciousness or memory of what had passed. He talked as if there had been no quarrel at all. The colour came back to his face, the light to his eyes.

"One more go like that, Lou," he said, "and I'll be all right."

I wasn't at all sure what King Lamus would have said; but it was my own responsibility, and I couldn't refuse him.

He went off to sleep very soon after. In the morning I found out what had happened to him. He had been round to some of the men he used to know in the hospital to get them to give him some H., but they hadn't dared to do it. They were suffering from a sense of insult about the new law, the Diabolical Dope Act. They had undergone a long and expensive training and had diplomas which made them responsible for the health of the community; and now they weren't allowed to prescribe for their own patients. It was natural enough that they should be indignant.

The fourth man to whom Peter had gone told the same story, but had been very cordial. He thought he'd help things by standing Peter a dinner and filling him up with alcohol, with the idea that that would help him to support the lack of the other stimulant. It seems that I had to pay for the prescription.

No, Lou, you're a naughty girl. You mustn't be bitter like that. It's your fault for getting born into a world where ignorance and folly are in constant competition for the premiership of the minds of the educated classes. The commonest ploughman would have had more horse-sense than that doctor.

I gave Peter the tablet with plenty of water when he began to get restless. It soothed him a great deal. I wished I had one for myself. I felt my irritability returning; but I didn't break out because it couldn't be long till Basil came round. I looked forward to his coming as to a certain end to all our troubles. . .

What actually happened was quite different. I hardly know how to write it down. The shame and the disappointment are blasting. I feel that the doors of hope have been slammed in my face. I can imagine the grinding of the key as it turns in the lock, the screech of the rusty bolt as it is driven home.

The moment Basil appeared, Peter's insanity blazed up. He poured out a stream of insults, and accused Basil to his face of trying to get me away.

If Basil had only known how eagerly I would have gone! A man in sexual mania is not fit to consort with human beings. I never realised before why women despise men in their hearts so deeply. We respect men who have mastered their passions, if only because we are ourselves ultimately nothing but those passions. We expect a man to show himself superior. It will not do to kill passion, like Klingsor; the sexless man is even lower than "the wounded king," Amfortas, the victim of his virility. The true hero is Parsifal, who feels the temptations. "A man of like passions with ourselves." The more acutely alive he is to love, the greater are his possibilities. But he must refuse to surrender to his passions; he must make them serve him. *"Dienen! Dienen!"*

Who would kill a horse because he was afraid to ride him? It is better to mount, and dare the brute to bolt.

After the man is thrown, we pick him up and nurse him, but we don't adore him. Most men are like that. But what every woman is looking for is the man with the most spirited horse and the most complete mastery of him. That's most symbolic in *The Garden of Allah,* where the monk who cannot ride takes a stallion out into the desert, determined to fight the thing out to a finish.

Basil was not moved by the savage spite of Peter. He refused to be provoked. Whenever he got a chance to put a word in, he simply asserted the purpose of his visit. He did not even take the trouble to deny the main accusation.

It tired Peter to dash himself so uselessly against the cliff of Basil's contempt. I don't mean that it was contempt, either, but his calm kindness was bound to be felt as contempt because Peter couldn't help knowing how well he deserved disdain. He was aware of the fact that his abuse became weaker and emptier with every outburst. He simply pulled himself together with a last effort of animosity toward the friend who could have saved us, and ordered him out of the house. He made himself more ridiculous by posing as an outraged husband.

Lofty morality is the last refuge when one feels oneself to be hopelessly in the wrong.

It was the first time I had ever known Peter play the hypocrite. His professions of propriety were simply the measure of his indignity.

There was nothing for Basil to do but to go. Peter pretended to have scored a triumph. It would not have deceived anybody, but—if there *had* been a chance—he cut away the pulpit from under his own feet when he swung back into the room and snapped with genuine feeling:—

"God damn it, what a fool I am! Why didn't you tip me the wink? We ought to have played up to him and got some heroin out of him. . ."

This morning has taken everything out of me. I don't care about saving myself. I know I can't save Peter. Why must a woman always have a man for her motive? All I want is H. Both Cockie and I need it hellishly.

"Look here, Lou," he said with a cunning grin, such as I'd never seen before, quite out of keeping with his character. "You doll yourself up and try the doctors. A man told me last night that there were some who would give you a prescription if you paid them enough. A tenner ought to do the trick."

He pulled some dirty crumpled notes out of his trousers' pocket.

"Here you are. For God's sake, don't be long."

I was as keen as he was. All the will to stop had been washed out of me when Basil went. My self-respect was annihilated.

Yet I think it was reluctance to go that kept me hanging about on the pretence of attending to my toilet.

Peter watched me with approval. There was a hateful gleam in his eye, and I loved it. We were both degraded through and through. We had reached the foul straw of the sty. There was something warm and comfortable about snuggling up to depravity. We had realised the ideal of our perversion. . .

I went to my own doctor. Peter had put me up to symptoms; but he wasn't taking any. He talked about change of climate and diet and the mixture to be taken three times a day. I saw at once it was no good by the way he jumped when I mentioned heroin first.

All I could do was to get out of the old fool's room without losing face. . .

I didn't know what to do next. I felt like Morris What's-his-name in *The Wrong Box* when he had to have a false death certificate, and wanted a "venal doctor."

It annoyed me that it was daylight, and I didn't know where to go. Suddenly, out of nowhere, there came the name and address of the man who had helped Billy Coleridge out of her scrape. It was a long way off, and I was horribly tired. I was hungry, but the thought of lunch made me sick. I felt that people were looking at me strangely. Was it the scar by my eye?

I bought a thick veil. The girl looked surprised, I thought. I suppose it was rather funny in September, and might attract still more attention; but it gave me a sense of protection, and it was a very pretty veil—cream lace with embroidered zig-zags.

I took a taxi to the doctor's. Doctor Collins, it was, 61 or 71 Fairelange Street, Lambeth.

I found him at home; a horrid, snuffy old man with shabby clothes; a dingy grimy office as untidy as himself.

He seemed disappointed at my story. It wasn't his line, he said, and he didn't want to get into trouble. On the other hand, he was frightened of me because of what I knew about Billy. He promised to do what he could; but under the new law, he couldn't do more than prescribe ten doses of an eighth of a grain apiece. Four or five sniffs, the whole thing! And he wouldn't dare to repeat it in less than a week.

However, it was better than nothing. He told me where to get it made up.

I found a cloak-room where I could put the packets into one, and started.

The relief was immense. I went on, dose after dose. Cockie could get his own. I should tell him I had drawn blanks. I felt I could eat again, and had some light food and a couple of whiskies and sodas.

I felt so good that I drove straight back to Greek Street, and poured out a mournful tale of failure. It was delicious to deceive that brute after he'd struck me.

It was keen pleasure to see him in such pain; to imitate his symptoms with minute mimicry; to mock at his misery. He was angry all the same, but his blows gave me infinite pleasure. They were the symbols of my triumph.

"Here, you get out of this," he said, "and don't come back without it. I know where you can get it. Andrew McCall is the man's name. I know him to the bottom of his rotten soul."

He gave me the address.

It was a magnificent house near Sloane Square. He had married a rich old woman, and lived on the fat of the land.

I had met him once myself in society. He was a self-made Scot, and thought evening dress *de rigeur* in Paradise.

Peter sent me off with a sly snigger. There was some insane idea at the back of his mind. Well, what did I care? . . .

Dr. McCall was a man of fifty or so, very well preserved and very well dressed, with a gardenia in his buttonhole. He recognised me at once, and drew me by the hand into a comfortable arm-chair. He began to chatter about our previous meeting; about the duchess of this and the countess of that.

I wasn't listening, I was watching. His tact told him that I wasn't interested. He stopped abruptly.

"Well, well, excuse me for running on like this about old times. The point is, what can I do for you today, Miss Laleham?"

I instantly saw my advantage. I shook my head laughingly.

"Oh, no," I said, "it's not Miss Laleham."

He begged my pardon profusely for the mistake.

"Can it be possible? Two such beautiful girls so much alike?"

"No," I smiled back, "it's not as bad as that. I was Miss Laleham, but now I am Lady Pendragon."

"Dear, dear," he said, "where can I have been? Quite out of the world, quite out of the world!"

"Oh, I'm not quite such an important person as that, and I only married Sir Peter in July."

"Ah, that accounts for it," said the doctor. "I've been away all the summer in the heather with the Marchioness of Eigg. Quite out of the world, quite out of the world. Well, I'm sure you're very happy, my dear Lady Pendragon."

He always mentioned a title with a noise like a child sucking a stick of barley sugar.

I saw at once the way to appeal to him.

"Well, of course, you know," I said, "in really smart circles one has to offer heroin and cocaine to people. It's only a passing fashion, of course, but while it's on, one's really out of it if one doesn't do the right thing."

McCall got out of the chair at his desk, and drew up a little tapestried stool close to mine.

"I see, I see," he muttered confidentially, taking my hand and beginning to stroke it gently, "but you know, it's very hard to get."

"It is for us poor outsiders," I lamented, "but not for you."

He rolled back my sleeve, and moved his hand up and down inside of my forearm. I resented the familiarity acutely. The snobbishness of the man reminded me that he was the son of a small shopkeeper in a lowland village—a fact which I shouldn't have thought of for a second but for his own unctuous insistence on Debrett.

He got up and went to a little wall safe behind my back. I could hear him open and shut it. He returned and leant over the back of my chair, stretching out his left arm so that I could see what was in his hand.

It was a sealed ten-gramme bottle labelled "Heroini Hydrochlorid," with the quantity and the maker's name. The sight of it drove me almost insane with desire.

Within a yard of my face was the symbol of victory. Cockie, Basil, the law, my own physical pangs:—they were all in my power from the moment my fingers closed over the bottle.

I put out my hand; but the heroin had disappeared in the manner of a conjuring trick.

McCall leant his weight on the back of my chair and tilted it slightly. His ugly shrewd false face was within a foot of mine.

"Will you really let me have that?" I faltered. "Sir Peter's very rich. We can afford to pay the price, whatever it is."

He gave a funny little laugh. I shrank from the long wolf-like mouth hanging over me greedily open, with its bared two white rows of sharp, long fangs.

I was nauseated by the stale whisky in his breath.

He understood immediately; let my chair back to its normal position, and went back to his desk. He sat there and watched me eagerly like a man stalking game. As if inadvertently, he took out the bottle and played with it aimlessly.

In his smooth varnished voice he began to tell me what he called the romance of his life. The first time he saw me he had fallen passionately in love with me; but he was a married man, and his sense of honour prevented his yielding to his passion. He had, of course, no love for his wife, who didn't understand him at all. He had married her out of pity; but for all that he was bound by his sense of right feeling, and above all by realising that to give rein to his passion, God-given though it was, would mean social ruin for me, for the woman he loved.

He went on to talk about affinities and soul-mates and love at first sight. He reproached himself for having told me the truth, even now, but it had been too strong for him. The irony of fate! The tragic absurdity of social restrictions!

At the same time, he would feel a certain secret pleasure if he knew that I, on my part, had had something of the same feeling for him. And all the time, he went on playing with the heroin. Once or twice he nearly dropped it in his nervous emotion.

It made me jump to think of the danger to that precious powder. But there was clearly only one thing to be done to get it: to fall in with the old fellow's humour.

I let my head fall on my breast and looked at him sideways out of the corners of my eyes.

"You can't expect a young girl to confess everything she has felt," I whispered with a deep sigh, "especially when she has had to kill it out of her heart. It does no good to talk of these things," I went on. "I ought really not to have come. But how could I guess that you, a great doctor like you, had taken any notice of a silly kid like me?"

He jumped to his feet excitedly.

"No, no," I said sadly, with a gesture which made him sit down again, very uneasily. "I should never have come. It was absolutely weakness on my part. The heroin was only my excuse. Oh, don't make me feel so ashamed. But I simply must tell you the truth. The real motive was that—I wanted to see you. Now, let's talk about something else. Will you let me have that heroin, and how much will it cost?"

"One doesn't charge one's friends for such slight services," he answered loftily. "The only doubt in my mind is whether it's right for me to let you have it."

He took it out again and read the label. He rolled the bottle between his palms.

"It's terribly dangerous stuff," he continued very seriously. "I'm not at all sure if I should be justified in giving it to you."

What absolute rubbish and waste of time, this social comedy! Everyone in London knew McCall's hobby for intrigues with ladies of title. He had invented the silly story of love at first sight on the spur of the moment. It was just a gambit.

And as for me, I loathed the sight of the man, and he knew it. And he knew, too, that I wanted that heroin desperately badly. The real nature of the transaction was as plain as a prison plum-pudding.

But I suppose it does amuse one in a sort of way to ape various affected attitudes. He knew that my modesty and confusion and blushes were put on like so much paint on the cheeks of a Piccadilly street-walker. It didn't even hurt his vanity to know that I thought him an offensive old ogre. He had the thing I wanted, I had the thing he wanted, and he didn't care if I drugged myself to death tomorrow, provided I had paid his price today.

The callous cynicism on both sides had one good effect from the moral point of view. It prevented me wasting my time in trying to cheat him.

He went on with his gambit. He explained that my marriage made a great difference. With reasonable caution, for which we had every facility, there was not the slightest risk of scandal.

Only one thing stuck in my conscience, and fought the corrosive attack of the heroin-hunger. After King Lamus had gone this morning, Peter and I had quarrelled bitterly. I had given up Basil, I had given up all idea of living a decent life, I had embraced the monster in whose arms I was struggling, gone with my eyes wide open into his dungeon, devoted myself to drugs, and why? I was Sir Peter's wife. The loss of my virtue, independence, self-respect, were demanded by my loyalty to him. And already that loyalty demanded disloyalty of another kind.

It was a filthy paradox. Peter had sent me to McCall with perfect foresight. I knew well enough what he expected of me, and I gloried in my infamy—partly for its own sake, but partly, unless I am lying to myself, because my degradation proved my devotion to him.

I no longer heard what McCall was saying, but I saw that he had taken a little pocket-knife and cut the string of the bottle. He had levered out the cork, and dipped the knife into the powder. He measured out a dose with a queer cunning questioning smile in his eyes.

My breath was coming quickly and shallowly. I gave a hurried little nod. I seemed to hear myself saying, "A little bit more." At least, he added to the heap.

"A little mild stimulant is indicated," he said, with an imitation of his bedside manner. He was kneeling in front of my chair, and held up his hand like a priest making an offering to his goddess.

The next thing I remember is that I was walking feverishly, almost running, up Sloane Street. I had a feeling of being pursued. Was it true, that old Greek fable of the Furies? What had I done? What had I done?

My fingers worked spasmodically on the little amber-tinted bottle of poison. I wanted to get away from everyone and everything. I didn't know where I was going. I hated Peter from the depths of my soul. I would have given anything in the world—except the heroin—to be able never to see him again. But he had the money, why shouldn't we enjoy our abject ruin as we had enjoyed our romance? Why not wallow in the moist, warm mire?

V

Towards Madness

I found I was attracting attention in the street by my nervous behaviour. I shuddered at the sight of a policeman. Suppose I were arrested, and they took it away from me?

And then I remembered how silly I was. Maisie Jacobs had a flat in Park Mansions. I knew she would stand for anything, and keep her mouth shut.

She was in, thank goodness. I don't know what tale I told her. I don't know why I was stupid enough to trouble my head to invent one. She's a real good sport, Maisie, and doesn't care what you do as long as you don't interfere with her.

She had some white silk, and we sewed up the H. in little packets, and stitched them in the flounces of my dress. I kept about half, and put it in an old envelope she had. That was to make my peace with Peter. But I needed two or three good goes on the spot.

I had a fit of hysterical crying and trembling. I must have fainted for a bit. I found myself on the sofa with Maisie kneeling by me and holding a glass of champagne to my lips.

She didn't ask any questions. It wasn't her business if my story was all lies.

I felt a bit better after a while. She began to talk about King Lamus. She had fallen for him the first time she met him, about a year ago, and had become an enthusiastic pupil. She could do what she liked; she was free, plenty of money of her own, no one to interfere.

In a way, I hated her for her independence. It was really envy of her freedom.

I felt that Basil was the only man that mattered, and I had missed my chance with him through not being worthy. I had ended by losing him altogether; and the irony of it was terrible, for I had lost him through loyalty to Peter at the very moment when I thoroughly loathed and despised him.

Yet I knew that Basil would admire and love me for that very loyalty itself. It was the first thing that I had ever had to show him. My only asset had made me bankrupt forever!

Maisie had been talking quietly while I was thinking these things. I slid out of my concentration to hear her voice once more. She was in the middle of an explanation of her relations with Basil.

"He claims to be utterly selfish," vibrated her tense tones, "because he includes every individual in his idea of himself. He can't feel free as long as there are slaves about. Of course, there are some people whose nature it is to be slaves; they must be left to serve. But there are lots of us who are kings and don't know it; who suffer from the delusion that they ought to bow to public opinion, all sorts of alien domination. He spends his life fighting to emancipate people in this false subjection, because they are parts of himself. He has no ideas about morality. His sense of honour, even, means nothing to him as such. It is simply that he happened to be born a gentleman. 'If I were a dog,' he said to me once, 'I should bark. If I were an owl, I should hoot. There's nothing in either which is good or bad in itself. The only question is, what is the natural gesture?' He thinks it his mission in the world to establish this Law of Thelema."

She saw my puzzled look.

"Do what thou wilt shall be the 'whole of the Law,'" she quoted merrily. "You must have heard those words before!"

I admitted it. We laughed together over our friend's eccentricity.

"He says that to everyone he meets," she explained, "not only to influence them, but to remind himself of his mission and prevent himself wasting his time on anything else. He's not a fanatic; and in the year that I have known him, I've certainly got on more with my music than I ever did in any five years before. He proved to me—or, rather, showed me how to prove to my own satisfaction—that my true Will was to be a singer. We began by going through all the facts of my life from my race and parentage to my personal qualities, such as my ear and my voice being physiologically superior to that of the average musician, and my circumstances enabling me to devote myself entirely to training myself to develop my powers to the best advantage. Even things like my guardian being a great composer! He won't admit that was an accident."

"He claims that the coincidence of so many circumstances affords evidence of design; and as so many of these are beyond the control of any human intelligence, it leads one to suppose that there is some individual at work somewhere beyond our limitations of sense who has made me a singer instead of a milliner."

"Oh, yes, Maisie," I interrupted, "but that's the old argument that the design of the Universe proves the existence of God; and people have stopped believing in God chiefly because the design was shown to be incompatible with a consistent character."

"Oh, certainly," she admitted without a qualm. "The evidence goes to show that there are many different gods, each with his own aim and his own method. Whether their conflicting ambitions can be reconciled (as seems necessary from a philosophical point of view) is practically beyond the scope of our present means of research. Basil implored me not to bother my head about any such theories. He simply laughed in my face and called me his favourite nightingale. 'Thou wast not born for death, immortal bird,' he chuckled, 'but neither wast thou born to take a course of Neo-Platonism.' His whole point is that one mustn't leave the rails. If I had convinced myself that I was a singer, would I kindly refrain from meddling with other affairs?"

"I know," I put in, "as the captain said when the first officer interrupted him, 'What I want from you, Mr. Mate, is silence, and precious damned little of that!'"

Again we found ourselves laughing together. It was really very extraordinary the way in which talking to Basil or his pupils exhilarated the mind. I began to see why he was so distrusted and disliked. People always pretend to want to be lifted out of themselves, but in reality they're terribly afraid of anything happening to them. And Basil always strikes at the root of one's spiritual oak. He wants one to be oneself, and the price of that is to abandon the false ideas that one has of oneself. People like the sham teachers that soothe them with narcotic platitudes. They dread having to face reality in any form. That is the real reason for persecuting prophets.

Of course, I was full of H., but Maisie had made me forget all about it for a moment.

"Who's that thin girl that's always there?" I asked her.

It was an automatic spurt of jealousy.

"Oh, Lala," said Maisie, "she's rather a dear. She's a queer girl, one of the queerest ever. Swiss or something, I fancy. He's trained her for the last three years. He met her, I don't know how, and asked her to pose for him. She told me once how startled she was at the reason he gave. 'Did you write that psalm,' he asked her, '"I can tell all my bones, they look and stare upon me?"' You know the girl hasn't got an ounce of flesh on her body. She's perfectly healthy; she's just a freak of nature. And while he sketched her he asked her to suggest a title for the picture. 'Paint me as a dead soul,' she answered. He caught up the phrase with fiery enthusiasm, and began to work on an enormous screen, a triptych with the strangest beasts and birds and faces, all arranged to lead up to her as the central figure. She is standing naked with a disproportionately large head grinning detestably. The body is almost a skeleton covered with greenish skin. It made a perfectly grisly sensation. I wonder you haven't seen it."

As a matter of fact, I had seen a photograph of it in some newspaper, and now I remembered that Bill Waldorf had pointed her out, roaring with laughter, as the Queen of the Dead Souls. Basil had said that London was full of dead souls.

"It's nothing to do with that story of Gogol's," said Maisie. "Basil thinks—and it's only too ghastly true—that most of the people we see walking about, and eating and drinking and dancing, are really dead—'dead in trespasses and sins,' as my old uncle used to say—in the sin of not knowing themselves to be Stars, True and Living Gods Most High——"

I sighed with sadness. I, too, was a dead soul—and I had given up the Lord of Resurrection that morning out of loyalty to another dead soul. And—the same afternoon! Faugh! what a charnel-house Life is! How chill and damp and poisonous is the air! How the walls sweat the agony of the damned!

"And look at Lala now!" Maisie went on. "He had to put her through the most frightful ordeals—for she was very dead indeed—but she got to the other end of the tunnel all right. She's a Great Soul, if ever there was one in the world, and he has raised her mortal into immortality. Her corruptibility has put on incorruption—and she radiates light and life and love, leaping through the years in utter liberty——"

"But what does she do now?" I asked with a dull pain at my heart.

"Why, her True. Will, of course!" came back the flaming answer. "She knows that she came to this planet to bear witness to the Law of Thelema in her own person, and to help her Titan in his task!"

Maisie was really stupefying. Everyone knows that she was in love with Basil from the first, and is, and always will be. How was it that she could speak of another woman who loved him without jealousy, and, as things were, without envy? It was true, perhaps, after all, that he had some huge hypnotic power, and held them helpless, filed away like so many letters. But Maisie was bubbling over with energy and joy; it was absurd to think of her as vampirised, as a victim. I asked her about it point-blank.

"My dear Lou," she laughed, "don't be too utterly gaga! My Will is to sing, and Lala's is to help him in his work—why should we clash? Why should there be any ill-feeling? She's helping me by helping him to help me; and I'm helping her by showing that his Law has helped me, and can help others. We're the best friends in the world, I and Lala; how could anything else be possible?"

Well, of course, she was herself doing a notoriously impossible feat. The point of view of Basil and his crowd is simply upside down to all ordinary people. At the same time, one can't deny that the result is amazingly invigorating to contemplate. I could quite understand his idea of developing mankind into what is practically a new species, with new faculties, and the old fears, superstitions, and follies discarded forever.

I couldn't stand it another second. Maisie had given him—and herself—up, and yet she possessed both herself and him: I had clung to him and to myself, and I had lost both—Lost, lost forever! I got up to go home; and before I reached the street I realised with desolate disgust and despair the degree of my degradation, of my damnation; and I hugged desperately my hideous perverse pride in my own frightful fate, and rejoiced as the horrible hunger for heroin made itself known once more, gnawing at my entrails. I licked my lips at the thought that I was on my way to the man whom my love had done so much to destroy—and myself with him.

To begin with, no more of this diary—why should I put myself out for King Lamus? "Every step he treads is smeared with blood," as Gretel once said. Yes, in some infernal way he had made me one of his victims. "All right—you shall get enough magical diary to let you know that I'm out of your clutches—I'll put down just those things which will tell you how I hate you—how I have outwitted you—and you shall read them when my Dead Soul has got a Dead Body to match it."

September 14

I expected Peter would be in; impatient to know if I'd wangled McCall. Instead, he turned up after twelve, full of champagne and—Snow!

My aunt, what a lucky day!

He was boiling with passion, grabbed me like a hawk.

"Well, old girl," he shouted, "what luck with McCall?"

I produced my package.

"Hurrah, all our troubles are over!"

We opened our last three half-bottles of fizz to celebrate the occasion, and he gave me some coke. And I thought I didn't like it! It's the finest stuff there is. A sniff to the right and a sniff to the left and a big heap right on my tongue; and that wasn't all.

"I tell you what's been wrong," he said in the morning. "Who the hell could expect to be right in a place like this? I've got right on to the ropes. We need never run short anymore. We'll go down to Barley Grange and have another honeymoon. You're my honeysuckle, and I'm your bee."

He went and flung open the door and shouted for the woman to pack our things while we went out to breakfast, and have the bill ready.

"What infernal fools we are," he cried as we went sailing down the street to the Wisteria, where you can get real French coffee and real English bacon.

We looked at ourselves in the long mirror. We could see how ill we had been, but all that was gone.

Decision and self-confidence had come back; and love had come back with them. I could feel love mingling its turbulent torrent with my blood like the junction of the Rhone and the Arve in Geneva.

We walked into a shop and bought a car on the spot, and took it away then and there. There was one at the Grange, but we wanted a racer.

We drove back to Greek Street in a flood of delight. It was a bright, fresh autumn morning; everything had recovered its tone. Winter could never come. There was no night except as a background for the moon and the stars, and to furnish the scenery of our heavenly hell.

September 17

The Grange is certainly the finest house in the world. There is only one drawback. We didn't want callers. County society is all right in its way; but tigers don't hunt in packs, especially on the honeymoon. So we had to send the word around that the precarious state of my health made it impossible for us to receive. Rather an obvious lie, motoring the way we were. The 'plane had come back from Deal, but we didn't do any flying.

Cockie gave various reasons; but they were unconvincing. We roared with laughter at their absurdity. The truth was that he was nervous.

It didn't make us ashamed. After what he had done, he could rest on his oars. It was only temporary, of course. We'd made ourselves rottenly

ALEISTER CROWLEY

ill in that gaga place in Greek Street. We couldn't expect to get back to the top of our form in a week.

Besides, we didn't want that kind of excitement. We had enough in other ways. We found we could see things. That ass, Basil, was always talking about the danger of magic, and precaution, and scientific methods and all that bunk. We were seeing more spirits and demons everyday than he ever saw in ten years. They are nothing to be afraid of. I should like to see the old Boy himself. I'd——

September 18

We found a book in the library one rainy afternoon. It told us how to make the Devil appear.

Cockie's grandfather was great on that stuff. There's a room in the north tower where he did his stunts.

We went up after dinner. Everything had been left more or less the way it was. Uncle Mortimer never troubled to alter anything.

There was a legend about this room too. For one thing, grandfather was a friend of Bulwer Lytton's. We found a first edition of *A Strange Story*, with an inscription.

Lytton had taken him for the model of Sir Philip Derval, the white magician who gets murdered. Lytton said so in this copy.

It was all very weird and exciting. The room was full of the strangest objects. There was a table painted with mysterious designs and characters and a huge cross-hilted sword; two silver crescents separated by two copper spheres and a third for the pommel. The blade was two-edged, engraved with Arabic or something.

Cockie began to swing it about. We thought flashes of light came from the point, and there was a buzzing, crackling sound.

"Take this," said Cockie, "there's something devilish rum about it."

I took it out of his hand. Of course, it was only my fancy; but it seemed to weigh nothing at all, and it gave a most curious thrill in one's hand and arm.

Then there was a golden cup with rubies round the brim. And always more inscriptions.

And there was a little wand of ebony with a twisted flame at the top; three tongues, gold, silver, and some metal we'd never seen before.

And there were rows and rows of old books, mostly Latin, Greek, and Hebrew.

There was a big alabaster statue of Ganesha, the elephant god.

"This is the place," I said, "to get hold of the devil."

"That's all right," said Cockie, "but what about a little she-devil for me?"

"Oh," I said, "if I'm not satisfactory, you'd better give me a week's salary in lieu of notice."

We laughed like mad.

Something in the room made our heads swim. We began kissing and wrestling.

It's all very well to laugh at magic, but after all certain ideas do belong to certain things; and you can get an idea going, if you're reminded of it by a place like this. . .

(Lady Pendragon's Diary is interrupted by a note written on some later occasion in the handwriting of Mr. Basil King Lamus. Ed.)

Lou means all right, bless her! She makes me think of Anatole France—La Rôtisserie de la Reine Pédauque—old Coignard has been warned by the Rosicrucian not to pronounce the word Agla, and the moment he does so, a wheel comes off his carriage, with the result that he gets murdered by Moses.

Then, again, all the Rosicrucian's predictions come true; and he himself goes up in a flame like the Salamander he has been invoking. He looks upon his own death as the crown of his career—the climax towards which he has been working.

Anatole France is, in fact, compelled to write as if the Rosicrucian theories were correct, although his conscious self is busily exposing the absurdity of magic.

It looks as if the artist's true self were convinced of the actuality of magic, and insisted on expressing itself despite every effort of the sceptical intellect to turn the whole thing into ridicule. There are numerous other examples in literature of the same conflict between the genius and the mind which is its imperfect medium. For instance—at the other end of the scale—Mr. W. S. Maugham, in "The Magician," does his malignant utmost to make the "villain" objectionable in every way, an object of contempt, and a failure. Yet in the very moment when his enemies succeed in murdering him and destroying his life's work, they are obliged to admit that he has "Accomplished the Great Work"—of creating Living Beings! "Every man and every woman is a star."

B. K. L.

I don't like that room. I said nothing about it to Peter; but the old man was there walking about as large as life. You have to be specially prepared to see these things.

Cockie was never spiritually minded.

September 18

An alarm of burglars last night. We roused the house—but no traces could be found. The servants here are frightfully stupid. They irritate me all the time.

One can't sleep in this house. It's too old. The wood cracks all the time. Just as one is on the verge of sleep some noise makes one more wide-awake than ever.

I can't bear the idea of being touched. My skin is very sensitive. It's part of the spiritualising of my life, I suppose.

I'm glad, though, that the new honeymoon didn't last more than three or four days.

It is irritating to one's vanity. But that is merely a memory. How can vanity co-exist with the spiritual life?

I saw the Spirit of heroin today when I went up to the magic room. It is tremendously tall and thin, with tattered rags fluttering round it, and these turn into little birds that fly off it, that come and burrow in one's skin!

I just feel the prick of the beak, and then it disappears. They were messengers from the other world. There is a little nest of them in my liver. It is very curious to hear them chirping when they want food. I don't know what they'll do so far away from their mother.

It is horrible not being able to sleep. That, too, must be a preparation for the new life.

I wandered up all alone to the magic room, and sat with my hands on the table opposite the old man, trying to get him to talk.

His lips move, but I can't hear what he says.

I was disturbed, of course. I always am being disturbed. I am so tired. Why won't they let me alone?

This time it was a shot. The magic room has windows all around it.

I went to see who could have fired. It was very bright moonlight; but I could see nothing.

Then there came another flash and report. I went round to the side it came from, and watched. It was by the lake. I watched a long time. Then a crouching figure hidden among the reeds sprang up, put a gun to its shoulder and fired twice in rapid succession. Then it screamed, and ran to the house throwing away its gun. I wonder what it could be.

I have found a manuscript in grandfather's room that tells you how to invoke the Devil. It needs two people, and I don't feel sure about Peter.

He can't see into the spiritual world at all. On the contrary, he is getting a little queer in the head, and imagines he sees things which don't exist at all. He's constantly scratching himself.

He behaved very strangely at dinner. I think the butler noticed it.

At midnight we went up to the old man's room and began to go through the ritual. A lot of it seems silly, but the climax is fine.

You keep on saying, over and over:—

"Io Pan Pan! Io Pan Pan! Ai Pan Pan!
Io Pan Pan! Io Pan Pan! Pan Pan Pan!
    Aegipan, Aegipan, Aegipan, Aegipan, Aegipan, Aegipan, Io Pan Pan!"

You go on till something comes. We used two black robes that we found hanging up there.

They were lovely silk robes with hoods.

You take candles in both hands and dance while you make the incantations.

We got frightfully excited. It was as if a strange force had got hold of us. It seemed to lead us all round the house and then into the grounds.

We were shouting at the top of our voices.

Once or twice we saw a servant putting out a nose through a chink of a door. It would always be shut with a little squeal, and we could hear keys turning and bolts being pushed.

We wanted to roar with laughter, but we had to keep on with the invocation. The book said you mustn't stop it while you were outside the magic room, or the Devil could get you.

The strange thing is that I don't remember at all what happened. Did the Devil come or not?

I don't even remember getting back to the magic room. I must have gone to sleep, for I've woken up frightfully hungry.

Cockie's awake too. He's kneeling at the window with a shot gun. He aimed it two or three times, but didn't fire. He came back to me after putting the gun in a corner.

He said, "It's no good. They're too spry. The only chance to get them is at night."

He was hungry too. We rang for some food. Nobody answered the bell.

We rang again and again.

Then Peter got angry and went to see what was wrong.

There isn't a soul in the place!

It's perfectly incomprehensible. What could have happened to them all?

Peter says it's the Germans. Part of a plot to persecute him for what he did in the war. But I don't think so at all.

It says in a book that you have to get rid of everyone if you're going to start the spiritual life.

I expect my spiritual guide put it into their minds to go, but I'm very doubtful about Cockie. He's not ready for any high development. Men are always revoltingly gross.

Think how they are even about love. I must say this for Cockie, he's all right about that. The very flower of purity—a perfect knight!

Yet we went through a period of a very evil character. No doubt we had to be purged of all our baser elements.

There is a great sympathy between us at times, and it is not soiled by any animality.

The only thing is I'm not sure whether it hasn't been too great a strain for his mind—the process of purification.

He certainly has some very queer ideas. Sometimes I catch him looking at me with some deep suspicion in his eyes. His mind is harping on the Germans. He broke out just now into a denunciation of Gretel Webster as a German spy, and rambled on from that to say something that I couldn't properly understand. But the gist of it was apparently that as Gretel had introduced us more or less, I was being used to do him some harm.

Of course ideas like this come to one when one's hungry, and all this sprang up owing to the mysterious disappearance of the servants.

There was nothing for it but for Peter to go to the inn and have food sent in. But I had the devil's own job to get him to do it. His character lacks decision.

I made him take two or three sniffs of snow. That put him right, and now he's gone off to the inn.

I'm very glad to be alone. I always felt those servants were spying. The house is delightfully quiet.

As I write there are two beautiful people looking over my shoulder. They have been sent to watch over me and guide me, and prepare me for the great destiny which is in store for me.

Here comes Peter with the waiter and a tray. I must hide this book. The secrets of the spiritual life must be kept from the profane.

It's all right. Peter is my soul-mate after all. We couldn't eat much. It's only natural; all base appetites have to be killed out before one is ready to go on. Peter ate very little himself; and then he said:—

"I know why we couldn't get the Devil to come the other night. It was having those servants about. I remember now that grandfather only had two in the house, and he used to send them away when he had anything big on. Let's see what we can do tonight."

That was delightful. That was his old self.

We thought it would be a good plan to coke up pretty hard before starting.

VI

Cold Turkey

I don't remember what happened. I know why. Basil told me long ago that the mind only kept count of material things. So these spiritual events are recorded in a higher kind of mind of which we are not conscious until we get accustomed to spiritual life. So all I can put down is that we had a complete success.

The Devil, of course, needs a human interpreter if he is to communicate with this world, and so he took possession of Peter. He has been preparing Peter to represent him. He will make Peter pope, and I am to be in the Vatican disguised, to help him because he can't do without me.

My own spiritual guide is named Keletiel. She is a wonderful being, wears peacock blues and greens. She has white wings like a swan, and carries a sheaf of many-coloured flowers. She has long, loose, black curling hair down to her waist. There is a golden band round her forehead, studded with sapphires, with her name on it. I can always tell her by this.

There has to be a token, because she changes her size so much. Sometimes she is a tiny thing, not up to my knee, and sometimes she is two or three times as high as the North Tower.

Peter and I are covered with blood. We came out of the circle before the Devil had gone, and he scratched us all to pieces. Luckily we got back before he killed us, but we lost consciousness and woke up a long while later. That's why we can't remember what happened.

I have some idea that I had a terrible quarrel with Peter, but I can't remember any details.

I think he does, though, but he won't tell me.

I don't know why he should act like that. The only thing I can think is that Gretel Webster may have come down to see him perhaps in her astral body, and put him against me somehow. . .

He was lying on the sofa in his pyjamas. I wanted to be kissed, and went over to him with some cocaine. But he didn't move. He looked at me with wide open eyes. There was some dreadful fear in them, and he said,—

> *"Black, the plague of the pit,*
> *Her pustules visibly fester."*

Of course, I knew he didn't mean it, but I was hurt. I gave him the cocaine.

It roused him. He sat up and then he held me by the shoulders and looked straight at my face and said:—

> *"Dragon of lure and dread,*
> *Tiger of fury and lust,*
> *The quick in chains to the dead,*
> *The slime alive in the dust,*
> *Brazen shame like a flame,*
> *An orgy of pregnant pollution*
> *With hate beyond aim or name—*
> *Orgasm, death, dissolution!"*

And then he began shrieking, and ran out of the house down to the lake and dived right in. He swam a few strokes and then came out and walked slowly up to the house.

I found some towels in the linen chest. I was afraid of his catching a chill, so I rubbed him hard all over. He seemed to have forgotten everything. He was quite nice and normal but just a little scared.

I can't make out what's the matter with him. He acts as if he had learnt some terrible secret which he had to keep from me. He always seems afraid of being spied on or overheard.

I went up to the magic room tonight. Peter was sitting in the old man's chair writing in a book. I couldn't understand it at first. I had come straight up, and he was fast asleep downstairs! Then, of course, the whole mystery became clear.

While he's asleep, his astral double comes up and does magic. I knew it was very dangerous to disturb any one's astral double, so I tiptoed out of the room; but the double followed me noiselessly. Everytime I looked over my shoulder he was there, though he was very quick at dodging back round the corner or into a doorway. . .

Peter has been very preoccupied for sometime. He writes out telegrams on forms, and then tears them up; and then he seems to think that isn't safe, and picks the pieces up and burns them. I asked him about it; but he would say nothing, and got very angry.

I think I know what it is, though. I found a sheet of paper which he had forgotten to destroy—a letter to the War Office, warning them against German plots, and telling somethings that have happened down here. I could hardly read it; his handwriting is absolutely gaga.

HE TALKS A GREAT DEAL to himself. I overheard some of it. He thinks there may be a German spy in the War Office and is afraid to trust the post or telegraph.

He kept on saying, "I'm at my wits' end." Then he went off into muttering about the plots against him.

I am sure I could help him out if he would only trust me. I wonder if it's all delusion on his part. He certainly has some funny ideas.

For one thing, he pretends to see spiritual guides, which is impossible, because he is not pure enough. Besides, the things he says he sees are all horrible and disgusting.

But he says nothing at all now, anymore. He begins to speak to me and checks himself. . .

It is very dark tonight. Rain is falling. Peter has gone down to the lake with his gun.

I have taken this book from its hiding place. I am horribly frightened.

I had no appetite at lunch, and Peter wouldn't eat. He burst out in a hysterical appeal to me, reminded me of our love, and said he couldn't believe it was all a sham. Why had I gone into the plot to drive him to death? He doesn't eat, because he thinks the food is poisoned; and when he saw that I wasn't eating, it convinced him that I was in the plot against him.

I tried to tell him this was all nonsense. I told him that I was not in any plot against him. It didn't set his mind at ease. I had to tell him my great secret that I am the woman clothed with the sun in the Book of Revelations, and that he must protect me.

I proved to him that this was the only explanation. The reason why he couldn't live with me as my husband was that my angel had told me that I was going to bring the Messiah into the world.

We went into a heated argument. I don't remember what happened; but as usual, it turned into a quarrel.

One must be concentrated on the spiritual life, so the slightest interruption from the senses, if it's only the wind in the trees, is a terribly irritating thing. "Satan is the prince of the power of the air," it says in the Bible, so he sends these noises in the air to disturb my mind.

How can I give birth to the Messiah if I am not caught up into the Seventh Heaven, and unconscious of material things?

The world, the flesh, and the Devil. One in three and three in one. This evil trinity must be abolished. It knows that; and that's why it tries to interrupt me either by means of Peter or the pains of the body, or the sights and sounds of nature.

Nature is under a curse because of sex, and so this world is in the power of the Evil One. But I am chosen to redeem it, and the Holy Spirit overshadows me and sends angels to guard me. That is how we got rid of the servants.

PETER SUDDENLY ATTACKED ME. HE got me down, and put his knee on my chest, and tried to strangle me. But the angel smote him suddenly, and all his muscles relaxed and he rolled over.

His eyes were wide open, but I could only see the whites. That is a sign that he is possessed by the Devil, and that the angels are protecting me.

He has fired two or three times, and now I see him coming up from the lake. I must hide this book, and then I will go to the garage, and hide till the morning.

Keletiel tells me that this is the critical night. I will get into the big car under the sheet. He won't look for me there, and the angels will be on the watch. . .

It came out all right. I slept on the seat of the car. I had a dreadful nightmare, and woke sweating all over. Then I went to sleep again. I was with six angels who carried me through the air to a place which I mustn't describe. It is a great and wonderful mystery.

It is awful and miraculously wonderful to be the woman clothed with the sun. The sublimity of it would have frightened me only a few weeks ago. I have been gently and wisely prepared for my exalted position.

This vision initiated me into the most marvellous secrets.

When I woke Keletiel came and told me that the crisis was over. I was shivering with cold, and went into the house for some heroin. That's the only thing that keeps one warm however hot the weather is. This is because what keeps the body warm is the rush of animal life, and when one has got to the stage where one becomes wholly spiritual, the body becomes cold like a corpse. . .

A dreadful thing has happened. We have used up all the heroin, and there is hardly any cocaine. I remembered what I had sewn away in my white frock, and went to get it. It was on the floor in a corner of the drawing-room.

It was all shrunk and rumpled and dirty, and it was still quite wet. I suppose I must have gone a long walk in the rain, though I don't remember anything about it.

All the heroin was washed away. There wasn't a grain left. Peter came in and found me crying. He understood at once what had happened. All he said was:—

"You'll have to go back to McCall."

I couldn't even be angry. Men are too grossly animal to understand. How could I do such a thing, seeing who I was?

He wanted some H. badly; finding it gone, made him want it insanely.

He took one of the packets and began to chew it.

"Thank God," he said, "it's quite bitter. There must be a lot in the dress."

I was shivering and faint. I got another packet, and put it in my mouth. He went wild and clutched me by the hair, and forced open my jaws with his finger and thumb. I struggled and kicked and scratched; but he was too strong. He got it out and put it in his own mouth. Then he hit me in the face as I sat. I went flat and limp, and began to howl. He picked up the dress and the packets, and started to go. I caught at his ankles desperately; but he kicked himself free, and went out of the room with the dress.

I was too weak and hurt to go after him, and my nose was bleeding.

But I had got some H., and I remembered who I was. This was all part of the ordeal. At any moment I might manifest my glory, and he would fall down at my feet and worship me. After all, he has a wonderful destiny himself; like St. Joseph—or else perhaps he may be the Dragon that will try to destroy me and the Messiah.

In my position the actual H. isn't really necessary anymore than food is. The spiritual idea is sufficient. That I suppose is the lesson I had to learn. I had been relying on the stuff itself. It says in the Bible "Angels came and ministered unto him." My angels will bring me the manna that cometh down from heaven.

I am perfectly happy. It is sublime not to be dependent anymore on earthly things. Keletiel came and told me to go and prophesy to Peter, so I will hide away the diary. I must think of a new place everytime, else Peter will find out where I keep it, or the old man may be hunting around in his astral body and take it away. I have been very careful what I wrote; but he might discover some of the secrets and ruin everything.

There's another trouble. I can only remember spiritual things clearly. The material world is fading out. It would be disaster if I forgot where I hid it.

Basil would never forgive me.

I will hide it in the chimney, then I can always look up where I put it. . .

WHAT IS DREADFUL IS THE length of time. With H. or C. or both, there is never a dull moment; without them the hours, the very minutes, drag. It's difficult to read or write. My eyes won't focus properly. They have been open to the spiritual world, they can't see anything else. It's hard, too, to control the hands. I can't form the letters properly.

This waiting is hellish. Waiting for something to happen! I can think of nothing but H. Everything in the body is wrong. It aches intolerably. Even a single dose would put everything right.

It makes me forget who I am, and the wonderful work to be done. I have become quite blind to the spiritual world. Keletiel never comes. I must wait, wait, wait for the Holy Spirit; but that's a memory so far, far off!

There are times when I almost doubt it, yet my faith is the only thing that prevents my going insane. I can't endure without H.

The sympathy of suffering has brought Peter closer. We lie about and look at each other; but we can't touch, the skin is too painful. We are both restless as it is impossible to describe. It irritates us to see each other like this, and we can't do anything; we constantly get up with the idea of doing something, but we sit down again immediately. Then we can't sit, we have to lie down. But lying down doesn't rest us; it irritates us more, so we get up again, and so on forever. One can't smoke a cigarette; after two or three puffs it drops from one's fingers. The only respite I have is this diary. It relieves me to write of my sufferings; and besides, it is important for the spiritual life. Basil must have the record to read.

I can't remember dates, though. I don't even know what year it is. The leaves in the park tell me it is autumn, and the nights are getting

ALEISTER CROWLEY

longer. The night is better than the day; there is less to irritate. We don't sleep, of course, we fall into a torpor. Basil told me about it once. He called it the dark night of the soul. One has to go through it on the way to the Great Light.

The light of day is torture. Every sense is an instrument of the most devilish pain. There is no flesh on our bones.

This perpetual craving for H! Our minds are utterly empty of everything else. Rushing into the void come tumbling the words of that abominable poem:—

> *"A bitten and burning snake*
> *Striking its venom within it,*
> *As if it might serve to slake*
> *The pain for the tithe of a minute."*

It is like vitriol being thrown in one's face. We have no expression of our own. We cannot think. The need is filled by these words. . .

The impact of light itself is a bodily pain.

> *"When the sun is a living devil*
> *Vomiting vats of evil,*
> *And the moon and the night but mock*
> *The wretch on his barren rock,*
> *And the dome of heaven high-arched*
> *Like his mouth is arid and parched,*
> *And the caves of his heart high-spanned*
> *Are choked with alkali sand!"*

We are living on water. It seems for the moment to quench the thirst, at least part of it. Peter's nervous state is very alarming. I feel sure he has delusions.

He got up and staggered to the mantelpiece and leant against it with his arms stretched out. He cried in a hoarse, dry voice:—

> *"Thirst!*
> *Not the thirst of the throat,*
> *Though that be the wildest and worst*
> *Of physical pangs that smote*
> *Alone to the heart of Christ,*

> *Wringing the one wild cry*
> *'I thirst' from His agony,*
> *While the soldiers drank and diced."*

He thought he was Jesus on the Cross instead of the Dragon, as he really is. It makes me very nervous about him.

When he had finished reciting, his strength suddenly failed him, and he collapsed. The clatter of the fire-irons was the most hideous noise that I had ever heard. . .

When I can summon up enough strength to write in my diary, the pain leaves me. I see that there are two people here. I, myself, am the Woman clothed with the Sun, writing down my experiences. The other is Lou Pendragon, an animal dying in agony from thirst.

I said the last word aloud, and Peter caught it up. He crawled away from the grate towards me croaking out:—

> *"Not the thirst benign*
> *That calls the worker to wine;*
> *Not the bodily thirst*
> *(Though that be frenzy accurst)*
> *When the mouth is full of sand,*
> *And the eyes are gummed up, and the ears*
> *Trick the soul till it hears*
> *Water, water at hand,*
> *When a man will dig his nails*
> *In his breast, and drink the blood*
> *Already that clots and stales*
> *Ere his tongue can tip its flood."*

His mind had gone back to infancy. He thought that I was his mother, and came to me to be nursed.

But when he came near, he recognised me and crawled away again, hurriedly, like a wounded animal trying to escape from the hunter. . .

Most of the time, when we have energy to talk at all, we discuss how to get more H. and C. The C. has been finished long ago. It's no good without the H. We could go to Germany and get it; or even to London, but something keeps us from decision.

I, of course, know what it is. It is necessary for me to undergo these torments that I may be purified completely from the flesh.

ALEISTER CROWLEY

But Peter doesn't understand at all. He blames me bitterly. We go over the whole thing again and again. Every incident since we met is taken in turn as the cause of our misery.

Sometimes his brutal lust revives in his mind. He thinks I am a vampire sent from Hell to destroy him; and he gloats over the idea. I cannot make him understand that I am the woman clothed with the sun. When he gets those ideas, they arouse similar thoughts in me. But they are only thoughts.

I am afraid of him. He might shoot me in a mad fit. He has got a target pistol, a very old one with long, thin bullets, and carries it about all the time. He never mentions the Germans now. He talks about a gang of hypnotists that have got hold of him, and put evil thoughts in his mind. He says that if he could shoot one of them it would break the spell. He tells me not to look at him as I do; but I have to be on the watch lest he should attack me.

Then he mixes up my hypnotic gaze with ideas of passion. He keeps on repeating:—

> *"Steadily stares and squarely,*
> *Nor needs to fondle and wheedle*
> *Her slave agasp for a kiss,*
> *Hers whose horror is his*
> *That knows that viper womb,*
> *Speckled and barred with black*
> *On its rusty amber scales,*
> *Is his tomb—*
> *The straining, groaning rack*
> *On which he wails—he wails!"*

He takes an acute delight in the intensity of his suffering. He is wildly proud to think that he has been singled out to undergo more atrocious torments than had ever been conceived of before.

He sees me as the principal instrument of the torture, and loves me with perverse diabolical lust for that reason, yet the whole thing is a delusion on his part, or else it is a necessary consequence of his changing into the Dragon.

It is only natural that there should be strange incidents in a case of that sort, especially as it never happened before. It is wonderful and terrible to be unique. But, of course, he is not really unique in the way that I am. . .

WE HAVE LIGHTED A HUGE fire in the billiard-room. We sleep there so far as we sleep at all. We got the waiter to bring down blankets and quilts from the bedroom, and he leaves the food on the table.

But fires are no good. The cold comes from inside us. We sit in front of the blaze, roasting our hands and faces; but it makes no difference. We shiver.

We try to sing like soldiers round a camp fire, but the only words that come are the appropriate ones. That poem has obsessed us. It fills our souls to the exclusion of everything else except the thirst.

> "*Every separate bone*
> *Cold, an incarnate groan*
> *Distilled from the icy sperm*
> *Of Hell's implacable worm.*"
> *We repeated them over and over. . .*

I don't know how one thing ever turns into another. We are living in an eternity of damnation. It is a mystery how we ever get from the fire to the table or the two big Chesterfields. Every action is a separate agony rising to a climax which never comes. There is no possibility of accomplishment or of peace.

> "*Every separate nerve*
> *Awake and alert, on a curve*
> *Whose asymptote's name is 'never'*
> *In a hyperbolic 'forever!'*"

I don't know what some of the words mean. But there is a fascination about them. They give the idea of something without limit. Death has become impossible, because death is definite. Nothing can really ever happen. I am in a perpetual state of pain. Everything is equally anguish. I suppose one state changes into another to prevent the edge being taken off the suffering. It would be incredibly blissful if one could experience something new, however abominable. The man that wrote that poem has left out nothing. Everything that comes into my mind is no more than an echo of his groans.

> "*Body and soul alike*
> *Traitors turned black-hearted,*

> *Seeking a place to strike*
> *In a victim already attuned*
> *To one vast chord of wound."*

The rhythm of the poem, apart from the words, suggests this *moto perpetuo* vibration. Yet the nervous irritability tends to exhaust itself as such. It is so unendurable; the only escape seems to be if one could transform it into action. The poison filters through into the blood. I am itching to do something horrible and insane.

> *"Every drop of the river*
> *Of blood aflame and a-quiver*
> *With poison secret and sour—*
> *With a sudden twitch at the last*
> *Like certain jagged daggers."*

When Peter crosses the room, I see him

> *"With blood-shot eyes dull-glassed*
> *The screaming Malay staggers*
> *Through his village aghast."*

It is natural and inevitable that he should murder me. I wish he were not so weak. Anything to end it all.

The medical books said that if one didn't die outright from abstention, the craving would slowly wear off. I think Peter is already a little stronger. But I am so young to die! He complains constantly of vermin under his skin. He says he could bear that; but the idea of being driven mad by the hypnotists is more than any man can be expected to stand. . .

I FELT I SHOULD SCREAM if I went on a moment longer; and by scream I don't mean just an ordinary scream, I mean that I should scream and scream and scream and never stop.

The wind is howling like that. The summer has died suddenly— without a warning, and the world is screaming in agony. It is only the echo of the wailing for my own lost soul. The angels never come to me now. Have I forfeited my position? I am conscious of nothing but this tearing, stabbing, gnawing pain, this restless raging trembling of the body, this malignant groping of a mad surgeon in the open wound of my soul.

I am so bitter, bitter cold. Yet I can't stand the room. Peter is lying helplessly on the couch. He follows me about with his eyes. He seems to be afraid that he will be caught out in something. It's like it was when we had dope. Though we knew we were taking it, offering it to each other openly, yet whenever we took it ourselves, we were afraid lest the other should know.

I think he has something that he wants to hide away, and is trying to get me out of the room so that I shan't know where he has put it.

Well, I don't care, I'm not interested in his private affairs. I'll go out and give him a chance. I'll hide this book in the magic room, if I have strength to get there. The old man might be able to give me some elixir. I wouldn't mind if it killed my body; if my spirit were free I could fulfil my destiny. . .

Just as I closed the book I heard an answering shot. It must have been the door, for the old man has come in. He has a marvellous light in his eyes, and he radiates rainbow colours throughout the world. I understand that my ordeal is over. He stands smiling and points downwards. I think he wants me to go back to the billiard-room. Perhaps there is someone waiting for me; someone to take me away to fulfil my destiny. I know now what it was that I thought was a shot, or a door closing. It was really both of these things in a mystical sense; for I know now who the old man is, and that he is the father of the Messiah. . .

VII

The Final Plunge

Sunday

The church bells tell me the day. I have been through another terrible ordeal. I don't know how long ago since I came down from the north tower. The noise was really a shot. I found Peter on the floor with the pistol by his side, and blood pouring from a wound in his breast.

I understood immediately what I had to do. It was impossible to send for a doctor. The scandal of the suicide would make life impossible ever after, and he would immediately discover that it was due to dope. The burden must be on my own shoulders. I must nurse my boy back to life.

I remember that I had been too weak to walk down from the north tower. I climbed to the balustrades and gasped, and slid myself, sitting, from step to step. I was almost blind, too. My eyes seemed unable to focus on anything.

But the moment I saw what had happened, my strength came back to me, at least, not my strength but the strength of nature. It flowed through me like the wind blowing through a flimsy ragged curtain.

The cartridges were very old, and the powder must have lost its strength; for the bullet turned on his breast bone and ran round the ribs. It was really a trifling wound; but he was so weak that he might have died from loss of blood. I got some water, and washed the wounds, and bound them up as best I could. When the waiter came, I sent him for proper things from the chemist, and some invalid food. For the first time I was glad of the war. My Red-Cross training made all the difference.

There was a little fever, due to his intense weakness, and occasionally he had delirium. The obsession of the poem still enthralled him. While I was dressing the wounds he said feebly and dreamily:—

> *"She it is, she, that found me*
> *In the morphia honeymoon;*
> *With silk and steel she bound me;*

> *In her poisonous milk she drowned me,*
> *Even now her arms surround me."*

"Yes," I said, "but it's your wife who loves you and is going to nurse you through this trouble, and we're going to live happy ever afterwards."

He smiled very faintly and sweetly and dozed off. . .

Wednesday

I count the days now. We are having an Indian summer. Nature is lovely. I go out for little walks when Peter is asleep.

Friday

There have been no complications, or I should have had to get a doctor in at whatever risk. What troubles me is that as he gets stronger, the delusions of persecution have begun to return. I know now how deeply I was myself obsessed by ideas of grandeur, and how my need to be a mother determined their form.

But is it a delusion that I should be thinking constantly of Basil? I seem to hear him saying that I was cured from the moment that I forgot myself altogether in the absorption of my love for Peter; the work of bringing him back to life.

And now that I have ceased to look at myself and feel for myself, I have become able to see him and feel for him with absolute clearness. There is not the slightest possibility of error.

All the time he has been able to realise dimly that he was slipping down the dark slope to insanity. He has mixed it all up with the idea of me. He had begun to identify me with the phantom of murderous madness which he recognised as destroying him. A look of trouble comes into his face every now and then; and he begins to repeat plaintively in a puzzled voice with his eyes fixed on mine:—

> *"Know you now why her eyes*
> *So fearfully glaze, beholding*
> *Terrors and infamies*
> *Like filthy flowers unfolding?*
> *Laughter widowed of ease,*
> *Agony barred from sadness,*
> *Death defeated of peace,*
> *Is she not madness?"*

Over and over again he said it, and over and over again I told him the answer. I had indeed been a personification of the seductress, of the destroying angel. But it had been a nightmare. I had awakened, and he must awake.

But he saw not me anymore, but his ideal enveloping me congealed into my form. No matter what I said, his fixed idea became constantly stronger as his physical strength came back.

> *"She waits for me, lazily leering,*
> *As moon goes murdering moon;*
> *The moon of her triumph is nearing;*
> *She will have me wholly soon."*

The rhythm of the poem was still in my own blood; but it seemed to have worked itself out into another channel. I had forgotten the acute personal anguish of the earlier part of the poem. I could not even remember the lines anymore. I was wholly occupied by the last two paragraphs where the subject changes so suddenly.

I began to realise what my governess used to call *Weltschmertz*; the universal sorrow wherein "Creation groaneth and travaileth until now."

I understood Basil's wish that we should undertake the fearful experiment which had brought us to such extremity. My insanity had been the result of my selfish vanity. I was not singled out for a unique destiny. The realisation of my own suffering had led me to understand that everyone else was in the same boat. I could see even the false note of the contempt of the poet for those who had not experienced his own sublimity of horror.

> *"And you, you puritan others,*
> *Who have missed the morphia craving,*
> *Cry scorn if I call you brothers,*
> *Curl lip at my maniac raving,*
> *Fools, seven times beguiled,*
> *You have not known her? Well!*
> *There was never a need she smiled*
> *To harry you into hell!"*

The pride of Satan, in the deepness of damnation, has a fall when he realises that others are in a same calamity—without having been at such perverse pains to get there. He only attains the truth when he becomes wholly impersonal, in the final paragraph.

> *"Morphia is but one*
> *Spark of its secular fire.*
> *She is the single sun—*
> *Type of all desire!*
> *All that you would you are—*
> *And that is the crown of a craving.*
> *You are slaves of the wormwood star.*
> *Analysed, reason is raving.*
> *Feeling, examined, is pain.*
> *What heaven were to hope for a doubt of it!*
> *Life is anguish, insane;*
> *And death is—not a way out of it!"*

I saw that all feeling, however it might seem to casual scrutiny, must be of the nature of pain, because it implied duality and imperfection; and that the nature of thought of whatever kind, must ultimately be insanity, because it expresses the relations between things, and never the things in themselves.

It became evident that the sorrow of the Universe was caused by the desire of manifestation, and that death could not do more than suppress one form of existence in favour of another. Of course, the *impasse* is complete. There seems to be no solution of the problem. It is a vicious circle.

At the same time, by acquiescence in actuality, the insane insistence on one's individual anguish is abated. Sympathy with universal suffering brings one into a certain sombre serenity. It does not show us the way of escape, if such there be, but at least it makes the idea of escape thinkable. As long as one is trying to get out of the burning theatre for one's own sake, the panic makes concerted action impossible. "Every man for himself and the devil take the hindmost" is not the kind of order that is likely to secure victory. It does not even ensure the safety of anyone man.

How quickly I had recovered my own well-being when I was forced to forget about it!

Peter is still desperately striving to save himself. "He that loveth his life shall lose it." I must dedicate my miraculously restored faculties to his salvation. Only I don't see how to set to work.

If only Basil were here. He would know. He has worked out the technique. All I can do is to love and labour blindly. After all, there must have been angels looking after me in some sense which I don't pretend to understand. Why should they not be even more vigilant on his behalf?

I am only a foolish flapper not worth throwing into the waste-paper basket. He is a splendid man with a glorious past and endless possibilities for the future. It won't do to let him go under; and they must know that.

I won't trouble my silly head about it, I'll keep on loving and trusting.

October 26

I have forgotten about my diary all this time. I have been too busy with Peter. My memory is frightfully bad. I don't seem able to fix things at all. Peter got stronger all the time. He is practically quite well now, and took me out and taught me to shoot pheasants this morning. It was terribly exciting. I actually got one, my very first day. I got a man and wife and their daughter to come in and do for us, so we're really very comfortable, in a countrified way. I couldn't have anyone while Peter was raving.

The waiter from the inn is a Swiss. He kept his mouth shut; and I saw to it that he had no reason to regret the policy.

What I can't remember is how Peter began to get better: mentally, I mean. I ought to have kept this diary properly, I know, but as he improved, he took up more and more of my time, and then I had to do so many things to have things ready for him when he was able to get up.

And now, I can't think how it came about; but I believe the first sign of improvement was that the poem dropped out. He began to talk naturally about ordinary affairs. He was terribly weak and ill, and it had scared him. He was like an ordinary convalescent, I suppose—signs of returning interests in the affairs of life. I had ceased to be a symbol. I was just his nurse.

Part of the time he had forgotten who I was. He was back in the base hospital; the time they winged him.

Our honeymoon and its sequel is mostly blotted out. I can't say how much he knows. He says things sometimes which make me think it's quite a lot.

And then again, other things which make me think he doesn't even remember that I am his wife. This morning, for instance, he said: "I must go to London to see about a settlement I'm making in case I ever get married."

And then, not half an hour afterwards, he referred to an incident of our life in Capri. I am careful not to contradict him or alarm him about the state of his mind, but it's very difficult to know what to do. There are so many things I forget myself.

"How did we get down here?" Then again, "Where is Alice?" The name keeps on popping up, and yet I don't know anyone at all intimately or importantly with that name.

I had forgotten this diary—I found it by accident and immediately began to read it through to refresh my memory.

Most of the handwriting is unreadable. I puzzled and puzzled before I could make out the words. And then when I got the words, they were so senseless. I can't believe that all that happened to me. Some of it came back slowly; curiously, the unimportant things came first.

I was amazed to find that Mabel Black was dead. I wrote her a letter only yesterday. Poor old girl!

The part, too, about Dr. McCall. I could swear quite honestly that never happened. And yet it must have; for I found scraps of the dress in the cushions of the blue Chesterfield chewed to a pulp. . .

October 27

We have been shooting again; but it was cold and damp. We were neither of us interested and we were too weary to walk. Peter said nothing; but all the time I can feel how disgusted he is. We're so rottenly let down. This afternoon I picked up that article of Sieveking's. He is talking about the sensation of walking after a flight.

> "One has an infinitely distressing sensation of being clamped down to the ground—manacled by the very grass-blades!"

We have been living so long at such a terrific bat, life is intolerable on any other terms.

I don't feel any physical need of drugs anymore. On the contrary, I feel a delightful bodily buoyancy at having got free. It's an extraordinary thing, too, how normal appetite has returned. We've been eating five meals a day, one feeding like forty instead of Wordsworth's forty feeding like one. We had been starving ourselves for months, and we had to make up for it. The most delicious sensation of all is the re-birth of healthy human love. Spring coming back to the earth!

But it doesn't satisfy, even so. The intervals between one's emotions are appallingly long. I think drugs intensify the high lights for one thing; but for another, and this is really more important, they fit up the interstices of shadow.

It's hard, I imagine, in the ordinary way, to come off one's honeymoon back into regular life. I often wonder how a poet feels when he isn't absorbed in the ecstasy of inspiration. That may be why so may of them go off the deep end, the interstices bore them.

I may as well face the facts. We've had a pretty narrow escape. We've got out of the mess more by good luck than by good judgment. But if it weren't for that, I'm not sure that we shouldn't be inclined to take another chance. Of course, as things are, it's quite out of the question. It may be not the least of our luck that the lesson was so severe as it was.

October 30

The fact is, we're too young. We don't think of the obvious thing. Of course, we're bored stiff down here with the leaves all fallen, and the mist steaming up from the lake and swamping the house like a gas attack. We ought to be in London, and do the theatres, and look up a few of the old crowd. I ought really to see Maisie Jacobs and tell her how grateful I am.

Funny, I can't think what I have to be grateful about. But luckily it's in the diary.

Peter has got more silent and morose everyday, like the weather. He seems to have something on his mind. I wish he'd tell me what it is. . .

He brightened up at dinner. "Let's go to town tomorrow, Lou," he said. "We'll just take small bags. We needn't be away more than two or three days. What we need is a few decent meals in a restaurant, and take in a show or two, and perhaps get a bunch down here to liven us up a bit. The birds are pretty good this year after all."

October 31

It only struck us when we got into the train that we couldn't possibly go to the Savoy with no clothes. Peter thought it would be a joke to go round to that place of ours in Greek Street.

It certainly will be amusing to look at it from the new point of view. He will take the bags on there, while I get one or two nice people together. We ought to give a little dinner to celebrate.

Here's London at last. I'll lock this up in my dressing case. . .

Later—I can pocket the creature's insolence at the price. It must have been on my mind. The first address I gave to the chauffeur was McCall's. He looked shocked when I was announced.

"My dear Lady Pendragon," he almost shouted at me very fast. "I know you'll forgive me. I'm frightfully busy this afternoon."

(There wasn't a soul in his waiting-room.)

"If you'll allow me, I think this is what you want, and I hope you will come and see me again soon. Always at your service, dear Lady Pendragon."

While he was talking he half emptied a ten-gramme bottle into a piece of paper, twisted it up like a grocer, thrust it almost rudely into my hand, and bowed me out volubly and effusively into the street.

I went faint all over. The taxi was still there. I called him, and drove to Mme. Daubignac's. I don't know why, but I felt that I needed a treatment. I was trembling all over. It was worse when I went in: for I could see that she was as shocked as McCall.

Then I got in front of a glass. How is it that in all the times I've looked at myself in these months I've never seen what they see in a second?

Good God! it's too awful to talk about. My face is drawn and haggard and pale and wrinkled. I might be sixty. Well, what do I care? I've had three beautiful sniffs!

Madame dolled me up as well as she could. Already I looked much better, and I felt superb.

Peter was out when I got to Greek Street; so I opened my dressing case and wrote this up, and had a few more sniffs. The only trouble before was simply our own foolishness. We didn't take ordinary precautions. This time we're going to watch out. . .

Peter is back, furious. His pedlar has been pinched. So I came to the rescue.

"We'll go out to dinner and make a night of it."

November 6

We've arranged for a regular supply; but the hellish thing is that the stuff doesn't work anymore. We get the insomnia and those things all right, but we can't get any fun out of it. We've tried all sorts of dodges. It's no good. Being with it simply dulls the pain of being without. That's the best I can say. What are we to do?

(There are three more entries in this diary; but they are illegible, quite beyond conjecture. The only words decipherable are "sleep" near the beginning of the first; the name "Basil" in the second; and the word "poison" in the third.)

BOOK III
PURGATORIO

(NOTE.—The Abbey of Thelema at "Telepylus" is a real place. It and its customs and members, with the surrounding scenery, are accurately described. The training there given is suited to all conditions of spiritual distress, and for the discovery and development of the "True Will" of any person. Those interested are invited to communicate with the author of this book.)

I

King Lamus Intervenes

It is only three months ago; but it seems a lifetime. My memory is now very good, and I remember more details of the past everyday. I am writing this account of the past three months, partly because my best friend tells me that it will strengthen it if I exercise it by putting down what has occurred in sequence. And you know, even a month ago, I couldn't have recalled anything at all with regard to certain periods.

My friend tells me that memory fails me in part because nature mercifully wishes to hide from us things which are painful. The spider-web of protective forgetfulness is woven over the mouth of the cave which conceals the raw head and bloody bones of our misfortunes.

"But the greatest men," says King Lamus, "are those that refuse to be treated like squalling children, who insist on facing reality in every form, and tear off ruthlessly the bandages from their own wounds."

But I have to think very hard to write down the incidents of the dinner at the Wisteria when Lou and I had made up our minds to end our lives.

I had got some prussic acid from the chemist's more than a week before. It took us that time to make up our minds to get up and to acquire Dutch courage enough to take the plunge.

Some instinct prevented us dropping out of existence in a place like those lodgings in Greek Street. When all one's moral sense is gone, there remains a racial instinct in men and women of good blood which tells them, like Macbeth and Brutus, to die positively and not negatively.

I believe it was this alone that dragged us up from the dirty bed from which we had not moved for weeks, sunk in a state which was neither sleep nor waking.

It was by a gigantic effort that I got up and put some clothes on, and went out and got shaved. Nothing but excitement and the idea of death enabled me to do it. I found the same thing in the war; and so did lots of men.

It seems as if the soul is tired of the body, and welcomes the chance to be done with it once and for all. But it wants to offer itself gallantly in a flight or a charge. It objects to dying in a ditch passively. I am sure that nothing less would have got us up from that fœtid stupor.

We had some champagne before starting, and then tottered giddily over the unfamiliar streets. There was something faintly attractive about the bustle of humanity. There was a momentary regret about leaving it. Yet we had already left it so long, so long ago, in every intelligible sense of the word. We should, I suppose, have been classed as human beings by statisticians, but surely by nobody else. We could never return to their midst. And even in the midst of our wretchedness, we felt a repulsion of contempt for the ruck of humanity which made us content to widen the gap between them and ourselves. Why preserve the outward semblance of these futile insects? Even their happiness disgusted us; it was so stupidly shallow.

We could see that the people of the Wisteria were shocked at our appearance. The *maitre d'hotel* bustled over and made some sympathetic remarks about our not having been there for a long time. I told him that we had both been very ill; and then Lou put in, in a hollow voice:—

"We shall be better tonight."

Her intonation was so sinister that the man almost jumped. I was afraid for the moment that everything would be spoilt, but I saved the situation by some silly joking remark. However, I could see that he was very uncomfortable and glad to get away from our table.

We had ordered a wonderful dinner; but, of course, we couldn't eat anything. The mockery of having all those expensive dishes brought, one after the other, and taken away again untouched, was irritating at first, and then it began to be amusing. I vaguely remember something in history about funeral feasts. It seemed singularly appropriate to start west in such conditions.

Yes, we, were participating in some weird ceremony such as delighted the ancient Egyptians. The thought even came to my mind that we had already died, that this was our mocking welcome to Hades, the offering of dishes of which we were unable to partake. And yet, between us and the unknown was the act of drinking the contents of the little bottle in my waistcoat pocket.

It was nearly an hour and a half since we had some heroin, and already the loathsome fumes of abstention were suffocating us. We had as much as our bodies could tolerate. We didn't want anymore actively. It would do us no good to take more, but nature had already begun her process of eliminating the poison.

In the body, morphine and heroin become oxydised, and it is the resulting poisons, not the drugs themselves, that are responsible for the appalling effects. Thus the body begins to give off these products through the secretions; therefore the nose begins to run; there are prolonged foul sweats; there is a smell and a taste which cannot be called unpleasant even, it can only be called abominable in the proper sense of that word: that which is repugnant to man. It is so detestable as to be unendurable. One might get relief by cleaning one's teeth or by having a Turkish bath, but the energy to do such things is lacking.

But if you take a fresh dose of the drug, it puts a temporary stop to the efforts of nature to eliminate it. That is why it is such a vicious circle; and these premonitory symptoms of abstinence are merely the fœtor of the foul breath of the dragon who is on his way to crunch you.

If you make up your mind to endure the disgusting symptoms, the demon soon proceeds to more serious measures.

Lou has explained in her diary more or less what these are. But even with the help of the poet, one cannot give any idea of what it is like. For example, the question of cold. The reader thinks at once of the cold of winter. If he has travelled a little and has some imagination, he may think of the chill spells of fever. But neither of these give much idea of the nature of the cold produced by abstinence.

Our poet, whoever he is (his name is not given in the magazine) certainly succeeds in conveying to his reader the truth, that is, provided his reader already knows it. I can't imagine how it would strike anyone who had not experienced it. For he conveys his meaning, so to speak, in spite of the words. This business of expression is very curious.

How could one describe, say, a love affair to a person who had never had one or imagined one? All expression does is to wake up in the reader the impressions in his own experience which are otherwise dormant. And he will interpret what is said or written only in terms of that experience.

Lamus said the other day that he had given up trying to communicate the results of his researches to people. They couldn't even be trusted to read words of one syllable, though they might have taken the best degrees in Humane Letters at Oxford. For example, he would write, "Do *what* thou wilt" to somebody, and would be attacked by return of post for having written "Do *as* thou wilt."

Everyone interprets everything in terms of his own experience. If you say anything which does not touch a precisely similar spot in another man's brain, he either misunderstands you, or doesn't understand you at all.

I am therefore extremely depressed by the obligation under which King Lamus has put me to write this section, with the avowed object of instructing the world in the methods of overcoming the craving for drugs.

He admits frankly that he feels it quite useless to do it himself, for the very reason that he is so abnormal a man. He even distrusts me, on the ground that he has had so much influence on my life and thought.

"Even a mediocrity like yourself, Sir Peter," he said to me the other day, "dull as you are, cannot be trusted in my neighbourhood. Your brain unconsciously soaks up the highly charged particles of my atmosphere. And before you know where you are, instead of expressing yourself— what little self you have to express—you will be repeating, in a debased currency, the words of wisdom that from time to time have dropped from my refined lips."

There was a time when I should have resented a remark like that. If I don't do so now, it isn't because I've lost my manhood, it isn't because I feel such gratitude to the man who pulled me through; the reason is that I have learned what he means when he talks like that. He has completely killed out in himself the idea of himself. He takes no credit for his marvellous qualities, and has even got over kicking himself for his weaknesses. And so he says the most serious things in the language of absurdity and irony. And when he talks in a serious strain, his language merely accentuates the prodigious sense of humour which, as he says himself, saves him from going insane with horror at the mess into which humanity has got itself. Just as the Roman Empire began to break down when it became universal, when it was so large that no individual mind could grasp the problems which it postulated, so today, the spread of vulgar education and the development of facilities for transport have got ahead of the possibilities of the best minds. The increase of knowledge has forced the thinker to specialise, with the result that there is nobody capable to deal with civilisation as a whole.

We are playing a game of chess in which nobody can see more than two or three squares at once, and so it has become impossible to form a coherent plan.

King Lamus is trying to train a number of selected people to act as a sort of brain for the world in its present state of cerebral collapse. He is teaching them to co-ordinate the facts in a higher synthesis. The suggestion is that of his old teacher, Prof. Henry Maudsley, with whom he studied insanity. Herbert Spencer, too, had a similar idea. But King Lamus is the first to endeavour to make a practical effort to embody this conception in a practical way.

I seem to have wandered a long way from our farewell dinner party; but my mind is still unable to concentrate as it should. Heroin and cocaine enable one to attain a high degree of concentration artificially, and this has to be paid for by a long period of reaction in which one cannot fix one's mind on a subject at all. I am very much better than I was, but I get impatient at times. It is so tedious to build oneself up on biological lines, especially when one knows that a single dose of heroin or even morphine would make one instantly the equal of the greatest minds in the world.

We had decided to take the prussic acid in our coffee. I do not think we were afraid of death; life had become such an infinitely boring alternation between a period of stimulation which failed to stimulate and of depression which hardly even depressed.

There was no object in going on. It was simply not worth while. On the other hand, there was a certain hesitation about stopping because of the effort required. We felt that even to die required energy. We tried to supply this with Dutch courage, and we even succeeded in producing a sort of hilarity. We never had a moment's doubt about carrying out our programme.

The waiter brought two Pêches Melba; and as he retired we found that King Lamus was standing at our table.

"Do what thou wilt shall be the whole of the Law," came his calm voice.

A sudden flush of hostility suffused my face.

"We've been doing it," I answered with a sort of surly anger, "and I suppose the great psychologist can see what's come of it."

He shook his head very sadly; and sat down without being invited on the chair opposite to us.

"I'm afraid not," he said. "I'll explain what I mean on a more convenient occasion. I can see you want to get rid of me; but I know you won't refuse to help a man out when he's in trouble like I am."

Lou was all sympathy and tenderness at once; and even in the state in which I was, I was aware of a feeble movement of hate both towards her and him. The fact is that the man's mere presence acted as a powerful stimulant.

"It's only a trifle," he said, with a curious smile, "just a little literary difficulty in which I find myself. I was hoping you might remember my giving you a poem to read a little while ago."

His tone was airy and supercilious; but yet there was an undercurrent of earnestness in his voice which compelled the attention.

Lou nodded easily enough; but I could see that in her heart, no less than in mine, an arrow had struck, charged with acid venom. The reference recalled the dreadful days at Barley Grange; and even the Bottomless Pit of Nothingness into which we had since fallen seemed less outrageous than the lake of fire through which we had passed.

The poem rang through my brain, snatches of the anthem of the damned.

His elbows were upon the table, his head between his hands; he watched us intently for a few moments.

"I want to quote that poem in something I'm writing," he explained, "and can you tell me the last line of it?"

Lou answered mechanically, as if he had pressed a button:—

"Death is not a way out of it!"

"Thank you," he said. "It's a great help to me that you should have been able to remember."

Something in his tone caught my imagination vividly. His eyes burnt through me. I began to wonder whether there were any truth in what was said about the diabolical powers of the man.

Could he have divined the reason for our coming to the café? I had the absolute certainty that he knew all about it, though it was humanly impossible that he should.

"A very strange theory, that about death," he said. "I wonder if there's anything in it. It would really be too easy if we could get out of our troubles in so simple a fashion. It has always seemed to me that nothing can ever be destroyed. The problems of life are really put together ingeniously in order to baffle one, like a chess problem. We can't untie a real knot in a closed piece of string without the aid of the fourth dimension; but we can disentangle the complexities caused by dipping the string in water—and such things," he added, with an almost malicious gravity in his tone.

I knew what he meant.

"It might very well be," he continued, "that when we fail to solve

ALEISTER CROWLEY

the puzzles of life, they remain with us. We have to do them sooner or later; and it seems reasonable to suppose that the problems of life ought to be solved during life, while we have to our hands the apparatus in which they arose. We might find that after death the problems were unaltered, but that we were impotent to deal with them. Did you ever meet anyone that had been indiscreet about taking drugs? Presumably not. Well, take my word for it, those people get into a state which is in many ways very like death. And the tragic thing about the situation is this; that they started taking the drugs because life, in one way or another, was one too many for them. And what is the result? The drugs have not in the least relieved the monotony of life or whatever their trouble was, and yet they have got into a state very like that of death, in which they are impotent to struggle. No, we must conquer life by living it to the full, and then we can go to meet death with a certain prestige. We can face that adventure as we've faced the others."

The personality of the man radiated energy. The momentary contact with his mind had destroyed the current of thought which had been obsessing ours. Yet it was a fearful pang to be torn away from the fixed idea which had imposed itself as the necessary conclusion of a course of thought and action extending over so long a period.

I can imagine a man reprieved at the foot of a scaffold experiencing an acute annoyance at being wrenched away from the logical outcome of his tendencies.

"Cowards die many times before their death." And those who have decided whether with their will or against it, to put an end to their lives, must resent interference. As Schopenhauer says, the will to die is inherent in all of us, as much as the will to live.

I remember a lot of fellows in the trenches saying that they dreaded being sent to the base; they would rather have it over than take a temporary respite. Life had ceased to be precious. They had become accustomed to face death, and had acquired a fear of life of just the same quality as the fear of death that they had had at first. Life had become the unknown, the uncertain, the dreadful.

A hot, fierce wave of annoyance went through me like a flush of fever.

"Damn the fellow," I muttered, "why must he always butt in like this?"

And then I noticed that Lou had taken the little bottle from my waistcoat pocket, and handed it to King Lamus.

"I believe you're right, Basil," she said. "But if you take that bottle away from us, the responsibility lies with you."

"Is that calculated to frighten me?" he answered smiling, and rose to his feet. He dropped the bottle to the ground, and stamped his heel deliberately on it.

"Now," he said, "let's get down to business," resuming his seat.

The fumes of the acid enveloped the table.

"Hydrocyanic acid," he remarked, "is an excellent pick-me-up when absorbed into the system in this diluted form, but to take it in large doses is an indiscretion."

There is no doubt that the man had a tendency to what in a woman is called nagging. He constantly used the word "indiscretion" as if it were a weapon.

We both winced.

"You accept me," he went on, "as responsible for getting you out of this mess?"

There was nothing else to do. It went against the grain. However, I blurted out something about being grateful.

"You needn't talk that nonsense," he retorted severely. "It's my business to help people to do their wills. The gratitude is on my side. I want you to understand from the beginning that you are helping me to justify my existence by allowing me to do what I can to straighten out this tangle. But my conditions are that you give me a fair chance by doing what I say."

He did not even wait for acquiescence.

"You are a bit excited nervously," he went on. "Depression is only another form of excitement. It means a variation from normal tone. So when you have had your coffee, I will join you in a cup, we will go around to my studio and try what some of those tablets will do. Then, where are you living?"

We told him we had gone back to our old place in Greek Street.

"Hardly a salubrious neighbourhood," he remarked. "I think we ought to celebrate the occasion by making a night of it in my studio, and tomorrow morning we must see about getting you some decent rooms."

I remembered that our supply of heroin was in Greek Street.

"You know, Lamus," I stammered, "I'm ashamed to admit it, but we really can't get on without H. We tried—in fact, once we got clean away—but we couldn't possibly go through that again."

"Nothing to be ashamed of, my dear man," returned our physician. "You can't get on without eating. That's no reason for stopping. All I ask you to do is to do it sensibly."

"Then you won't cut us off?" put in Lou.

"Certainly not, why should I? You take as much as you want, and when you want, and how you want. That's no business of mine. My business is to remove the want. You say you cured yourselves, but you didn't. You only cut off the drug; the want remained. And as soon as the opportunity for starting again arrived, you started again. Perhaps, in fact, you made the opportunity."

The man was really uncanny. I must confess it put me off, being hit everytime like that when I wasn't expecting it. But Lou took it in quite a different way. She was glad to be so thoroughly understood. She clapped her hands. I was amazed. It was the first time in months that I had ever seen her make the slightest movement that wasn't absolutely necessary.

"You're quite right," she said. "We said nothing to each other about it, and I hadn't the slightest conscious intention of doing what I did. But the moment I got to London I drove to the place where I knew I could get heroin. And when I got back, I found that Peter had been out trying to find the man who had sold him the cocaine before. I assure you it wasn't deliberate."

"That's exactly the trouble," retorted Lamus. "It leads you by the nose, and prevents your doing your will. I remember once when I was making experiments with it myself, how I would go out with the intention of keeping away from the stuff all day, and how, without my knowing it, I took advantage of all sorts of little incidents that cropped up to get back to the studio some hours before I had intended. I found myself out at once, of course, having learnt some of the tricks of the mind. And I sat and watched myself finding excuses for starting in. One gets into an absolutely morbid state, in which everything that happens has some bearing on the question, 'Shall I or shall I not take it?'; and one gets so pleased with oneself for saying 'no' so often that one is tempted to reward oneself by saying 'yes' just once. I can promise you a very interesting time watching your minds and spotting all the little dodges. The great thing I want you to remember is that you have to learn to take pleasure in what is really the most pleasurable thing in the world— introspection. You have got to find amusement in observing the details of the discomfort of being without the drug. And I don't want you to overdo it, either. When the discomfort becomes so acute that you can't enjoy it properly, then is the time to take a small dose and notice the effects. I hope, by the way, you've been a good little girl and kept that magical diary."

Lou was astonishingly pleased to be able to say "yes."

"Some of it's done very fully," she said, "but you know there were days and weeks when I couldn't think, I couldn't move. Life was a perpetual struggle to get back to——" she hesitated for a word, and then ended with a pained little laugh, "oh, to anywhere."

King Lamus nodded gravely. We had finished our coffee.

"Now," said he, "to business," and led the way to the door.

I stayed behind for a moment to pay the bill. There was still a faint smell of bitter almond in the air. It reminded me of how the dinner might have ended, and I trembled all over like a man in an ague fit.

What was happening in me? Had I suddenly fallen in love with life, or had I simply become aware of the fear of death?

When we reached the fresh air, I knew it was the former. Lamus had made me feel. The effect of the drug had been to kill all feeling in me. My impulse to kill myself had not been so wholly negative as I had thought. It was a positive craving for what I supposed to be the anæsthesia of death. The pain of life had been too much to endure, and the influence of King Lamus had been to brace me to meet life face to face, whatever it might have in store, and conquer it.

I did not fear death anymore than I had done in the old days, flying over the lines. I didn't mind dying at all; but I wanted to die fighting.

Lou was talking quite briskly to King Lamus on the steps of the restaurant while the commissionaire called a taxi. And I realised too that I loved her, that she was worth fighting to recover, that I had been a cad to drag her down with me. I understood my jealousy of King Lamus. His colossal strength, even his callousness about women, attracted them. The man himself had made me sit up and match myself against him.

I wasn't going to have Lou see me constantly at a disadvantage.

We drove around to the studio.

The atmosphere invigorated us. I got an entirely new point of view about Lala. Before, she had seemed to me little more than part of the furniture, but tonight she was the resident spirit of the place. She informed it, gave it a meaning. The intimacy between her and her master was not in anyway personal. She was the medium by which his thoughts became perceptible.

The fantastic appointments of the studio were projections in terms of material substances of his mind interpreted through her consciousness. I had an uncanny feeling that if it were not for her, King Lamus would be invisible.

In his mind, there was no difference between any two things, but through her mediation he was able to pretend that there was.

The studio was divided into several parts by arrangements of curtains. There was a perpetual soft noise of laughter, singing, and dancing; interrupted only by periods of intense silence which was somehow more significant than the sound. The firelight threw doubtful shadow pictures upon the glass roof; and from time to time figures moved with intimate softness through the dark corners and out into the courtyard. These swathed and muffled forms possessed an uncanny quality of unreality.

The studio was full of subtle incense. No smoke was visible; it was as if the atmosphere had somehow been impregnated with it.

Our little party fell very silent. He had given Lou and myself some tablets which had the effect of silencing the nervous restlessness which had begun to seize us after even so short an abstinence from heroin.

"I want you to hang on a little," explained our host. "The sting of abstinence will make the indulgence worth while. You have noticed, I am sure, that the vast majority of doses fail to produce any definite active effect."

It was quite true. We had been cursing the drug for its failure to reproduce the original sensations. We had tried to overcome the difficulty by increasing the quantity. But a time had come when we were immune to its action; horridly aware of its absence, without obtaining any satisfaction from its presence.

"That stuff I have given you," Lamus explained, "dilutes your symptoms, and enables you to some extent to bear the discomfort. I want you to take advantage of the fact to watch your discomfort as if it were somebody else. When you find that you can enjoy this instead of blindly rushing to heroin for relief, you will already have gone a long way in the direction of acquiring mental control."

Several times during the night Lala intervened vigorously in such a way that it was impossible for us not to give her our attention. We found out later that this was part of the plan, that we were being watched for symptoms of acute disquietude, and that whenever these appeared, she interfered to prevent our dwelling on the subject.

I was astonished to find it about four o'clock in the morning, when King Lamus said:—

"I've just been thinking that we should all be the better for a little heroin," and proceeded to hand it around.

The effect was extraordinary. I was aware of an infinite sense of relief; but it was evanescent. It could only have been a few instants before I sank into a dreamless slumber.

II

First Aid

When I woke, the winter sun was already high. It streamed upon my face through the glass skylight of the studio. The sensation of waking was itself a revelation. For months past I had been neither awake nor asleep; simply passing from the state of greater to one of less unconsciousness. But this was a definite act.

King Lamus had gone out, and Lala had only just returned, for she was taking off her furs as I woke.

I had been covered with blankets. She came and took them off, and told me it was time to go and get my things from Greek Street and take them to the new rooms which she had engaged for us that morning.

Lou, it seemed, was already there; and had fallen asleep again, said Lala, only a few minutes before she left.

I could not help feeling a dislike for the way in which everything was being managed for me. I must have shown something of this in my manner. Lala, after bundling me into the automobile which I had driven to Barley Grange on that first tremendous night, began to turn the conversation so as to answer my unspoken resentment.

She made a pleasant little excuse for not offering me the steering-wheel. I knew too well that I couldn't have driven that car a hundred yards through traffic. I had abdicated my manhood. I must resign myself to be driven where anyone was willing to take me. I might count myself lucky if I had fallen into reasonably good hands.

At Greek Street we met with a surprise. It appeared that a few minutes before our arrival, a lady and gentleman had called and were very anxious to see me. They would come back in half an hour. I couldn't imagine who on earth it could be, and the matter slipped from my mind. I was hot and eager to get out of the disgusting atmosphere of those rooms. I wouldn't let Lala come in; but I found that I wasn't strong enough to pack my stuff. The smell of the den was foul beyond all belief.

Lou has not described a hundredth part of the dark abominations which had become habitual.

In fact, I was overcome by the fœtor. I had no strength left. I sunk helplessly into a chair, and began to look feebly about me for the heroin to buck me up.

I must have gone off into a sort of swoon; for I don't know how it happened, but the fresh, cold air was blowing on my face. Our things had been packed as if by magic, and had been taken out to the motor. The bill had been paid.

As I set foot in the car, I heard the landlady asking what she should do if the lady and gentleman came back. I gave the address of my new rooms. As I stumbled into the seat the clear incisive tones of Lala rang across.

"You'd better tell them that Sir Peter's far from well. He will probably not be able to see anyone this week."

I sat limply, shaken by the vibrations of the car. I was an empty vessel; but I felt that, as we got out of the twisted network of streets, and the automobile bounded forward, I was escaping from some infernal labyrinth.

I found Lou at the new rooms. She was sitting in a big lounge chair holding tight to the arms. Her face told the same tale as my own. We felt that we had come through a great illness by a miracle. It struck me as dreadfully unfair that instead of being gently nursed back to health, a demand was to be made upon us for the exercise of the utmost moral and physical strength and courage.

It was impossible for either of us to put forth the slightest effort without the help of the drug. It seemed logically impossible that we should be able to stop drugs by our own efforts; and we knew only too well from experience that we had got to a state where even a few moments delay in taking a dose might result in complete collapse and death.

"I shall leave you children alone for an hour to get settled in, and then we might drive down and have lunch in the country, don't you think? But of course you'll be needing heroin all the time, and I notice that you have a plentiful supply, so there's nothing to worry about there. It's not taking the drug that does the harm, it's the not knowing what you take. So I brought you a couple of charts marked off into hours; and what I want you to do is to promise to make a cross in the proper space everytime you take it."

The condition was easy enough. What we had been dreading, in spite of what Lamus had said, was the forcible suppression which we had experienced at Barley Grange, and which had brought us to such extremities.

But Lala's last remark removed all our apprehensions. The matter was left entirely in our own hands. All we were asked was to keep a record of what we were doing.

I couldn't see how the fact of putting a thing down could make any difference to the act itself.

At that moment King Lamus came in, and kept us amused for half an hour with a perfectly absurd story of some trifling adventure that had happened to him that morning. But despite his vivacity and the interest which he excited, I found my hands instinctively going to the little wooden box in which I kept my heroin.

I took a dose. Lamus immediately broke off his remarks.

"Go on," I said feebly. "I didn't mean to interrupt." "That's all right," said Lamus. "I'm only waiting for you to put it down."

Lala had pinned my chart to the wall. I looked at my watch, and went over and scrawled a cross in the proper section.

As I returned, I noticed that Lamus was watching with a smile of singular amusement. I know now that it was due to his recognising the nature of my annoyance.

He finished his story in a few words, and then asked me point-blank how the cure was going.

I said I didn't see how I could even begin to be cured, and pointed out the nature of the deadlock.

"Well," he said, "you aren't making any allowance for something that the doctors all talk about and forget nine-tenths of the time, which is yet the only thing that saves them from being found out as the ignorant meddlers they are. Do you know that the post-mortems on people who die in New York hospitals show that about fifty percent, of the cases have been wrongly diagnosed? No, Sir Peter, while you and I are wasting our time discussing our troubles, there's one thing working for us, never stops day or night, and that is *Vis medicatrix naturæ*."

Lala nodded emphatically.

"Didn't you notice that even in the Red-Cross?" she said to Lou. "The cases that got well were those that were left alone. All the surgeons did was to repair, as well as possible, the interference with nature caused by the wound. Anything beyond that was a mistake."

"We'll be back in about an hour," said Lamus, "and take you to lunch at Hindhead. Have you a pocket-knife, by the way?"

"Why, yes," I said with surprise. "Why?"

"Otherwise I would have left you mine. You may need one to sharpen your pencil."

Lou and I fell to talking as soon as they were gone. We were already better in this respect, that we had begun to take an interest in ourselves once more. We resorted once or twice to heroin during the absence of our friend; and we made a kind of little family joke of keeping each other up to the mark in the matter of recording the facts.

I discovered what had amused King Lamus on the first occasion. I was conscious of a distinct shade of annoyance at having to get up and make a little cross. It had never occurred to me to break my word. There was a fascination in watching the record.

The drive was a revelation. It was like coming out of a charnel house into the fresh air. A keen cold wind beat against our faces, almost blinding us.

It was not until we reached the inn that we remembered that we had come out without any heroin. Lamus was immediately all sympathy when he heard of our plight. He offered to go out and get some immediately; but Lala protested that she was dying of hunger, and she was sure that lunch would restore our strength just as well, and King Lamus could go out immediately we were finished eating.

We agreed. We could hardly do anything else. As a matter of fact, the fresh air had excited in us both a very keen appetite. The meal did us a lot of good, and at its conclusion our host slipped out unostentatiously and returned in ten minutes with a little packet of powder.

It struck me as very extraordinary that he should have been able to procure it at so remote a place without a prescription. But Lou's eyes were fixed on him with an expression of delighted curiosity. I felt as though somehow or other she had divined the secret.

She seemed intensely amused at my perplexity, and stroked my hair in her most patronising manner.

"You poor brainless creature," she seemed to be saying with her finger-tips.

Well, we all had heroin with our second cup of coffee, and my spirits rose immediately.

Lamus produced two little note books which he had bought in the village, so that we might record our doses while we were out and copy them on our charts when we got back.

We drove back to London, and had tea on the way in a cottage where the people seemed to know our friends very well. It was kept by a little old man and his wife who had the air of being family retainers. The cottage stood well away from the road in grounds of its own. Two mighty yew trees stood one on either side of the gate. Lala told us that the place belonged to the Order of which King Lamus was the head, and that he occasionally sent people down here for certain parts of his training which could only be carried out in solitude and silence.

A great longing came upon me to experience the subtle peace which indwelt this simple habitation. For some reason or other I felt a natural disinclination to take the dose of heroin which was offered to me. It seemed out of keeping with the spirit of the surroundings. I took it and enjoyed it; but the act was mechanical, and the effect in some obscure fashion unsatisfactory.

We drove back to town, and had dinner in my new apartment, where they had an excellent restaurant service.

I found that during the day I had had fifteen sniffs of heroin. Lou had only had eleven. The reaction in my mind was this: If she can get on with eleven, why shouldn't I? though I hadn't sufficient logic to carry on the argument to the people, millions of them, who hadn't had any at all, and seemed to be thriving!

We were both pretty tired. Just as Lamus and Lala rose to leave I took a final sniff.

"What did you do that for?" he said, "if you don't mind my asking."

"Well, I think it was to go to sleep!"

"But this morning you told me you took it to wake up," he retorted.

That was true, and it annoyed me; especially as Lou, instead of being sympathetic, gave one of her absurd little laughs. She actually seemed to take a perverse pleasure in seeing me caught out in a stupidity.

But Lamus took the matter very seriously.

"Well," he said, "it certainly is extraordinary stuff if it does two precisely opposite things at the will of the taker."

He spoke sarcastically. He refrained from telling me what he told me long afterwards, that the apparently contradictory properties that I was ascribing to it were really there, that it can be used by the expert to produce a number of effects, some of which seem at first sight mutually exclusive.

"Well, look here, Sir Peter," went on Lamus. "You can't have it both ways. You really ought to make up your mind as to the purpose of taking a dose."

I replied rather piteously that we had found out long ago that we couldn't sleep without it. Mabel Black had told us that.

"And the result of that delusion," returned Lamus "is that she's dead. I think your experience has been influenced by her foolish remark. You have told me yourself that the delightful result, in the first instance, was to keep you lying awake all night in a state of suspended animation, with a most fascinating flow of fancies filling your brain."

I had to admit the truth of what he said.

"Heroin," he explained, "is a modification of morphine, and morphine is the most active of the principles of opium. Now surely you remember what Wilkie Collins says in *The Moonstone* about opium and its preparations, that they have a stimulating effect followed by a sedative effect. Heroin is much more positive in its action than opium; and the reasonable thing to do, as it seems to me, would be to go ahead with it pretty hard in the morning and keep yourself going by that means, but to leave it entirely alone for some hours before you go to bed, so that the sedative effect may send you nicely to sleep at the proper time. I know the objection to that. The abuse of the drug has left you full of nervous irritability. The reason why you want heroin at night is to deaden yourself to that. When you take it in the morning after a night's rest, you are giving it to a more or less healthy person refreshed by sleep; it is able to stimulate you because your sleep has given you some reserves of force on which it can work. When you take it at night, you are administering it to a sick person, which is a very different thing. However, what you should do is to replace it at night by these tablets, with a nice warm drink of whisky or rum and water, and you will find yourself asleep before you know it. Then in the morning, you awake much fresher than usual, and the heroin will have something more to catch hold of. The result of this will be that you will find quite a small quantity do you as much good as a big one did last week, and more."

Well, all that seemed pretty sensible to me. We took his advice. We did not go to sleep at once. I felt my thoughts too varied. They wandered from one thing to another without reasonable sequence. There seemed to be gaps of unconsciousness between two sets of thoughts; but eventually the irritation subsided, and I knew no more till the morning.

We woke very late, completely exhausted. But as Lamus had prophesied, the heroin took hold immediately; the first two doses made us lively, and with the third we were out of bed and having a bath for the first time in—I'm ashamed to say how long.

Lou fell into a rage at the condition of our underwear, and of our outer clothes, too, for the matter of that. It was all soiled and dirty and stained. We must literally have stunk. And with the realisation of this came an acute feeling of disgrace that we should have been going about with Lamus and Lala in such a condition. If they had said anything about it to us, we might have worked up an artificial indignation about it. But that they should have said nothing was absolutely damnable.

We could not tolerate the idea of ourselves. And yet, only forty-eight hours before, nothing mattered at all.

Lou, in a state of almost insane excitement, was calling up Barley Grange on long distance. The housekeeper was to send up something to wear that morning. While she shouted the order, I suddenly recollected that Lamus and Lala were coming in after lunch; the clothes couldn't possibly reach us till after three o'clock. The best thing to do was to have some dressing-gowns sent up from Piccadilly.

They sent people round with a selection at once, and what with that and sending out for some toilet things, and having in the hairdresser, we made ourselves fairly presentable by half-past one.

That morning gave me the impression of a vaudeville turn or a farce. We had to dodge about from one room to another according as male or female angels ministered unto us.

The excitement kept our minds off heroin very successfully; but it obtruded itself constantly on our notice none the less by insistent physical attacks. Of course, we warded them off at once by taking suitable doses. I cannot say that there was any real diminution. For one thing, taking the stuff by the nose, you can't tell exactly how much you are getting, and a good deal of what you take is wasted.

But the whole atmosphere had changed. We had been taking it till now in a steady, regular manner. It had become a continuous performance. But this morning each patch of craving and each dose were definite incidents. The homogeneity of the vice had been broken up into sections. The dull monotony of the drug had developed dramatic qualities. We were reminded of our early experiences with it. We had, to a certain extent, recovered what addicts call "drug virginity." That alone was sufficient to fill us with a keen sense of exhilaration. We had regained the possibility of hope.

On the other hand, we were brought very sharply up against ourselves by the efforts of the hairdresser and the haberdasher. The smart new dressing-gowns contrasted so strikingly with the deadly illness of our appearance!

However, we could see the daylight afar off, and we sat down to lunch with a certain pleasure. Our appetites had not returned, of course, and we ate very little of the light and exquisite food we had ordered. But at least the idea of food did not disgust us, as had been too long the case.

Lamus came in in time to join us at coffee. It was easy to see that he was pleased at the result so far obtained. Lala was not with him. Instead, he had brought Maisie Jacobs.

I found myself wondering acutely whether there was any serious reason for the change. I had got to the state where I suspected the man's slightest action of having some occult significance, especially as he gave no explanation. Decidedly his manners were not calculated to reassure the unwary. It was easy to understand why his name had become the focus for a host of ridiculous inventions.

After all, it is not pleasant to feel oneself in the presence of an intelligence capable of out-manœuvring one's own at every point without even taking the trouble to do so. The way he took everything for granted was in itself annoying.

He strolled over to the charts, and stood studying them for a long time while he puffed at a cigar. Even the cigar was offensive. It was the kind that millionaires have specially made for themselves. Lamus smoked no other kind; and yet he was a comparatively poor man.

Of course, the explanation was perfectly simple. He really understood and really appreciated good tobacco, and preferred to indulge in cigars disproportionately.

It was the man's own business what he smoked; and yet he had managed to get himself an absolutely bad name in London on that one trait alone. People felt that it was monstrous for him to dine on a mutton chop and a piece of Stilton, and then pull out a cigar that cost half as much again as his dinner.

He studied our charts as if they had been maps and he was trying to work out his overland route from Bokhara to Khatmandu!

Ultimately he said, "There seems a very long gap here—fifteen hours—9 to 12, that's right, isn't it?"

He turned to Maisie for confirmation. He was, so he said, quite unable to trust himself to calculate.

Maisie entered into the spirit of the absurdity and counted it solemnly out on her fingers.

The tone of his voice had been mournful, as if his plans had been seriously disconcerted. That was another trick of his that put people off. It was Lou's sparkling eyes that told me what he meant.

And then I was brought up with a tremendous shock to realise what it meant to me. I went to the chart myself with excited curiosity, quite as if I had never seen it before.

It did not need a mathematician to put the situation into English. The crosses for the last thirty-six hours were crowded into a few spaces, leaving large empty gaps. In other words, the indulgence had become irregular. I stared at the chart as if it had been a ghost.

Lamus turned his head and looked down at me over his shoulder with a queer grin. Then he uttered the extraordinary word: *"Kriegspiel."*

I was completely taken aback. What in the name of thunder was the man talking about? And then it slowly dawned upon me that there was an analogy between the chart and the distribution of the troops in the war. It was obvious as soon as the idea struck one.

As long as the armies were evenly distributed along the line, it was a matter of trench warfare. Great victories and defeats were impossible in the nature of things. But once the troops were massed at points of vantage, aggregated in huge mobile units, it became possible to destroy them on the large scale.

When a British square is broken, the annihilation of its defenders does not come from any diminution in the fighting power of the individual soldiers; its military value is not sensibly diminished by the loss of the few men at the point of attack. It has become worthless because their regular arrangement has been thrown into disorder.

"At the Battle of Waterloo," said King Lamus, turning from the wall and going back to his coffee, "Napoleon sent forward the Old Guard. A few minutes later he cried, 'They are mixed,' and drove in despair from the field. He did not have to wait to see them destroyed."

Lou's breath was coming in great gasps. She had understood the essence of our friend's tactics.

We looked abominably ill; we were actually suffering at the moment from the craving, and embarrassed by the presence of Maisie Jacobs. We did not want to take it in front of her. And yet we knew that we had won the victory. It might be a matter of weeks or months; we didn't even care. We were content to have mastered the principle of the thing. It would be easy to attack those clusters of crosses, and eliminate them little by little.

King Lamus asked Maisie to sing. Luckily there was a baby grand in the room. He sat down and began to accompany her. I found myself enthralled by watching the man's mind work. It taught me something constantly.

This last act, for example. We couldn't go out as we were, and the singing would be an alternative distraction. At the same time, he wanted Maisie's back turned so that we could take our heroin.

We wanted it very badly indeed; and yet—so strange is nature!—we were just as ashamed to take it secretly as a moment before we had been to take it openly.

The thought hit me between the eyes.

It has already been mentioned that Lou and I both had the impulse to conceal the act from each other even while we were taking it openly together. We wanted to pretend that we were taking less than we were. The use of drugs develops every morbid kink in the mind.

Meanwhile, Maisie was singing in her rich contralto voice an English translation of one of Verlaine's most exquisite lyrics: "With muted strings."

> *"Calm in the twilight of the lofty boughs*
> *Pierce we our love with silence as we drowse;*
>
> *Melt we our souls, hearts, senses in this shrine,*
> *Vague languor of arbutus and of pine!"*
>
> *"Half-close your eyes, your arms upon your breast;*
> *Banish forever every interest!*
>
> *The cradling breeze shall woo us, soft and sweet,*
> *Ruffling the waves of velvet at your feet."*
>
> *"When solemn night of swart oaks shall prevail*
> *Voice our despair, musical nightingale!"*

The exquisite images, so subtle and yet so concrete, filled my mind with memories of all my boyhood's dreams. They reminded me of the possibilities of love and peace. All this was familiar to me, familiar in the most intense and alluring form. That was what nature had to offer; this pure and ecstatic rapture was the birthright of mankind. But I, instead of being content with it as it was, had sought an artificial Paradise and bartered the reality of heaven for it. In nature, even melancholy is subtly enthralling. I thought of Keats' ode to her, and even of James Thomson's "Melancholia that transcends all wit," whom he adored, and on whose altar lay his bleeding heart. Well might Verlaine say:—"Voice our despair, musical nightingale!"

But in our chemical substitute for natural stimulus, our despair could be sung by no nightingale. Could even the carrion buzzard give any idea of the hoarse and horrible discord of our disenchantment? The shreds of our souls were torn by filthy fish-hooks, and their shrieks were outside the gamut of merely human anguish.

Was it still possible to return? Had we forfeited forever our inheritance "for a mess of beastlier pottage than ever Esau guzzled?"

Lamus had been watching us intently while Maisie sang. Lou's eyes were full of tears. They ran down her thin, worn face. She made no effort to wipe them away. I do not know whether she felt them. Heroin dulls all physical sensation, leaving only the dull intolerable craving, the acrid irritation, to break in upon the formless stupor which represents the height of well-being.

But I had no inclination to weep; mine was the bitter black remorse of Judas. I had sold my master, my True Will, for thirty pieces of poisonous copper, smeared with the slime of quicksilver. And all I had bought was a field of blood in which I might hang myself and—all my bowels gushed out.

King Lamus rose from the piano with a heavy sigh.

"Forgive me for nagging," he said slowly, "but you spoilt your enjoyment of the song by being ashamed to put yourself in the proper condition to do so by taking the heroin that you need. How often must I tell you that there is nothing to be ashamed of, and everything to be proud of? You know yourself that you are running a greater risk than you ever did when you flew over the Boche lines. I don't want you to swank about it, of course; but you certainly don't want to act like a schoolboy puffing his first cigarette behind a hedge. For God's sake, man, can't you see that half the danger of this business lies in the secrecy and duplicity which go with it?"

"Suppose we made all the fuss about eating that we do about drinking and loving, can't you see what evils would immediately arise? Remember the food restrictions during the war."

"By Jove, I never thought of that," I said, as a hundred half-forgotten incidents bounced into my mind. There were all sorts of stratagems for dodging the regulations, on the part of people who in the ordinary way were plain straightforward law-abiding citizens.

"Of course, we must have restrictions about love and drink and drugs. It is quite obvious how frightfully people would abuse their liberty if they had it."

"I'm sorry to have to disagree," said Lamus. "And as you know, I've got into endless trouble of one sort or another for holding the views I do. But I'm afraid I do honestly think that most of the troubles spring directly from the unnatural conditions set up by the attempts to regulate the business. And in any case, the state of mind brought about by them is so harmful indirectly to the sense of moral responsibility that I am really not sure whether it would not be wiser in the long run to do away with the Blue laws and the Lizzie laws altogether. Legislative interference with the habits of the people produces the sneak, the spy, the fanatic, and the artful dodger. Take finance! Swindling has become a fine art, and is practised on a gigantic scale in ways which would have been impossible when there were no laws intended to protect the public."

It was a very strange view to take. I could hardly believe that Lamus was serious; and yet it did seem to me that the modern criminal millionaire was actually assisted by the complexity of the Company laws. It is impossible for the plain man to understand them, so that an unscrupulous man armed with expert knowledge is much more likely to get the better of his unwary fellows than in the old days when his activities were confined to thimble-rigging and pulling favourites.

"Oh, Basil," put in Maisie, "do tell our friends what you were saying the other day about the South Sea Islands."

Lamus laughed merrily.

"Good for you, kid, very much to the point!

"I've wandered a good deal through queer parts of the world, as you know, and in some of those places there are still taboos about eating and hunting and fishing—all sorts of things which we in England take quite simply, in consequence of which they give no trouble.

"But where a man has to think of a thousand things before he has his dinner: what he eats, and how it was killed, and who cooked it, and so on forever and ever, he gets no chance to develop his mind in more important ways. Taboo is responsible for the low mental and moral development of the peoples whom it afflicts, more than anything else. An appetite should be satisfied in the simplest and easiest way. Once you begin to worry about the right and wrong of it, you disturb the mind unnaturally, and begin to think awry in all sorts of ways that have apparently nothing to do with it.

"Think of the Queen of Spain who was being dragged by her horse, and lost her life because of the absence of the official appointed by etiquette to assist her to dismount!"

We all laughed; the girls frankly, but I with an ill-defined, uncomfortable feeling that Lamus was getting on to dangerous ground.

"What is modern fiction?" he asked, "from Hardy and Dostoevski to the purveyors of garbage to servant girls, but an account of the complications set up by the exaggerated importance attached by themselves or their neighbours to the sexual appetites of two or more bimanous monkeys."

"Most sexual troubles and offences so-called would do very little harm if nobody attached any importance to what was or was not going on."

Of course, there is an answer to this type of argument; but I don't know what it is. I felt very uneasy. He was laying his axe to the root of the tree of civilisation. That was evident.

Lou must have caught my thought. She quoted sarcastically:—

> *"O woodman, spare that tree,*
> *Touch not a single bough,*
> *In youth it sheltered me*
> *And I'll protect it n-yow!"*

Since the war, women are taking a very peculiar attitude. I didn't like the tone of the conversation. I instinctively looked to Maisie Jacobs for support.

The Jewish tradition, which is, after all, the foundation of the so-called Christian point of view, could surely be trusted. But Maisie merely retorted with some verses from Heine which showed that she was entirely on the enemy's side.

Lamus noticed my annoyance, and hastily changed the conversation.

"I'm afraid the only thing you can do," he said to me, "is to chain yourself to Buckingham Palace and then go on hunger-strike, until they give you permission to vote more early and often than ever, after which you won't care to go to the polls at all. That's another example of the same old story. However little we want a thing, we howl if we discover that we can't get it; and the moment we've got it the whole business drops out of sight."

"You'll find it's the same with your drugs. You've practically hypnotised yourself into thinking you can't do without them. It's not a real need, as you know. It's a false and perverse appetite; and as soon as you get out of the way of thinking that it's vitally important, you'll begin to forget how much you depend on it."

Well, of course, I could see the sense of that; and I was glad to see how gay and light-hearted Lou had become under the influence of the idea.

Maisie called Lamus away to the piano to sing another song.

> *"I love you because you're as crazy as I,*
> *Because all the shadows and lights of the sky*
> *Of existence are centred in you;*
> *The cross-jaggéd lightning, the roar of typhoon*
> *Are as good as the slumber of time as we swoon*
> *With the sun half asleep in the blue.*
>
> *You're a dream, you're a mystery, empress and slave,*
> *You're like life, the inscrutable beat of its wave,*
> *You are always the all-unexpected!*
> *When you've promised yourself, then you push me away;*
> *When you scorn me, you suddenly kindle and slay;*
> *You hate truth as the lies She rejected!*
>
> *I love you because you are gallant and proud,*
> *(Your soul is a sun and your body a cloud)*
> *And you leap from my arms when I woo you;*
> *Because you love earth and its worms, you caress*
> *The stars and the seas, and you mock my distress*
> *While the sorrows of others thrill through you!*
>
> *I love you because my life's lost in your being;*
> *You burn for me all the night long, and on seeing*
> *Me, jest at your tears—and allot mine!*
> *Because you elude me, a wave of the lake,*
> *Because you are danger and poison, my snake,*
> *Because you are mine, and are not mine!"*

Just as she had finished, Elsie arrived from Barley Grange with our trunks. Maisie and Lamus said they would leave us to unpack, and went off.

She and Lala dropped in from time to time in the course of the next five days to take us motoring, or to dinner, or the theatre, or to parties.

I thought they made rather a point of keeping off the subject which was the real reason of their visits.

III

The Voice of Virtue

Basil had gone out of town; but he turned up on the fifth day at eleven o'clock in the morning, and he came in his most serious professional manner. After a very brief greeting, he went straight to the charts and inspected them attentively.

Lou and I both felt very uncomfortable. He noticed it at once.

"You've still got heroin on the brain, I see," he remarked severely. "You insist on considering yourselves as naughty children instead of as pioneers of humanity undertaking a desperate adventure for the good of the race."

I began a sort of apology; I don't quite know for what.

"Nonsense," he interrupted. "I know perfectly well why you're ashamed of yourself. You've had what you call a relapse. After getting down to five, six and seven doses, you've suddenly gone back. Yesterday, I see, Lou had fourteen and you sixteen—more than you were taking ever since you have been in this place. You think that's a bad sign. I don't.

"To begin with, you've been honest with yourselves; and that's the thing that matters most. Then it's a good sign again that the daily variation is as large as it is. I'd much rather see 'two eighteen' than 'eight eight' in spite of the four extra doses. And that for exactly the same reason as applies to the hourly distribution.

"It's the same with drink. The man who goes on the bust occasionally is very much easier to manage than the steady soaker. Every child in the Fourth Standard knows that. I believe it's written in golden letters round the chancel in Westminster Abbey. If it isn't, it ought to be.

"Now don't worry. And above all things, don't get a fit of repentance and take too little today and tomorrow. If you do, you'll have another relapse. I know it sounds as though I were contradicting myself. Make the most of it, I don't care. I'm going to do it again in the following elegant manner.

"I want you to get the whole subject of heroin out of your mind; and that is the reason why I insist so strongly on your keeping a record of everytime you take it. It's a psychological paradox that the best way to forget about a thing is to make a memorandum of it.

"Now, goodbye, and come to dinner tonight at the studio. Perhaps you'll feel like dancing."

He went off with an airy wave of the hand.

When we came back from the dance the porter told us that a lady and gentleman had called to see us. They hadn't left their names. They would call again in the morning.

It struck me as curious; but I gave the matter little enough thought. The fact is that I was in rather a bad temper. I had used a good deal of heroin off and on during the last few days, and it had certainly not cost me anything to cut off the cocaine. Morphine and heroin give one a physical craving; but the pull of cocaine is principally moral and when one is taking H. one doesn't care such a lot about taking it.

But that night, raw as it was, I almost made up my mind to drive back and try to get a little snow for a change.

We were getting over the heroin, the first stage of diminution, without too much suffering. But there was something exceedingly tedious about the process.

We had had a very pleasant evening; but I couldn't help comparing it with the same sort of thing in honeymoon days. The sparkle had gone out of the champagne of life.

It was our fault, of course, for trying to outwit nature. But at the same time, one couldn't shut one's eyes to the facts, and I knew Lamus would have had no hesitation in giving us a little snow, feeling the way I was.

I don't know why I felt such a disinclination to go back and ask him. It may have been the instinctive dislike of bothering him; and besides, it was rather humiliating to have to admit. There was also a trace of sturdy British feeling that the thing to do was to stick it out and trust a night's rest to tone up my nerves.

Lamus had advised us to take Turkish baths if we felt unduly depressed. We had found them very useful.

We had got down to three goes a day two days running, chiefly by following his advice to take one of the white tablets instead of the heroin whenever the craving became irresistible. He made rather a point of that, by the way.

It was a bad thing, he said, to yield to stress. It wasn't nearly so harmful to take the heroin when one didn't feel so badly in need of it.

Even after all this time I hadn't quite got on to the peculiarities of the man's mind. I had never reached the stage where I could be sure what he could say next.

One day we were talking about Lou's Chinese appearance; and he said quite seriously that he must have some Chinese blood in him or was the reincarnation of a Chinese philosopher. Ko Yuen, I think he said the name was. He said that he owed it to his European reason to explain categorically why his thoughts had such an Asiatic cast.

They certainly had. From our point of view it was simply perversity. And yet, as a rule, it seemed to work out all right in the end. But it gives one a pain in the neck to try to follow the way his mind works. And he takes a Satanic pleasure in taking hold of one's most obviously reasonable ideas and putting up a series of paradoxes which bewilder one with their strangeness, yet to which there seems to be no answer.

Yet in spite of all this subtlety he had a downright British doggedness; the most perverse train of reasoning would suddenly pull out into a bulldog kind of conclusion that would leave one wondering whether he had been really thinking at all on the lines he pretended.

The upshot in my own case was to keep me up to the mark. So I went to bed, meaning to get up early and go to the Turker in the morning. But as it happened, we both slept late. By the time we were dressed we were getting hungry for lunch.

I was annoyed at this. I had wanted to get out of the house and change my ideas as completely as possible. The Hot Room is an excellent place for the purpose. While I'm there, I find I can't think of anything at all but the immediate effects of the temperature.

I was annoyed, too, to find Lou comparatively cheerful. I decided I would go out after all and have lunch in the Cooling Room, when the porter called up to ask if we could see a lady and gentleman.

These people had begun to obsess me. I demanded their names. There was a pause as if a discussion were taking place at the other end of the wire; and then he announced that it was Mrs. Webster and a friend.

Why the mystery? I didn't want to see her. What did she want with me? I had taken a strong dislike to the woman. I had come to blame her for putting us on to the drug business. It was so much easier than blaming myself.

However, we couldn't exactly refuse to see her, so I told the porter to show them up.

"So it was you," we both said in a breath as we advanced to meet each other. We were referring to the night of the suicide dinner at the Wisteria. As I was going out of the room I had thought I recognised her; but I had supposed she was out of London. She had been a couple of months before; but my mind had gotten into such a state that it never occurred to me that she might have come back.

That's the sort of thing that heroin does to one. One gets an idea about something, and it's too much trouble to change it.

She, on her side, had only half recognised me; and goodness knows she needed no excuse for that.

"We heard you were in London," she began volubly, in a tone which somehow rang false, "and of course I couldn't rest till I had come and welcomed you and Lou in person. We heard you were in a little place in Greek Street from one of the crowd; but you had gone the very morning I called, and they told us you were ill and couldn't see anyone for a week. But Billy Bray and Lady Rhoda came in last night and said they'd seen you at a dance. So I wouldn't waste a minute in coming to see you."

She rattled off all this as if she was in a violent hurry, punctuating her remarks by kissing Lou extravagantly.

I could see that Lou resented the woman even more than I did, but she naturally took care not to show it.

Hanging fatuously on the outskirts of the group was no less a person than the famous philanthropist, Jabez Platt. But he, too, had changed since we had seen him at the time of our marriage. Then he had been the very type of a smug, prosperous, contented Chadband; a placid patriarch with an air of disinterested benevolence and unassuming sanctity. If ever a man was at peace with himself and the world, it was Mr. Jabez Platt on the occasion of our first meeting.

But today, he was a very different individual indeed. He seemed to have shrunk. His black clothes had fitted him like the skin of a well-conditioned porpoise. Now they hung loosely like a toad's. He resembled that animal in several other respects. The virtue had somehow gone out of him. There was a hungry, hunted look in his eyes. Of course, I could see instantly what was the matter with him; he had been taking heroin.

"Dear me," thought I, for my dislike for the creature was instinctive, "how are the mighty fallen!"

Excuse a digression. There is a great deal of discussion about various pleasures—whether they are natural or unnatural. Lamus has since told me that the true test of the perversity of a pleasure is that it occupies a disproportionate amount of the attention.

According to him, we have no right to decide offhand that it is an unnatural pleasure to eat sawdust. A man might be constituted so that he liked it. And as long as his peculiarity doesn't damage or interfere with other people, there's no reason why he shouldn't be left alone.

But if it is the man's fixed belief that sawdust eating is essential to human happiness; if he attributes almost everything that happens either to the effects of eating it or not eating it; if he imagines that most of the people he meets are also sawdust-eaters, and above all, if he thinks that the salvation of the world depends entirely upon making laws to compel people to eat sawdust, whether they like it or not, then it is fair to say that his mind is unbalanced on the subject; and that, further, the practice itself, however innocent it may appear, is in that particular case perverse. Sanity consists in the proper equilibrium of ideas in general. That is the only sense in which it is true that genius is connected with insanity.

The conviction of Michael Angelo that his work was the most important thing in the Renaissance was not quite sane, even although in a way time has justified his belief.

That is what is wrong with the majority of vaccinationists and anti-vaccinationists and vegetarians and anarchists and the "irascible race of seers" in general, that they over-play their hands. However right they are in their belief, and in thinking that belief important, they are wrong in forgetting the equal or greater importance of other things. The really important things in the world are the huge silent inexorable things.

"What are the wild waves saying?"—that the pull of the tides is gradually slowing down the earth's rate of rotation. And that was what was wrong with me. I had a tendency to see heroin everywhere.

That was not what was wrong with Mr. Jabez Platt!

Gretel Webster was a mistress of the social arts, yet all her skill in small talk could not camouflage the artificial character of the visit. She saw it herself, and took advantage of the fact to ask Lou to take her in her bedroom and "talk clothes and leave dear Sir Peter and Mr. Platt to get better acquainted with each other."

But the process did not promise to be rapid. Dear Sir Peter and Mr. Platt seemed to have nothing to say to each other; dear Sir Peter did his best to offer cigars, cigarettes, and various drinks to relieve the tension, but Mr. Platt's Roman virtue did not permit him to indulge in such things.

Mr. Platt, however, was so sensible of the hospitality of dear Sir Peter that he felt obliged to ask dear Sir Peter's opinion of—and he suddenly whipped a ten-gramme bottle of cocaine out of his coat-tail pocket.

"We believe," he said, "that this is a particularly pure sample. There is strong scientific reason to believe," he explained, and the atmosphere of the pulpit positively radiated from him, "that it is not the drug itself but the impurities so often associated with it by careless manufacture that are responsible for the deplorable effects occasionally observed in persons who take it, whether for legitimate or other reasons."

To say that I sat stupefied is a gross understatement of the case. My astonishment prevented me recognising for a moment that my heart was bounding and leaping within me at the sight of the drug.

"I should really value your opinion as a connoisseur," continued Platt.

There was something tremulous in his voice, as if he were keeping hold on himself by some incredible effort of will.

I positively stammered.

"Why, Mr. Platt," I said, "I thought you were so anxious to stop the use of the drug altogether. I thought it was you who were chiefly responsible for putting through the Diabolical Dope Act."

"Ignorance, pure ignorance, my dear Sir Peter," he cried. "We live and learn, we live and learn. Used in moderation, we find it to be positively wholesome. A stimulant no doubt, you will say. And all stimulants may undoubtedly be dangerous. But I'm afraid people will have them, and surely the wisest course is to see that what they have is as little deleterious as possible."

While he spoke he kept on nervously jerking the bottle in my direction as if afraid to put it into my hands outright. And then I realised how very badly I wanted it.

"Well, certainly, Mr. Platt," I replied, entering into the spirit of the thing, "I shall be only too glad to give you my opinion for what it may be worth."

I could not conceal the feverish eagerness with which I shook out a dose. My pretence at sniffing with a critical air was ludicrously feeble. A child could have seen that I was shaken, body and soul, by the feverish lust to get it into my system after so long an abstinence.

Time had purged my system of the poison. It found the house "empty and swept and garnished"; and seven devils entered into me instead of the ejected one. My malaise passed like a cloud swept by the wind from the face of the sun. I became physically buoyant as I had not been for months. I was filled with superb self-confidence. My hesitation vanished. I played the game with all the sublime intoxication of recovered divinity.

"I must admit that it seems to me excellent," I pronounced with lofty calm, though my blood was singing in my ear.

I handed back the bottle.

"Keep it, I beg of you, my dear Sir Peter," protested Platt enthusiastically. "One never knows when a little household medicine may not come in handy."

Something set me off into roars of internal laughter. I couldn't see the joke, but it was the biggest joke in the world.

"It's really awfully kind of you, my dear Mr. Platt," I said with unction, feeling that I was cast for the star part in some stupendous comedy.

"The obligation is entirely on my side," returned my guest. "You have no idea how your kind approval has set my mind at ease."

I took another sniff. I was fainting away into an inexpressible ecstasy. I re-corked the bottle and put it in my pocket, thanking Platt profusely.

"I can't imagine your mind being ill at ease," I went on with a note of irony, which was however, absolutely genial. I was friends with everyone in the world. "If there was ever a man with a conscience void of offence toward God and man, that man is surely Jabez Platt."

"Ah, conscience, conscience," he sighed. "You have no idea, Sir Peter, how it has tormented me of late. The moral responsibility, the appalling moral responsibility."

"Whatever it is," I answered, "you are certainly the man to shoulder it."

"Well," he said, "I think I may say without boasting that I trust I have never tried to shirk it. Your approval has absolved me of the last shred of hesitation. I must explain, my dear Sir Peter, that I have always been a poor man. The service of humanity demands many sacrifices from its devotees, and I assure you that in that bottle there lies not only, as I now feel assured, the salvation of mankind from one of its direst dangers, but an enormous fortune."

He leant forward and tapped my knee with his forefinger.

"An enormous fortune," he repeated in awed tones. And then lowering his voice still further, "Enough, more than enough, for both of us."

"Why, how do I come in?" I asked in surprise, while a little thrill of avarice tickled my heart-strings.

I reflected that what with one thing or another, I had made a disagreeably large hole in my capital. Only two mornings ago I had had a rather irritating letter from Mr. Wolfe on the subject. It would suit me perfectly well to make an enormous fortune.

He drew his chair closer to mine, and began to talk in a quiet, persuasive voice. "It's this way, my dear Sir Peter. The workings of Providence are indeed strange. Just before the passing of my Act, I had invested what little fortune I possessed in the purchase of a Cocaine Factory in Switzerland, with the intention of putting an end to its nefarious activities. Now here is an instance of what I can only refer to with reverent gratitude as the Moving of the Divine Finger. On the one hand, my chemical manager informed me of the marvellous scientific discovery which I have already mentioned—I am sure you feel no ill effects from what you have taken?" His voice took on a tone of grave concern, almost paternal.

"Not much!" I countered cheerfully, "it's splendid. I can do with another sniff right now!" I suited the action to the words, like Hamlet's ideal mummer. "Won't you be persuaded?" I queried maliciously.

"Ah, no, I thank you, dear Sir Peter! Your remarks have raised me to the highest pinnacle of happiness."

I took a fourth dose, just for luck.

"Well, on the other hand, I discovered that, thanks to the very Act which I had so arduously laboured to put upon the Statute Book, that little bottle of yours which costs me less than five shillings to manufacture, and was sold retail for a matter of fifteen shillings, can now be sold—discreetly, you understand—in the West End for almost anything one cares to ask—ten, twenty, even fifty pounds to the right customer. Eh? What do you say to that?" He laughed gleefully. "Why, ill-natured people might say I had put through the Act for the very purpose of making a bull market for my produce!"

"And you save humanity from its follies and vices at the same stroke!" The cocaine had cleared my mind—it was like one of those transparent golden sunsets after a thunderstorm in the Mediterranean. I revelled in the ingenuity of Mr. Platt's proceedings. I gloated with devilish intensity upon the jest of carrying out so magnificent a scheme beneath so complete a camouflage. It was the vision of Satan disguised as an angel of light.

"Yes, indeed, the whole affair is eminently gratifying from every point of view," answered Platt. "Never in all my life have I been permitted to see with such luminous clarity the designs of providential loving-kindness."

"Alas! my dear Mr. Platt," I replied gloomily, as the stage directions seemed to indicate, "I am a very young and ignorant man, and I am unable at present to see any part for me in the design. My mere approval of your product——" I took it out and treated myself to a long, languishing kiss—yes, kiss, there is no other word for it! My long-lost love, home to my heart once more!

Platt in his turn assumed an air of Stygian melancholy. "My dear Sir Peter," he pursued, with a heavy sigh, "you can easily understand that, huge as my fortune, thanks to the inscrutable ways of Destiny, now is, time is necessary to realise it fully—and, by a singular and most unfortunate conjunction of circumstances, not only time is required, but—Capital."

"Unfortunate conjuncture of circumstances?" I echoed dreamily—my mind was royally racing in the Circus of Infinity, a billion leagues from where anybody sat.

"Unfortunate, that is, for me," corrected Platt, "no, no, I won't say that, since it is fortunate for my friend—for you!"

"For me?"

"For you, my dear Sir Peter! I told Mrs. Webster of the state of the case—and she immediately suggested your name. She has come to the rescue splendidly herself, I need hardly tell you—took all the shares she could—but there is still a matter of three thousand pounds to find. And remember, after insuring against all risks, and so forth, we shall be paying at the very least four thousand percent."

I have never been any sort of a business man; but a child of twelve could grasp the gigantic nature of the proposition.

"I have brought the papers for your inspection, my dear Sir Peter. You will see that the capital is only £20,000 in shares of £1 fully paid up—and I am offering you £3000 at par."

"It's princely, my dear sir," I exclaimed. "You overwhelm me. But—excuse me—I don't see why you need the money at all, or why you don't sell the shares through a broker."

At this moment Lou popped into the room. It annoyed me. Did I show it? Her face went suddenly white as marble. She stood in the doorway of the bedroom for a moment, swaying; and then went swiftly and softly through the room to the hallway. The portière swung to behind her—and I instantly forgot her existence, after vaguely supposing that she had gone to get her furs to show to Gretel, returning to the bedroom by the other door so as not to disturb us.

Platt was explaining the situation. "A most unfortunate affair,

Sir Peter! I fear I am overmuch preoccupied with the welfare of my fellows—and in consequence neglect my own. I certainly was surprised, when I went to my bank to see if I had enough money to purchase these chemical works, to find my balance so large—I am only too accustomed, alas! to find that my impulsive charity has denuded my little savings. But I only discovered last month that £3000 of the amount did not belong to me at all; it was part of a fund of which I am trustee. I am not allowed by our foolish laws to invest trust funds in such securities as this *Schneezugchemischerwerke* of ours; and I must replace the £3000 by the end of the month, or the consequences may be really most disastrous." He broke off short, trembling with fear. He was not playing a part about this. He undoubtedly felt that it might be difficult to explain to an unsympathetic jury how a Trust Fund had lost its way to the extent of wandering into the Trustee's private account without his suspecting it had behaved in so erratic a manner.

"You are a man of the world, Sir Peter," he declared, almost blubbering, "and I feel sure you understand."

I am not altogether a man of the world, as a matter of fact; but, whether helped by the cocaine or not, I really did think I understood fairly well what had happened.

"But why not go to the City?" I repeated, "they ought to fight like wolves over such a plump little doe as the *Schneezug*!"

"My *dear* Sir Peter!" He raised his hands in horrified surprise. "Surely, surely you realise that it may take years and years to educate the public to appreciate the difference between our Pure Cocaine, a wholesome household tonic, and the Impure Cocaine, which is a Deadly and Deleterious Habit-forming Drug! I felt I could approach you, because you are a man of the world, and a connoisseur, and—to be frank with you—because I took a liking for you the first time I saw you, so handsome and splendid with your beautiful young bride! But what, oh what, would people say if it became known that Jabez Platt had the majority of the shares in a Cocaine Factory? My dear Sir Peter, we are in England, remember!"

I wasn't deceived by any of the nauseating humbug of the scoundrel, but it was evident that his proposal was a genuine good thing.

The *Schneezugchemischewerke* had been paying well enough in the ordinary way when he bought them.

I determined to sell the necessary securities and take over the shares. My state of mind was exceedingly complex. My reasons for the purchase were not merely various but mutually exclusive. For one thing, the Satanistic idea of working evil for its own sake; for another, the schoolboy delight in doing things on the sly; then there was the simple and straightforward money lust. Again, my hatred of hypocrisy had turned into a fascination. I wanted to enjoy a taste of so subtle and refined a vice.

On the top of this there was a motive which really encroached on the category of insanity. On the one side I was exuberantly delighted to find myself in possession of boundless supplies of cocaine; on the other I was enraged with mankind for having invented the substance that had ruined my life, and I wanted to take my revenge on it by poisoning as many people as I could.

These ideas were tossed about in my mind like pieces of meat in boiling soup. The fumes intoxicated me. I shook Platt's hand and promised to go down to my bank at once and make the necessary arrangements.

I swelled with the delirious pride of the great man of affairs who sees the golden opportunity and grasps it. More crazily still, I enjoyed the sensation of being the generous benefactor to a brother man in misfortune.

Platt pulled out his watch. "We could drive down at once and have our lunch in the city. Bless my soul," he interrupted himself, "I shall never forgive myself for being so rude. I had quite forgotten Lady Pendragon and Mrs. Webster."

"Oh, they'll be delighted," I tittered. "They'll have a horrible lunch on cream buns and watercress and mince pies and champagne and go shopping afterwards like good little millionairesses."

"Yes, indeed," said Platt heartily and quite genuinely, "they're that all right. As for us, we'll lunch at Sweeting's on oysters and stout and drink to the prosperity of Parliamentary Institutions."

I laughed at the little joke, like a madman, and shouted wildly:—

"Come in, girls, and hear the news. We're all going to be elected to the Diamond Dog-collar Club."

Gretel appeared in the doorway. She was wearing a worried look which was perfectly incomprehensible.

"Where is Lou?" she said at once, her shrill voice off pitch with agitation.

"Isn't she with you?" I snapped back idiotically.

A sudden spasm of alarm set me shivering. What the devil could have happened?

Platt was more upset than any of us, of course. He had pulled off a delicate and dangerous intrigue; and at the moment of success he saw that his plan was in some incomprehensible danger. His mind's spy-glass showed him a bird's-eye view of the Old Bailey. The fact that there was no tangible reason for alarm only intensified the feeling of uneasiness.

"She must be hiding for a joke," said Gretel in a hard, cold voice, mastering her anxiety by deliberate violence.

We hunted over the apartment. There was no sign of her; and her fur coat and cap were missing from the hall. I turned to Mrs. Webster.

"What happened?" I asked curtly.

The woman had resumed her mask. She threw a defiant glance at Platt, whose eyes shot a venomous question.

"I can't understand it at all," she said slowly. "She seemed very uneasy all the time she was in the bedroom. I thought she was missing her dope. If I had had any on me, I'd have given her a big jolt. *Dummer Esel!* I'll never go out without it again so long as I live. I forget what excuse she made. I thought it was just camouflage to go and get her heroin."

Silence fell between us. Platt was afraid to say what he wanted to say. I was honestly puzzled. The incident had destroyed the effect of the cocaine I had taken. (It's extraordinary how easy it is to break the spell). I went to the Tantalus and poured out three brandies, dropping a pinch of snow into mine to make sure of getting back to where I was.

Mrs. Webster had recovered her equipoise.

"We're really very foolish children," she said gaily, as she sipped her brandy, "making all this fuss about nothing at all. There are a thousand and one reasons why she may have taken it into her head to go out. Why, of course—it's awfully hot in here, she probably thought she'd take a turn in the fresh air. Anyhow, you don't have to bother about me. You boys had better get down to the city and do your business. I'll wait here for her until she turns up, and spank her hard for frightening us all like this."

Platt and I put on our hats and coats. We were just shaking hands with Gretel, telling her to order herself a good lunch from downstairs, when we heard the latch-key put into the lock.

"There she is," cried Gretel gaily. "What babies we have been!"

The door opened; but it was not Lou who came in. It was Maisie Jacobs, and her face was stern and set. She gave two quick formal bows to the others, took my hand, and said in a deep, tense voice:—

"You must come with me at once, Sir Peter. Lady Pendragon needs you."

I went white. Once again I had been brought back from a complex chaos of conflicting emotions to the bed-rock truth which had been buried so elaborately and so often.

The deepest thing in myself was my love for my wife. I resented the realisation, and yet I could not bring myself to admit it. I asked, stupidly enough:

"Is anything wrong?" as if Maisie's face, to say nothing of her appearance, were not sufficient guarantee of the seriousness of the situation.

"Come with me," she repeated.

Gretel had been watching the dialogue like a cat. She flashed forked lightning at Platt, thinking that his fears might betray him into saying something irrevocably stupid.

"Of course, there's only one thing to be done," she said hurriedly, summing the psychology of the situation in a brilliant synthesis. "You must go at once with Miss Jacobs, Sir Peter. I needn't say how terribly anxious I feel; but I hope there is nothing really wrong. I'll look in late this afternoon with Mr. Platt for news; and if everything is all right—I won't allow myself to think that it can be otherwise—we can make an appointment for the morning over our business affairs. Don't let's lose anytime."

I shook hands hastily and slipped my hand into Maisie's arm. She ran downstairs with me, leaving the others to wait for the lift.

IV

OUT OF HARM'S WAY

L amus's motor was at the door. Maisie sprang to the wheel and drove off without saying a word. I shivered at her side, filled with inexplicable qualms. The exaltation of the cocaine had completely left me. It seemed to increase my nervousness; and yet I resorted to it again and again during the short drive.

When we got to the studio, Lala was sitting as usual at the desk, but Lamus was walking up and down the room with his hands behind his back; his head bowed in thought so deep that he seemed not to notice our arrival. Lou had not removed her furs. She was standing like a statue in the middle of the room. The only sign of life was that her face continually flushed from white to red and back again. Her eyes were closed. For some reason or other she reminded me of a criminal awaiting sentence.

Lamus stopped short in his stride and shook hands with me.

"Take your things off, and sit down, Sir Peter," he said brusquely. His manner was completely different from anything I'd ever seen in him. He turned away and flung himself into a chair, searched in his pockets for an old black pipe, filled it and lit it. He seemed the prey of a peculiar agitation. That again was utterly unlike him. He cleared his throat and got up, with an entire change of behaviour. He offered me one of his millionaire cigars and motioned to Lala to get me a drink.

"This is the latest fashion in the studio," said Lala gaily. She was obviously trying to relieve the tension. "Basil invented it last night. We call it Kubla Khan No. 2. As you see, it's half gin and half Calvados, with half a teaspoonful of crêmede menthe and about twenty drops of laudanum. You filter it through cracked ice. It's really the most refreshing thing I know."

I accepted the luxuries automatically, but I couldn't help fidgeting. I wanted to get down to business. I could feel that something urgent was on hand. I didn't like the way Lou was acting. She stayed so absolutely still and silent, it was uncanny.

Lamus had taken three matches to light his pipe and it kept on going out between almost every puff. By-and-by he threw it angrily on the carpet and lighted a cigar. There was a club fender round the grate. Maisie was sitting on it swinging her legs impatiently. We all seemed to be waiting for something to happen and it was as if nobody knew where to begin.

"Tell him, Lou," said Lamus suddenly.

She started as if he had struck her. Then she turned and faced me. For the first time in my life I realised how tall she was.

"Cockie," she said, "I've come to the cross-roads." She made a movement of swallowing, tried to go on, and failed.

King Lamus sat up in his chair. He had completely recovered himself; and was watching the scene with impersonal, professional interest. Lala bent over his chair, and whispered long and earnestly in his ear. He nodded.

Again he cleared his throat, and then began to speak in a strained voice.

"I think the simplest way in the long run is for Lady Pendragon to tell Sir Peter, as she has already told us, exactly what has happened, as if she were in the witness-box."

Lou began to twist herself about uneasily.

"I'm fed up," she burst out at last.

"The witness will kindly control herself," remarked Lamus, judicially.

The callousness of his tone restored Lou not merely to herself, but to herself as she might have been before I ever knew her.

"When those people arrived this afternoon," she said quite calmly, "I saw at once that they were up to some game. I knew why Gretel wanted to get me out of the room, and I tackled her about it point-blank. She told me the truth, I think, as nearly as a woman of that sort can ever get to it. Something about buying shares in a chemical works?"

"Yes, certainly," I returned, and I could feel the hostility creeping into my voice. "And why not? It's a wonderful investment and the chance of my life financially, and I don't see why women have to poke their noses into men's business which they don't understand and never will. Between you, you may have made me miss my chance. Confound you! If I knew where to find Platt, I'd go around and sign the contract this moment. As it is, I can go down to the bank and arrange to get the money."

I pulled out my watch.

"I can't even have my lunch, I suppose," I went on, working myself up deliberately into a fury.

Lou walked a few steps away and then turned back and faced me.

"Accept my apologies, Sir Peter," she said, in icy, deliberate tones. "I have no right whatever to interfere with your plans. After all, they don't concern me anymore."

I rose to my feet and flung away the half-smoked cigar into the fireplace.

"What do you mean by that?" I said passionately. I had something else in mind to say, but all of a sudden my whole being seemed to falter. I sat down weakly in the chair, gasping for breath. Through my half-shut eyes I could see Lou take an impulsive step towards me; and then, controlling herself, she recoiled as a man might who had approached what he thought was a beautifully marked piece of fallen timber and recognised it for a rattlesnake.

The pulse of my brain was beating feebly and slowly; but she went on with pitiless passion, and swept me away with the tempestuous rush of her contempt.

"I made an excuse, and came to see what was going on. I found you had utterly forgotten the facts. You were sniffing cocaine, not as an experiment, not because of any physical need, but as a vice pure and simple. You were already insane with it. I might have stood that, for I loved you. But that you should plan to become the partner of that murderous villain with his hypocritical piety, that was another matter. That was a matter of honour. I don't know how long I stood there. I lived a lifetime in a second, and I made up my mind once for all to be done with such dirt. I slipped out and came here. I'm half insane myself at this moment with craving for H.; but I won't take it till I've seen this thing through. The pain of my body helps me to bear up against the mortal anguish of my soul. Oh, I know it's heroics and hysterics—you can call me what you like—what you say doesn't count anymore. But I want to live; and I have asked Basil to take me away as once he promised to do long before I met you. He has promised to cure me, and I hold him to that. He has promised to take me away, and I hold him to that. You can get a divorce. You'd better. For I never want to look upon your face again."

The other three people in the room did not exist for me. I had to brace myself to meet Lou's attack. There was absolute silence except for the sound of my sniffing. I became my own master again, and broke out into a fit of yelling laughter.

"So that's the game, is it?" I answered at last. "You are selling me out to buy a third share in that cad!"

I stopped to try to think of some viler insults; but my brain refused to work. It merely prompted me to abuse of the type usually associated with bargees. I spluttered out a torrent of foul language; but I felt even at the time that I was not doing myself justice. My remarks were received with complete indifference. Even Lou merely shrugged her shoulders, and looked at Lamus as much as to say, "You see I was right."

Lamus slowly shook his head. As a matter of fact, I could hardly see. My eyesight was disturbed in some peculiar way which frightened me, and my heart began to protest. I took out the cocaine once more. To my astonishment, Lamus bounded from his chair and took the bottle from my hands. I wanted to get up and kill him; but a deathly faintness seized me. The room swam. Lamus returned to his chair, and once again silence fell on the studio.

I think I must have lost consciousness for a while; for I do not remember who put an ice-cold towel round my head or how it came about that the freezing moisture dripped down my spine.

I came to myself with a heavily heaved sigh. Everyone was in the same position as before, except that Lou had taken off her furs and curled herself up on the settee.

"If you feel well enough, Sir Peter," said Lamus, "you may as well hear the end of the story."

Lou suddenly choked with sobs and buried her head in the cushions. Lamus gave a gesture which Lala apparently understood. She came forward and stood in front of me with her hands behind her back like a child repeating a lesson.

"Sir Peter," she said in a gentle voice, "Basil explained to Lady Pendragon that she was taking a very wrong view of the matter. He told her that when people are getting over drug-habits they were liable to say and do things entirely foreign to their characters. We all know how abundantly you have shown your courage and your sense of honour. We know your race, and we know your exploits. What happened at the interview with Mr. Platt didn't count. You were a sick man. That was all. Maisie suggested that she should go round and fetch you; and thank heaven she got there in time!"

Lou twisted herself round, and turned savagely on King Lamus.

"I hold you to your promise," she cried violently. "I hold you to your promise."

"That, once more," he said calmly, "is simply because you are a sick woman as much as he is a sick man."

"So it's honourable to break your word to a sick woman, is it?" she flashed back like a tigress.

A curious smile curled his lips.

"Well, what does Sir Peter say?" he asked with a kind of lazy humour.

I suddenly became acutely conscious of what a ridiculous figure I was cutting, sitting there like a sick monkey with a towel round my head. I tore it off and dashed it to the ground.

Lala came forward immediately and picked it up. I felt the action as an insult. I was being treated as a person who is a nuisance making a mess in another man's studio. The effect was to induce a surly mood.

"What I say doesn't seem to matter," I answered gruffly. "But since you ask, I say this. Take her and keep her and let me hear no more of her. And I'll say thank you."

My own voice made me wince. Could it really be I who was indulging in this vulgar repartee? It was an extraordinary thing the way everything that happened seemed to make my position less and less dignified.

The thought was interrupted by Lou's gleaming tones.

"There, Basil, he sets me free. I come to you without a stain. You can keep your promise without breaking your faith."

She got up from the sofa and went across to his chair. She threw herself at his feet, and buried her face in his knees; while her long arms reached up and groped for his face to stroke it.

He patted her head affectionately.

"Yes," he said, "we're free, and I'll keep my promise. I'll cure you, and I'll take you away with me. But will you let me make one condition?"

She lifted her face to his. In spite of the physical wreckage of the last few months, love was able to transform her bodily. She was radiantly beautiful. She only waited for him to take her in his arms. She was trembling all over with ecstatic passion.

I gripped the arms of my chair in futile rage. Before my very face the only woman I had ever loved had disowned me, cast me off with contempt, and was offering herself to another man with the same impulsive ardour that she had once shown toward me. No, by all the powers of hell, it was worse! For I had wooed her rapturously; and he had made no effort.

"One condition?" her voice rang high and clear through the studio. "I'm giving you myself, my Lord and lover; body and soul to have and to hold. What do conditions matter to me?"

"Well," said King Lamus, "it's really only a small condition; and to prove that I keep my promises, I must keep them all round. You see, I promised to cure Sir Peter, too, and so my condition is that he comes with us."

She sprang to her feet as if a cobra had struck her. Her long arms wrestled against the unresisting air. The humiliation was unspeakable. Lamus put his pipe away in his pocket, rose to his feet, and stretched himself like some great lazy lion. He took her in his arms and held her firmly, fixing his eyes upon her tortured face; the long jagged scarlet mouth stretched to a tragic square through which the scream refused to come.

He shook her shoulders gently. Her rigid muscles began to relax.

"It's a deal, then, little girl," he said.

Her mouth closed, and then curled itself into a smile of exquisite happiness. The sombre fire of lust died out of her eyes. They kindled with the light of understanding.

He put his arm around her waist, and brought her over to me, his right hand fastened under my arm-pit. And he lifted me bodily out of my chair as if he had reached down like Hercules into the darkest depths of hell, and dragged forth a damned soul into the light of heaven.

He put her hands in mine and closed his own over them.

"Whom God hath joined together," he said solemnly, "let no man put asunder."

He turned on his heel and became a man of quick decisive action.

"Maisie," he said, "you have the key. Go over and have their things packed and leave them in the cloak room at Victoria. Lala, 'phone for reserve places and a cabin for these good people on the boat. London's no place for us—too many philanthropists about seeking whom they may devour. Ring up Dupont and have him send in dinner for five for seven o'clock. We'll catch the ten o'clock and be in Telepylus *sabse jeldi*."

Maisie was already out of the studio and Lala at the telephone before he had finished talking. He turned to us with the same affectation of hustle.

"Here, young people," he said breezily. "Your nerves are all shot to pieces, and no wonder. White tablets for two and a little H. to sweeten them. And you've missed your lunch! That's too bad. We'll have an old-fashioned high tea. I know there's something to eat in the coal scuttle or somewhere, and Lala can cook something while I make the buttered toast. You sit down and talk and make your plans for honeymoon number eight, or whichever it is. And don't get in my way, because I'm going to be a very busy man. In fact, it's rather lucky that I've acquired the habit of starting for three years' trips around the world at three minutes notice."

It was half an hour before tea was ready. Lou and I sat on the sofa, shaken and sore by what we had gone through. Morally, mentally, physically—we were both aching with the most cruel fatigue. And yet its waves surged vainly against the silent and immovable rock of our sublime felicity. It did not find expression. We were far too weary. And yet we were aware in some deepest part of our consciousness, laid bare for the first time by the remorseless stripping off of all its upper layers, that it existed. It always had existed "before the beginning of years," and always would exist. It had nothing to do with conditions of time and space. It was an ineffable union, in infinity, of our individualities.

I must not describe our journey to Telepylus in any detail. If once the beauty of the place were discovered, it would soon be spoilt. There is no harm, however, in indicating what the place itself is like, especially as not less than three thousand years ago it became one of the most famous places in the world. And one of its chief claims was that even then it was famous for the ruins of forgotten civilisations. Today, the hand of man has left ephemeral scribbles all over the great rock which dominates the city.

Approaching Telepylus from the west, we were astounded when that mighty crag burst into view as the train rounded a corner. Like another Gibraltar it stood out against a background of sky twelve hundred feet above the sea. It stretched out two great paws over the city like a crouching lion playing with its prey which it was about to devour—as indeed it is.

The biggest morsel there is a magnificent cathedral dating from the Normans. It stands on an eminence below the edge of the overhung cliff, and beneath it the town is spread like a fan. It is reduced to insignificance by the cathedral as the cathedral is by the rock; and yet one's familiarity with the size of an ordinary house makes one run up the scale instead of down it.

The town is witness to the stupendous size of the cathedral; and as soon as one has realised the cathedral, it, in turn, becomes a measure of the grandeur of the rock.

We walked up from the station to the residence of King Lamus, high on the hillside above the neck of land which joins it to the rock.

The cliffs towered above us. They were torn into huge pinnacles and gullies; but above the terrific precipices we could see the remains of successive civilisations; Greek temples, Roman walls, Saracen cisterns, Norman gateways, and houses of all periods were perishing slowly on the gaunt, parched crags.

It was very hard work for Lou and myself to climb the hill in the wretched condition of our health. We had to sit down repeatedly on the huge boulders which lined the paths that wound among the well-tilled fields dotted with gnarled gray olives.

The air of the place was a sublime intoxication, and yet its enchantment merely rubbed into our souls the shame of our wretched physical condition. We had to take several goes of heroin on the way. We didn't see why we couldn't have had a carriage part of the way. But it was part of King Lamus's plan, no doubt, that we should be stung with the realisation of our impotence in so divine a spot, where every voice of nature swelled the chorus that spurred us to physical activity. Our invalidism had not seemed so horribly unnatural in London as it did in this consecrated temple of beauty.

Lamus himself seemed invigorated to an extraordinary degree by his home-coming. He gambolled like a young goat while we plodded gaspingly up the slope. And while we rested he told us the history of the monuments that crumbled on the crags.

"This place will help you to correct your ideas," he said, "of what is permanent, so far as anything is permanent."

We were indeed filled with a feeling of the futility of human effort as we contemplated the layers of civilisations, and looked down upon that last of them which was still flourishing, although the signs of decay were only too obvious. The modern town was not even built with the idea of defying the centuries. It was essentially flimsy and ramshackle, and the events of the last few hours had given repeated evidence not only of the state of social unrest which was likely at any moment to lay the modern structure in ruins, but of general lassitude and lack of energy on the part of everybody with whom we came into contact.

Our little party obviously represented undreamed-of possibilities of doing good business. But no one seemed to want to fulfil even that last of human ambitions: the acquiring of the good will of prosperous travellers.

"Don't be downhearted," laughed Lamus. "Your trouble is that you are looking for permanence in the wrong place. Do you see those two men?"

On the road below us were two goatherds, one driving his flock up from the town after having been milked, the other driving them down for that purpose.

Lamus quoted two lines of Greek poetry. I did not remember enough to be able to translate them, but the words had an extraordinarily familiar ring. Lamus translated.

"'The city Telepylus, where the shepherd who drives his flock into the town salutes another who is driving them out, and the other returns his salute. A man in that country could earn double wages if he could do without sleep, for they work much the same by night as they do by day.'

"That was written three thousand years ago, and even the name of the woman who wrote that poem, albeit it is one of the most famous poems in the world, is lost. But there are the shepherds saluting each other today as they did then. ΠΑΝΤΑ ΡΕΙ said Heracleitus, 'all things flow.' And everything that tries to escape that law, that relies on its strength, that becomes rigid, that endeavours to call a halt, is broken up by the irresistible waves of time. We think steel stronger than water; but we cannot build a ship to resist its action. Compare the soft-flowing winds with the inflexible rock. We breath those winds into our lungs today— the air is as fresh as ever. But see how those temples and strongholds, nay, the very crags themselves, have been worn down by the languorous caresses of this invigorating breeze. That is one of the reasons why I came to live here, though one hardly needs support after one glance at the incomparable beauty of the place; a beauty which varies everyday and never tires. Look at the sunset every night. It is good for two hours of grand opera. It is almost stupefying to sit on the terrace of the villa and watch the ever-changing glories of night-fall. And night itself! There stands the Pole Star over the rock. As the months move the Great Bear wheels about its stable splendour, and one's mind begins to work on a totally different scale of time. Each revolution of the heavens about the Pole is like the second hand of one's spiritual watch."

We listened with enthralled attention. The beauty of the place beat hard upon our brains. It was unbelievable. Patches of cancer like London and Paris were cut ruthlessly out of our consciousness. We had come from the ephemeral pretentiousness of cities to a land of eternal actuality. We were re-born into a world whose every condition was on a totally different scale to anything in our experience. A sense of innocence pervaded us. It was as if we had awakened from a nightmare; our sense of time and space had been destroyed; but we knew that our old standards of reality had been delusions. Clocks and watches were mechanical toys. In Telepylus, our time-keeper was the Nature of which we were part.

We walked on for another five minutes; but again weakness overcame us. The scenery was blotted out by the persistent ache for heroin. We satisfied the craving, but the act now seemed abominable. There was no one to see us; and yet we felt as if Nature herself were offended by the presence of a monstrosity.

"I'll go on to the Abbey," said Lamus. "You'd better take it easy. I'll tell them to get some refreshments ready and send someone down to bring you along."

He waved his hand and strode up the hill with the steady swinging step of the practised mountaineer.

Lou's hand crept into mine. We were alone with nature. A new feeling had been born in us. The sense of personality had somehow faded out. I drew her gently into my arms; and we exchanged a long kiss such as we had never done before. We were not kissing each other. We were parts of the picture, whose natural expression it was to kiss.

"Hadn't we better go on?" said Lou after a while, releasing herself.

But at this moment we found ourselves confronted by a very extraordinary person indeed. It was a fair-haired boy of five years old, bare-footed but dressed in a short robe of rich blue with wide sleeves and a hood; the lining was of scarlet. He had a very serious face, and accosted us with a military salute:—

"Do what thou wilt shall be the whole of the Law," said the little fellow stoutly, and held out his hand. "I've come to take you up to the Abbey."

Even Lou realised that it was quite impossible to pick up such an important little person and kiss him. We entered into the solemnity of the occasion with proper dignity, and got up and shook hands.

Then, running down behind him, came an even smaller boy.

"Love law, love will," he said. It was obviously a point of politeness.

"They don't know what to say," explained the elder boy in a lenient tone. "My name is Hermes," he said to Lou, "and this is my friend Dionysus."

We broke into a fit of uncontrollable laughter which Hermes evidently thought highly improper. But Dionysus said to Lou, "I'll dive you a bid tiss."

She caught up the astonishing brat, and returned his salute with interest. When she put him down, he gave each of us one of his hands while Hermes led the way up the hill in an extremely business-like manner, looking back from time to time to make sure that we were all right.

Dionysus seemed to think it his business to entertain us with an account of the various objects along the road.

"That's the nice man's house down there," he said, "I'll take you to lunch with him if you promise to behave properly. And that's where the doat-woman lives," he went on, apparently assured by our guarantees of proper conduct.

The solemnity of the elder boy and the rollicking disposition of the other carried us from spasm to spasm of suppressed laughter.

"We seem to have walked straight into a fairy tale," said Lou.

"The Big Lion says that that's the only true kind of tale," replied Hermes, evidently prepared to argue the subject at great length if necessary. But I admitted the truth of his statement without difficulty.

"That's the Abbey," he went on, as we turned the corner of the hillside. And a long, low, white building came into sight.

"But that isn't an Abbey," I protested. "That's a villa."

"That's because you're looking with the wrong kind of eyes," objected Hermes. "I used to think the same myself before I was educated."

"Do you think Mr. Lamus will be able to educate us?" I asked, overpowered by a sense of the comicality of the situation.

"Oh, he isn't Mr. Lamus here," retorted Hermes loftily. "Here he's the Big Lion, and of course he can train anybody that isn't too old or too stupid. I was very stupid myself when I first came here," he continued in an apologetic tone. "It was the turning point of my career."

The child was certainly not more than five years old, and his conversation was absolutely incredible. The feeling grew that we had somehow strayed into an enchanted country. At the same time the country was enchanting.

Dionysus was all on fire to get us up to the Abbey, and tugged at our arms.

"Now Di," said Hermes, "you know it's wrong to pull at people like that. It's one of the rules," he explained to Lou, "not to interfere with people. The Big Lion says that everyone would get on all right if only he were left alone."

He seemed to think the statement required explanation.

"Cypris is reading Gibbon to us this week; and she shows us how all the trouble came from people meddling with other people's business."

I shouted with laughter. "Gibbon?" I cried, "What next, I wonder?"

"Well, one must know Roman history," explained Hermes, in the tone of a head master addressing an educational conference.

"And what did you read last week?" said Lou, though she was rocking with laughter as much as I was.

"Shelley was being read to us," he corrected. "We don't read ourselves."

"The Tenth don't dance," I quoted.

"Don't be an ass, Cockie," said Lou.

"Well, Hermes, but why don't you read?"

"The Big Lion doesn't want us to learn," he said. "We have to learn to use our eyes, and reading spoils them."

"But why?" asked Lou, in surprise. "I don't understand. I thought reading was the best way to get knowledge."

Dionysus put his foot down.

"Enough of Betause, be he damned for a dod."

It wasn't physical fatigue this time. These amazing children had made us forget all physical sensation. But when one is walking up-hill it is impossible to laugh as we wanted to laugh. We sat down on a patch of grass ablaze with flowers and rolled over and over, tearing up tufts of grass and biting them to overcome our emotions.

Dionysus evidently thought it was a game and began to romp; but Hermes, though evidently eager to join in the fun, was held back by his sense of responsibility.

"Where on earth did you learn such extraordinary language?" cried Lou at last, the tears running down her cheeks.

Hermes became more serious than ever.

"It's from the Book of the Law. Change not so much as the style of a letter," he said.

We began quite seriously to wonder whether we had not got into one of those fantastic waking dreams with which heroin had made us familiar. But this was a dream of a totally different quality. It had a strain of wholesomeness and actuality running through its incredible tissue of marvels.

At last we sat up and drew a long breath. Hermes hastened to assist

Lou to her feet, and the action, natural as it was, coming from such an extraordinary quarter, set us off laughing again.

Dionysus was regarding us with big serious eyes.

"You'll do," he suddenly decided; and began to execute a little step-dance of his own.

But we could see that Hermes, with all his unwillingness to interfere with other people, was impatient; and we scrambled to our feet. This time, Lou took his hand, and left me to bring up the rear with Dionysus, who poured forth an unending stream of prattle. I could not even hear it; the whole thing was too much for me.

We came out on to the terrace of the villa; King Lamus was standing in the open doorway. He had changed his travelling clothes for a silken robe of the brightest blue, with scarlet linings to the hood and sleeves like that of the boys. But on the breast in golden embroidery was an Egyptian eye within an equilateral triangle which was surrounded by a sun-blaze of rays.

Behind him stood two women in robes similar to those of the boys. One was about twenty-five years old, and the other nearer forty. Both had bobbed hair; the younger woman's of flaming chestnut, the elder's a rich silvery gray.

"That's the Bid Lion," said Dionysus, "with Athena and Cypris."

Hermes drew back and told us confidentially: "Now you be the first to say 'Do what thou wilt' to show you're more awake than they are."

We nodded encouragingly, and carried out the programme with success.

"Love is the law, love under will," answered the three people in the doorway. "Welcome to the Abbey of Thelema!"

In a moment, as by the breaking of a spell, the seriousness broke up. We were introduced warmly to the women, and began jabbering as if we had known each other all our lives. Basil had taken the two gods on his knees, and was listening happily to Hermes' story of how he had acquitted himself of his responsibility.

A table had been brought out on to the terrace, and we sat down to a meal. Athena put us in our places, and then explained that it was the custom at the Abbey to eat in silence; "as soon," she said, "as we have said Will."

What did she mean by "saying Will?" We had heard of saying grace before meat, but it was a long while since either of us had said it. However, the little mystery was soon explained.

She knocked on the table with the handle of a Tunisian dagger, its steel blade inlaid with silver. She knocked three times, then five, then three times more. Some significance was apparently attached to this peculiar method. She then said:—

"Do what thou wilt shall be the whole of the Law."

Dionysus showed signs of strong agitation. It was his turn to answer, and he was terribly afraid of forgetting his words in the presence of strangers. He looked up to Cypris pleadingly, and she whispered into his ear.

"What is dy will?" with a sudden burst of confidence and pride.

"It is my will to eat and drink," replied Athena gravely.

"To what end?" inquired Dionysus doubtfully.

"That my body may be fortified thereby."

The brat looked about him uneasily, as if the answer had taken the wind out of his sails. Cypris pressed his hand, and he brightened up again.

"To what end?" he repeated boldly.

"That I may accomplish the Great Work," replied Athena.

Dionysus seemed to have got on to his game. He retorted without the slightest hesitation.

"Love is the law, under will."

"Love is the law, *love* under will," corrected Cypris; and the baby repeated it solemnly.

"Fall to," cried Athena cheerfully, and sat down.

V

At Telepylus

L unch consisted of fish of a kind that we had never seen before; long, thin bodies with beaks like swordfish. We were very hungry; but they would have tasted exquisite under any circumstances. The meal continued with cheese, honey, and medlars; and ended gloriously with real Turkish coffee; not one cup but as many as we wanted; and Benedictine.

We had drunk the rough, strong wine of the country with the meal; and to us it tasted as if it had been the best red wine ever made. It had not been submitted to any chemical process. There was a sort of vitality inherent in it. It was primitive like all the arrangements of the Abbey, but the freshness and naturalness of everything made more than amends even to our cultivated palates. We were apparently sitting down to lunch with a choice selection of Olympian Deities; and the food seemed to be in keeping!

Besides that, we had no time to be critical; we were overwhelmed by the beauty of our surroundings.

Far away to the west, a line of hills ran out into the sea, the farther peaks were over fifty miles away, yet in that translucent atmosphere of spring they stood out sharply. We could even see in front of the range a small, dark line of crags which jutted out parallel with them and about ten miles nearer. Thence the coast line swept towards us in a complex curve of indescribable beauty and majesty. Telepylus being itself on a promontory, there was nothing to break the mighty stretch of sea between us and the distant range with its twin cones which overhang the principal city of the country; the city from which we had started that morning.

To the left of the coast line, a range of tumbled mountains, fantastically shaped and coloured, reached thence to the very hillside on which we were sitting. In front the ocean reached to the horizon. The light played upon its waves like some mysterious melody of Debussy's. It varied in hue from the most delicate canary yellow and glaucous green through infinite changing shades of peacockry to lilacs and deep purples. Ever-changing patches of colour wandered about the surface in kaleidoscopic fantasy.

A little to the right again, the limitless prospect of water was cut off by a precipitous cliff crowned by the ruins of a church, and up again to the right, the sheer crag reared its perpendicular terror to the skyline; a jagged line of quaintly carven pinnacle. Beyond these the slope suddenly eased off, and thence the rock took a final leap to its summit on which stood the remains of ancient Grecian temples.

With even greater suddenness the right hand precipice plunged clear into the sea. But on this side the view was closed in by groves of olive, cactus, and oak. The terrace before us was edged by a rock garden where flowered enormous geraniums, bushes of huge daisies, tall stems of purple iris, and a clump of reeds twice a man's height that swayed like dancers to the music of the gentle breeze that streamed up from the slopes of the sea.

Below the terrace were mulberry, cherry, and apple tress in blossom, together with a number of many-coloured trees whose names I did not know.

Between the house and the hill that overhung it on the south was a grassy garden shadowed by a gigantic tree of unfamiliar leaves, and behind this stood two Persian nuts, like cyclopean telegraph poles tufted with dark green leaves which reminded one of a guardsman's busby.

With the arrival of the coffee the rule of silence was broken. But Lamus had already left of the table. Athena explained that the theory of meals in the Abbey was that they were deplorable interruptions to work, and that "Will" was said before beginning to eat in order to emphasise the fact that the only excuse for eating was that it was necessary to keep one's body in condition to assist one in the performance of the Great Work, whatever that might be in any particular case. When anyone had finished he or she got up and went away without ceremony, the interruption being over.

Lamus now came out of the house in a flannel shirt and buckskin riding breeches. He sat down and began to drink his coffee and Benedictine. He was smoking a thin, black cigar, so strong that its very appearance was alarming.

"I hope you'll excuse me this afternoon," he said, "I have to go and inspect the other houses. This house is the antechamber, so to speak, where we receive strangers. In the other houses, various courses of training are carried on according to the Wills of their inhabitants. You will sleep here, of course, and considering the reason for which you have come—No, Dionysus, this isn't the time to say 'He shall fall down into the pit called Because, and there he shall perish with the dogs of Reason'—I will sleep down here for the present instead of in my lonely little tower, as I usually do."

We noticed that Cypris and the boys had slipped away quietly; but Athena sat engrossed in studying us.

"In the absence of Lala," he said, "Sister Athena is our chief psychologist. You will find her knowledge very useful to you and your work. I will leave her to talk things over with you for the next couple of hours. But, of course, the first thing is to get you rested from your journey."

He got up and walked off round the corner of the house. We didn't feel that we needed rest, we were much too interested by the atmosphere of the place. It was not merely the curious customs that stimulated our imaginations; there was an indefinable atmosphere about the place and the people which left us at a loss. The mixture of simplicity and elegance was in itself bizarre but still more so was the combination of absolute personal liberty with what was evidently in some ways a rather severe discipline. The automatic regularity with which everything was done seemed to imply an almost Prussian routine.

Lou saw the point at once, and with her usual frankness asked Sister Athena outright to explain it.

"Thank you for reminding me," said Sister Athena. "The Big Lion said you had better rest. Suppose you lie down in the studio. I know you don't want to go to sleep, but we can talk there just as well as we can here. So you'd better make yourselves comfortable while I explain our funny little ways."

The arrangements for repose were as primitive as everything else. The studio was furnished with narrow mattresses on steel springs on the floor. They were covered with comfortable cushions. We threw ourselves down with a certain hesitation; but immediately discovered that we were much more at home than if we had been at a higher elevation. It made the room seem larger, and the sensation of rest was more in evidence. There was a sort of finality about being so low, and it was certainly much more convenient to have our drinks and cigarettes on the floor than on a table. We found out that we had always gone about the world with a subconscious fear of knocking things over. I began to understand why a picnic on the grass gives such a sense of freedom. It was the absence of a worry which had annoyed us none the less because we had not been aware of it.

Sister Athena stretched herself out on a folding chair, also very low. It was no trouble for her to pick up her glass from the ground.

"About what you asked," she began, "it's perfectly true that we have vanadium steel discipline in this place; but we are made to think out everything for ourselves and the regulations don't bother us, as soon as we see their object.

In civilised life, so-called, at least two-thirds of everyone's time is wasted on things that don't matter. The idea of this place is to give everyone the maximum time for doing his own Will. Of course, if you come here with the fixed determination to resent everything that is different to what you are accustomed to, you can work yourself up into a constant irritation, which is all the worse because there is nothing to interfere with your indulgence. When I came here two years ago, every detail was an annoyance and an insult. But I came around gradually, through seeing that everything had been thought out. These people were enormously more efficient than I was, through economising the time and trouble which I had been accustomed to waste on trifles. I could no more fight them than Dionysus could fight Jack Dempsey. There is absolutely nothing to do here in the way of amusement except walking and climbing and reading, and playing Thelema; and, of course, bathing in the summer. The housework occupies practically no time at all because of the simplification of life. There is nowhere to go and nothing to do. The result is that with eating and everything else thrown in there is not much more than an hour of our waking time which is occupied by what one may call necessary work. Compare that with London! Mere dressing accounts for more than that. These robes are decorative enough for a royal banquet and yet they're absolutely practical for anything but rock climbing. To dress or undress is a matter of thirty seconds. Even our climbing clothes—it's merely a shirt and a pair of breeches, stockings and tennis shoes instead of these sandals— and off we go."

Lou and I listened sleepily to this disquisition. We were so interested that we simply had to keep awake. We each took a big sniff of heroin for the purpose. Sister Athena jumped up from her chair.

"That reminds me," she said, "I must get you your charts."

She went to a cabinet and produced two forms. We languidly marked our little crosses in the proper section.

"Excuse the interruption," she said, "but the Magical Record is always the first consideration in the Abbey."

The heroin woke me completely.

"I see the point, I think. All your rules are intended to reduce the part of life that has to be run by rules, as much as possible."

"That's it," she nodded emphatically.

"But I say," said Lou, "it's all very well; but I don't know whatever I'm to do with myself. The time must hang frightfully heavy on your hands."

"God forgive you," cried Athena. "One never has a minute one can call one's own!"

We laughed outright.

"It's easy to see you're a pupil of King Lamus. You have acquired his talent for paradox in a very complete manner."

"I know what you mean," she said, smiling. "If you're a lazy person, this is the worst place in the world for getting bored, and the lazier you determine to be the more bored you get. We had two people last year, absolutely hopeless rotters. They called themselves writers, and imagined they were working if they retired solemnly after breakfast and produced half a page of piffle by lunch. But they didn't know the meaning of work; and the place nearly drove them insane. They were bored with the Abbey, and bored with each other, and were very insulted because everybody laughed at them. But they couldn't see the way out, and wouldn't take it when it was shown them. It made them physically ill, and they went away at last to everyone's relief to an environment where they could potter about indefinitely and pose as great geniuses. The Big Lion does more in a day than they will ever do in their lives if they live into the next century. I'm sorry, too, as sorry as sorry can be. They were delightful personally, when they weren't pinned to a cork by their fixed ideals of what we ought to be doing. They had come one thousand miles to be trained, and then wouldn't give us a chance to train them. But they have good brains, and the stamp of this Abbey never wears off. They're better and wiser for their stay here, and they'll better and wiser still as soon as they allow themselves to admit it!"

"You don't encourage us much," said Lou in a really alarmed tone. "I haven't got even the consolation of these people. I can't fool myself that I am a *Wunderkind*. You probably know without my telling you that I've done nothing all my life but potter. And if I've nothing to potter about, I go off into the blackest boredom."

Sister Athena acquiesced.

"Yes, this place is kill or cure," she admitted, with a laugh. "But I'm glad to say that it's cure for most people. The two I was telling you about only failed because their vanity and selfishness was so extreme. They interpreted everything wrong, and expected the world to fall down and worship them for being wastrels. And at every turn they found the Big Lion in the way, to bring them back to reality. But the truth was too bitter medicine for them. If they had accepted the facts, they could have altered the facts; and learnt to do something worth while. But they preferred to cherish delusions of persecution. They persuaded themselves that they were being crucified when they were only having their faces washed. But the paint of self-esteem had been put on too thick; so away they went, and said how badly they'd been treated. Well, they had asked for the treatment themselves; and it will do them some good yet when they see the thing in perspective and discover that the adulation of their silly little clique of cranks in Soho is not really so good for their souls as the accurate abuse of their friends in this Abbey."

"Yes, I see that all right," said Lou, "and I know Basil too well to make that kind of fool of myself. But I'm still a little worried about this horrid efficiency of yours. Whatever am I to do with myself? Don't you understand that it was really boredom or the dread of it that drove me to heroin to pass away the time?"

"That's just it," said Athena very seriously. "This is all kinds of a place for driving a fellow to drink. And that's why the Big Lion insists on our going through the mill. But it takes us a very short time to realise that there is not enough heroin in the world to tide us over a single day in such a ghastly place, so we quit."

Here was another of Basil's paradoxes in full working order. But they came quite differently from the lips of a steady-going serious-minded person of this kind. The personality of the Big Lion is his greatest asset in one way, but in another it handicaps him frightfully. His cynical manner, his habitual irony, the sensation he produces that he is making fun of one; all these make one inclined to dismiss everything that he says as "mere paradox" without investigation. Lamus is too clever by half; but Sister Athena spoke with such simple earnestness and directness that although she too had a sense of humour of her own, Basil's ideas were very much more effective when they had passed through the machinery of her mind than when they frothed fresh from his. I had always been inclined to distrust King Lamus. It was impossible to distrust this woman who trusted him, or to doubt that she was right to trust him.

He never seemed able even to take himself seriously, perhaps because he was afraid of appearing pompous or a prig; but she had taken him seriously and got the best out of him.

"Well, Sister Athena," said Lou, "if even heroin's no good, what is?"

"I'm afraid I'll have to treat you to another paradox," she said, lighting a cigarette. "I'm afraid that at first sight you'll think there must be something wrong. It's really such a revolutionary reversal of what seems obvious. But I've been through it myself, and the plain fact is this: finding ourselves here with so much more time on our hands than we ever had in our lives, we get desperate. In a big city, if we're bored, we simply look around for some diversion, and there are plenty of them. But here, there's no alleviation or the possibility of it. We must either go under completely or decide to swim. Here's another case where the Big Lion, who must certainly be Satan himself, economises time. One has to be very stupid not to discover within forty-eight hours that there is no possibility of amusing oneself in any of the ordinary ways. In London one could waste one's life before bringing one's mind to the point where Big Lion wants it. So one finds oneself immediately up against the fact that one has got to find something to do. Well, we go and ask Big Lion; and Big Lion says: 'Do what thou wilt.' 'But, yes,' we say, 'what is that?' He replies rudely, 'Find out.' We ask how to find out; and he says, 'How do you know what is the good of a motor-car?' Well, we think a bit; and then we tell him that we find out the use of a motor-car by examining it, looking at its various parts, comparing it and them with similar machines whose use we already know, such as the bullock wagon and the steam engine. We make up our minds that an automobile is constructed in order to travel along the high road. 'Very good,' says Big Lion, 'go up top. Examine yourself, your faculties and tendencies, the trend of your mind, and the aspirations of your soul. Allow me to assure you that you will find this investigation leaves you very little time to wonder what in the devil to do with yourself.' 'Thank you very much,' we say, 'but suppose our judgment is wrong, suppose that what we have decided is an automobile intended to go, is in reality a coffin intended to contain a corpse?' 'Quite so,' says Big Lion, 'you have to test your judgment; and you don't do that by asking the opinion of people who are probably more ignorant than yourself; you get into the beastly thing and press the proper button, and if it goes it's an automobile, and you've made no mistake. Didn't you read what it says in the Book of the Law: "Success is your proof?" And allow me again to assure you that when you've got yourself going, doing your True Will, you won't find you have anytime to get bored.'"

She threw away her cigarette after lighting another from the butt. She seemed to be brooding, as if much deeper thoughts were passing through her mind than even those to which she was giving such airy expression.

We watched her intently. The heroin had calmed and intensified our thought, which was intensely stimulated by her explanation. We had no wish to interrupt. We wished she could have gone on talking forever.

Her self-absorption became still more marked. After a very long pause she went on slowly talking, so it seemed, to herself more than to us and with the intention to giving form to her own idea, that of instructing us.

"I suppose that must be the idea," she said.

She had a curious mouth, with square-cut lips like one sees in some old Egyptian statues, and a twist at the corners in which lurked incalculable possibilities of self-expression. Her eyes were deep-set and calm. It was a square face with a very peculiar jaw expressing terrific determination. I have never seen a face in which courage was so strongly marked.

"Yes, I think I see it now. He forces one to come to what I might call the point of death. The whole of life is reviewed in perspective, and its meaning seized. But instead of being snatched away to face the unknown, as in the case of death, one has the opportunity and the necessity to take up the old life from the point at which one left off, with a clear apprehension of the past which determines the future. That is the meaning of what he calls initiation. I understand 'Thou hast no right but to do thy will.' That is why the old hierophants shut up the candidate in silence and darkness. He had the choice between going mad or knowing himself. And when he was brought out into light and life, restored to love and liberty, he was in very truth a Neophyte, a man new-born. Big Lion puts us through it without our knowing what he's doing. Though I've been through it myself, I didn't know in this clear way what had really happened until I tried to explain it to you."

The sense of being enchanted came over me again very strongly. I looked across at Lou, and I could see in her eyes that she felt the same. But she was trembling with excitement and eagerness. Her eyes were fixed on the face of Sister Athena with devouring ardour. She

ALEISTER CROWLEY

was looking forward to undergoing this terrific experience. My own mood was slightly different. Already my past life surged up before me in a series of pulsating pictures. I was revolted by the incoherence and fatuity of the past. The achievements of which I was proudest had lost their savour because they pointed to nowhere in particular. The words of Lewis Carroll came into my mind:—

"A wise fish never goes anywhere without a porpoise." And quite inconsequentially my brain took up the time:—

> *"Will you, won't you, will you, won't you,*
> *Won't you join the dance?"*

When I woke it was, I suppose, about midnight. Rugs had been thrown over me where I lay. I was quite warm, despite the breeze that came in through the open door. It struck me as very strange that it should be open. The country was notoriously infested with brigands.

King Lamus was sitting at his desk writing by the light of a lamp. I watched him idly, feeling very comfortable and disinclined to move.

Presently I heard the deep booming of a bell in the far-off cathedral. It was twelve o'clock.

He immediately rose and went to the doorway, down the steps and on to the moonlit terrace. He faced the north. In a deep solemn voice he recited what was apparently an invocation.

"Hail unto thee who art Ra in thy silence, even unto thee who art Kephra the beetle, that travellest under the heavens in thy bark in the midnight hour of the sun. Tahuti standeth in his splendour at the prow, and Ra-Hoor abideth at the helm. Hail unto thee from the abodes of evening!"

He accompanied the speech with a complicated series of gestures. When he had finished he returned and noticed that I was awake.

"Well, did you have a good sleep?" he said softly, standing over my mattress.

"I never had a better one."

It would be impossible to give the details of even one day at Telepylus. Life there has all the fullness of the heroin life with none of its disillusions. I must simply select such incidents as bear directly on our Purgatorio.

I dropped off to sleep again after a short chat with Basil about indifferent affairs, and woke in the morning very much refreshed, and yet overpowered by the conviction that it was impossible to get up without heroin.

But the bright spring sun, his rays falling so freshly on the crags green-gray and dun opposite, reminded me that I had come to Telepylus to renew my youth. I held back my hand. Little by little, strength came back to me; but as it did so the feeling of helplessness in the absence of heroin was replaced by the presence of craving for it.

I dragged myself from the mattress and got unsteadily to my feet. Lou was still sleeping, and she looked so lovely in the pure pale light that filtered into the room that I took a firmer resolve to break off the habit that had destroyed our love. It was only in sleep that she was beautiful at all in these last months. Waking, the expression of tenseness and wretchedness, the nervous twitching of her face and the destruction of her complexion by the inability of the liver to throw off the toxic effects of the drug, made her look not only twice her age but ugly, with that ugliness of vice and illness which is so much more repulsive than any merely æsthetic errors of nature.

Lou, more than any girl I ever knew, depended for her beauty upon her spiritual state. The influence of an idea would transform her in a moment from Venus to Echidna or the reverse.

It was deep spiritual satisfaction that made her so lovely this morning. But even as I stood and looked, the horrible restlessness of the heroin craving nearly drove me to take the stuff without my body telling me what it was doing. But I detected the movement in time.

I thought a brisk walk might help me to pass through the critical moment. Just as I got out of the house, I was met by Sister Athena.

"Do what thou wilt shall be the whole of the Law," she said.

It was the regular morning greeting at the Abbey. Accustomed as I was to the phrase, it still took me rather aback.

"Good-morning," I said in a rather embarrassed way.

"The answer is 'Love is the law, love under will,'" she smiled. "We exchange this greeting so as to make sure that the sight of our friends doesn't distract us from the Great Work. Now we can talk about whatever we like. Oh, no, we can't, I must first inspect your yesterday's chart."

I brought it out, and we sat down at the table together. Of course, there was only the one cross. She assumed a very severe look.

"This is extremely irregular, brother," she said. "You haven't filled in column two."

I discovered later that it was part of the system of the Abbey to pretend to be very severe about any infraction of the rules, and then to show by some pleasant remark that it wasn't meant in anger. The object was to fix in one's mind that the offence was really grave, so that the pretended scolding had all the effect of the genuine article.

Not knowing this, I was surprised when she continued:

"That's all right, Cockie, we know you're a new chum."

But her finger pointed sternly to column two. It was headed, "Reason for taking the dose."

Well, Dionysus had shown me the way out of that, so I turned impudently around and said:—

"Enough of Because, be he damned for a dog!"

The effect was electric. We both broke into a duet of low musical laughter that seemed to me in exquisite harmony with the beauty of the April morning.

"The devil can quote scripture," she retorted, "that business about Because refers to something entirely different. The point about this (she was very serious now) is that we want you to know what is going on in your own mind. We all do so many stupid things, for bad reason or no reason at all. 'Forgive them, Father, they know not what they do' applies to nine-tenths of our actions. We get so much work done in this Abbey because we have learnt to watch our minds and prevent ourselves wasting a moment on what is worthless, or cancelling out one course of action by another, and so getting nowhere. In the case of this experiment of yours, in learning to master a drug so powerful that hardly one man in ten thousand stands a dog's chance of coming out, it's especially important because, as I'm afraid you will find out, I mean, as I hope you will find out very soon, your brain has developed certain morbid tendencies. You are liable to think crooked. Big Lion has told me already how you got to the stage where you took one dose to sleep and another to wake up again, and where you would try to conceal the amount you were taking from the very person with whom you were taking it openly. Another point is that privation always upsets the mental balance. A man who lacks food or money finds very queer thoughts come into his mind, and does things, not necessarily connected with his necessity, obsessing though that be, which are entirely out of keeping with his character."

I took a pencil, and wrote at once against the cross in column two "In order to make the most of Sister Athena's illuminating discourse."

She laughed merrily.

"You see, it's Adam and Eve all over again! You're trying to shift the blame on to me. By the way, I see your body is nervous at this moment. If you don't want to take heroin, as you don't, else you wouldn't have let yourself get as shaky as you are, you'd better take a white tablet. It won't put you to sleep, as you've had a night's rest, and the poor little thing won't have anything to do but run around your solar plexus and stroke all your little pussy-cat nerves the right way."

I took the advice and felt much better. At that moment King Lamus appeared, and challenged Sister Athena to a set of Thelema. I brought Lou out; and we sat in the courtyard and watched them play.

Thelema is so called because of the variety of strokes. It is a sort of Fives played with an association football, but there are no side walls, only a low wall at the back over which, if the ball goes, it is out of play, as also if it strikes outside the vertical lines painted on the wall or below a ledge about a foot from the ground. The ball may be struck with any part of the body so long as it is struck clean, and the game is bewilderingly fast to watch.

After two games, the players were perspiring violently. The score was kept somewhat as in tennis, but each point had a monosyllabic name to economise time. It also had a certain startling implication—with the object of familiarising the mind with ideas which normally excited.

The whole system of King Lamus was to enable people to take no notice, that is, no emotional notice, of anything soever in life. A great deal of the fascination of drugs arises from the fuss that is made about them; the focusing of the attention upon them. Absinthe, forbidden in France, Switzerland, and Italy, is still sold freely in England, and no one ever met an English absinthe fiend. If anyone took it into his head to start a newspaper campaign against absinthe, it would become a public danger in very short order.

King Lamus emancipated people's minds by adopting the contrary formula. He had all sorts of dodges for compelling people to accept the most startling sights and sounds as commonplace. The very children were confronted with the most terrifying ideas while they were still too young to have acquired settled phobias.

Hermes, at the age of five, was already accustomed to witness surgical operations and such things, to face the dangers of drowning and falling from cliffs, with the result that he had completely lost his fear of such things.

These principles were explained to us during the breathing spaces between the sets. Sister Cypris and three or four others came down from the other houses to take part in the game.

The intense activity and lightheartedness of everybody amazed us. We were asked to join in the game, and our incompetence was a keen source of annoyance. We were too enfeebled by our indulgence in drugs to hold our own; and the result was to inspire us with a passionate determination to emancipate ourselves from the thraldom.

But the tribulations of the morning had only begun. It was the custom of the Abbey to celebrate the arrival of new-comers by a picnic on the top of the rock. From the Abbey, a path leads through a patch of trees to a rough narrow track between two walls. At the end of this is an aqueduct across the road, and both Lou and I were too nervous to walk along the narrow causeway. We had to go round, feeling more and more ashamed of ourselves with every incident.

On the other side, the hill rises steeply. A tongue of grass leads to a gully which is filled by the wall of the old city which crowned the rock two thousand years or more ago, when the world was less arid and the population could depend on rainfall instead of having to cluster in the neighbourhood of springs and streams for its water.

King Lamus tied himself on the middle of a rope with Dionysus at one end and Hermes at the other; while we, under the guidance of Cypris and Athena, toiled up the goat track which made a zigzag on the grassy tongue. Their party attacked the rock buttress on our right.

King Lamus made Hermes lead up the most astonishingly precipitous crags, with little advice and no assistance. But his hand was always within reach of the boy; so that if he made a mistake and fell, he could immediately be caught without hurting himself.

But the child himself did not know how carefully he was being watched and guarded. Basil treated him in every way as a responsible leader.

Their progress was necessarily slow; but so was ours. Both Lou and I found it impossible to go more than twenty paces or so without a rest. We had plenty of time to watch them, and it was amazing to see the working of the mind of Hermes as problem after problem presented itself to him.

There were many occasions on which it would have been easy for him to go around an obstacle, but he never attempted to do so. King

Lamus had already implanted in his mind the idea that the fun of rock-climbing consisted in tackling the most difficult passages.

The child would occasionally stop at the foot of a pitch, and contemplate it as if it were a mathematical problem. Once or twice he decided that it was too hard for him. On these occasions, King Lamus would go up first, calling out instructions to note the exact places where he put his hands and feet; and when it was the turn of Hermes to follow, as often as not he did so on a slack rope. His leader's example had taught him how to negotiate the difficulty.

As for Dionysus, his methods were entirely different. He had neither the intellectual power of the elder boy nor his prudence, and he climbed with a sort of tempestuous genius.

At the top of the tongue, the goat track bends suddenly to the right, under the wall, to a point where there is a breach where one can crawl through very comfortably. Here we rejoined the climbers.

"Tomorrow," said Hermes, "I shall take you up the Great Gully," with the air of a full-fledged alpine guide.

Dionysus shook his little head. "I don't know if he tan det through the hole," he lamented.

King Lamus had taken off the rope and made it into a coil by winding it around his knee and foot. We plodded painfully over very rough ground to the top of the rock. It was both exhilarating and disheartening to see the way the two boys scrambled from boulder to boulder.

At last we reached the top. The two brethren who had carried up the provisions in knapsacks had already begun to spread them out on a level patch of grass.

VI

THE TRUE WILL

L ou and I were both utterly exhausted by the climb; and King Lamus reminded us that this was the formula of the Abbey of Thelema at Telepylus, that everyone had to reach the top, step by step, through his own exertions. There was no question of soaring into the air by alien aid; and in all probability coming to earth with a bump.

We had found ourselves repeatedly out of breath during the ascent, though it had only occupied three-quarters of an hour, and we should certainly never have reached the top without recourse to heroin.

But all the time we were lost in amazement at the behaviour of the boys; their independence, their fearlessness, and their instinctive economy of force. We had no idea that it was possible for children of that age to achieve, even physically, what they had done, apparently without effort.

And as for their moral attitude, it was entirely outside our experience. I said something of the sort; and King Lamus retorted at once that it was the moral attitude which made possible the physical attainment.

"You will find that out for yourself in the case of your own experiment. It will do you very little good to break off your present practice. When you begin to tackle a subject, you must endure to the end, and the end never comes until you can say either yes or no, indifferently, to physical considerations."

But for all that, both Lou and I were exalted by our physical triumph over the rock, trifling as it was; and our situation on the summit reminded us of some of the sensations of flying. There was the same detachment from the affairs of the world, the same visions of normal life in perspective; the ruddy brown roofs of the houses, the patches of tilled land, the distant hillsides with their fairy-like remoteness, the level plain of the sea, the receding coast line; all these things were so many witnesses of one great truth—that only by climbing painfully to a spot beyond human intervention, could one obtain a stable point of view from which to regard the Universe in due proportion.

At once we drew the moral analogy to our physical situation, and applied it to our immediate problem. Yet, in spite of what Lamus had said, we were both obsessed by the idea that we must stop taking heroin.

The next few days passed in strenuous efforts to reduce the number of the doses, and it was then that we began to discover the animal cunning of our bodies. Do what we might, there was always a reason, an imperative reason, for taking a dose at any given moment.

Our minds, too, began to play us false. We found ourselves arguing as to what a dose was. As the doses became fewer, they became larger. Presently, we arrived at the stage where what we considered a fair dose could not be conveniently taken at a single sniff. And then, worst of all, it broke on me one day, when I was struggling hard against the temptation to indulge, that the period between doses, however prolonged it might be, were being regarded merely in that light. In other words, it was a negative thing.

Life consisted in taking heroin. The intervals between the doses did not count. It was like the attitude of the normal man with regard to sleep.

It suddenly dawned upon me that this painful process of gradually learning to abstain, was not a cure at all in any right sense of the word.

Basil was perfectly right. I must reverse the entire process and reckon my life in positive terms. That's what he means by "Do what thou wilt." I wonder what my true will is? Is there really such a thing at all? My mathematics tells me that there must be. However many forces there may be at work, one can always find their resultant.

But this was all terribly vague. The desire to take heroin was clear-cut. It no longer produced any particular effect to take it. Now that I was getting down to two or three doses a day, at the most, it seemed as though there were no particular object in taking it, even as dulling the craving for it. I found it increasingly difficult to fill column two.

King Lamus descended on me one morning, just after I had taken a dose, and was raking my brain for a reason for my action. I was alternately chewing the end of my pencil and making meaningless marks on the paper. I told him my difficulty.

"Always glad to help," he said airily; went to a filing cabinet and produced a docket of typed manuscripts. He put it in my hand. It was headed, "Reasons for taking it."

1. My cough is very bad this morning.
   (Note: (*a*) Is cough really bad?

(*b*) If so, is the body coughing because it is sick or because it wants to persuade you to give it some heroin?)

2. To buck me up.
3. I can't sleep without it.
4. I can't keep awake without it.
5. I must be at my best to do what I have to do. If I can only bring that off, I need never take it again.
6. I must show I am master of it—free to say either "yes" or "no." And I must be perfectly sure by saying "yes" at the moment. My refusal to take it at the moment shows weakness. Therefore I take it.
7. In spite of the knowledge of the disadvantages of the heroin life, I am really not sure whether it isn't better than the other life. After all, I get extraordinary things out of heroin which I should never have got otherwise.
8. It is dangerous to stop too suddenly.
9. I'd better take a small dose now rather than put it off till later; because if I do so, it will disturb my sleep.
10. It is really very bad for the mind to be constantly preoccupied with the question of the drug. It is better to take a small dose to rid myself of the obsession.
11. I am worried about the drug because of my not having any. If I were to take some, my mind would clear up immediately, and I should be able to think out good plans for stopping it.
12. The gods may be leading me to some new experience through taking it.
13. It is quite certainly a mistake putting down all little discomforts as results of taking it. Very likely, nearly all of them are illusions; the rest, due to the unwise use of it. I am simply scaring myself into saying "no."
14. It is bad for me morally to say "no." I must not be a coward about it.
15. There is no evidence at all that the reasonable use of heroin does not lengthen life. Chinese claim, and English physicians agree, that opium smoking, within limits, is a practice conducive to longevity. Why should it not be the same with heroin? It has been observed actually that addicts seem to be immune to most diseases which afflict ordinary people.

16. I take it because of its being prohibited. I decline being treated like a silly schooboy when I'm a responsible man.
    (Note: Then don't behave like a silly schoolboy. Why let the stupidity of governments drive you into taking the drug against your will?—K. L.)
17. My friend likes me to take it with her.
18. My ability to take it shows my superiority over other people.
19. Most of us dig our graves with our teeth. Heroin has destroyed my appetite, therefore it is good for me.
20. I have got into all sorts of messes with women in the past. Heroin has destroyed my interest in them.
21. Heroin has removed my desire for liquor. If I must choose, I really think heroin is the better.
22. Man has a right to spiritual ambition. He has evolved to what he is, through making dangerous experiments. Heroin certainly helps me to obtain a new spiritual outlook on the world. I have no right to assume that the ruin of bodily health is injurious; and "whosoever will save his life shall lose it, but whoever loseth his life for My sake shall find it."
23. So-and-so has taken it for years, and is all right.
24. So-and-so has taken it for years, and is still taking it, and he is the most remarkable man of his century.
25. I'm feeling so very, very rotten, and a very, very little would make me feel so very, very good.
26. We can't stop while we have it—the temptation is too strong. The best way is to finish it. We probably won't be able to get anymore, so we take it in order to stop taking it.
27. Claude Farrère's story of Rodolphe Hafner. Suppose I take all this pains to stop drugs and then get cancer or something right away, what a fool I shall feel!

"Help you at all?" asked Lamus.

Well, honestly, it did not. I had thought out most of those things for myself at one time or another; and I seemed to have got past them. It's a curious thing that once you've written down a reason you diminish its value. You can't go on using the same reason indefinitely. That fact tends to prove that the alleged reason is artificial and false, that it has simply been invented on the spur of the moment by oneself to excuse one's indulgences.

ALEISTER CROWLEY

Basil saw my perplexity.

"The fact is," he said, "that you're taking this stuff as the majority of people go to church. It's a meaningless habit."

I hated to put that down on my paper. It was confessing that I was an automaton. But something in his eye compelled me. I wrote the word, and broke out as I did so into a spasm of internal fury. I recollected a story from my hospital days, of a man who had committed suicide when it was proved to him that he couldn't move his upper jaw.

Meanwhile Lamus was looking at my average. I had got down to less than two doses daily. But the rest of the twenty-four hours was spent in waiting for the time when I could indulge.

I knew that Lou was ahead of me. She had gone on what Basil called his third class. She was taking one dose a day; but everyday she was taking it later and later. She had about an hour of real craving to get through, and Sister Athena or Sister Cypris, or Sister someone would always intervene, as if by accident, and take some active steps to keep her mind off the subject during those critical minutes.

As soon as one had reached an interval of forty-eight hours between doses, one entered class four and stopped altogether unless some particular occasion arose for taking a dose.

I was very annoyed that Lou should have got on faster than myself. Basil told me he thought I needed more active exercise, though already I had begun to take some interest in the sports of the place. I had even got through a whole game of Thelema without having to sit down and gasp.

But there was still an obscure hankering after the drug life. It had been burnt into me that normal interests were not worth while.

King Lamus had taken me out climbing several times; but while I experienced profound physical satisfaction, I could not overcome the moral attitude which is really, after all, expressed in Ecclesiastes, "Vanity, vanity, all is vanity!"

My relations with Lou herself were poisoned by the same feeling. The improvement in our physical health, and the intoxicating effect of the climate and the surroundings urged us to take part in the pageant of nature. Yet against all such ideas we could not help but hear the insistent voice of Haidee Lamoureux, that the end of all these things is death. She had deliberately renounced existence as futile, and there was no answer to her pleadings.

Besides this, my mind had eaten up its pabulum. I had literally nothing to think of except heroin, and I discovered that heroin appealed to me behind all veils, as being an escape from life.

A man who has once experienced the drug-life finds it difficult to put up with the inanity of normal existence. He has become wise with the wisdom of despair.

The Big Lion and Sister Athena exhausted their ingenuity in finding things with which I might occupy my weary aimless hours. But nothing seemed to get me out of the fixed idea that life was heroin with intervals that did not count.

For about a week King Lamus tried to get me out of my groove by giving me cocaine, and asking me to employ my time by writing an account of my adventures from the time when I began to take it. The drug stimulated me immensely; and I was quite enthusiastic for the time. I wrote the story of my adventures from the night of my meeting Lou to our return to England from Naples.

But when the episode was over, I found the old despair of life as strong as ever. The will to live was really dead in me.

But two evenings later King Lamus came to smoke a pipe with me on the terrace at sunset. In his hand was the Paradiso record which I had written. Sister Athena had typed it.

"My dear man," he said, "what I can't see is why you should be so blind about yourself. The meaning of all this ought to be perfectly obvious. I'm afraid you haven't grasped the meaning of 'Do what thou wilt.' Do you see how the application of the Law has helped you so far?"

"Well, of course," I said, "it's pretty clear I didn't come to this planet to drug myself into my grave before my powers have had a chance to ripen. I've thought it necessary to keep off heroin in order to give myself a show. But I'm left flat. Life becomes more tedious everyday, and the one way of escape is barred by flaming swords."

"Exactly," he replied. "You've only discovered one thing that you don't will; you have still to find the one thing that you do will. And yet there are quite a number of clues in this manuscript of yours. I note you say that your squad commander, who didn't become that without some power of dealing with men, told you that you were not a great flyer. How was it exactly that you came to take up flying?"

That simple question induced a very surprising reaction. There was no reason why it should produce the intense irritation that it did.

Basil noticed it, rubbed his hands together gleefully, and began to hum "Tipperary." His meaning was evident. He had drawn a bow in a venture; and it had pierced the King of Israel between the joints of his harness. He got up with alacrity, and went off with a wave of the hand.

"Think it over, dear boy," said he, "and tell me your sad story in the morning."

I was in a very disturbed state of mind. I went to look for Lou, but she had gone for a walk with Cypris, and when she came back, she wore an air of wisdom which I found insupportable. However, I told her my story. To my disgust, she simply nodded as if highly appreciative of some very obscure joke. There was no getting any sense out of her. I went to bed in a thoroughly bad temper.

Almost immediately, the usual struggle began, as to whether I should or should not take a dose of heroin. On this occasion, the controversy was short. I was so annoyed with myself that I took a specially large sniff, apparently less to soothe myself than to annoy somebody else indirectly. It was the first I had had for a week. I had been supplying its place with codeine.

Partly from this and partly from the psychological crisis, its effects were such as I had never before experienced. I remained all night in a state between sleep and waking, unable to call for assistance, unable to control my thoughts; and I was transported into a totally unfamiliar world. I did not exist at all, in any ordinary sense of the word. I was a mathematical expression in a complex scheme of geometry. My equilibrium was maintained by innumerable other forces in the same system, and what I called myself was in some mysterious way charged with a duty of manipulating the other forces, and these evaded me. When I strove to grasp them, they disappeared. My functions seemed to be to simplify complex expressions, and then to build up new complexes from the elements so isolated as to create simulacra of my own expression in other forms.

This process continued, repeating itself with delirious intensity through endless æons. I suffered the intolerable pang of losing my individuality altogether by confusing it, so to speak, with some of the expressions that I had formulated. The distress became so acute that I felt the necessity of getting Lou to assist me. But I could not discover her anywhere in the system.

And yet, there was something in the nature of the curves themselves which I identified with her. It was as if their ultimate form in some way depended upon her. She was concealed, so to speak, in the expression of the ideas. She was implicit in their structure; and as the worst of the excitement and the anxiety subsided, I found a curious consolation in the fact that she was not an independent and conflicting unit in this complicated chaos of machinery, but was, as it were, the reason for its assuming its actual appearance in preference to any other. And as the night went on, the enormous complexity of the vision co-ordinated itself. There was a sensation of whirling and rising communicated to the entire universe of my thought. A sort of dizziness seized upon my spirit. It was as if a wheel had been set in motion and gradually increased its pace so that one could no longer distinguish the spokes. It became an indefinite whirr. This feeling invaded my entire consciousness little by little, so that it was reduced to an unchanging unity; but a unity composed of diverse forces in regular motion. The monotony devoured consciousness so that my waking sleep merged into true sleep.

The strangest part of the whole experience was that I woke up an entirely new man. I found myself engrossed in abstruse calculations, loosely knit together, it is true, but very intense, with regard to an idea which had not entered my mind for months. I was working out in my mind a plan for constructing a helicopter, the invention of which had occupied me deeply when I was out of a job. It had been driven completely out of my mind by my becoming heir to Uncle Mortimer's estate.

As I regained full wakefulness, I found myself extremely puzzled by my surroundings. In fact, I could not remember who I was. The question seemed in some extraordinary way to lack meaning. The more I regained consciousness of myself, of Telepylus, and of the immediate past, the more these things became unreal. The true "I" was the mathematician and engineer working on the helicopter, and the interval had been an elaborate nightmare.

I threw it all off like a retriever coming out of a pond with a stick in his mouth, and bent myself to my work. I was disturbed by some person or persons unknown kissing me on the back of my neck, and putting a tray with my breakfast at my side. I was aware of a vague subconscious annoyance that the food was cold.

When the tom-tom sounded for the noonday Adoration, I got up and stretched myself; my brain was completely fagged out. I joined the little party on the terrace at the salutation to the sun.

"Hail unto thee who art Ahathor in thy triumphing, even unto thee who art Ahathor in thy beauty; that travellest over the heavens in thy bark at the mid-career of the Sun. Tahuti standeth in his splendour at the prow, and Ra-Hoor abideth at the helm. Hail unto thee from the abodes of morning!"

One of the party made a very singular impression on me. There was something indefinably Mongolian about her face. The planes were flat; the cheek-bones high; the eyes oblique; the nose wide, short, and vital; the mouth a long, thin, rippling curve like a mad sunset. The eyes were tiny and green with a piquant elfin expression. Her hair was curiously colourless; it was very abundant; she had wound great ropes about her head. It reminded me of the armature of a dynamo. It produced a weird effect—this mingling of the savage Mongol with the savage Norseman type. Her strange hair fascinated me. It was that delicate flaxen hue— so fine. The face was extraordinarily young and fresh, all radiant with smiles and blushes.

"Peter, my boy," I said to myself, "you'd better get busy and finish that helicopter and make some money, because that's the girl you're going to marry."

This conviction seized me with the force of a revelation; for the girl was mysteriously familiar. It seemed as if I had seen her in a dream or something like that. I was very annoyed to find an arm familiarly slipped through mine, while a voice said in my ear:—

"We may as well walk over to the refectory for lunch. You haven't answered my question about how you came to take up flying."

"When you asked me, I wasn't at all clear in my mind, but the chain of causes is sufficiently obvious now."

I had never taken kindly to medicine. Its unscientific procedure, its arrogance, its snobbishness, and its empiricism all combined to disgust me. I had simply gone to the hospital because my father was bent on it, and wouldn't put up the money for anything else. I wanted to be an engineer. I was keen as mustard on bicycles and automobiles. Even as a boy I had had a sort of workshop of my own. The greatest pleasure of my childhood had been the rare visits to my mother's father, who in his time had been a great inventor and done an immense amount of work relative to the mechanical perfection of railway travelling.

When the war broke out I had gone straight to the engineering shops; and I became a flying man rather against my will, on account of my weight and the dearth of pilots.

I broke off in my enthusiastic harangue, because King Lamus had stopped on the crest of the ridge which divided the strangers' house at the Abbey from the main buildings.

"The climb has put you out of breath," he said. "Take a sniff of this; it will put you all right in a second."

I pushed the man's hand away impatiently, and the little heap of powder fell to the ground.

"Oh, it's like that, is it?" said Basil laughing.

I realised how rude I had been, and began to apologise.

"That's all right," he said. "But, of course, you aren't going to get out of it as easily as that. You don't give up eating mutton because you ate too much one day and got indigestion. You'll find heroin pretty useful when you know how to use it. However, your gesture just now was automatic. It was evidence that your unconscious or true will objects to your taking heroin. So far so good for the negative side. But the question is, what does your true will actually want you to do in a positive way?"

"Confound the fellow and his eternal metaphysics," I thought.

"I haven't the least idea," I answered sharply, "and what's more, I've no time to waste on this occult stuff of yours. Don't think I'm rude. I'm very grateful for all you've done for me."

Strangely enough, the memory of the last few months had just returned to my mind. Yet it was merely the background of the burning flame of thought that filled my consciousness.

Basil did not answer, and as we walked down the hill together I began to explain my ideas about the new helicopter. Almost without knowing it, we had reached the door of the large house which the Abbey used for a refectory, and we sat down on the stone seats which lined its north-eastern wall, and gazed over the marvellous prospect.

The refectory was set on a steep slope. The ground fell sharply away from below our feet. On the left, the great rock towered even more tremendously than on the other side; and on the right, the hills above the coast-line danced away into dim purple. In front was a strange jagged headland crowned with a fantastic cluster of rocks, and beyond this the great sea stretched away, in masses of greens and blues and violets, to where a number of volcanic islands slumbered dimly on the horizon.

Basil annoyed me intensely by interpolating remarks about the beauty of the scenery. I couldn't seem to interest him in the helicopter at all. Was I really talking such rubbish?

"I'm too old to be snubbed, Sir Peter," (Oh, yes, I was Sir Peter now! Of course I was.) he interjected, shaking me gently by the shoulder.

I had paused to clear up a point in my mind about one of the gauges.

"And I must remind you that you are a gentleman; and that when you came to this Abbey the first thing you did was to sign a pledge-form."

He repeated the words:—

"I do solemnly declare that I accept the Law of Thelema, that I will devote myself to discover my True Will, and to do it."

"Yes, yes, of course," I said hurriedly. "I'm not trying to get out of it; but really, I am at the moment most frightfully preoccupied with this idea about the helicopter."

"Thank you, that will do," said King Lamus briskly. "The meeting will now adjourn."

I felt a little irritation at his offhand manner, but I followed him in to lunch. He stood at the end of the table, facing Sister Athena at the other.

"There will be champagne," he said, "for lunch today."

The remark was received with a hilarity which seemed positively indecent, and altogether out of proportion to the good news announced. The whole Abbey seemed to have gone wild with delight.

Following the example of the Big Lion, everyone pointed a forefinger downwards to the left, swung it sharply across to the right. This gesture was repeated three times and accompanied by the words:—

"Evoe Ho! Evoe Ho! Evoe Ho!"

They began to clap hands but checked the movement before contact and only allowed the clash to take place on the third syllable of the great cry

IAO

This was followed by very rapid clapping three times three, in silence.

I was entirely bewildered by this demonstration, but had no opportunity to make inquiries, for Sister Cypris immediately said "Will" with Hermes, and lunch began in the invariable silence, a silence somewhat modified by the exuberant hilarity of the entire assembly.

The champagne would not account for it all. The unrestrained glee reminded me of my early days with cocaine. However, I had something better to think about. The question was how to reduce W to an indefinitely small quantity in the formula:—

$$S^{-1} = \sqrt{I - \dfrac{\frac{tm^2}{t+w}}{t}}$$

Confound it, what was the use of making a rule of silence at meals when everybody was breaking it in the spirit if not in the letter? I got hot and red behind the ears. Everybody from Big Lion with his tumbler full of champagne to Dionysus with his liqueur glass of the same was holding it out to me as if drinking to my health. I availed myself of the rule which permits us to leave the table without ceremony. I would go back to the other house and work.

But a sudden thought struck me just as I got outside the door. I sat down again on the stone seats, whipped out a note-book and began my calculations. I saw my way to a solution, jotted down my idea, and snapped the book to in triumph.

It was then that I became aware that Big Lion was putting a cigar in my mouth, and that everybody was crowding around me and shaking hands. Was this another of the buffoon's stupid jokes?

"To what end?" said Big Lion, as he lighted my cigar.

I had sunk back in the bench in a sort of lazy triumph. Nothing bothered me now. I could see my way to solve my problem.

"You must say 'attomplish great wort.'" said Dionysus, in a tone of dignified reproach.

"Confound the Great Work!" I replied pettishly, and then became sorry for myself.

I picked up my Pagan friend, took him on my knee, and began to stroke his head. He snuggled up to me delightfully.

"You must excuse us," said Hermes very seriously, "but we're all so glad."

VII

LOVE UNDER WILL

I began to laugh despite myself.

"Well," I said, puffing at my cigar, "I do really wish you'd let me know what this is all about. Has Lloyd George resigned?"

"No," said Big Lion, "it's just you!"

"What about me?" I retorted.

"Why, your success, of course," said Sister Cypris.

Something, of course, quite obvious to them was hidden from my dull understanding.

I turned on Basil point-blank.

"What success?" I said. "It's true I do see my way through a formula that's been bothering me. But I don't see how you know about it. Do Hermes and Dionysus comprise a knowledge of the differential calculus in their attainments?"

"It's very simple," said the Big Lion. "It involves a knowledge of nothing but the Law; and the Law, after all, is nothing but the plainest common sense. Do you remember my asking you before tiffin what was your true will?"

"Yes," I said, "I do. And I told you then, and I tell you again now, that I haven't the time to think about things like that."

"That fact," he retorted, "was quite enough to assure me that you had discovered it."

"Look here," I said, "you're a good sort and all that, but you are really a bit queer, and half the time I don't know what you are driving at. Can't you put it in plain English?"

"With all the pleasure in life," he returned. "Just look at the facts for a moment. Fact one: Your maternal grandfather is a mechanical genius. Fact two: From your earliest childhood, subjects of this sort have exercised the strongest fascination for you. Fact three: Whenever you get off those subjects, you are unhappy, unsuccessful, and get into various kinds of mess. Fact four: The moment the war gives you your opportunity, you throw up medicine and go back to engineering. Fact five: You graduate reluctantly from the bench to the pilot's seat, and your squad commander himself sees that it's a case of a square peg in a round hole. Fact six: As soon as the Armistice throws you on your beam ends, you get busy again with the idea of the helicopter. Fact seven: You are swept off your feet by coming into a fortune and immediately go astray with drugs—clear evidence that you have missed your road. Fact eight: As soon as your mind is cleansed by the boredom of Telepylus of all its artificial ideas, it returns to its natural bent. The idea of the helicopter comes back with such a rush that you let your breakfast get cold, you don't know your wife when she brings it, and you can talk about nothing else. For the first time in your life your self-consciousness is obliterated, You even start to explain your ideas to me, though I know nothing whatever of the subject. It doesn't require any particular genius to see that you have discovered your true will. And that accounts for the champagne and applause at lunch."

I scratched my head, still hardly comprehending. But one clause in the Big Lion's roar had struck me with appalling force. I looked round the circle of faces.

"Yes, I've discovered my will, all right," I said, "I know now what I'm good for. I understand why I came to this silly planet. I'm an engineer. But you said 'my wife.' That doesn't fit in at all. Where is she?"

"Well, you know," returned Big Lion, with a grin, "you mustn't imagine me to be a cold storage warehouse for other people's wives. If I might hazard a guess, however, your wife's discovered what her own will is, and has gone off to do it."

"Oh, damnation," said I. "Here, you know, I say I can't allow that sort of thing!"

The Big Lion turned his sternest gaze upon me.

"Now, Sir Peter," he said incisively, "pull yourself together. You've only just discovered your own will, and you naturally want to be let alone to do it. And yet, at the very first opportunity, you butt in and want to interfere with your own wife doing hers. Let me tell you point-blank that it's none of your business what she chooses to do. Haven't you seen enough harm come from people meddling with other people's business? Why, hang it, man, your first duty to your wife is to protect her."

"Another of your paradoxes," I growled.

As a matter of fact, I was torn between two attitudes. Lou had been an ideal companion in debauchery of all sorts. A woman like that was bound to be the ruin of a hard-working engineer. At the same time I was madly in love with her, especially after seeing her for the first time that morning; and she belonged to me.

ALEISTER CROWLEY

It was only too clear to me what he meant by saying she had discovered her true will. She had shown that plainly enough when she had begged him to take her away. He had simply worked one of his devilish tricks on me, and got rid of me, as he thought, by getting me absorbed in my helicopter.

I was to be the complacent husband, and allow my wife to go off with another man right under my nose, while I was busy with my calculations. I was to be the *mari complaisant,* was I?

Well, the fiend was ingenious, but he had calculated wrong for once. I got up and deliberately slapped him in the face.

"Before breakfast," he said to Sister Athena, "we shall require pistols for two and coffee for one. But while we are waiting for the fatal rendezvous," he added, turning to me with one of his inscrutable grins, "I must continue to keep my oath. As it happens, one of the brethren here is himself a mechanic. That little house on the headland (he pointed as he spoke) is fitted up as a fairly complete workshop. We might stroll down together and see you started. There will probably be a lot of things that you need which we haven't got and you can make a list of them, and we'll telegraph Lala to buy them in London and bring them down here. She is coming in three days' time. I will also ask her to stop in Paris for one of those nice iron wreaths with enamelled flowers to put on my nameless grave."

The man's nonchalance made me suddenly furiously ashamed of myself. I had to spit out between my teeth that he was an unutterable scoundrel.

"That's right, Sir Peter," retorted the Big Lion, "reassure yourself, by all means. 'The unspeakable Lamus' is the classical expression, and it is customary to give a slight shudder; but perhaps a genius like yourself is justified in inventing new terms of abuse."

I was disconcerted abominably by the attitude of the audience, whose faces were fixed in broad grins, with the exception of Dionysus, who came straight up to me and said:—

"Sonna mabitch," and hit me in the eye. "If you shoot my Bid Lion," he added, "I'll shoot you."

The entire company broke into screams of uncontrollable laughter. Lamus rose with assumed indignation, and observed ferociously:—

"Is this your idea of doing your wills, you wasters? Did you come to this planet to turn the most serious subjects into mockery? You ought all to be weeping, considering that within twenty-four hours you will have to bury your beloved Big Lion or our esteemed guest, who has endeared himself to all of us by his unconscious humour. Come along, Sir Peter," and he slipped his arm through mine. "We have no time to waste with these footlers. As to Unlimited Lou (he began to sing):—

> *Has anyone seen my Mary?*
> *Has anyone seen my Jane?*
> *She went right out in her stocking feet*
> *In the pelting pouring rain.*

> *If anyone sees my Mary,*
> *He'll oblige me, I declare,*
> *If he'll send her back in a packing case,*
> *'This side up, with care.'"*

We were already far down the slope, striding like giants. From above came a confused chorus of shouts and laughter.

One has to be an athlete to run down-hill arm in arm with Big Lion. He didn't seem to mind the cactus, and when we came to a ditch, it had to be jumped. And when the path took a little turn up-hill, he used our momentum to take us over the crest like a switchback. It made me positively drunk. Physical alarm was combined with physical exhilaration. I was sweating like a pig; my sandals slipped on the hard dry grass; my bare legs were torn by brambles, gorse, and cactus.

I kept on slipping; but he always turned the slip into a leap. We never checked our career till we pulled up at the door of the house on the headland.

He let go of me suddenly. I flopped, and lay on my back panting for breath. He was absolutely cool; he had not turned a hair. He stood watching me while he pulled out his pipe, filled it and lit it.

"Never waste time on the way to work," he observed, in a tone which I can only describe as pseudo-sanctimonious. "Do you find yourself sufficiently recovered," he added in mock anxiety, "to resume the vertical position which distinguishes the human species from other mammals? I believe the observation is due to Vergil," he continued.

There was a twinkle in his eye which warned me that he had another surprise in store for me; I had begun to realise that he took a school-boyish delight in pulling people's legs. He seemed to enjoy leading one on, putting one in a false position, and making a mystery out of the most commonplace circumstances. It was extremely idiotic and extremely annoying; but at the same time one had to admit that the result of his method was to add a sort of spice to life.

I remembered a remark of Maisie Jacobs: "Never dull where Lamus is."

The events had been of an ordinary and insignificant character, and yet he had given a value to each one. He made life taste like it does when one is using heroin and cocaine, yet he did it without actual extravagance. I could understand how it was that he had his unique reputation for leading a fantastic life, and yet how no one could put a finger on any particular exploit as extraordinary in itself.

I picked myself slowly together, and, after removing a few thorns from my bare legs, was sufficiently master of myself to say:—

"So this is the workshop?"

"Once again, Sir Peter," replied Lamus, "your intuition has proved itself infallible. And once again your incomparable gift of expression has couched the facts in a tersely epigrammatic form, which Julius Cæsar and Martial might despair of editing."

He opened the door of the house, repeating his old formula:—

"Do what thou wilt shall be the whole of the Law."

Till that moment I had found the phrase by turns ridiculous, annoying, or tedious. It had completely lost these attributes. The dry bones lived. I thrilled to the marrow as he uttered it. A soft, sweet voice, strangely familiar, answered him out of the vast, dim room. Dim, for the blinding sunlight of the open air was unable wholly to illuminate the interior to my contracted pupils.

"Love is the law, love under will."

I thrilled again, this time with a combination of surprise and exultation which was curiously unintelligible. Then I saw, in one corner of the room, behind the array of benches and tables crowded with neatly disposed apparatus, a glimmering form. The back was turned to us; it was on the floor busily occupied in cleaning up.

"This is Sir Peter Pendragon," said Big Lion, "who is coming to take charge of the laboratory."

My eyes were still unaccustomed to the gloom, but I could see the figure scramble to its feet, curtesy, and advance to me, where I stood in the shaft of sunlight that came through the half-open doorway.

It was dressed in a knickerbocker suit of black silk. It wore sandals and black stockings.

I recognised Lou.

"Big Lion said you might want to begin work this afternoon, Sir Peter," she said with dignity, "so I have been trying to put the place in some sort of order."

I stood absolutely aghast. It was Lou, but a Lou that I had never seen or known. I turned to King Lamus for an explanation, but he was not there.

A ripple of laughter ran over her face; the sunlight blazed in her magnetic eyes. I trembled with indescribable emotion. Here was an undecipherable puzzle. Or was it by any chance the answer to a puzzle—to all my puzzles—the puzzle of life?

I could think of nothing to say but the most lame and awkward banality.

"What are you doing here?" I inquired.

"My will, of course," came the answer, and her eyes twinkled in the sunshine as unfathomably as the sea itself.

"Thou hast no right but to do thy will," she quoted. "Do that and no other shall say nay."

"Oh, yes," I retorted, with a trace of annoyance. I had still a feeling of reaction against the Book of the Law. I hated to submit to a formula, however much my good sense, confirmed by my experience, urged me to surrender.

"But how did you find out what your will was?"

"How did *you* find out?" she flashed back.

"Why," I stammered, "Big Lion showed me how my heredity, my natural inclination, and the solution of my crisis, all pointed to the same thing."

"You said it," she answered softly, and fired another quotation. "The Law is for all."

"Tell me about it," I said.

My stupefaction and my annoyance were melting away. I began to perceive dimly that the Big Lion had worked out the whole situation in a masterly fashion. He had done with his material—us, what I was doing with my material, the laws of mechanics.

"I discovered my will four days ago," she said very seriously. "It was the night that you and Big Lion climbed Deep Ghyll and took so long over Professor's Chimney, that you missed the champagne dinner."

"Yes, yes," I said impatiently, "and what was it?"

She put her hands behind her back and bent her head. Her eyelids closed over her long slanting eyes, and her red, snaky mouth began to work tremulously.

"While you were asleep after tiffin," she said, "Big Lion took me up to the semicircular seat on the hill above the Strangers' House, and put me through my paces. He made me tell him all my early life and especially the part just before I met you, when I thought I loved him. And he made me see that all I had done was to try to please myself, and that I had failed. My love for him was only that of a daughter for her father. I looked to him to lead me into life, but nothing meant anything to me till the night I met you. At that moment I began to live. It was you, and not Gretel's beastly cocaine, that filled my soul with that Litany of Fuller's. I had chanted it often enough, but it had never touched the spot. That night I used it to get you. I had only lived that I might one day find you. And all my life curled itself, from that moment, round you. I was ready to go to hell for you. I did go to hell for you. I came out of hell for you. I stopped taking heroin only because I had to fit myself to help you to do your will. That is my will. And when we found out this morning what your will was, I came down here to get the place ready for you to do it. I'm going to keep this place in order for you and assist you as best I can in your work, just as I danced for you, and went to McCall for you, in the days when you were blind. I was blind too about your will, but I always followed my instinct to do what you needed me for, even when we were poisoned and insane."

She spoke in low, calm tones, but she was trembling like a leaf. I didn't know what to answer. The greatness of her attitude abashed me. I felt with utmost bitterness the shame of having wronged so sublime a love, of having brought her into such infamy.

"My God!" I said at last. "What we owe to Big Lion!"

She shook her head.

"No," she said, with a strange smile, "we've helped him as much as he's helped us—helped him to do his will. The secret of his power is that he doesn't exist for himself. His force flows through him unhindered. You have not been yourself till this morning when you forgot yourself, forgot who you were, didn't know who kissed you and brought you your breakfast."

She looked up with a slow half-shamefaced smile into my eyes.

"And I lost you," said I, "after tiffin, when I remembered myself and forgot my work. And all the time you were here helping me to do my work. And I didn't understand."

We stood awhile in silence. Both our hearts were seething with suppressed necessity to speak. It was a long, long while before I found a word; and when it came, it was intense and calm and confident.

"I love you."

Not all the concentration given by heroin, or the exaltation of cocaine, could match that moment. The words were old; but their meaning was marvellously new. There had never been any "I" before, when I thought "I" was I, there had never been any "you" before when I thought of Lou as an independent being, and had not realised that she was the necessary complement of the human instrument which was doing "my" work. Nor had there been any love before, while love meant nothing but the manifold stupid things that people ordinarily mean by it. Love, as I meant it now, was an affirmation of the inevitable unity between the two impersonal halves of the work. It was the physical embodiment of our spiritual truth.

My wife did not answer. There was no need. Her understanding was perfect. We united with the unconscious ecstasy of nature. Articulate human language was an offence to our spiritual rapture. Our union destroyed our sense of separateness from the universe of which we were part; the sun, the sky, the sea, the earth, partook with us of that ineffable sacrament. There was no discontinuity between that first embrace of our true marriage, and the occupation of the afternoon in taking stock of the effects of the laboratory, and making notes of the things we should ask Lala to bring us from London. The sun sank behind the ridge, and far above us from the Refectory came the sonorous beat of the tom-tom which told us that the evening meal was ready. We shut up the house, and ran laughing up the slopes. They no longer tired and daunted us. Half-way to the house, we met the tiny Dionysus, full of importance. He had been deputed to remind us of dinner. Sister Athena (we laughed to think) must have realised that our honeymoon had begun; and—this time—it was no spasmodic exaltation depending on the transitory excitement of passion, or stimulants, but on the fact of our true spiritual marriage, in which we were essentially united to each other not for the sake of either, but to form one bride whose bridegroom was the Work which could never be satiated so long as we lived, and so could never lead to weariness and boredom. This honeymoon would blossom and bear fruit perennially, season by season, like the earth our mother and the sun our father themselves, an inexhaustible, frictionless enthusiasm. We were partakers of the eternal sacrament; whatever happened was equally essential to the ritual. Death itself made no difference to anything; our calm continuous candescence burst through the chains of circumstance, and left us free forever to do our wills, which were one will, the will of Him that sent us.

The walk up to the Refectory was one long romp with Dionysus. Oh, wise dear Sister Athena! Was it by chance that you chose that sturdy sunlight imp to lead us up the hill that night? Did you suspect that our hearts would see in him a symbol of our own serene and splendid hope? We looked into each other's eyes as we held his hands on the last steep winding path among the olives, and we did not speak. But an electric flame ran through his tiny body from one to the other, and we knew for the first time what huge happiness lay in ambush for our love.

The silence of dinner shone with silken lustre. It lasted long—so long—each moment charged with litanies of love.

When coffee came, Big Lion himself broke the spell. "I am going to the tower to sleep tonight; so you will be in charge of the Strangers' House, Sir Peter! The duties are simple; if any wanderer should ask our hospitality, it is for you to extend it on behalf of the Order."

We knew one wanderer who would come, and we would make him welcome.

> *"A bright torch and a casement ope at Night*
> *To let the warm Love in."*

"But before you go across, you will do well to join us, now that you have discovered your true wills, in the Vesper Ceremony of the Abbey, which we perform every night in the Temple of my tower. Let us be going!"

We followed, hand in hand, along the smooth, broad, curving path that bordered the stream, cunningly bended to run along the crest of the ridge so that its power might be used to turn various mill-wheels. The gathering shadows whispered subtle lyrics in our ears; the scents of spring conveyed superb imaginations to our senses; the sunset squandered its last scarlet on the sea, and the empurpled night began to burst into blossom of starlight. Over the hill-top before us hung the golden scimitar of the moon, and in the stillness the faint heart-beat of the sea was heard, as if the organ in some enchanted cathedral were throbbing under the fingers of Merlin, and transmuting the monotonous sadness of existence into a peaceful pæan of inexpressible jubilance of triumph, the Te Deum of mankind celebrating its final victory over the heathen hordes of despair.

A turn in the path, and we came suddenly upon a cauldron-shaped depression in the hillside; at the bottom a silver streak of foam darted among huge boulders piled bombastically along the bed of the valley. Opposite, jutting from the grassy slopes, there stood three stark needles of red rock, glowing still redder with some splash of crimson stolen from the storehouse of the sunset; and above the highest of these there sprang a sudden shaft of stone against the skyline. A blind dome of marble rimmed with a balcony at the base crowned the tower, circular, with many tall windows Gothic in design, but capped with fleurs-de-lys; and this was set upon eight noble pillars joined by arches which carried out the idea of the windows on a larger scale. When we reached the tower, by a serpentine series of steps, megalithic stones laid into the mountain side, we saw that the floor of the vault was an elaborate mosaic. At the four quarters were four thrones of stone, and in the centre a hexagonal altar of marble.

Four of the principals of the Abbey were already robed for the ceremony; but they furnished themselves with four weapons—a lance, a chalice, a sword, and a disk—from a pillar which had a door and a staircase which formed the only means of access to the upper rooms.

Basil seated himself in one of the thrones, Sister Athena in another; while a very old man with a white beard, and a young woman whom we had not yet seen, took their places in the other two. Without formality of any sort beyond a series of knocks, the ceremony began. The impression was overwhelming. On the one hand, the vastness of the amphitheatre, the sublimity of the scene, and the utter naturalness of the celebrants; on the other, the amazing distinction of the prose, and the sharp clarity and inevitability of the ideas.

I can only remember one or two clauses of the Credo: they ran thus:—

"And I believe in one Gnostic and Catholic Church of Light, Life, Love and Liberty, the Word of whose Law is THELEMA.

"And I believe in the communion of Saints.

"And, forasmuch as meat and drink are transmuted in us daily into spiritual substance, I believe in the Miracle of the Mass.

"And I confess one Baptism of Wisdom, whereby we accomplish the Miracle of Incarnation.

"And I confess my life one, individual, and eternal, that was, and is, and is to come."

I have always told myself that I had not a spark of religious feeling, yet Basil once told me that the text "The fear of the Lord is the beginning of wisdom," ought to be translated "The wonderment at the forces of nature is the beginning of wisdom."

He claims that everyone who is interested in science is necessarily religious, and that those who despise it and detest it are the real blasphemers.

But I have certainly always been put off by the idea of ceremonial or ritual of any kind. There again, Basil's ideas are fantastically different to other people's. He says; what about the forms and ceremonies used in an electric light plant?

I gave a little jump when he made the remark. It was so destructive of all my ideas.

"Most ritual," he agreed, "is vain observance, but if there is such a thing as the so-called spiritual force in man, it requires to be generated, collected, controlled, and applied, by using the appropriate measures, and these form true ritual."

And, in fact, the weird ceremony in progress in his Titan tower produced a definite effect upon me, unintelligible as it was to me for the most part, on one hand, and repellent as it was to my Protestant instincts on the other.

I could not help being struck by the first of the collects.

"Lord visible and sensible, of whom this earth is but a frozen spark turning about thee with annual and diurnal motion, source of light, source of life, source of liberty, let thy perpetual radiance hearten us to continual labour and enjoyment; so that as we are constant partakers of thy bounty we may in our particular orbit give out light and life, sustenance and joy to them that revolve about us without diminution of substance or effulgence forever."

The words were full of the deepest religious feeling and vibrated with a mysterious exultation, and yet the most hardened materialist could not have objected to a single idea.

Again, after an invocation of the forces of birth and reproduction, all rose to their feet and addressed Death with sublime simplicity, masking nothing, evading nothing, but facing the huge fact with serene dignity. The gesture of standing to meet Death was nobly impressive.

"Term of all that liveth, whose name is inscrutable, be favourable unto us in thine hour."

The service ended with an anthem which rolled like thunder among the hills and was re-echoed from the wall of the great rock of Telepylus.

It was a very curious detail of life at the Abbey, that one act merged into the next insensibly. There were no abrupt changes. Life had been assimilated to the principle of the turbine, as opposed to the reverberatory engine. Every act was equally a sacrament. The discontinuity and abruptness of ordinary life had been eliminated. A just proportion was consequently kept between the various interests. It was this as much as anything else that had helped me to recover from the obsession of drugs. I had been kept back from emancipation by my reaction against the atmosphere, in general, and my latent jealousy of Basil, in particular. Lou, not having been troubled by either of these, had slid out of her habit as insidiously, if I may use the word, as she had slid into it.

But the culminating joy of my heart was the completeness of the solution of all my problems. There was no possibility of a relapse, because the cause of my downfall had been permanently removed. I could understand perfectly how it was that Basil could take a dose of heroin or cocaine, could indulge in hashish, ether, or opium as simply and usefully as the ordinary man can order a cup of strong black coffee when he happens to want to work late at night. He had become completely master of himself, because he had ceased to oppose himself to the current of spiritual will-power of which he was the vehicle. He had no fear or fascination with regard to any of these drugs. He knew that these two qualities were aspects of a single reaction; that of emotion to ignorance. He could use cocaine as a fencing-master uses a rapier, as an expert, without danger of wounding himself.

About a fortnight after our first visit to the tower, a group of us was sitting on the terrace of the Strangers' House. It was bright moonlight, and the peasants from the neighbouring cottages had come in to enjoy the hospitality of the Abbey. Song and dance were in full swing. Basil and I fell into a quiet chat.

"How long is it, by the way," he said, "since you last took a dose of anything?"

"I'm not quite sure," I answered, dreamily watching Lou and Lala, who had arrived a week since with the apparatus I required for my experiments, as they waltzed together on the court. They were both radiant. It seemed as if the moon had endowed them with her pure subtlety and splendour.

"I asked you," continued Big Lion, pulling at a big meerschaum and amber pipe of the Boer pattern, which he reserved for late at night, "because I want you to take the fullest advantage of your situation. You have been tried in the crucible and come out pure gold. But it won't do for you to forget the privileges you have won by your ordeal. Do you remember what it says in the Book of the Law?"

"'I am the Snake that giveth Knowledge and Delight and bright glory, and stir the hearts of men with drunkenness. To worship me take wine and strange drugs whereof I will tell my prophet, and be drunk thereof! They shall not harm ye at all.'"

"Yes," I said slowly, "and I thought it a bit daring; might tempt people to be foolhardy, don't you think?"

"Of course," agreed Basil, "if you read it carelessly, and act on it rashly, with the blind faith of a fanatic; it might very well lead to trouble. But nature is full of devices for eliminating anything that cannot master its environment. The words 'to worship me' are all-important. The only excuse for using a drug of any sort, whether it's quinine or Epsom-salt, is to assist nature to overcome some obstacle to her proper functions. The danger of the so-called habit-forming drugs is that they fool you into trying to dodge the toil essential to spiritual and intellectual development. But they are not simply man-traps. There is nothing in nature which cannot be used for our benefit, and it is up to us to use it wisely. Now, in the work you have been doing in the last week, heroin might have helped you to concentrate your mind, and cocaine to overcome the effects of fatigue. And the reason you did not use them was that a burnt child dreads fire. We had the same trouble with teaching Hermes and Dionysus to swim. They found themselves in danger of being drowned and thought the best way was to avoid going near the water. But that didn't help them to use their natural faculties to the best advantage, so I made them face the sea again and again, until they decided that the best way to avoid drowning was to learn how to deal with oceans in every detail. It sounds pretty obvious when you put it like that, yet while everyone agrees with me about the swimming, I am howled down on all sides when I apply the same principles to the use of drugs."

At this moment, Lala claimed me for a waltz, and Lou took Basil under her protection. After the dance, we all four sat down on the wall of the court and I took up the thread of the conversation.

"You're quite right, of course, and I imagine you expected to be shouted at."

"No," laughed Lamus, "my love for humanity makes me an incurably optimistic ass on all such points. I can't see the defects in my inamorata. I expect men to be rational, courageous, and to applaud initiative, though an elementary reading of history tells one, with appalling reiteration, how every pioneer has been persecuted, whether it's Galileo, Harvey, Gauguin, or Shelley; there is a universal outcry against any attempt to destroy the superstitions which hamper or foster the progress which helps the development of the race. Why should I escape the excommunication of Darwin or the ostracism of Swinburne? As a matter of fact, I am consoled in my moments of weakness and depression by the knowledge that I am so bitterly abused and hated. It proves to me that my work, whether mistaken or not, is at least worth while. But that's a digression. Let's get back to the words 'to worship me.' They mean that things like heroin and alcohol may be and should be used for the purpose of worshipping, that is, entering into communion with, the 'Snake that giveth Knowledge and Delight and bright glory' which is the genius which lies 'in the core of every star.' And, 'Every man and every woman is a star.' The taking of a drug should be a carefully thought out and purposeful religious act. Experience alone can teach you the right conditions in which the act is legitimate, that is, when it assists you to do your will. If a billiard player slams the balls around indiscriminately, he soon takes the edge off his game. But a golfer would be very foolish to leave his mashie out of his bag because at one time he got too fond of it and used it improperly, and lost important matches in consequence. Now with regard to you and Lou, I can't see that she has any particular occasion for using any of these drugs. She can do her will perfectly well without them, and her natural spirituality enables her to keep in continual communion with her inmost self, as her magical diary shows clearly enough. Even when she had poisoned herself to the point of insanity, her true instincts always asserted themselves at a crisis; that is, at any moment when you, the being whom it is her function to protect, was in danger. But there must be occasions in your work when 'the little more and how much it is' could be added to your energy by a judicious dose of cocaine, and enable you to overcome the cumulative forces of inertia, or when the effort of concentration is so severe that the mind insists on relieving itself by distracting your thoughts from the object of your calculations, a little heroin would calm their clamour sufficiently long to enable you to get the thing done. Now, it's utterly wrong to force yourself to work from a sense of duty. The more thoroughly you succeed in analysing your mind, the more surely you become able to recognise the moment when a supreme effort is likely to result in definite achievement. Nature is very quick to warn one when one makes an error. A drug should act instantaneously and brilliantly. When it fails to do so, you know that you shouldn't have taken it, and you should then call a halt, and analyse the circumstances of the failure. We learn more from our failures than from our successes, and your magical record will tell you by the end of the year so accurately what precise circumstances indicate the propriety of resorting to any drug, that in your second year you must be a great fool if you make even half a dozen mistakes. But, as the Book of the Law says, 'Success is your proof.' When you resort to such potent and dangerous expedients for increasing your natural powers, you must make sure that the end justifies the means. You're a scientific man; stick to the methods of science. Wisdom is justified of her children; and I shall be surprised if you do not discover within the next twelve months that your Great Experiment, despite the unnecessary disasters which arose from your neglecting those words, 'to worship me,' has been the means of developing your highest qualities and putting you among the first thinkers of our generation."

The mandolin of Sister Cypris broke into gay triumphant twitterings. It was like a musical comment upon his summary of the situation. The moon sank behind the hill, the peasants finished their wine and went off singing to their cottages; Lou and I found ourselves alone under the stars. The breeze bore the murmur of the sea up the scented slopes. The lights in the town went out. The Pole Star stood above the summit of the rock. Our eyes were fixed on it. We could imagine the precession of the Equinoxes as identical with our own perpetual travelling through time.

Lou pressed my hand. I found myself repeating the words of the creed.

"'I confess my life, one, individual, and eternal, that was, and is, and is to come.'"

Her voice murmured in my ear, "I believe in the communion of Saints."

I made the discovery that I was after all a profoundly religious man. All my life I had been looking for a creed which did not offend my moral or intellectual sense. And now I had come to understand the mysterious language of the people of the Abbey of Thelema.

"Be the Priest pure of body and soul!"

The love of Lou had consecrated me to do my will, to accomplish the Great Work.

"Be the Priest fervent of body and soul!"

The love of Lou not only kept me from the contamination of ideas and desires alien to my essential function in the universe, but inspired me to dynamic ecstasy.

I do not know how long we sat under the stars. A deep eternal peace sat like a dove, a triple tongue of flame upon our souls, which were one soul forever. Each of our lives was one, individual, and eternal, but each possessed its necessary and intimate relation with the other, and both with the whole universe.

I was moreover aware that our terrific tragedy had been necessary, after all, to our attainment.

"Except a corn of wheat fall into the ground and die, it abideth alone. But if it die, it bringeth forth much fruit."

Every step in evolution is accompanied by colossal catastrophe, as it seems when regarded as an isolated event, out of its context, as one may say.

How fearful had been the price which man had paid for the conquest of the air! How much greater must be the indemnity demanded by inertia for the conquest of the spirit! For we are of more value than many sparrows.

How blind we had been! Through what appalling abysses of agony had we not been led in order that we might say that we had conquered the moral problem posed by the discoveries of organic chemistry.

"The master of tide and thunder against the juice of a flower?"

We had given the lie to the poet.

"This is the only battle he never was known to win."

We no longer looked back with remorse on our folly. We could see the events of the past year in perspective, and we saw that we had been led through that ghoulish ghastliness. We had followed the devil through the dance of death, but there could be no doubt in our minds that the power of evil was permitted for a purpose. We obtained the ineffable assurance of the existence of a spiritual energy that worked its wondrous will in ways too strange for the heart of man to understand until the time should be ripe.

The pestilence of the past had immunised us against its poison. The devil had defeated himself. We had attained a higher stage of evolution.

And this understanding of the past filled us with absolute faith in the future.

The chaos of crumbled civilisations whose monuments were on the rock before us, had left that rock unmarred. Our experience had fortified us. We had reached one more pinnacle on the serrated ridge that rises from the first screes of self-consciousness to a summit so sublime that we did not even dare to dream how far it soared above us. Our business was to climb from crag to crag, with caution and courage, day after day, life after life. Not ours to speculate about the goal of our Going. Enough for us to Go. We knew our way, having found our will, and for the means, had we not love?

"Love is the law, love under will."

The words were neither on our lips nor in our hearts. They were implicit in every idea, and in every impression. We went from the court up the steps, through the open glass doors, into the vaulted room with its fantastic frescoes that was the strangers' room of the Abbey of Thelema; and we laughed softly, as we thought that we should never more be strangers.

A Note About the Author

Aleister Crowley (1875–1947) was an English poet, painter, occultist, magician, and mountaineer. Born into wealth, he rejected his family's Christian beliefs and developed a passion for Western esotericism. At Trinity College, Cambridge, Crowley gained a reputation as a poet whose work appeared in such publications as *The Granta* and *Cambridge Magazine*. An avid mountaineer, he made the first unguided ascent of the Mönch in the Swiss Alps. Around this time, he first began identifying as bisexual and carried on relationships with prostitutes, which led to his contracting syphilis. In 1897, he briefly dated fellow student Herbert Charles Pollitt, whose unease with Crowley's esotericism would lead to their breakup. The following year, Crowley joined the Hermetic Order of the Golden Dawn, a secret occult society to which many of the era's leading artists belonged, including Bram Stoker, W. B. Yeats, Arthur Machen, and Sir Arthur Conan Doyle. Between 1900 and 1903, he traveled to Mexico, India, Japan, and Paris. In these formative years, Crowley studied Hinduism, wrote the poems that would form *The Sword of Song* (1904), attempted to climb K2, and became acquainted with such artists as Auguste Rodin and W. Somerset Maugham. A 1904 trip to Egypt inspired him to develop Thelema, a philosophical and religious group he would lead for the remainder of his life. He would claim that *The Book of the Law* (1909), his most important literary work and the central sacred text of Thelema, was delivered to him personally in Cairo by the entity Aiwass. During the First World War, Crowley allegedly worked as a double agent for the British intelligence services while pretending to support the pro-German movement in the United States. The last decades of his life were spent largely in exile due to persecution in the press and by the states of Britain and Italy for his bohemian lifestyle and open bisexuality.

A Note from the Publisher

Spanning many genres, from non-fiction essays to literature classics to children's books and lyric poetry, Mint Edition books showcase the master works of our time in a modern new package. The text is freshly typeset, is clean and easy to read, and features a new note about the author in each volume. Many books also include exclusive new introductory material. Every book boasts a striking new cover, which makes it as appropriate for collecting as it is for gift giving. Mint Edition books are only printed when a reader orders them, so natural resources are not wasted. We're proud that our books are never manufactured in excess and exist only in the exact quantity they need to be read and enjoyed.

Discover more of your favorite classics with Bookfinity™.

- Track your reading with custom book lists.
- Get great book recommendations for your personalized Reader Type.
- Add reviews for your favorite books.
- AND MUCH MORE!

Visit **bookfinity.com** and take the fun Reader Type quiz to get started.

Enjoy our classic and modern companion pairings!

Printed in the USA
CPSIA information can be obtained
at www.ICGtesting.com
JSHW022210140824
68134JS00018B/977